To J

When or if you
have ~~time~~ to

# Glove Her Hands

Read this, I
hope you enjoy

## MARY KINZELBERG

it as much as
I liked your
Valentine!
Mary

# Glove Her Hands

ISBN: 9781521962435

# DEDICATION

In memory of my parents; Florence and Addison Olian.
And to Jay, my husband and Matt, my son.

For my inspiration I would like to thank Richard Hawley for his song:

## "Who's Gonna Shoe Your Pretty Little Feet?"
### By Richard Hawley

Who's gonna shoe your pretty little feet
And who's gonna glove your little hands
And who's gonna kiss your ruby red lips
mmmmm mmmmmm mmmmmm

Papa's gonna shoe your pretty little feet
And mama's gonna glove your little hands
And I'm gonna kiss your ruby red lips
mmmmmm mmmmmm mmmmmm

Who's gonna rock your little rocking chair
And who's gonna sing you to sleep
And who's gonna wipe away your little tears
mmmmmm mmmmmm mmmmmm

Papa's gonna rock your little rocking chair
And mama's gonna sing you to sleep
And I will wipe away your little tears
mmmmmm mmmmmm mmmmmm

Papa's gonna rock your little rocking chair
And mama's gonna sing you to sleep and
I will kiss your ruby red lips
mmmmmm mmmmmm mmmmmm
And I will kiss your ruby red lips
mmmmmm mmmmmm mmmmmm

# ACKNOWLEDGMENTS

Thank you to my husband; Jay, and my son; Matt, for their endless encouragement and readings. To my mentor; Neil Landau, my editor(s); Elaine Partnow and Rebecca Mansdorff and my assistant and marketing director; Chelsea Ford. I'd also like to thank my many friends and family members who have supported me by reading the book: Wendy R., Mady J., Richard L., Jeri P., Florence O., Kiela H-M. Barbara W., Jan C., Connie H., Larry K., Buz O., and Evin W.

Book cover design by Kiela Hine-Moriarty and graphic design by Fred Zolan of Running Images.

# A NOTE FROM THE AUTHOR

This novel is set in 1959-1962 during a time of great racial tension in America. Attitudes regarding matters of personal freedoms, work, gender roles, family life, race, religion and government as described in this story were of their time. The use of specific language to describe immigrants, people of color and religious groups is now considered to be outdated and offensive, and words we presently use to describe one another have evolved. While inspiration for this novel has been taken from the author's own life and history, the names, characters, places, events and incidents are either products of the author's imagination or used in a fictitious manner. Depiction of dialect and actual historical events may not be entirely accurate. The locations, characters and experiences contained in this story are influenced by actual events. However, as this book is a work of fiction, any character resemblances to actual persons, living or dead, are entirely coincidental.

# CONTENTS

# 1
# BIRTHDAY
# SUMMER 1959

Dad always sits at the head of the table—even today on my birthday. Dad has straight, thick black hair that he slicks back like Clark Gable. I have never seen him without a mustache. He is six feet tall, slender, and drives around in a sports car with the top down. My mom has blondish-brown wavy, medium long hair that she wears either in a French twist or down in rich waves across one eye and down her back. She used to be a model and she has kept her figure. I know because I've seen pictures of her in magazines. Mom is glamorous, like Dad. They look like gorgeous movie stars. All my girlfriends tell me that, especially about my dad.

From the front stairs I can see Dad, Mom, Nana and Grandma all sitting in their places. Grandma, my mom's mom, is a widow. My grandfather is only a glimpse in my memory. Grandma comes over most nights for dinner. Nana is my dad's mom. She has lived with my parents since we moved into this house when I was three months old. Before that my folks lived in a smaller house which Nana moved into when my Grandpa died.

They are waiting for me to come down, but I'm not going to until everyone is seated. I want to make an entrance so everyone looks at me at once. I don't want Annie, my older sister by nine years, or Rusty, my younger brother by four years, to see me sneaking a look so I run back to my room to find Jessy, but she must have taken the back stairs that go through the kitchen. Our dog Mister isn't allowed in the dining room so he's probably lying on the carpet or on the couch in the living room. Mister is a brown and white boxer. He knows his place is not upstairs. If I ever have a dog he will be allowed to be anywhere. No one pays much attention to Mister, including me. I pet him, but I don't really play with him—but I love him.

Jessy and I share a room until Annie gets married in the fall. We are only nineteen months apart and in school she is one year ahead of me. Jessy is dark in color, like my dad. They always look tan, but that's because they have olive skin—probably because the olive tree is abundant in Israel and it is a symbol of peace, not because their skin color is green or black like olives. My hair is auburn like Nana's and my skin is pale and freckled. Grandma's skin is milky white and burns like toast the minute she sits in the sun. Grandma's hair is bright red, like a clown. Nana is short and stocky with twinkling eyes that squint when she smiles to make her look kind. She covers me up at night but I pretend I am asleep because I have nothing to say to her. Grandma's plump short body is sprinkled with auburn freckles framed by her milky white skin. She laughs heartily in a soprano tone. They are both outgoing and rock solid opinionated. I have heard the best grandma fights when they play cards in our library with their friends.

Jessy is outgoing like Mom, funny and not afraid to say anything, except when Dad is around. Even though it is my birthday, I know I will be shy at the table, like I always am. I enter the dining room wearing a bright yellow and orange capris outfit that Peggy, my best neighborhood friend, lent me because we decided my own outfits don't look like birthday colors. The white flats are mine.

Jessy shouts, "Rachael, you look pretty! Whose clothes are those?"

I answer, "Peggy's."

Jessy says, "You look different."

Nana and Grandma tell each other how beautiful and grown up I look, but they never tell me. And they say to Mom that I look gorgeous. I glance over their way and say thank you. As I pull my chair out and sit down I hear Mom, Dad, Rusty and Annie say I look pretty and Happy Birthday but my eyes look down at the chair longer than normal so I won't have to see everyone looking at me. I love the attention but it makes me feel uncomfortable.

Nana and Grandma sit on either side of Dad at one end. They shout in Yiddish across him to each other. Everyone is left out when they do this. Yiddish is the Jewish language, a combination of German and Hebrew. It was brought to the U.S. by Jews fleeing the oppression in Europe but mostly only older Jews only speak it. I can only guess what they might be saying.

Even though we are Jewish and celebrate Passover by having an extended family dinner at our home, we also celebrate Christmas and Easter, without the religious part. Just the tree, gifts and decorations for Christmas, and an Easter egg hunt in our back yard with all the cousins. We don't even light the Chanukah lights and we don't light the Sabbath candles or say the prayers over them on Friday nights. We do go to temple once a year for the High Holidays which are Rosh Hashanah for the Jewish New Year and Yom Kippur, for the Day of Atonement. I go to Temple for classes on Sundays during the school year so I will be confirmed at the end of ninth grade as Annie did, and Jess and Rusty do also. I do feel inside I am Jewish even though we don't practice many of the ceremonies or keep a kosher house. We belong to an all-Jewish country club and, most of my and my parents' friends are Jewish.

Annie and Jessy sit on either side of Mom at the other end. Rusty and I have the middle seats facing each other. I wish I faced the swinging kitchen door because I like to see who is coming into the dining room first or glimpse of what Ethel, our cook, is doing. We only have breakfast in the dining room for special occasions. Formal rooms are for grownups not family, except today the room feels like it belongs to me. Other times, when the room is empty, the chairs look like erect soldiers and the mahogany table is shined like soldiers' boots. There is a silver tea service on the buffet in front of the large gold framed mirror that I have never seen moved from its spot in thirteen years. The wallpaper is a floral print and each flower has its name in Latin. I love it because the drawings are intricate designs that warm up the cold room.

Since he said happy birthday, Dad hasn't looked at me. He is staring out the window onto the large front yard and street and he looks worried. It scares me when he looks like this.

Our house is on a quiet residential road and every time

a car goes by at least one of us knows who it is. There are about a hundred houses in our neighborhood. They are all extremely large—like they have at least fifteen or twenty large rooms. Most are red brick, like ours, but there are some in white brick or white stone. Ours is in English Tudor style so there is some wood trim around the windows, like a Hansel and Gretel house. There are two pointed cupolas on the roof with windows. In the attic I love to look out from them.

Dad jumps slightly and stares glossily when Ethel brings in pancakes with birthday candles on them and starts singing "Happy Birthday". Ethel knows I love pancakes. When I blow out the candles, I wish today will be the best day of my life. I also wish I could say something to the family that is witty or funny like Jessy so everyone will laugh.

Dad looks like he is memorizing every morsel of his pancakes as he cuts each piece, swimming in syrup, and puts it in his mouth.

Annie suddenly says, "After Donald and I are married we will be coming to your parties together, Rachael. Oh, and yours, too, Jessy."

Jessy jumps in, "Why mine? Signs at my parties will say, 'Adults Omitted,'

I say louder than usual, "I wish you were both coming tonight, Annie."

Rusty chimes in, "Rachey, I could come."

"I know, Rusty. Maybe next year you can stay up for my party."

Dad startles me when he looks up and says, "Slim, I

will be at the party a little late. I have a meeting with the buyers from New York."

I answer, "Okay, Dad," but I am not sure I hid all the disappointment in my face.

Now I don't feel hungry any more. When I am worried my appetite disappears. Dad calls me "Slim" because I am skinny. Jessy and Rusty are a little pudgy and Annie is thin like me.

Mom looks over at me and says, "Honey, I have to work at the store while Dad is meeting those men and then I'm off to the beauty shop. I'll be home later to help you look your prettiest."

Jessy pushes my leg under the table and we look at each other and roll our eyes. We know Mom puts the beauty shop before God. I don't want to start our usual giggling after our eye rolling because Dad always sends us away from the table when we do. This is not going to happen today. But I know Jessy wants to see if Dad would do it on my birthday. Nothing is going to ruin this day.

I say, "Okay, Mom, but Ruby is doing my hair. Remember I decided not to go to the beauty shop with you, so please remind them. I really like the way Ruby does it, but can you help me with my dress?"

Mom reminds me, "The Caseys are having you and Jessy over for swimming today."

"I know, Mom, I already talked to Peggy about it yesterday."

I wish Mom had kept a diary when she was a teenager, like Anne Frank. In school we read *The Diary of Anne Frank*, about a teenage Jew during the war. Mom lived through war and the Depression as a teenager but she never talks to me about what it was like. She only says we didn't have any relatives killed in the concentration camps. Maybe she's afraid if she did talk about the Holocaust, it might happen to our relatives.

Every birthday Mom tells me I had colic until I was four months old and a nursemaid had to rock me all the time to keep me from crying all day and night. Nursemaids are like maids but they are only for babies' care. I'll bet mom and I know more about Anne Frank than we do about each other.

Birthdays are a time to think about what you want to change.

Mom presses the buzzer under her foot to signal Ethel to start clearing the dishes. The sound is silent in the dining room but I can still hear it in the kitchen. Ruby and Ethel come in through the swinging door like wind-up dolls in their starched white uniforms and stockings limply hanging unevenly over their comfortable white shoes.

Nana and Grandma are pushing out their chairs as they continue to talk loudly in Yiddish. They realize that I'm looking at them. They both say "Happy Birthday" and come over to kiss me and give me savings bonds in blank envelopes. I kiss their cool, damp, stale smelling cheeks and thank them. I don't look at the bonds, but I know they will each be generous. They continue their Yiddish as they leave the dining room and walk toward the living room. Dad comes over and kisses my cheek and says he will bring his movie camera to the party. He always takes movie pictures on holidays or birthdays but I only remember once when we all looked at them.

I hope he takes some when Tommy and I are dancing.

Mom starts talking to Ethel about the household duties and interrupts herself to tell me to have fun swimming as she and Ethel walk into the kitchen. Annie, Rusty, and Jessy trounce upstairs, but I just want to sit here quietly.

The flowers in the center of the table are my colors: pink and orange, and the napkins are the black and white checkered ones, my favorites. Ruby and Ethel did this because they know what I love. The presents are all stacked on the buffet but I told everyone I would rather open them after my birthday party at the country club. The beautiful wrappings excite me because they hold surprises and mysteries. I wonder what Tommy's wrapping will look like?

Tommy is coming to my party as one of Jessy's guests because he is in her class. He is really cute with a perfectly round face, dark chocolate brown eyes, extra long eyelashes, and full lips that are always smiling. He sports a flattop haircut that goes straight up like a flat two inch table. That's what's in style with all the older boys now. There is some puberty pudge on his hands and arms, but his legs are lanky like a colt. Whenever he talks to me he jokes, and I wonder what he is thinking behind the jokes. In the hall at school before we got out for the summer, he said, "Let's practice dancing at your birthday party."

I answered, "Why, practice for what?"

"I want to take you to the Temple dance before you leave for camp."

"You're leaving for camp, too," I said, ignoring answering him because I was afraid he might not mean it and would forget he said it.

"Thunderbird Camp is also having a dance at your camp this summer," he said, looking down.

My heart was thumping so hard, I could barely speak. I murmured, "I have to go to class."

Last night my friend Peggy and I talked about Tommy for the first time. She called to tell me she was coming to the birthday party today.

"Peggy, I have to tell you a secret. I like Tommy. He's a grade higher than me, but when I talk to him I get all nervous. He'll be at my party tomorrow night," I said excitedly.

"Okay. I won't tell anyone. I hope he dances with you," Peggy said sweetly.

After we hung up I called Jane since she is my best school friend and I don't want her to feel left out of the secret.

"Jane, you know Tommy in my sister's class? Well, I really like him and it's a secret because I don't want him to know in case he doesn't feel the same," I confided in her. "He will be at my party tomorrow night because I let Jessy invite some friends."

"Okay, Rachael, your secret's good with me. He is cute. I hope he likes you back." Jane said it like she meant it. Sometimes I think she is jealous of me because we live in a big house and she lives in a tiny apartment.

Tonight Tommy may give Jessy most of his attention because he will be sitting at her table with the kids she invited. She always gives me disapproving looks when I talk to her friends. Usually, I don't even care about going to the country club because none of my friends belong, but tonight it could be a magical place and if Tommy gives me my first real kiss there I will always think of it as a castle. I can almost feel him touching my mouth as I jump to the sounds of dishes clanking.

The sweet smell of caramel comes from the direction of the swinging kitchen door. Ethel promised my favorite cake as her gift—the recipe she brought from her Mississippi roots. Her family traveled north during the Industrial Revolution to make more money than they could on the farms and plantations of the South. Once she told me why it's traditional for Negroes to make caramel icing on cake. Slaves and sugarcane from the Caribbean were traded for rum and caramel a hundred years ago. Caramel and rum were made from the sugarcane in the South. Rum needed the caramel for flavor, so they started using caramel for desserts.

I yell from the table, "I'm coming in there, Ethel, to find that sticky caramel bowl."

Ethel shouts, "You better hurry or it will be sudsy."

As I run in through the swinging door I tell Ethel, "I need to lick it."

"Your mommy won't like you licking icing for breakfast."

I run over to where Ethel has hidden the bowl under a damp kitchen towel. Ethel races to intercept the prize but I grab the mixing bowl and circle it with my arms like it is liquid gold. As I sit in the middle of the floor I scrape every drop off the sides and scarf it up as I look up at Ethel's strong body.

Even though I am finally almost as tall as she is, her towering over me right now feels good, like I am still her baby. She is about my mom's age, but her medium brown skin is velvety smooth and soft. The kitchen has a black and white linoleum floor with wear and tear stains holding memories that resonate with a warm place in my heart. Contrasting this are shinny white tiles and freshly painted cabinets that make each day seem to start crisply. The back door is opened by the milkman, Ray, who fills up the wire basket with fresh eggs, cream and milk.

When I first arrive in the kitchen, Ethel's face looks serious because she has a lot to do. When two people are in the kitchen it seems crowded so I hop up on the counter and we talk about southern recipes from Mississippi, my school work, and my summer experiences with my friends, but we always end up laughing. One time I asked Ethel about why no one seems to cook for their own family. Ethel cooks for us, her mom cooks for her, and it just doesn't make sense to me. When I tell her I will cook for my own family with her recipes one day and she will come to dinner she often says, "Uh huh," like she doesn't believe me. She writes her recipes down for me and puts them in a secret place that only she and I know. Ethel doesn't smile a lot so I don't feel right unless her face looks happy by the time I scoot out of the kitchen. Sometimes I watch the kitchen door swinging back and forth from different rooms. It means someone is going in and out of Ethel's domain and I wonder what they talk about. I like to come into the house through the back door because it leads into the cozy kitchen instead of the formal front hall. Ethel's kitchen is the heart of the house.

Ruby, the upstairs maid, visits Ethel on her way to the basement laundry room. Ruby is joyful and is younger than Ethel. She has pretty eyes that water when she talks, probably because her words don't come out smoothly and she needs to work hard to speak. Ruby and I talk more because her room, where she sleeps six nights a week, is right off mine. Ruby is always smiling— her cheeks are like cherubs. She is in her twenties and her skin is the color of caramel icing.

When I find Ruby and Ethel in the kitchen at the same time it is my most favorite time. Sometimes they are talking about our family as I barge in, or arguing like sisters. I love to talk about my day because they are always interested. I suddenly realize I never ask them about their lives. Today I am thirteen and I want to think about their families and their homes. They make me feel so special. I wonder if they ever feel special.

I hug Ethel and she gives me a bear hug back that feels yummy like her caramel icing and then I run upstairs to my room.

Jessy is putting on a two-piece bathing suit as I stare enviously while I pull on my one-piece. When I am fourteen I will be allowed to wear a two-piece. This unwritten rule was unanimously decided by the neighborhood moms.

We run down the stairs and I yell to Ethel, "See you later. We're going."

Ethel loudly says, "Okay. Don't you go getting too burned now 'fore your party."

Tantalizing sparks run around my body thinking of the cute boys that may be at the pool as Jessy and I run hand-in-hand to the Casey's pool, taking shortcuts through intervening yards. They have the only pool and tennis court and everyone is always welcome to come over.

Drinks and snacks are out on tables with comfortable chairs all around the deck. One of their colored maids supervises us. In the winter the pool is frozen over for ice skating. We love to watch their pet monkey, named Monkey, play in his locked cage on a table outside. We aren't allowed to let him out because he might escape, but I wish he could be free and wild in the jungle. The cage is always clean so he won't spread disease. I will ask Jill, one of the Casey daughters, if I can come over when they clean the cage so I can hold Monkey.

I see Peggy, Mary Ann, Jill, Barbara, Burton, and other neighborhood friends waving as we get closer. Peggy is always the most beautiful girl at the pool. She is Jewish, but has no Jewish features. Dad has a big nose, like Nana, but it isn't hooked the way a lot of Jewish noses are. Actually, no one in our family looks particularly Jewish, but Peggy's combination of blonde hair, little turned-up nose and blue eyes aren't the usual characteristics of Jewish people.

We wave back as Peggy yells, "Hey, Rachael, Happy Birthday, teenager!"

I yell, "Thanks."

As she runs up and puts her arm around my shoulders, I softly say, "Cute suit."

Peggy whispers back, "Don't feel bad, no one will make fun of your one piece. If they do, I'll kill them."

I look over her shoulder to see the other kids. The girls my age are all in one-piece bathing suits and I feel better already. Gently, I push Peggy in the pool and jump in after her. We both laugh. I love her so much; I wish she were my real sister. She is always sweet to me and says something just as I was thinking the same thing. Sleeping over at each other's houses without Jessy is my favorite neighbor thing to do, but sometimes Jessy has to come too because she is Peggy's age.

Self-consciously I climb out of the pool and grab a towel to cover up from my waist down and sit down to join the other kids. They all say Happy Birthday. I am looking at the older girls as they move their mysterious bodies freely and confidently. The boys move awkwardly around the girls, but I have not seen this clumsiness in Tommy. Carefully I remove my towel and expose my whole suit. Peggy gives me a look of approval while no one else notices what is transpiring.

Some of us start to play kickball on the tennis court. I play only to be part of the group, not because I love the game. The yelling about plays is so much more fun than conversation around the pool. Even with Jessy playing I was shouting too, rather than being the quiet sister. Next time we play I will pretend it is my birthday again and yell. And then the worst thing that could happen happens.

As I run after the kickball, I slam right into a rope that's been strung up where the tennis net would normally be. I guess they put it up to delineate the two sides of the court for dodge ball, but I didn't see it. Now my body is splayed on the hot asphalt. The maid runs inside to get ice and salve. Everyone stops playing. I carefully sit up. The maid calls Mom, then tells me she is coming over to get me. The kids all say my neck is bright red and how do I feel and they are sorry. My legs are shaking when I get up and queasily go to look in the pool house mirror at the swelling and cherry redness. I put on the salve and hold the ice against my neck. The air conditioning feels good and I really want to stay inside away from the heat and humiliation, but I go out and sit on a lounge chair and ice my neck with Peggy and Jessy sitting on either side of me.

"I want to cry," I say to them quietly. "I ruined my

birthday."

Peggy quickly says, "Stay here and swim; the cool pool will make it feel better."

Jessy adds, "You'll forget about your neck if you stay."

After what seems like an hour I finally see Mom running over to me in her heels and dress, her hair in curlers with a net over them.

Mom says, "Oh, darling, I'm so sorry. It does look awful. I'll take you home to rest for tonight, but first we'll go to the doctor. Here's a cream you must put on."

I really want to go home but I don't want to look like a baby.

Peggy confidently tells Mom, "Mrs. Hirsch, she will be fine. I will walk her home if she isn't, I promise. We'll sit in the shade and cool off in the pool. Please don't let this ruin her day."

Mom looks amazed and says, "Peggy, I agree with you. You are a bright fourteen-year-old. Jessy, will you watch your sister and make sure she puts the cream on?"

Jessy answers, "Of course, Mom, a gallon of it."

Mom and I laugh about her hair up in rollers and she says she better go back to the beauty shop and finish her hairdo for my party. Then she says she has to work at the store for a little while. Mom works at the store near to our house. We own both and they are expensive clothing stores. She doesn't work every day.

The day turns out to be fun and my neck and suit don't bother me because no one is teasing me about it. In fact I feel more relaxed than I have the whole day because I don't have to try to act perfect now. My accident put an end to that. Still, thinking about Tommy hangs on like the humidity.

Jessy and I say our goodbyes and gather up my gifts. We hold hands as we run through the yards and laugh like I want us to all the time not just today. Jessy's bed and mine are separated by a night table with two lamps. Stains and tears from age speckle the red plaid wallpaper. Mom loves wallpaper; it's everywhere. Even the halls have grass cloth. Our spreads and dust ruffles and pillow covers are all the same plaid. Only one window looks out to the backyard but it is hard to see out in the winter because the radiator is below it and can be steaming hot to lean on.

My heart jumps when I see the white sleeveless fitted bodice shaped to meet the blue taffeta skirt covering the three layers of crinoline spread out on my bed. I rub the crinolines against each other and hear the rustle, and then I hold the dress up to the full length mirror on my closet door. Slowly I am dancing, holding the dress, dreaming of Tommy in my arms. I hang the dress and petticoats on the front of the closet door so I can see the dress awake, not sleeping on my bed. Did the seamstress, when she was sewing it, imagine a teenager wearing this dress filled with thoughts of becoming a woman?

Ruby startles me from her adjacent room saying, "Rachael, I saw youse dancin' in front your mirror in that party dress. Honey, youse look so beautiful, even before it's on you, I got tears. Why, you's all growed up!"

Ruby's room has the most sunlight of any room in the house. To enter Ruby's room one must pass through my room because there isn't a separate entrance. We have another maid's room in the basement where Bernice and her husband, Bill, stay sometimes. When I see Ruby joyfully bouncing through our room in the morning my day starts out happy. Two sides of her room are almost floor to ceiling windows and the walls are painted white with no wallpaper. If it were a guestroom there would be wallpaper. The bare necessities are the only pieces of furniture: her small bed and a wooden dresser with a mirror over it plus a cozy sofa that used to be in the basement up against a wall. I asked Mom if Ruby could have it in her room. Now I have somewhere to sit when Ruby and I talk. Sounds of her quick footsteps on the wood floor stop when her feet touch the oval, white braided area rug by the dresser or the one by the bed. There is an unfinished feel in Ruby's room. There's no spread for the bed and only white shear curtains on some of the windows.

The smell of Ruby's hair pomade soothes me as it permeates her room. Colored women use it to make their hair straight. Ruby's hair always looks like it has a layer of icing. An *Ebony* magazine sits next to Ruby's hairbrush and comb. The simplicity of the room is calming and inviting.

I run into her room and hug her, "Oh, Ruby, what are you going to wear?"

"Now youse know I'm not going. Why youse ax me what I'm wearing?"

"Because I just want you there. I thought you could be there tonight. Just this once."

"No, honey. Now hold that there dress up again. My! Bernice did a mighty fine job starching them slips to poof out alright."

"I know and I want to go thank her. Come on with me, please," I beg her.

"Oh, okay, but I still have lots to do before yo' mama come home," she says as she hangs up the dress and crinolines on the front of the closet door, covering the full length mirror

We race down the back kitchen stairs and then the basement stairs. I go first. I love to hear Ruby's steps behind me—it makes me feel cared for. When we get to the laundry room the door is shut and it is pitch black through the glass window in the door.

I open it and Ethel and Bernice shout, "Surprise."

How did they know I was coming? I give my best happy smile and hug them.

Bernice is the laundress and receives the laundry through the chute that comes from the second floor. I wish I could slide down the chute. The steam from the iron makes her face moist. She is the oldest of the three but the grey hair around her face hardly shows. Her eyes have yellow patches in the white part, like sunlight came in and stayed. She is taller than Ruby or Ethel so she can reach to hang up clothes on the lines that I can't reach unless I jump. Her skin has brown and white splotches on her arms and legs. I hope they weren't burned from the iron. The candy smell from her must be from all the stuff used on laundry and sheets to make them smell sweet. In the summer the clothes are hung on the line in the backyard unless there is a shower coming. A special gift to Bernice is when I can help her gather the clothes and sheets on the line quickly before a sudden surprise storm hits and help her put them back up on the line in the laundry room.

After turning on the lights, Bernice smiles and says, "Here, honey, I made you this for tonight."

I open a crocheted white shawl wrapped in a hair net like Ethel wears when she cooks.

"Oh, Bernice, thank you so much." I try it on around my shoulders and prance around showing off. "It's so romantic—just like I pictured me one day wearing."

I move to hug her moist cool arms and she hugs back tightly. I don't let go until she does.

Bernice retorts, "Honey, it may be romantic, but don't let them boys get romantic when you bend down and shows yo' underwear because them petticoats'll stick out like they was a diving board."

Laughing I say, "Bernice, why don't you come and make sure that doesn't happen."

Ethel adds disapprovingly, "Why'ja iron them so stiff if you want her respectable, Bernie?"

I never noticed before that Ethel calls her Bernie, like Bernice is maybe too formal.

Ethel and Bernice nod to one another without smiling. I feel their tension and want them to make up but I stay quiet. It's my fault because it's my dress they're arguing about.

Ethel opens the door to leave without saying anything. I should have asked Ethel to come tonight too, but I didn't get a chance. Or maybe she has something cooking in the oven. I don't think she likes Bernice because I never see her down here. Today was an exception, for me. Ethel probably looks down on Bernice because she works in the dungeon laundry room, not the immaculate huge house.

Ruby and Bernice start dancing to the rhythm and

blues music playing softly on the radio. I join in and we all laugh as I slowly dance my way out of the room. I never want to leave this moment. Three sweet maids are hard to find in one household. Mom knows how to hire help that love me, even if they don't love each other.

I race to my room up the back stairs. I think of Tommy going to the party as Jessy's guest. She senses I like him or maybe she likes him too or why did she just happen to ask him and one other boy, Mitch, of all the boys in her class? I'm afraid to ask her because then she might tell Tommy. I can never predict what Jessy will do. Even today when I was talking to Peggy she was looking at me exasperated and jealous because Peggy is friends with both of us even though she's Jessy's age. I'll be angry at Jessy if she takes up all of Tommy's time at the party.

Mitch is my best guy friend. He is also Tommy's best friend. I've known him since the first grade. He always makes me feel like a princess. I know he likes me more than a friend and I wish I felt the same. I can tell him anything. He's very funny and silly and always makes me laugh. I'm happy Jessy asked him.

I lay on my bed thinking about tonight until it's time to get ready. I try to think of my friends who will be at the party but the only thing entering my thoughts is Tommy.

Mom is helping me and Jessy get ready in our room, zipping up our zippers, adjusting our slips. She brings in some lipstick and rouge to put on us.

Only last year my girlfriend Jane and I smeared lipstick on Nana's mirror and all over our faces. We slept in her room when she was out of town. When she saw lipstick all over her carpet and bathroom she didn't even tell Mom or get mad at me. If Jessy had done the same thing she would have made sure Jessy was punished because she is mean to Jessy. Jessy looks the most like Mom, so Nana gets angry at Jessy instead of Mom. Nana can't get mad at Mom because she is living in Mom's house.

"Mom, I'm going to put this on myself," I declare, looking in the dressing table mirror.

"Okay, honey, but not too much or you'll look like a fancy lady."

Jessy laughs at her as I roll my eyes and look at Jessy.

"Mom, you look so pretty," I tell her.

"Honey, I am in my robe."

"I know, but you already look pretty."

"This is your night and you are going to look like Cinderella."

Jessy says, "Am I going to look like the wicked stepsister?"

No, honey, you are going to look like Snow White."

Mom hands me a wrapped gift before she leaves our room. The wrapping is satin white paper tied with a blue ribbon that matches my skirt exactly. Inside are white long satin gloves; they are so perfect and grownup. My eyes are watering. My dress, crinolines, and gloves are on. I stand with my back to the full length mirror, then slowly turn and face myself. I like that I look pretty.

Ruby does my hair in a French twist with a wave over my forehead like Mom's instead of bangs and a ponytail, my usual hairdo. Bernice starts talking real fast and soft so that

21

I can hardly hear her. Sometimes in the laundry room, before she knows I'm there, I hear her talking to herself just like this. I hope the laundry detergent isn't affecting her brain.

Finally, I hear her say loudly, "Honey, tonight don't be 'fraid to show love. You's a lady now and I knows you shy but you be like a flower. When a flower is alive it smells sweet and it don't never run out of smell to give and give 'til it die. And dear, youse never run out of love. We don't have no short supply of love just to give to only a few but we have love to give on and on and on 'til we die."

Bernice has never offered her wisdom to me before, but then I never asked her. I think she may feel she is only good at the laundry and now she is happy to come up from the basement to do something special. I don't even know the last time she saw my bedroom or has been on this floor. The only windows she looks out while she's working are facing concrete steps or parts of the foundation of the house and almost every day when she leaves it is dark. It's like being in a prison all day, only to see a black night with stars and shadows to look forward to. I must ask her to come up here more often for something, even if I make it up.

I look in the mirror to see all the angles of my hair and glance at my shoulders and back, gleaming from the sweetness of sun. My neck is hardly red and blends in with my light raspberry sunburn. Pain from the rope burn and sunburn are traded for distress about Tommy. Jessy looks grown up in her strapless, straight red dress and acts very sophisticated until we laugh in front of the mirror and do the can-can, screaming with delight.

Bernice watches, then walks toward the door. Before she leaves, she turns around and says, "Jessy, you are a beauty too in that dress and much too growed up."

# 2
## COUNTRY CLUB PARTY

After what feels like an eternal drive with Mom, the white stone walls of the club driveway appear at last. Not having Dad with us in the car chips away at my mood of high hopes. Mom isn't talking very much to Jessy and me—just as well. All the way there my thoughts are only of Tommy.

We are greeted by the colored men. We walk into the fancy entrance to the lounge. Mom says thank you to Edward and Jones, who hold the glass and wood door for us, and I see Jessy curtsey to them while they laugh.

The separate room for my party is in the back of the lounge. It's usually used for meetings or card games, but tonight it's set up with a dance floor, a place for the band, tables and chairs. Blue and pink streamers of crepe paper, balloons and flowers, decorate the room. I told Mom that it had to be these colors because all-girl colors were too prissy.

Only one friend from my class belongs to this exclusive country club, Paul. My close friends in school mostly don't live in huge houses—only apartments or small houses—and they are always making comments about how lucky I am to belong to this club and live in a mansion with central air-conditioning, which they call the "Popsicle Stand" because two people can stand in front of it to cool their bodies. Jessy's two closest friends and some other kids in my class do live in big houses. And all my sister Annie's friends belong to the club because she goes to private school. When Mom tried to get me and Jessy in, they already had their quota of Jewish girls.

I don't ever look forward to going to the country club; in fact, when we are going I feel sad because I know none of my friends are going to be there. Today is an exception. At least Mom and Dad picked the only Jewish country club that has Easter egg hunts. I know this because I have asked friends who belong to the other Jewish clubs. In this town even the Jews are divided by where their ancestors came from, even if they were all born right here in the good old U.S. of A.

The Jews from Eastern Europe belong to separate clubs than those from Western Europe. I guess they're proud to be from a certain area and want to socialize with people that have similar backgrounds. We are in a club with Jews from Eastern Europe. One time my Nana told me her mother came from Romania but her father came from Spain—Spanish Jews are called Sephardic Jews. The other ones are called Ashkenazi Jews. No one in our family ever mentions the Spanish part because the Eastern part of Europe is supposed to be a fancier place to be from. My Dad looks like all the Spaniards I see in pictures and I don't know how my parents can get away with this type of secret. Someday I will tell my children the truth because if the Jews

25

can share holidays with Christians why can't they at least share country clubs with other Jews? I don't understand how, after Hitler, the Jews wouldn't want to stand together as a strong unit and not show prejudice toward their own people.

Mom checks all the place settings while I check all the name tags, since Jessy has disappeared. Tommy will be seated right next to Jessy at her table with her friends. Our seventh and eighth grades are in one school before we go to high school so Jessy's class and mine are together this year. I change Tommy's tag so he is the farthest away from her just as Jessy enters the room.

Smiling, Jessy says, "Oh, Rachael, everything looks perfect. Don't worry about a thing. I saw the band arriving and Jane is here."

"Oh, great. She's early."

Listening, Mom comments, "Best friends should arrive early and stay late."

Jane is the most popular and prettiest girl in my class, but I'm not jealous of her because she is my best friend at school. If I weren't pretty too I would be envious. Jane looks beautiful and we talk quickly about the party because I want her to know that I am still so nervous about Tommy. I look up from our secret conversation to see kids coming in the door holding gifts. I go over to greet them.

From across the room, without obviously looking his way, I see that Tommy finally arrives with Mitch. Hopefully, my excitement and the nervousness I feel in my stomach doesn't show. What if Tommy doesn't sign my dance card? I hate the stupid things. Little cards tied to our wrists with numbered lines that have to be signed by the boy who wants to dance with you. It might be great for the boys who want to dance with you, but what if you don't want to dance with them? Or what if someone you want to dance with doesn't sign your card? Or what if it gets all filled up before he has a chance to? I hate them. But it's what everyone does and everyone expects.

Dad gave me a wrist corsage because I told him a pin corsage may stick me. I put it on the wrist without the dance card. I wish Dad had told me to sign his name on my dance card for one dance but I guess he's too busy with work. Mom could have signed Dad's name but she's thinking about herself, not me—like always.

The band has come and is still tuning up as I see Tommy check out where he is sitting. Presents are being handed to me as my class mates say "Hi" and "Happy Birthday" and remarks about who is there and what they are wearing and if certain couples still like each other. There are conversations going on all around me. I am not used to being the center of attention ever except on my birthday. While I don't feel I'm worth being the center I do like the feeling. It's exciting. Gifts pile up taller than I can see over before Mom comes to take them.

My thoughts are interrupted by a boy saying, "Rachael, let me see your dance card."

I respond holding up my wrist, "Sure, Roy."

Roy is the shortest boy in my class but his engaging smile lights up the schoolroom. His body moves like a dancer, whether he's walking in the hallway or playing at recess. He still has a few boyhood freckles but I can also see tiny hairs starting above his mouth. He is like a baby brother to me because he only comes up to my neck. But even the tall boys in my class seem like babies.

27

Roy says, "Rachael, hope you don't mind—I signed the first dance and second to last."

"No, I don't mind," I say unenthusiastically.

Everyone is directed by Mom to sit down at their places to eat hamburgers and French fries, pickles, salad, and milk shakes. I sit between Jane and Carl.

Carl always stares at me way too long, but we are just friends. He wears his hair slicked back with a ducktail and the grease is practically dripping off it. The taps on his penny loafers can be heard across the dance floor. Even though that hairstyle makes Carl look like a hood, he is shy and doesn't get into trouble—he just wants to look tough.

Tommy walks over toward me and my heart is racing.

"Rachael, do you have a pencil?"

"I see one in the middle of the table."

"I want to sign my name on your dance card before it is filled up."

"Leave one dance for my dad."

"Where is he?"

"At a meeting—but he'll be here."

"I hope someday I'll be able drive around in a sports car and cap looking like Clark Gable."

"Where did you see Dad?"

"Everyone sees him; he has the only green convertible in town."

Dad drives a Jaguar. It's not an American car, like everyone else's. It's from Great Britain.

"I wish he had a Buick or Oldsmobile like everyone else."

"I have to sit at your sister's table to eat."

Rachael couldn't quite read the look in his eyes.

"You look pretty," he went on. Then, with some concern, "But what happened to your neck?"

My cheeks are probably as red as my neck as I confess, "I ran into a tennis rope playing kickball. It doesn't feel as bad as it looks."

Inside I'm crying. He can't ignore my red neck and he doesn't even say "Happy Birthday". I want to throw my dance card at him—but it is tied to my wrist. He holds the card without touching me and writes. It seems to take forever. As he writes I look at his long dark lashes outlining his dreamy eyes. His flat top makes him look taller tonight. When he's done, he walks away without another word.

Mom comes over and whispers in my ear that Dad has been held up and won't be able to come to the party. "Some buyers from New York came in. I'm sorry, honey," she says.

I run into the bathroom after Mom turns away. Jane follows me.

I sob in a stall with the door closed. Jane says, "What is it?"

"My dance card; I don't want to read it."

29

"Let me in there; I will read it."

"No."

"Rachael, everyone will know you're in here."

"I know." I slip the dance card off my wrist and hand it to Jane beneath the stall door. "Read it and tell me how many dances he signed."

Jane grabs the dance card and gasps, "He signed the last four before Roy who has the second to last and you signed your Dad on for the last."

I forgot I had done that.

"Jane, rub my dad's off, would you?"

"Why?"

"He isn't coming. He's working," I blurt out, trying to hold back tears. He had a meeting with some men who help buy clothes for the store, whatever that means."

"Now I know why you ran in here—not just to have me read your dance card. I'm sorry," Jane says.

Mom runs in then and says, "Rachael, I know you're in here. What are you doing?"

Blurry eyed I gurgle out from the stall, "My neck hurts a little and I wanted to look at it."

"Hurry, the kids will wonder what is happening in here."

"Okay, Mom," I say angrily, surprising myself. I open the stall door, dabbing at my eyes with toilet paper, and go over to a sink to rinse my face with cool water.

The three of us come out with me wearing a fake happy look. My card is filled up with friends and some boys I don't know that well because I had to invite my whole class. I dance all night—slow and fast. Even though he didn't bother to sign my dance card, Mitch cuts in a few times.

"Rachael, you look pretty pretty," Mitch says looking at me.

"Pretty pretty!" I laugh. "Are you having fun?"

"Yeah, I like hanging out with younger women."

I laugh, "You look nice in that shirt and tie."

"At least I didn't have to wear a monkey suit."

The dance ends.

Mom dances with a few of her men friends—she invited some of their couple friends— and doesn't seem to care that Dad isn't here. She's been drinking scotch and laughing all night.

I see Tommy everywhere and during every dance, even when he dances with Jessy, as I wait for the four he put his name on. I see Jessy's card and it's empty, like she's too grown up to even bother using it. I wish I could tear mine up. Her friends are real loud all night, like it's their party. They don't mingle with my friends—like we're going to give them polio if they even get near us. Sometimes I want to be at her table too, instead of waiting all night for my dances with Tommy.

The band finally takes a break after announcing they may only have time for one last dance. I can't believe it. Our dance cards were printed for 25 dances. How can they quit before we've had all of them? What if I don't get to

dance with Tommy? Mom should have printed the dance
cards with the right number of dances the band would play.
Again, I want to rip my card into a million pieces.

A few of the shy kids start saying thanks and goodbye
when they get picked up early. I start to lose my enthusiasm
for my fantasy evening with Tommy. I want to go get the
band to start again before everyone leaves but Jane
reassures me that everyone isn't leaving. If Peggy, my best
neighborhood friend was here she would tell me what to
do, but no one in her school was invited. I understand that
it would have been uncomfortable for her to come tonight.
She would tell me not to waste a minute thinking about
Tommy if he wasn't making sure he was showing everyone
that he especially likes me.

This last dance is twenty-five on my card and Tommy
signed starting with twenty. Tommy looks over and our
eyes meet. Paul, the club member, is walking my way for the
last dance even though he didn't sign my card. Paul isn't
following the rules. Tommy and I continue our stare. His
eyes are saying I want the last dance—so why isn't he
walking over here to rescue me from dancing with someone
else? It isn't the girl who's supposed to ride the white horse
and sweep the guy up on its back and ride away.

Paul—the skinniest, tallest, sweetest boy in the whole
class—is my last dance. It's a slow one. My eyes stay closed
as I lean on Paul's chest without looking Tommy's way
again but I can feel him staring at me. When I open my eyes
he's gone. He left without saying goodbye.

As Mom drives us home she's rocking the car with her
foot constantly on and off the gas pedal. It makes me
nauseous. The annoyance is worse in the front because I
can see her foot doing it. Mom is smoking and flicking the
ashes from the cigarette out of the open window, which fly

back onto Jessy's dress in the back seat. No one is talking but the radio is playing, as Ella Fitzgerald soothes the air. The presents are sliding around on the vinyl upholstery in back, sometimes landing on Jessy's lap. Some are in the trunk and clomp together whenever we turn sharply. I hope Tommy's wrapping didn't tear.

Thinking of opening all the presents feels like a burden instead of treasure waiting to be discovered. Dad's car is in the garage as we pull in next to it and go in through the back door. He surprises me by being in the kitchen to greet us.

"Hi, Slim, how was the party?"

"Hi, Dad. Okay. When did you get home?"

"A few minutes ago. I'm sorry I didn't make it, Slim."

"Dad, don't call me that anymore. I'm a grown up now. Please don't call me that," I say as sweetly as I can.

"Okay, Slim…I mean, Rachael."

Mom interrupts, "Let's all go into the living room and Rachael can open her gifts."

Mister is on the couch. He jumps off quickly with a thud when he hears us come in.

The living room has cushy chairs and a couch. There is a formality to the room but Mom and Dad let our friends sit in here when they come to visit. Annie and Rusty come downstairs. Rusty looks like Mom just woke him, which was not a good idea because he will not be amused by opening girl's things. Annie is still dressed from her date with Donald, her fiancé. She looks like a married lady already, with her matching shoes and dress: so prim and proper, like she is going to temple. Her scarf has a messed up "made out" look. Jessy and I sometimes sneak to watch Annie and Donald on the living room couch through the hall mirror. When we cannot hold our giggles any longer, we sneak back to our room and let them out like a blown up balloon.

We will be here all night if I open the presents alone. I ask everyone to help me. If they tear the nice wrapping paper I can still save part of it for my collection. Tommy's may be one that Jessy opens and I don't care. I make sure I put Dad's present under my feet. It is the only gift I really want to see. He always gives me one present alone, without Mom, because when Rusty was born he thought a father should give his son a separate gift. But Jessy, Annie and I told him we would like that as well. I tell everyone I want to open it alone later so my birthday will last until the moment before sleep. Everyone agrees that will make the day longer.

Finally, Tommy's gift is opened by Rusty. It is a necklace, a gold chain with an opal stone surrounded by a gold design. Everyone teases me because it is a romantic gift. It is my first jewelry from a boy. I will never lose it, my whole life, no matter what happens. The wrapping is nothing special but the gift is. Tommy wants me to wear a beautiful necklace and think of him as I wear it. Now I feel afraid because I like him more. What if he changes his mind and wishes he never bought it? Or maybe the gift is something his mom made him bring to be polite. Gifts are sometimes obligations because families are connected. My mom and his grandmother used to live close to each other when my mom was growing up. Mom would visit his grandmother to ask her about private things, like sex and periods. Mom told me the story when I asked her how she knew her. Mom couldn't ask her own mom about boy problems, so she asked Tommy's grandmother.

I thank everyone again and say goodnight with half-hearted hugs. Rusty, who has fallen asleep on the couch, is awakened because he is too big for Dad to carry him upstairs. He wobbles up the stairs. I carry the wrapping paper I want to save with some of the gifts. Jessy and Mom bring the rest of the gifts into my room. Mom tucks us in after we change and does the can-can dance for about a minute in front of our beds. Mom does this when she is drunk. Jessy and I laugh and then she says toodle-oo and leaves.

I wait for Jessy to fall asleep before opening Ruby's present and Dad's. I want to be alone to look at the gifts as long as I please without Jessy telling me to hurry up. Ruby left hers under the bed before she left for her day off. It's another doll with long legs and arms that she made. I call them all Amy and put her in the closet sitting on a shelf with the other Amys. Ruby says my long arms and legs were for a six foot boy but God made a girl at the last minute.

Dad's wrapping is a map of streets in St. Louis that he gets from the gas station for free. The ribbon is string from a kite. Inside the box is a velvety cream-colored holder shaped like an open envelope and inside the envelope is a beautiful shining silver compass. A compass is not what a Dad gives his daughter. He thinks I will get lost but I won't be driving for three more years. I'll put it away with anything else I received that I am not ready for, like the two-piece bathing suit Peggy gave me and the frilly pink underpants Carl gave me.

# 3
# THE TRAIN TO REBELLION

At the train station, summer after summer, I watched my older sisters pull away. I didn't know where they were going and I didn't care. I just wanted to get on that train, any train that was scheduled in chalk on the blackboard. Today is different.

Today the magic of the smoky smell, the roar of the wheels and the high pitched whistle meant hurry, something unpredictable lies ahead. This time the shiny locomotive will take me away from home, where camp memories wait to be made. This is the fourth summer in a row I've decided to go to Camp Hiawatha in Wisconsin.

It's a Jewish all-girls camp and I'm looking forward to the train ride, but I definitely don't have the same excitement I had the first time. I'm not sure why, but after that first summer there I never felt the cherished train ride was worth the destination, but I didn't tell anyone. Confronting Mom and Dad with a request to stay home was way too scary. Their decisions were not to be questioned. Even when Jessy refused to go back to Camp Hiawatha, they said she could pick another camp but staying home in the humid summer in St. Louis wasn't allowed. I guess their summer vacation was home without us!

I never think about what Mom or Dad do in the summers when I go away to camp. Maybe if they asked more about what activities or experiences I had for two months, I would be curious about what exactly they do in the summer. Mom always works in the store at least part of most days when I'm home. But I'm not even sure about that. How many days or hours—I really never think to ask, and she never tells me. What does Mom do when she doesn't work? Golf, ladies' luncheons, charity work? I don't know about Mom and she doesn't know about me. Dad works all the time except on Thursdays and Sundays when he plays golf. Maybe in the summer he does different things. When I stop to think about it, I don't know my parents very well at all.

I decide not to rock the boat and stay put at Camp Hiawatha. I like knowing the kids and counselors and daily activities. Besides, going to a new camp would be even more frightening. It's not like I ever feel comfortable at home with my own family anyway.

A few days before leaving I go with my friends to the public pool. We sit on the hot sizzling concrete without a chair or towel and enjoyed being together.

The good part of camp is my best friend Susie. We're affectionately dubbed the "Gold Dust Twins" by the camp directors because all summer we're rarely seen apart. Susie makes me feel happy, like my friends at school do. Without her I would feel lost. When we wrote letters to each other during the school year we decided to be daring teenagers and not be perfect sweet little campers this summer. We never said anything in our letters about what we would do exactly. If it wasn't for Susie returning to Camp Hiawatha this summer, I would be on a different train going to a different camp.

Susie lives in Memphis. She has curly brown hair, is light-hearted, and loves to laugh. She is very social in her hometown. I know this because I flew to Memphis on my very first airplane ride last Thanksgiving to visit her family and friends. We went to parties, kids' houses, and they came over to hers. I fit in with her friends. I could tell because we laughed together and they asked me a lot of questions about my life in St. Louis.

Barbara, one of her friends, is the most beautiful girl I have ever seen. I am even nervous talking to her, like I am with a boy. I could look at her all day—but I don't want to kiss her like I want to kiss Tommy. She is like a big smile that is joyous and silly. Every boy that meets her must be in love with her.

This Thanksgiving vacation, Susie is coming to St. Louis to stay with us. She will see I am also socially popular but, unlike her, quiet and uncomfortable around my family. Rather than looking forward to Susie's visit, I am already worried about impressing her— like Mom does with her friends. Susie doesn't try to make people like her. She is the leader and I follow. I don't know how to be any other way.

This week Mom, Ruby and I pack my trunk with all the required clothes, equipment, toiletries, and the compass Dad gave me for my birthday. Dad doesn't know this, but once I got lost going back to my tent when I was out gathering wood. I got really scared until I finally found my way back, so I am happy to have the compass this year.

When we first open the trunk, a stale aroma wafts out, saved along with the letters Mom had written to me—they smell musty too. Dad never wrote. I throw Mom's letters in my wastebasket—don't know why I kept them. The memories Susie and I make at camp are my only lasting ones. The others are lost, like the dust gathered in the corners of my trunk.

I also pack a small suitcase for the overnight train ride from Chicago to Mercer, a small town in Wisconsin. This overnight bag houses secret and magical memories—the first and last nights of camp—the ones on the train. These two nights are the magical part of the two months.

I pretend to be excited about the whole camp experience as I approach the train platform.

"Rachael," Mom loudly pronounces, "I want you to have the time of your life, darling."

In a place where Mom's friends are around, she uses darling a lot. I think it is called "putting on airs."

"I will, Mom," I say faintly, as my eyes tear up. "I really wish Dad could have come."

"He felt sick, dear—as I told you—but he wanted so much to see you off."

Dad would be talking to all the parents here and I would hardly say anything to him except goodbye. He loves to kid around with people he knows, and even strangers, just to make them laugh. Mom is so serious saying goodbye. My face looks unhappy so I look at the ground and force a smile before looking up. Mom sees me smiling and she smiles too. Dad hates to see me with a sad face and would make sure I smiled for him by making a joke.

"Mom, I have to go to the group by the train; they're calling us."

The group is all the girls going from St. Louis; some are thirteen like me, some are older, some younger. There are a few women counselors, too. I'm not close with any of the other campers going from here so I don't much care who I end up sitting with.

"Oh, dear, the time will fly by and we will see you at camp on visiting day."

"Write me the date so I will know way before," I say. "Can you stay longer than one day this time? I promise to get you and Dad liver and onions for lunch. You can eat mine, too." I laugh as we walk quickly toward the group.

"Dad and I will try to stay as long as we can," Mom promises. She hugs me as though I was a jagged piece of glass that might cut her, but I hug back really hard. She always promises to do lots of things when we're in public.

I wave and Mom looks back when she walks away. My eyesight is blurry with tears, but I am not sad about leaving her. I feel lonely without Ethel, Ruby and Bernice. Summer flowers at camp smell like Ethel's cakes, so I always have some by my bed to think of her.

My emotions feel trapped, like fireflies in a jar. I don't want to leave and I don't want to stay. As I climb the metal steps to the train, the Negro porter tips his hat to me and I smile back—not a fake one, but genuine. The shiny varnished wood seats face each other. I make sure to pick one that's backward to punctuate what I am leaving.

The whistle blows and the sound of chugging plays like familiar music. Already I feel better. The industrial parts of the city and the downtown office buildings are strangers to me as we pass by. It could be any city. I am not at all familiar with this part of St. Louis. My grandfather had his clothing store downtown where Dad worked until he was thirty. Then he moved it to the suburbs, but I have never seen exactly where. I even wonder what streets Grandpa and Dad walked and where they had coffee. I will ask Mom or Dad to show me where the stores were. I never knew Grandpa, but I can at least know where he spent most of his life working.

Soon we are passing farms with scratched and peeled-paint barns and silos, passenger trains going the opposite way flashing pieces of faces, small town train stations with their shingled pitched roofs and people meeting and leaving—they all flicker like arbitrary and mysterious silent films. I yearn to know who lives on the farms and why a crying boy dressed in a suit is saying goodbye to a man who looks like his grandfather. Who is that Oriental lady standing up in the aisle of that passing train, and where is it going? At home I don't wonder about people I pass in cars.

At our first stop, the aromas from pushcarts come in through the windows and mix with the smell of the train as it pauses to gather the waiting people and deposit others. I want to taste all the foods slowly and ask who cooked them and how they were prepared. There's music blaring in the station—it's Ella Fitzgerald singing to us.

The colored porter walks with a colored family way down the track to lead them to the last car. The dad and mom hold hands with three small children—a boy about five and two twin girls about three. The mom and girls have on white gloves and are dressed in party dresses. The boy and dad are in long sleeve dress shirts and khakis with dress shoes but no socks. They look like they are going to church or a wedding, not just riding on a train on a hot summer day. I think this ride must be very special to the family. It is probably their first time out of the town or they are going to see some relatives for the first time. The boy breaks free of his father and dances wildly to the music in the distance. The dad grabs the boy's hand again.

After they get on, I tell the counselor I'm going to the bathroom. I wind my way through the shaky, bumpy train, sometimes thrown off-balance, slapping myself against the walls, and when I open the door to the last car, I can see the family getting seated. Benny Goodman's band is playing on a radio in the dusty corner. They look up and see me watching them but I pretend to look for a porter while I look around. The colored boy is dancing freely again. The seats in the last car are wobbly and dirty and there aren't enough, so many of the families sit on the floor. I am sorry they are in that filthy car and wish I could bring them to where I sit.

The morning goes by faster than the train moves. We campers go to the dining car to eat lunch. The swagger of the train feels like an amusement park ride, especially when I step between the cars. The sound of the wheels' movements are louder here and it's thrilling to watch the ground sweep by. Kids laugh as they try to walk upright. As we order lunch, the salt and pepper shakers, bowls of pickles, and small ketchup holders slide around the table top like a pinball machine.

At the Chicago station where we change trains, all the campers from different cities meet. Susie and I hug and laugh. The letters we wrote to each other about boys, school, and what we dare to do this summer has cemented our friendship. She looks the same, but different. Her hair is longer—shoulder length—and she's taller. I wonder if I look different to her.

We go to the public restroom to look at each other's first bras. I tell her about the dance with Thunderbird Camp this summer and how I found out about it from Tommy, the boy I really like. I don't reveal to her what happened at my birthday dance when Tommy left without dancing with me, but I will later, maybe.

"What about you? Do you like anyone at home?" I ask as we leave the stall.

I want to find out a secret of Susie's to sew up the hole I am feeling in our friendship because Susie seems distracted and is not concentrating on our talk.

"No one in particular. There are some cute boys I have a crush on but I can't decide if any of them likes me," Susie gives nothing away.

"Like who? I know all the boys in your group." I say not wanting a vague

answer.

"I want to get out of this restroom. It smells," Susie says.

We both exit the restroom and the discussion is ended. Susie heads toward the berths. I follow. I feel sad that Susie didn't tell me anything about who she likes after I told her who I liked. Maybe she is jealous that I already know Tommy is coming to the dance and she doesn't know if anyone she likes will be coming.

We get our berth numbers for the overnight train. I always make sure I get an upper berth. Some years I have to lie about nausea, fear of crashing, sleepwalking, and breathing problems to make sure I get it. Mom backs me up with a note, just in case. She knows the only subject I talk about with enthusiasm is my love of the overnight train ride on the upper bunk. When I step on the ladder to climb up to my berth, it feels like I enter another dimension. The bunks are made up in crisp, bleached, white ironed sheets with blue musty-smelling blankets that say Pullman Car. I watch the Pullman porters help the other campers find their berths or carry linens and valises through the narrow aisle.

After I say goodnight to my friends, I close the curtains that are now streaked with age—curtains to the real world—and treasure the small, secure and safe rectangle. The rich lacquered mahogany walls separating the bunks look like they were used on a king's castle or a yacht.

Every stop is an adventure to be tasted, magnified by the blackness of night—summer lightning storms, glistening creeks and rivers shining in the moonlight, fireworks and sparklers from early Fourth of July parties, windows lit up. A man in a Korean War Navy uniform sees his family off. He is going to active duty while they are going to grandma's house in Chicago for the summer, I fantasize. They take flash pictures with a Brownie camera like the one I take to camp. They could have a picture all together—without one person left out—if I could just get off the train for a minute.

The circus train we pass is painted with Ringling Brothers in red on each car. The animals have bars at the top so they can't escape. Some of the compartments are tall for a giraffe or elephant. I went to the circus once in St. Louis. It was set up in a parking lot with apartment and office buildings all around, but I never saw one in a quaint town set up in a field next to the tracks where the circus people travel by the train's schedule.

Circus people must have problems that are so different from mine. Are the animal feeding schedules arranged so they can get enough sleep? Are the dwarfs able to room with the muscle men? Does the bearded lady get called names? Does the lion tamer practice cracking his whip when he can't sleep?

When we pull into the next station, it's very dark but I can see a hobo hiding in the corner of the station, shining his flashlight, ready to hop a freight train. A young softball team dressed in uniforms from Kansas City must be on their way to play a team in Chicago as they climb up the stairs of the train going the other way. Before they get on, one of the boys get his leather ballgame shoes shined by the colored man sitting on an unbalanced fruit crate. Maybe his mom gave him ten cents so his shoes can shine like a pro. Their suitcases delight me with their colors and designs— striped patterns on slick vinyl, grey metal streamlined aluminum, wooden trunks with stamps of places traveled, worn leather bags of browns and faded blacks mix in the low lights of the stations. Camper trunks are ordinary military brown metal. My mom has a white leather trunk that is as soft as melted chocolate and lined in butter yellow linen; I like to pet it like a baby kitten. Mysteries and adventures could be revealed if I could see inside their suitcases. I look through Mom's movie magazines for suitcase and trunk pictures to imagine who might buy them and where they will travel.

Hazy lights of towns and farms are like ruby, emerald, diamond and sapphire jewels. There are no bright city lights the rest of the ride. Stations and trestles are designed in Art Noveau, Art Deco, and Victorian or Colonial style. I learned about architecture at the St. Louis Art Museum on our school's yearly visit. While most of the kids giggled about the naked statues, I asked questions about periods of art. The boys in my class are immature and embarrassed about nudity at the museums. The girls want to be liked by

45

them so they laughed too. Nana, my dad's mom, taught me to appreciate art and the time it reflects. She buys furniture and tchotchkes for our home. "It is more fun to bid on an object in an auction than buy it in a store," Nana said.

I see names of towns—Rockford, South Beloit, Janesville, Wisconsin Dells, Tomah, La Crosse, Columbus, Portage—on the station signs. I keep a list of each town we stop at in my secret diary. At each stop, even at night when people are sleeping, music blares—Frank Sinatra, Cole Porter, or Billie Holiday.

It is one in the morning and the last thing I see before I drift off is a mom dressed in a suit, hat, heels, and black gloves with a baby in one arm while holding hands with a boy about nine. The boy sits on a bulging worn out suitcase and waves to the train conductor. He is dressed in a sport coat, tie, a white shirt that hangs out of his pants, a cowboy hat and riding boots. His mom kisses and hugs him, crying, while the conductor grabs his hand to take him to the train. He is going to visit his dad living on a ranch in Wisconsin, I decide, because his dad is getting settled before the rest of the family packs up to move. My story may be wrong but in the morning I am going through every car until I know that boy is safe. I wish I could lend him the compass Dad gave me for my birthday so he would at least know what direction he's going in.

Breakfast is in the elegant polished dining car, but before I can eat I have to find that boy. I walk through five cars until I see him from the glass window between cars. I enter the car. He's sitting with a porter, talking. Pretending to look for something I lost, I glance to make sure the smile the boy's wearing is genuine and not a scary smile for appeasement.

They are making up a funny story and taking turns

46

about what happens next.

"I saw a big tiger crossing the street in our neighborhood," the porter laughs.

"He was green with red dots. I saw him too," the boy says.

"Did you see what was on his back?"

"Yeah, a blue suitcase with a girl riding on top."

"I know. Maybe she had to save her baby sister from taking long naps."

"No, he wanted water and the girl was showing him where."

I would say, "All the animals were following behind them that they didn't see like a giraffe, an elephant, a dog, an ostrich, and a kangaroo. If they would turn around they would have a jolly time talking about where to find the water hole."

It would be fun to sit down and join them to curb my insatiable appetite for storytelling, but instead I run back through the four cars to the dining car, feeling joyous that the boy is fine.

One of the counselor's voice booms out, "Why are you late, Rachel?"

"I had a stomach ache," I lie, "I was in the bathroom."

Making up stories seems to be my favorite hobby. Susie sits at another table with Candy, a friend of ours from camp. Candy is pretty, with short hair that looks like she had it done at the beauty shop. She has a baby face with fat cheeks and talks calmly in a southern accent, smiling all the while.

Susie didn't save me a seat. She seems to be avoiding me to make closer friends with Candy and anyone else that happens to be near her. The other three summers she didn't do that. Last year Susie would have felt bad about Tommy not dancing with me at my party, but she's so different this summer—I'm not sure I can trust her with my secret. She probably wouldn't even care or listen to what I say—that I wonder if Tommy will write, if he will dance with me at the camp dance, why he didn't dance with me at my party and why he didn't even say goodbye.

This must be how that hobo I saw feels— begging for food, a place to sleep, alone in a crowd, and no one to share secret thoughts with. I could probably even leave the train at some obscure town, and I don't think anyone would notice for a while, not even Susie. Last year I didn't need an excuse to get her attention by telling her secrets I wouldn't tell anyone else.

We arrive at Mercer Train Station, the last stop. I wish the yellow school bus wasn't already waiting. The frightened feeling I have didn't start until now. The morning is cool with the familiar fresh smell of pines and damp wood mulch creaking as I walk to the bus with Susie. Maybe she feels badly about not saving me a seat at breakfast. I notice that Candy is walking with someone else. I still have a lump in my throat because I am trying to make her not leave me.

The bus ride is bumpy and uncomfortable. As soon as I see Bass Lake from the bus window, the dread of cold water swims with "leach checks" gives me a nauseous feeling. Leach checks are when another camper or counselor checks your whole body immediately after swimming in Bass Lake. A lot of the younger campers

scream the first time they see a leach on their body. Salt is
put on it to kill it. Leaches are brown- black slimy things,
about two to three inches long and two fingers wide. Some
kids cut them in half to make two new leaches, but that
makes me sick. When Mom and Dad visit we will walk to
the lake and I will tell them again about how frightened I
am of these beasts. My mom always checks my head when I
return from camp for any ticks. Ticks are disgusting, but
they don't seem prehistoric like leaches.

The camp buildings appear and dust swirls by the
windows as we swing around the driveway. When we get
off the bus, Susie walks away from me to join Candy.
Without Susie I go up the twenty-four steps (which seem
like a hundred and twenty four), to the main building, and I
sit on the floor next to her and Candy. I have decided right
now that I need to make other friends, not hang around
being ignored.

We listen about new and old activities, then sign up for
classes. We are also told which cabins we are in. Susie and I
are together in the same cabin with Candy. Susie and Candy
look at each other and scream, elated when they hear this,
but they don't look at me. I really just want to go home.
Instead I hold in my tears and try to pretend I don't care.

Candy is just a prissy girl who should be in a shirt dress
with flats, going to lunch at Famous-Barr, the department
store, instead of at camp. Susie will find out goody-two-
shoes Candy will not join us in being daring teenagers, even
if she says she will. I know she is a phony and Susie will
find out, too. Then Susie and I will be the "gold dust twins"
again.

I sign up for sailing, tennis, archery, crafts, and
swimming. They could just as well be sewing, painting or
ceramics because they're just distractions until I see Tommy

at the camp dance. Susie plans to take horseback riding with Candy but I would never! Horses scare me more than bats, leaches or ticks. They are gorgeous and elegant but their power and haughty looks feel like a tidal wave ready to hit the beach.

Making sure there isn't anyone around, I hesitantly go over to Sylvia, one of the camp directors, to ask her about the dance. She tells me it will be in August. I don't say a word to her or anyone about Tommy.

Maybe he'll send me a letter and at mail call I'll be blushing when I see his return address on the envelope. All my friends will ask who it's from but I will I run away to a secret place to read it. Everyone wants to get letters, but if someone gets one from a boy, that is the biggest thing to happen in the day. Mom usually writes about once a week and Annie or her fiancé Donald writes. He's an artist so he draws a picture over the whole front of the envelope in colored pencils.

In my letter I will ask Tommy why he didn't say goodbye at my party. The weird memories I have from the party are like gloomy night shadows on a Rembrandt painting that I want to redo with bright sunny colors from a Van Gogh. If he wants to be with me like I yearn for him, the camp dance will erase those dark memories.

We have snacks for lunch during sign up time. Some of the little kids, ten years old, cry because it is their first sleep-away. The only time I cry is when I get home. Mom says I am "camp-sick." I do want to be somewhere else, but not camp.

"Do we have to eat it if we don't like what is served?" One of the new campers asks.

Lon, the other director, answers, "Yes, you have to eat everything on your plate. Only take a little of something if you don't think you will like it, but you must try everything."

I detest the camp food. I have gagged trying to finish hot liver. If you don't finish what's on your plate, the directors will make you sit at their table until you do. When they serve that hot oily salad dressing on lettuce and or the rice pudding I try to sneak it to someone at my table. I pass the plates underneath the table, trying not to catch the dusty stalactites that hang there. Once I got caught and had to finish everything on my plate. I threw up and the vomit splashed onto Sylvia's shirt and shoes.

I go around the building to see who is working in the kitchen this summer. They come out the backdoor for a break where they talk, smoke, laugh, and pet a few scroungy dogs that roam the campgrounds. Molly, a colored girl about 20, is there every year and we smile at each other real friendly as we remember each other from last year. I recall she was always by herself and even now she's sitting by herself. I wonder if she's daydreaming because she has a distant look in her eyes. I remember that stare of hers like she wants to be somewhere else. I make believe that I'm working in the kitchen with her instead of being a camper and she's my friend. I hear a loud voice coming from the front of the building that makes me jump, like I was in a bad dream instead of being a camper being ignored by her former best friend.

Lon shouts from a loud megaphone on the other side of the building, "Okay, girls, off to your new cabins and get into your dress clothes for dinner."

I think, dress clothes at camp? Oh, then I remember—all whites.

We unpack, make our beds, play jacks, and get dressed in all whites—shirt, shorts, sailor hat and socks—our dress clothes for dinner. Our counselor, Loreen, is a large, muscular, fat, woman who looks like a man, with her short blonde haircut and no make-up. She must be five-foot-ten and looks old, like she's thirty-five. I know her from the other years and I am scared of her.

Loreen goes over all the rules. I think how much she looks like a fat old man. Susie and I giggle silently while we roll our eyes at each other. I want to tell Susie that she's different this year. Loreen leaves our area of the cabin and goes to her room. I smell cigarette smoke coming from the back door. Susie and I get together on my bed and whisper.

"Maybe we could steal her cigarettes," I say.

"What if she catches us?" Susie's eyes grow big.

"We'll wait till she's down by the lake and sneak up here together. She'll never know who took them."

"Have you got your period yet?" Susie asks.

"Not yet. Have you?"

"No. Me, neither."

We laugh that maybe smoking will make it start. Mom, Dad, and Annie all smoke.

"If we solo sail this year, the lake will be the best place to try smoking," I suggest.

"Candy got her period three months ago," Susie says.

Candy is putting her clothes away and smiles at me. She is never angry and doesn't seem jealous when Susie and I

52

talk. I'd want to be just like her if I didn't hate her so much.

After dinner, we have time to play records, ping pong, or board games. I leave and go in back of the dining lodge. There are some cars I don't recognize parked on the hill and new faces out on a break. The colored and white help are talking in separate groups, like last summer. As I wait for Molly to come out, Tim, a tall, cute, white guy who seems kind of shy and Ellen, a plump, pimply-faced white girl in her twenties, both say a friendly hello. They were here last year too.

When Molly finally comes out, to my surprise she hugs me really hard and laughs. I hope I hugged her just as hard. She is from Mississippi, has a drawl, is short, and looks heavier this year. She loves to come to Wisconsin for the cold nights. We plop down on a log.

"I have a present for you that I brought from home," I lie, because I want her to be my new friend.

Bernice taught me to crochet and I brought a scarf I made to give to Susie, but I've changed my mind and give it to Molly instead. I also lie and say I bought her my mom's favorite perfume, Channel No. 5, which I really brought for the dance so Tommy would never forget how good I smell. Mom doesn't know I took it and won't even notice because she has so many bottles of the same perfume.

Molly almost cries as she thanks me over and over. I was scared she would think it was weird that I had presents for her when I had never really talked to her before. I think she needs a best friend, too. I run to my cabin to get the items, come back, then we race to her room to put them away.

She lives upstairs above the main dining hall in a dingy

room with no bathroom or window. The bed looks lumpy and the dresser is a tin filing cabinet. She has stacks of paperback books all over the floor with pictures of men and women embracing on the covers. I see *Lady Chatterley's Lover*. This is a book I will ask Molly about borrowing. I know I have to read it secretly because I heard it has vivid love scenes in it. The naked light bulb hanging on a wire swings in the breeze from the open door. Maybe I can make her a shade for the bulb in arts and crafts. I'm no good at hiding what I'm feeling.

"Rachael, this is fine for me so don't look like you feel sorry for me," Molly says, reading my sad eyes.

"I'm so happy to see you this year. I was just expecting a little nicer place for you."

"I get away from home so I can have my own room here. There isn't a place in our house where I can be alone; just chaos of dirty diapers, liquor bottles and laundry piled up. Dad isn't home for days. Mom is overwhelmed with dishes and the baby, and my little brother Johnny runs around with a wild bunch after dark, so we all worry. Rachael, I love my freedom here. All I have to do is my job and save my earnings to help at home—and I don't have to do no one else's dirty laundry. I can just hibernate here."

"Okay, Molly, I'm sorry I shouldn't butt into your business."

"You didn't know. It's okay. Compared to where you live it probably looks like a bum wouldn't even live here."

We hug and I run off to the activity for the night thinking about what my room and house look like at home. I'm positive Molly wouldn't like me if she ever saw it. She would think I was a spoiled rich kid. I suppose I am.

I have never had a colored twenty-one year old friend. Mom and Dad think colored people should be help, not friends. They never say this but I have never seen Mom or Dad with a colored friend. I don't know if my parents even like them. They never talk about it. I wish they would say what they are thinking.

I stay up late and use a flashlight under my covers to write a letter to Tommy. I think about how cute he smiles and wonder what his lips taste like.

In the morning before breakfast, I go around in back of the kitchen to see if Molly is there to ask her if I should burn the letter or send it. Molly will know what to do. I already feel more myself with her than anyone at camp. I go around a different way to the kitchen, through a wooded area, so I can read over the letter before I let Molly see it. Oh, my God I see Molly making out with Tim in the back seat of his car parked where trees surround them and no one can see. I hadn't even seen them talk to each other on breaks. Rather than run away, I spy on them. The car windows steam over and their heads go down onto the back seat. Molly and I aren't close enough that I can tell her I saw her, but I hope she tells me that Tim is her new boyfriend. Then I will tell her about Tommy. She seems like a family away from home, even though she is only one person.

I go to a different wooded area and take out the letter I wrote last night. I don't want to watch Molly and Tim make out anymore. It feels like a betrayal. I read:

*"Dear Tommy,*

*I miss you so much. I wish we could have danced all night at my party. You looked so handsome and are the most fun boy in school. Why did you leave without even saying goodbye and then give me that beautiful necklace? I know we haven't spent very much time together but it seems like you like me. I cannot wait to see you at the camp dance.*

*Fondly,*

*Rachael Hirsch.*

Mom always signed her letters "fondly" and I want to sound grown-up.

This letter is the opposite of what I should write to be cool and not let him know how I feel, but I don't care if he knows. Anyway, I'll probably rip it up. I'll show Molly another time—not now.

# 4
## REBELLIOUS ESCAPADES

One morning, early in the session, Susie, Candy, and I walk together to Trude Lake for swim class and we pass the oldest girls' cabin. We step inside and see no one is there. The Kotex box in the bathroom screams "mature girls" to me. I am so jealous that every girl in this cabin has her period. Susie and I make the Kotex into bonnets and tie them under our chins. Candy runs ahead when she sees what we we're up to. She has no guts and I'm glad Susie sees it.

When we arrive at the lake a counselor spots us with our new "hats" and sends Susie and me to the director's cabin. Lon, the, masculine looking director, takes me to my cabin, makes me pack some of my clothes, and, as punishment, makes me move to Papoose, the cabin for the youngest girls.

"You're going to stay there a while, since you behave like a ten year old," she growls.

That's so cruel! I hate Lon and Sylvia.

Susie's only punishment is that she has to call her parents and tell them what she did. How come she didn't have to stay at Papoose? Maybe her dad gave the camp money so she wouldn't have to. If I had to call Mom and Dad they would probably tell Lon and Sylvia to do whatever they want as punishment.

When I visit Molly that evening, I tell her how I got punished and what I did to cause it. I don't say a word about seeing her in the car with Tim. She listens to me with a stiff face and then her voice soothes me like I was family. Molly agrees that it is a mean punishment to belittle me like that.

I sleep in Papoose for three more nights until Friday night when Lon says that, since it is the Sabbath, I can return to my cabin. I quickly pack and move back and laugh to myself that I will always remember this Sabbath and what it secretly meant to me.

*Dear Tommy,*

*I was moved to Papoose, the youngest cabin, because I stole something from another cabin that would make you laugh, but I don't think I could ever tell you what I stole. I hope you will dance only with me when you come to my camp, because I would like that.*

*Fondly,*

*Rachael Hirsch*

Two weeks go by without my getting into trouble. Susie and I hardly even talk to each other, but one evening she and I happen to walk to the dining hall alone together and decide on the way to go into Pill Inn—that's where sick campers are treated and sometimes sleep. Since no one is inside sick, it's empty and the nurse has already gone to dinner. Spontaneously, we jump on all the beds and mess them up but then, when bats start flying around the rafters, we run hysterically screaming out of the "Inn."

When we arrive at the dining hall, everyone is already eating at the tables. Sylvia stands and shouts, "Where have you two been?"

We remain silent.

"It's the Sabbath and you missed prayers. I say, where have you been?"

Susie speaks up. "We just stopped in at Pill Hill for some Asprin."

"Aspirin my foot," Sylvia replies, ordering one of the counselors to run to Pill Inn and see what we've been up to. When she comes back and tells Sylvia what a mess the place is in, Sylvia says, "Both of you will be restricted from getting any free time for a week. Plus I want you to write an apology to me, Lon, the nurse, and the whole camp to be read out loud at dinner tomorrow night."

Susie and I decide to not do more rebellious acts this summer because we might get kicked out of camp. This agreement doesn't last, though, because we both like the secret thrill of maybe getting away with being bad.

*Dear Tommy,*

*Camp is becoming a place to be different than I am at home. I know you think I am so quiet and shy but you should see me here. I am daring and rebellious. In fact, I might even kiss you first when I am with you at the dance. But we will have to find a secret place so no one will see us.*

*Fondly,*

*Rachael Hirsch*

I wonder if I will ever send any of the letters. I have hidden all of them under my towels on my shelf. Molly will tell me what to do.

Susie and I are the leaders in deciding to lock out Loreen, our counselor, because none of us in the cabin like her. We all pile up beds and furniture in front of the door one night while she is out. When Loreen can't open the door, she yells at us. Her booming voice scares us, so we let her in. The whole cabin is punished but, by our guilty faces and past reputations, Loreen knows that Susie and I are the leaders of this prank. She makes us clean her mud caked shoes. In addition, the whole cabin has to miss the weekly movie for Saturday evening.

While Susie is in Loreen's room cleaning her shoes, she steals her cigarettes.

I can't go to sleep thinking of the letters I've written to Tommy. I know I will never send them.

The next day at sailing, Susie and Candy and I are all on separate sailfish, which are flat-bottomed sailboats for one or two people. After three years of sailing experience at camp, we are finally trusted to sail solo.

I have my letters to Tommy with me and, once I'm out in the lake, I tear them into little pieces and toss them in the water. If I had a bottle I would have put them in it so another person someday would read my letters and wonder what happened to Rachael and Tommy.

After Susie and I tell Candy our plans to smoke the stolen cigarettes, she tells us she doesn't want to. Maybe she feels left out, since Susie and I planned this escapade without her. She seems more grown up than Susie and me, but I don't want to be grown up and not have fun.

I tie our sailfishes together with ropes and Susie lights up the cigarettes for us. Even though they got drenched from the water slopping over the sides of the boat as we sailed far from shore, they are now dry from the blazing sun. I take a drag. I don't inhale. It feels and tastes awful. I cough a lot. Susie is coughing, too. Still, just holding the cigarette makes me feel grown up. We laugh and agree to drag the smoke in, hoping it tastes better that way.

We are unaware that the sailing instructor has been watching us through a pair of binoculars. When we sail into the dock, she tells us what she saw. "Now you have to unrig all of the sailboats for the rest of the day," she commands.

Candy hears our punishment and, uncontrollably with her back turned to us, laughs.

Actually, I like coiling the ropes and putting the sails into neat folds by the masts. Every time I look at the rope, I think of Tommy. The last time a rope was the center of my life was in the Casey's backyard before my birthday party— when I had everything to look forward to. I thought that the day would be the best day of my life until the rope burn and the disastrous party changed that forever.

There are three weeks left of camp. Our parents are called about the smoking incident. Susie's parents are away in Europe so her only punishment is that she'll have to come to camp two weeks later next year—if she even decides to come back. But my parents are told I will be put on a train to come home two weeks early as a consequence for smoking and stealing cigarettes. They are told a porter will take care of me, make sure I get on and off the right trains, and watch over me the whole time.

My parents were getting ready to visit me in a few days so they tell me over the phone that they're canceling their visit. Mom isn't angry, but her voice sounds like she is talking to a stranger about the roof leaking or the toilet overflowing. I hear Dad in the background saying to get off because the call will cost a fortune. I wish my parents would get mad like other parents; likely they didn't want to visit me anyway. Probably they're relieved they don't have to interrupt all their parties and golf games.

I'm trying to imagine the train ride home alone with only a porter for company.

Everyone in my cabin says she will write me train letters and Molly promises she will give me some of her romance novels for the ride home. I already know about intercourse. My sister's friend, Jenny, told me what it was a few months ago.

I was standing with Jenny, Jessy's friend, waiting for a streetcar to take me to the drugstore where Mom was going to pick me up to take me home. Jenny was waiting for the same streetcar. She just started talking about intercourse like we were talking about the weather. I think she wanted me to know she knew. I kept a neutral look on my face as I listened but I was secretly in shock.

"Sounds to me like a doctor would have to do that to two people in the office," I said, "like an operation."

Jenny laughed.

The part I don't understand is how the man and

women manage to get into the position to do intercourse. The way I picture it, it doesn't seem romantic at all. I'm hoping Molly's books will explain it—and also how long you have to do it that way. I don't understand how it could be fun.

All the thirteen through fifteen year old girls are invited to the "Social with Thunderbird Camp." It's to be on a Thursday afternoon before dinner. Lon, the director, pulls me aside and says Susie informed her that no one in our cabin would go to the dance if I didn't get to go.

Susie also said that going home two weeks early is enough of a punishment. Susie tells Lon they really mean it and if I can't attend, all seven of them would pretend to be sick and lie in bed in their pajamas and not get ready. If they were made to go, they wouldn't dance when boys asked them. They would say no thank you and just sit there. I'm shocked that they all care about me that much.

Mail call comes without a letter or postcard from Tommy. Maybe he wrote some and never sent them, too. Every day this week Susie asks me if I'm excited to see him. I finally tell her about how much I like him and want to be his girlfriend but I still don't trust her that much. She might not feel badly for me if I told her how he humiliated me at my birthday party. She might tell Candy and they could make fun of me behind my back. Susie and I are still friends but we don't plan trouble together anymore, and we don't talk as much, and she still is with Candy more than me.

I am excited to see him, but my body feels like a gigantic train station with millions of locomotives crashing into it at once. I can't untangle the mess they are making inside me. The social with Thunderbird is today at four o'clock! Fear, excitement, loneliness, confusion, sadness and disappointment are all crowding my head and body at once.

I see Molly behind the kitchen after breakfast. I must talk to her about the dance today since she is my very best friend here and I need to tell her how scared I am about seeing Tommy.

After I tell her, Molly says, "Honey friends drift in and out of your life all the time. It's natural. You just be yourself with Tommy. He'll be lucky to dance once with you after what he did at your birthday party." Then Molly tells me she got fired because she missed too much work and was often late so, like me, she will leave soon. Molly stares at me like she wants to share more but maybe thinks I'm too young. Then she says that tomorrow she will tell me a secret. I feel so badly for her. She needs the money. Everyone in our cabin is dressed like we are in some kind of military service. We are all in white pants and white, crisply ironed, short sleeve shirts with sailor hats we brought to wear in the sun, not to a dance. I get dressed faster than anyone. If I could wear a pretty full skirt and dressy blouse I would tell Tommy how rude he was at my party. But dressed like this, like a boy, I don't want to tell him. I don't usually care much what clothes I have on unless boys I like are around. I'd rather be on the train going home in this outfit. My mom is always in pretty lady-like clothes for Dad, even when they stay home. Mom acts all flirty with Dad when she is in these outfits.

Walking to the dining hall for the dance, Susie and I talk about Tommy. I tell her how I'm not as nervous about seeing him because I don't want to tell her the truth. I'm so scared he will ignore me. She tells me I look gorgeous even in the stupid outfit and Tommy will like me today. I feel better she said something nice, but how does she know he will like me? Each stair I climb to the dining hall feels like my legs are heavier than my packed trunk.

The second I walk in I spot Tommy talking to another

boy, even though his back is turned away from the door. My heart is completely stopped and I can't breathe. Maybe I'm having a heart attack. I want to run away and never see him again. I want to cry because I'm afraid of him.

He turns and looks like a dazzling movie star standing with the other boys. His tan arms and white smile are taking my breath away. His madras shirt is tucked into his white shorts to show his slim body. Dad would call us both Slim now. Even though it isn't dark enough yet to see the romantic moonlight come through the glass windows, I feel like I'm in a trance. The counselors have put name tags on the table for dinner. Tommy and I wave at each other before we start to eat. I'm seated next to two boys whom I can barely look at. They're talking but their words sound like garbled sounds in my head. Maybe I should excuse myself and go to Pill Inn to lie down before I faint. I can't even tell whether it's pleasure or fear that I'm feeling. Tommy is all I can think of. It feels like hours before tables are cleared and chairs are moved for dancing. Then Tommy is walking over to me.

"Hello, pretty girl," he says loudly, a few feet before stopping in front of me.

"Hi," I say, and can think of nothing more to say.

"Do you want to dance?" he asks, taking my hand.

"I guess I'm going to," I answer as I walk trembling to the dance floor.

"Your old-fashioned stupid counselors are separating heads," Tommy whispers.

"Oh, my God," I say as I see the counselors go around and pull apart the heads of couples who are dancing cheek-to-cheek, as if they were actually making out madly on the dance floor.

I want to make conversation but I'm too embarrassed to tell him that I got kicked out of camp. He doesn't say anything to make me think he likes me or even wants to stay with me the rest of the dance. We haven't even tried to dance cheek to cheek and hardly say anything. I want to tell him about the trouble I got into so he can see I'm not a quiet girl with nothing to say. Now I wish I had mailed the letters so we would have something to talk about and he would understand me better. My fun personality doesn't come out around Tommy like it does around boys I don't especially like. I wish I could be like Jessy tonight. Her outgoing personality comes out with everyone.

When the music ends, I thank him and walk away. Tommy dances with other girls and I dance with other boys. I want to know what he is saying to them while they hold each other. Now I feel like crying because I want him to ask me to dance every dance and I know he would if I wasn't shy and quiet around him. I wish I didn't like him because he certainly doesn't show me that he likes me. We don't talk anymore except to say goodbye. This is what I waited for all summer—one lousy dance?

The morning finally comes when I have to leave camp. I say goodbye to my friends. Susie and I hug the most, but camp is already a memory in my diary. The enthusiasm for my night aboard the train isn't the same as usual. My excitement is that Molly talked Lon and Sylvia into allowing her to drive me to the train station so we could finally talk in private.

We drive in the camp van, just the two of us, and leave early so we'll have more time together.

"I'll be leaving, too, in just a couple of days," Molly says. "It'll be a relief 'cause I've been having morning sickness."

"Morning sickness? What's that?" I ask.

"Well, it's something that happens when you get pregnant. You feel kinda nauseated and you throw up."

I almost throw up when she tells me. Then I tell her, "I saw you with Tim in the car. I wasn't trying to spy, honest—but there you were, and I was curious about what you were doing." I worry that Molly might be angry with me, but she isn't even surprised. "Is that what you were doing with Tim in the car, getting pregnant?"

"No. If I am pregnant, then the father is my boyfriend back home. But I don't love him. I'm in love with Tim— but it can never be, because I'm colored and he's white," she says gazing down the winding road. Then she looks at me and says, "I think that's the real reason why I got fired. I think the directors didn't want a colored girl and a white boy liking each other."

"What does Tim think," I ask. "Does he love you?"

"I honestly don't know, hon. He never said he did."

I look at her with my eyes wide open without blinking. I figure I know what that feels like because Tommy never really said he liked me.

"I'm gonna have the baby," Molly says, "no matter what. I'd be afraid to have an abortion. The colored women I know who have had them, well…they don't know the best doctors to perform such a secret operation 'cause it's against the law to get one. Some of 'em get real sick…an' some of 'em die!"

"What's an abortion?" I ask.

I concentrate hard while Molly's telling me what an abortion is. This is a new life lesson and I'm trying to absorb it with every bit of my brain. When Molly tells me Tim will never know about the pregnancy because he is not the father, I bite my lips. Then she tells me she was probably pregnant when she left home but came to camp anyway hoping she would lose the baby naturally, working so physically hard in the kitchen. I thought the car shook when she said it but it was my body

"I slept with Tim because I fell in love with him last summer at camp. If I hadn't been pregnant before camp, I could be pregnant now with Tim's baby," she says longingly. "I do want to have children, but not until later, when I can give them all the best opportunities and not just have them to trap someone into marrying me," she says heatedly. "I'm gonna give this baby up for adoption—I'll find a good family."

I can see her trying to hold back her tears. How horribly awful, to give up a baby because you don't have the money to raise it. I feel smashed into tiny pieces; I feel like a piece of broken glass. Even if all the edges could magically go back together perfectly I will never again feel like I did before this day.

"I'll send you some money, Molly, to help you take care of yourself while you're pregnant." I have money in a secret box on my closet shelf that I've saved—probably one hundred dollars.

When we arrive at the train station, I give Molly a gift I wrapped in newspaper. She unwraps it and stares at it: it's my birthday compass from Dad. She refuses to accept it. "Anything your Dad gave you, you should keep forever," she says, adding, "I wish I had a dad to give me gifts. Thank you, Rachael, dear—you're a great girl. I can't believe you'd even think of me and the baby."

We exchange addresses and phone numbers and hug when she leaves me off with the porter. As I watch Molly walk away, I feel like the reflection of myself in a pond as the water swirls and changes me.

# 5
# PORTER JAMES

Porter James and I introduce ourselves and shake hands and he grabs my trunk by the handle and slides it onto a cart. James is colored and very dark. He's as tall as Daddy, but large like a football player, and his hands are strong and huge but not rough and scratchy. I figure he's about fifty or sixty years old.

"Miss Rachael, please ascend the stairs and wait for me," says James politely in a voice that sounds like an English teacher. It is clear, loud and protective, like I am his baby duckling.

"Okay, James," I say nervously, like I may never see him again and will be on my own.

"Rachael, you shouldn't have come with your friend into the station unless she is your maid in uniform. People were already asking me who you were with when you were hugging each other."

I look at James with alarm in my eyes, like he's telling me the station is on fire or something, but I don't say anything. He sounds different than Ethel, Ruby, Bernice and Bill. They don't talk as properly or pronounce each syllable so clearly. Sometimes they have a Southern drawl too. But I sense that James tries hard to have perfect pronunciation of each word.

"I want to tell you for the future, so as not to cause unnecessary trouble for you. We will be in this car and I will store your trunk over by that door, so please sit down here. We will have these four chairs to ourselves and you can choose if you want to ride forward or backwards for the ride to Chicago—or we can take turns."

"I want to ride forward please, James," I say quietly.

"Okay, I'll take your trunk to the end of the car."

I watch him take it and put it in a corner where the last seats are.

I never want to leave him even to go to the bathroom because it's scary being without anyone I know. Another porter comes by to talk to James and he looks familiar, but I am not sure. They talk softly so I can't hear.

James sits across from me and asks if I would like a blanket or a pillow or anything to drink. I say okay to everything, even if he has to go to the other car to get it, because I'm cold, uncomfortable and thirsty. He only has to go to a storage bin by the door for the blanket and pillow. Then he pulls a cord, like on a bus. About five minutes later the other porter that talked to James before comes in and asks James what he wants. James tells him two Cokes.

The train starts chugging slowly out of the station

toward Chicago. The familiar sound is like a sad song I memorized from my record collection of 45s, "Remember When" by the Platters. Out of the window I can see groves of Wisconsin birch trees and the bramble bushes look like the raspberry shrubs Susie and I picked from when we were supposed to be in archery.

When I wake up, James hands me an ice cold Coke in a nice glass. Our hands touch and I feel like we are friends now. I reach into the camp zipper bag Loreen gave me to store the train letters everyone wrote me. There are goodies in there, too. I feel a lollipop and a Sugar Daddy—my favorite. Maybe Molly or Loreen or Susie put it in the bag. I smile and look at James and he smiles back. As I eat my Sugar Daddy and drink my Coke I feel better, like I am in the Shady Oaks Movie Theater with my friends. I don't feel like reading the letters yet because they may make me sadder than I am. James tells me that lunch is going to be served early because Chicago isn't that far and the diner car has time for only one meal. We will go together soon.

Sometimes when I look up James has closed his eyes or he's looking at the people walking by. Every time another porter walks by they say hello by their first names. I never see any women porters or white porters. Maybe I will be the first white woman porter when I grow up or the first woman train conductor. I have never even seen a woman working on a train.

James tells me we are going to the dining car now. I bring my camp bag with me and follow him. We sit across from each other and look at the menu. We order but I am not hungry. I look at him and he looks back.

"Rachael, are you happy to return home?" James asks me.

"No, not really."

A long silence occurs which makes me uncomfortable because I don't want to be rude, but I don't know what to say.

"Where are you from, James?" I finally ask.

."I was born in Mississippi, but now I live in St. Louis," he says proudly.

"Where?" I ask.

"My family and I live in East St. Louis."

"I have heard of that from my sister, Annie," I say less shyly than I thought I would.

"What did your sister tell you about East St. Louis, if you don't mind me asking?"

"She said she goes there with other kids to hear Ike and Tina Turner, rhythm and blues, and soul music—and to dance. I can't wait to go, but I have to wait until I'm sixteen probably. Mom doesn't know Annie goes, but she's nineteen and engaged to be married so she doesn't ask. Annie tells me because she knows how much I love music and she knows I'll keep it a secret from Mom, too. One time she saw Lon Berry at the Cosmo Club. She told me she's going to see him at Club Bandstand, the only place colored and white kids are allowed to dance together. I didn't understand what she meant by that, but she didn't want to explain it to me because she said I was too young."

"I know what she means." James says sadly.

"Well, do you mind telling me? I am thirteen and I'm not too young—in fact I feel grown up. You, of course don't know me or my family, but I'm not as spoiled as you think. I've learned to care about people and how they are treated, because it bothers me when anyone treated unfairly. I know how that feels and it hurts more than I have ever said."

James looked at me a long moment, then speaks. "Colored and whites are not allowed to dance together, because some people think that colored people are not as nice as white people. But at that club they are all together and they can dance with each other without being arrested."

"My friend Molly at camp is colored, and she's very nice. She's the one who drove me here. Molly's in love with a white boy and she can't be with him," I add.

"Uh, huh," is all James utters.

"James, my maids at home are nicer to me than anyone I have ever known!" I say in a strong voice that shows anger. I kind of surprise myself, letting a stranger know how I feel. Everything inside me feels different than when I went to camp. My own little world of Susie and Tommy is now a big world of who is treating each other the right way.

Our food comes and I don't want to eat. I like talking more than eating. James starts eating and looks up to see what I'm doing. I can't stop thinking about what James just said. The rainstorm splashing by is like a flood of colors rushing in a stream in the intense summer light.

I think of the picture Ethel showed me of her husband in World War II. He was stationed in Guam. Every man in the picture was colored. I told her I noticed that there were no white men in the picture and they should put people in troops according to their blood type not the color of their skin because that is more important to save lives. Ethel

74

laughed and told me to write to President Eisenhower and say exactly that. When I get home I'm going to do that. If men are being separated by their skin color now in the Korean War, then nothing has been learned.

After what James told me I want to prove to him that white people are wrong—that colored people are as nice as white people. I want to apologize to James for all the people that think colored people are different. I don't want to get off this train until he knows how angry I am about what he told me.

James finishes his food and insists I eat my hamburger and fries and drink my milk, but I can only eat a few bites.

"Why aren't you eating?" he asks.

"I'm not hungry," I say solemnly.

"Why?" James repeats.

"When you told me about the colored and white not being able to dance together, it made me sick to my stomach. Also, I have two secrets that I want to tell you. I don't like being in my home except when I am with the colored maids that work in my house; and I like a boy, Tommy, who doesn't pay much attention to me." I say this last part softly, so no one else can hear.

"Rachael, sometimes children don't know how much parents love them. What about your parents?" James looks straight at me as he says this.

"Maybe they do love me without showing it, but I don't want them to know that I love the maids so much 'cause it might hurt them. Also, if they know about Tommy they might tell me I am being a silly girl, liking him when he doesn't pay much attention to me. I want to do things my own way. I want to know more about Molly and why she can't like a white boy and why my sister has to go to a secret place to dance with people." I stopped, exhausted from my confessions. "I don't want to think about my problems. Please, you tell me a secret now," I begged.

"Okay, I will—but I could lose my job talking to you about this subject so let's talk softly, please." He leaned across the table and lowered his voice. "There are many unfair things happening now to the colored people, but I don't know if I'm the one to educate you about this. Haven't your teachers or parents been talking to you about racial prejudice?" James asked as he looked intensely into my eyes.

"No, and I don't even know what those words mean," I said.

"Racial prejudice means people who don't like other people—like whites not liking coloreds or Orientals not liking Greeks. They see people as a group because of the color of their skin and not as each individual person." James spoke these words slowly, like I was stupid.

"At home, Mom and Dad said sometimes Jews are called 'kikes' and that is a dirty word for Jewish people. It means that Jews are different in a bad way," I add.

"Rachael, if someone calls you a kike, you can ignore them and pretend they didn't say it. The next place you go—maybe to see a church service for the first time, for instance—no one will call you a kike even if you are in their church and not your temple. Because they wouldn't even know you were Jewish. Colored people have darker skin so they cannot escape prejudice."

"I remember in school we read in Anne Frank—the

Jews had to wear yellow stars on their sleeve to show the Germans they were Jewish. We were white like the Germans so they had to make us different by a star. Then they could send us to a concentration camp and kill us because we had a Jewish star on our sleeve. James, I could have been one of those children because I am Jewish, but I guess you figured that out because I keep saying 'us'."

"Rachael, you are a smart girl. I don't think we should talk about this anymore because we have to go back to our seats. We are almost in Chicago."

"James, please tell me more. I am learning more than I have ever learned in my whole life."

James and I walk back to our seats and sit quietly until the conductor yells, "Chicago, next stop." His voice sounds operatic.

James gets my trunk and leads me off the car in a hurried fashion. We rush to another train, searching for the Pullman car going to St. Louis. The train cars are all charcoal grey like Daddy's suits, but the Pullman car has red curtains you can see in the windows from outside. James makes me feel safe, like I'm dreaming he rescued me from a terrible giant and is bringing me home, with all his power and might surrounding me.

Everyone working at the station knows James—even the people picking up the trash. Their faces light up when they see him, like he is a Superman of the trains. His voice is strong and clear and with no Southern twang. Maybe they hear that confidence in his voice like I do.

As we walk to the next train I see the water fountains with "Colored" and "White" signs and while James waits I drink out of the "Colored" one before he can stop me.

I turn around and see people, colored and white, whispering to each other. I am walking alongside the Superman of the trains, ready to fly with him to the next stop.

"James," I say showing him my hands, "I didn't even turn colored."

We both laugh heartily.

Finally we settle in the Pullman car. The beds on the bottom bunks are now seats, but later they will be made up for passengers to sleep in. James and I sit across from each other. He orders us Cokes in nice glasses with ice. We have a table by the window to put them on. Also we have some saltine crackers on a dish we share. I like sharing the same dish with him. I tell him I have to use the bathroom. I really go to get him another Coke with vanilla ice cream with my own money.

"Here, James, you finished yours so fast, I thought you needed one more before we have dinner," I say happily.

"Now, Rachael, I don't think anyone has ever waited on me on a train except another porter. Thank you."

"Next time, will you drink out of the white water fountain when I'm not there?"

James says, "I might just do that, Rachael, for you."

He tells me he has been a porter for eighteen years and he loves his job, even on dreary days when people are frustrated about being late or are on the wrong train. His favorite part of the job is making sure kids who travel alone are safely brought to their destination. James has seen all of the forty-eight states and reads history books about all the presidents we have had whenever he can. Once he met

78

President Eisenhower because James helped the President with his travel trunks and the President shook his hand. He tells me he had a kind smile and a Humpty Dumpty face. I ask him to tell me about some other presidents he read about.

"I'll do that, Rachael. The one I'm most interested in right now is President Thomas Jefferson, who owned slaves. Some people say he had some children with a slave he owned."

"I can't believe anyone would make people slaves in the United States after our Bill of Rights said everyone was equal," I protest. I know that six million Jews were tortured and killed by Hitler, and to me being a slave is only one step below what Hitler did.

James says the beginning of slavery was in 1607 and it lasted until 1865 when four million slaves were freed with the Thirteenth Amendment to the Constitution. I thought about the Isrealites, who were predecessors to the Jews were slaves to the Egyptians according to the Old Testament. I studied all this in history class but I never cared about these facts— except to memorize them for a class test—until lately.

James tells me more before I have to go to sleep. Lying in my upper berth, I think about slaves who, by law, weren't allowed to learn to read or write; of how many died on their way over to America because the conditions were worse than even animals were treated. People were chained tightly to each other and to the ships without food and water for long periods of time. That's when they started singing songs that are now called "The Blues"—sometimes called "Rhythm and Blues." Even white singers now sing songs that were originally from slaves working on plantations where they were whipped and the women were attacked. I know the word "rape," so when James says attacked I figure he can't say "rape" to me but that's what he means. I have seen that word in the newspaper and Jessy told me what it meant. Ethel, Ruby and Bernice's relatives were probably slaves but they have never even uttered a word of how they were treated or how their relatives were treated. How can they be so nice to me when my relatives did all this to their relatives?

When I think that James has to drink out of water fountains on some train stops that say "Colored," or sit in the back of the bus when he travels home, I just can't go to sleep. He told me that he and his colored friends had their senior high school pictures put in the back of all the other pictures in the yearbook because he went to school with whites. James and his friends were angry about being treated like they didn't count. Every night, when he prayed before bed, he would tell God he was good and kind and nice like the white kids. Finally, I fall asleep.

James's strong voice wakes me up to get ready for a buttered toast and juice. After breakfast, James tells me that a few years after he started working as a porter, he marched to Washington D.C. with the Brotherhood of Sleeping Car Porters. They protested against the way the colored people were treated in the military, being separated from the white soldiers. He also tells that he's one of the porters that smuggles Negro newspapers on train routes to other colored people in the Southern United States because they can't buy them in the South. He shows me one of the newspapers: it's called *The Defender*. Some people could be sent to jail for reading it in the South so the colored churches read it aloud to their congregations.

James wears an airplane pin on his lapel and the last thing he tells me that it is from World War II. When I press him to tell me more, he starts mumbling, like he doesn't want to brag, but he is so proud to say he was in the Army Air Corps called the Tuskegee Airmen from a station in Alabama and that it was an all-black combat unit. I gasp, overwhelmed that he was fighting for my family's freedom. Why, my parents may not even have had me if it weren't for men like him.

"James, did you have a family you were fighting for?" I ask.

"Yes, a wife and a baby on the way," he says proudly.

"Where are they now?"

"My wife sees me every four months, when I am off for a week, and my babies are grown with their own children. I am a grandpa and I see everyone during that week off."

For the first time I see James put his head down. He has tears in his eyes which make mine teary, too. I think he remembers all the horrible things he did and saw during that time.

I know there are thousands of things James hasn't told me. I feel a lot older than ten weeks ago.

When the conductor shouts that St. Louis is the next stop, I look out over the farm country. James is sitting opposite me looking out the other window over the heads of the people across from us. I think he is just staring into space and not really looking at the countryside. The view to him must be like a painting he can see with his eyes closed, he's taken this trip so many times. There is so much I want to tell Mom and Dad about him when they meet him but what I want to shout is, "Why didn't you show me real life instead of wrapping it up like a package that is scuff proof?

This is James, my friend, who is talking to me about the real world. You can care about me and teach me, too." I know I won't say this and they will all be polite and shake hands and thank James for bringing me home safe.

Which is exactly what happens. They meet and James and I shake hands for as long as he will hold on. As James walks away, I know some other child or adult will be lucky to talk to him for even a few minutes. He looks back at me and we wave like we're going to meet again someday. I notice another set of drinking fountains walking out of the station and I go over to the "colored" one and take a drink.

"Rachael, what did you do?" Mom says angrily.

"I was thirsty," I say with confidence.

"That was the colored fountain," Dad says.

"And so?"

My world goes from vivid hues to black and white.

Going home in the car my mom and Dad are quiet, either because I was kicked out of camp or I drank from the colored fountain, I don't know which. But I was happy to not talk to them. My anger is deep and I know I can never explain it to my parents. I don't know if I'm angrier because they wouldn't understand what I learned from Molly and James or because Molly and James are treated so unfairly and I don't know what I can do to help them. I take out my compass and hold it like it is my wishes, dreams, and future life showing me the way to help Ruby, Ethel, Bernice, Bill, James and Molly.

# 6
# RUBY

Something was wrong. All the way home from the train station Mom wasn't cheerful or talkative like she usually is when Dad is around. She just looked straight ahead the whole time, never turning to look at me like she usually did to say a few words about the weather or how disappointed she is about me getting into mischief at camp. Dad didn't even talk. He was probably thinking about how badly Mom and Dad's friends will think of me coming home from camp early.

Our station wagon has three rows of seats. I felt like a juvenile delinquent in the last row of seats. I wish I was still on the train with James.

Dad goes to work as soon as we get home. Usually when Dad leaves for work or comes home he kisses Mom on the mouth, but this time he just says goodbye and leaves without a kiss.

I wish Bill, our "man on the place" —that's what Mom

83

calls him—had come to pick me up. Bill is Bernice's husband, and he takes care of small repairs around the house, washes the cars, and does some gardening. Bill always says hello to me with a big smile.

No one else is home when we come in. Rusty and Jessy are still at camp and Annie is never home anymore. She's either with her fiancé, working somewhere on wedding plans, or at the store with Dad. The only welcome I get is Mister who wags his tail and jumps up on me like I've been gone a year. Only his slobbers linger on my blouse. I hear the house's lonely creaks when Mom and I walk across the wood floor in the foyer.

I scan each and every piece of furniture, wallpaper, mirrors, pictures—everything that is ingrained in my brain as home. I want to go to the kitchen and see Ethel but Mom insists we go sit for a private talk. The living room is serious, somber, with mostly green and muted grey, brown, and blue. Mom doesn't change things once they are placed into our house unless Nana goes to an auction and replaces an object or a piece of furniture. That isn't often and I like it that way. Familiar objects in the house are like friends I can count on.

The last time Mom and I sat on the couch, she told me I was going to be leaving the school I had gone to for five years and start attending Mary Institute, the private high school from which Annie graduated. I was in fourth grade and happy to be with the same friends since kindergarten. I didn't want to change. But Mom and Dad thought I would have a better education at Mary Institute. After weeks of misery waiting for it to happen, it turned out Jessy and I didn't get in because they had their "quota" of Jewish kids already. They didn't say that but everyone knew the reason. They only had three or four Jewish kids for each class and no Negroes in the entire school. When I heard the good news that we weren't going to change schools I ran around the house in circles until I dropped from being dizzy.

"Before you see Ethel, I need to talk to you, dear," Mom says coolly, like she's conducting a business meeting. Mom knows I want to see Ethel because I keep looking away from her toward the kitchen door. I know something's up.

"What's wrong, Mom?" My voice reflects my concern.

"Ruby had some family matters and she left while you were at camp," Mom sputters nervously.

"But she'll be back...won't she?" I'm starting to get really scared now.

"I'm afraid not," Mom says.

"Mom, what? I don't believe it. Why didn't you write me?" Mom holds me in her soft, perfumed arms.

"Dear, I know how much you enjoyed her and I am sorry. I didn't want to ruin your time at camp. We have found a new girl. Her name is June and she's from Sweden. She is very spry and always smiling. I think you will like her."

I just stare at Mom and start feeling my eyes watering again. I look up, surprised to see Ethel looking at me from the other end of the living room. I run into her arms.

Ethel never greets me at the door—probably because she doesn't want to interfere if Mom or Dad is there, but she knows I'm happier to see her than I am my parents. I have never talked to her about this. Truth is too dangerous sometimes.

"Mom," I try to control myself between sobs, "I want to talk to Ethel in the kitchen."

"Okay, dear, that's fine. I'll be on the telephone in my bedroom if you need me."

I can tell Mom is hurt by my wanting to be with Ethel, but I don't care.

Ethel and I walk with our arms around each other into the kitchen. We sit at the familiar, white Formica table across from each other on vinyl, cherry-red, cushioned chairs that let out air when you sit on them. We always laugh at the noise, but this time we don't.

"Ethel, I miss Ruby already. I can't live without her! I would say the same thing if you weren't here. I need you both, and Bernice, too. Why did she leave? Where is she?"

"Honey, I don't know why she left. It was a family matter. I's not sure where she went for work but maybe I can find out. I's gonna try to call her this weekend. I miss her too, hon. The new lady is nice, though. You's gonna like her. Let's go meet her upstairs. She can't wait to meet you." Ethel says, her begging eyes looking straight into my teary ones.

We hold onto each other as we walk up the stairs to my bedroom. A clap of thunder from a sudden summer storm makes me jump and almost trip on a stair. I remember thunder rumbled at camp this summer right before Molly and I talked for the first time. I hope I like June as much as I like Molly.

I see June through the glass doorway to her room. She's sitting on the chair reading a magazine, just like Ruby used to read *Ebony* magazine.

When I see she is white my heart starts beating faster. I didn't expect anything but a colored maid. She sees us and starts to get up from the chair. I look down as Ethel and I walk toward her, meeting in my room. I shake her large muscular hand. She has blonde hair and blue eyes that you can see through like the glass door. . She must be as tall as Daddy. Her breath smells like old books. I don't like her at all. She isn't Ruby.

The two walls that are all windows in her room are streaming with water from the thunderstorm. It looks just like my heart feels, like it's drowning.

"Hallo, Miss Rachael. I have been waiting to meet ya. I have heard that ya was pretty but you is prettier than all the roses in winter. Let me help ya unpack all ya camp items and we can get to know each other. Ya room's a beauty, just like ya. Would ya like me to get ya anything?" June rattles on nervously in a sing-song accent I have never heard.

"No thank you," I say looking down like a shy five year old.

"Well, I will start ya unpackin' after Bill brings ya trunk upstairs."

"Thank you," I murmur quietly like a mouse.

"June, I's gonna tell Bill ta bring Rachael's trunk up now," Ethel says before she follows me out of my room.

Bill and Bernice live in a tiny bedroom in the basement. They sleep over three or four nights a month.

Ethel and I walk down the stairs. I tell Ethel I hate June and that I'm going to be mean to her. She is ugly and smelly and says nice things just because she has to but she is really not a good person.

"Rachael, you don't even knows her. You done saw her for two minutes. I know'd her for a couple of weeks now and we get along fine. You just miss Ruby. You's mad at June for missing Ruby, girl. Give it a while and you will like her. I know you will."

I don't say anything back but I don't believe her. I miss Ruby and can't think about anything else. Now Ethel and I have a strange distance because we aren't thinking the same way. We go down the rest of the stairway on different steps, like we don't even know each other. I follow her into the kitchen. I want to get my closeness with Ethel back.

"Ethel, can I have a peanut butter and jelly sandwich?"

"Sho' thing, honey."

"I learned a lot this summer, Ethel."

"Like what you mean. Of course, you always learns lots away at camp."

"No, I mean, something else I learned."

Ethel looks up while she is spreading the smooth peanut butter on fresh white bread. She knows I only like the smooth, not the crunchy, and grape jam, not jelly. I get a warm feeling inside because she remembers what I like. Mom wouldn't know how to fix me what I like.

"I found out that you and many colored people are not treated nice by white people. It's called prejudice when people don't like other people that are different than they are. There are more poor colored people because they have schools that aren't good. Then they can't get jobs that pay more. Ethel, I don't know why I'm explaining this to you. You know. You should be living in this house and have people taking care of you! Why should you work for people that don't care about treating people the same? You put love into your cooking. I see it in your eyes and smile. That love is wasted on people that are mean. Maybe not Mom or Dad, but if I were you I wouldn't like any white people. I would only cook for Negroes until all the white people changed," I tell her.

"Honey, I have to cook dinner. You knows too much for a young girl just startin' out. Go and we's talk more about it later. Help June unpack yo' clothes."

When I get back to my room June has already put everything away. The room feels empty. I can't wait until Jessy gets home from camp so I can talk to her about June. She doesn't even know Ruby is gone. She probably won't care that much but I still need to tell her how upset I am. I always hope Jessy will make me feel better when I'm upset, but sometimes she makes me feel worse when she doesn't listen to me or understand that I can care about someone she hardly notices.

Jessy and I are different about Ruby. She doesn't lie on Ruby's bed and talk while Ruby's hair is covered with sticky cream before she combs it to make it straighter. Even now Ruby's room has the smell of that cream. Maybe she left a jar open somewhere in her room so I would still smell her. And when Ruby was in our room cleaning—if I was home—I always talked to her about school, girlfriends, clothes, hair and the family while I sat on my bed. Not Jessy, who always left the room as soon as she saw Ruby start to dust or vacuum.

June must be awfully poor to work for white people. I have never seen a white person work as help. Sometimes they are nursemaids when a baby is brought home from the hospital. Mom said I had colic for three months and my nursemaid was white. We were in a different house until I was a few months old and Mom said there was a porch where the nursemaid would rock me all day so I would stop crying. At three months old, exactly to the day, I stopped crying—just like the doctor had said. Maybe June should be a nursemaid at another house.

I remember Dad saying that Mom was from the "other side of the tracks"; he said it a few times, like it was a joke. I know Mom wasn't from a colored neighborhood. I'm going to ask him what he meant tonight at dinner.

"Dad, when you joke and say that Mom was from the wrong side of the tracks, does that mean Mom lived in a colored neighborhood?

Before Dad can answer, Annie explains. "No, of course not. It means Dad was from a richer part of town than where Mom grew up."

Mom says, "In some towns the railroad tracks separate the good part of town from the poor areas—that's how the saying started. It's true, Dad was from a more well-to-do family than I was from and he kids me about it, that's all."

Neither Mom or Dad looks at me to see if I understand what was just said, but I do.

Dad sits silent like a mannequin—dressed to a T—and he doesn't even smack Jessy and me on the back to sit up straighter when he leaves the table. I am so worried that Mom and Dad are in a fight. Dad didn't even look at Mom during dinner, but I couldn't stop looking at Dad. Except for a few moments when we talked about the railroad tracks no one said anything other than "pass the butter," "Ethel, the roast is really good," or "the air-conditioner is working, thank goodness." It was like I was dropped into a dining room, sitting at dinner with a family I had never met.

Today, I go into Mom's dressing room while she's putting herself together. It's lined with drawers and closets. There's a vanity table and mirror where she puts on her makeup while seated on a silk covered stool. Mom and I talk more in here than anywhere in the house because in here I know we're alone. She's in her silky, white slip and silk nude stockings with her hair perfectly coiffed in a French twist. I prefer Mom without makeup and with her hair down the most. Mom is so pretty I can't stop staring at her, I hope I will be as pretty when I'm older.

"Mom, I want to ask you something about Ruby."

"What dear?"

"I can't stop thinking about her not being here. I miss her. And June..." I want to tell Mom that June is clumsy when she cleans and does my hair and how she twitches and moves like a nervous rabbit., "...well, she just isn't Ruby."

Mom's eyes slice a look at me in her mirror. I take a deep breath and say, "Mom, I saw June take Dad's bottle of scotch from his closet and drink some of it when you and Dad were eating breakfast this morning. If you look right now you'll see some of it is gone. That is why I hate her, too. She's not trustworthy."

"Oh, dear, this is awful. I am so glad you told me, sugar."

Mom goes downstairs and checks the bottle. I follow her. My heart is pounding. She sees that the level is down from when she poured Dad's scotch last night.

"I will talk to Dad about this, dear. It is not your concern now," Mom says with a serious look on her face.

"Mom, could I please visit Ruby and meet her family and spend the night at her home? Maybe she'll tell me more about why she left. I don't even know if she wants me to visit, but can I find out. Mom, you don't see it, but I cry a lot about Ruby."

"Rachael, I'm so surprised that you want to do this. Whatever gave you the idea to go to her house?" Mom voice is so high she's almost singing her words. She looks shocked and her face has turned pale white even though she's just put on rouge. I don't think she's concentrating on what I'm asking, probably because I told her about June and the liquor.

"The colored people have been treated differently than white people, in the past and today, too. I never knew about any of this until this summer. It makes me angry, Mom, and I want to do something about it."

"What can you do, dear, you're only thirteen? And what does this have to do with sleeping at Ruby's home?" Mom asks, shaking her head disapprovingly. Her cheeks aren't pale anymore. In fact, she's blushing.

"I'm not sure, but I want to get to know Ruby's family better so I can find out what I can do, even if I am only thirteen," I say, frustrated.

"Dear, I will talk to your father about this. You know we treat the help very nicely."

"I know, Mom. But not everyone does. You don't know what life is like away from our house. It's not taught in history books, like a chapter on slavery. Discrimination is neatly tucked away. What's going on is unspoken except when someone cares to talk to colored people that are being affected. Maybe there might be an article in the back

92

pages of the newspaper hidden away among the Famous and Barr department store ads. Even if Ruby or Ethel could afford to buy a house where we live, the white people wouldn't let them live here. Remember the fountains in the train station that had signs for "Colored" and "White?" That's because white people think the coloreds are dirty and should stay away from our water. Mom, they take care of all of us. If they were dirty, why would you have them in our home?"

I am talking so fast, I have to stop to take a breath. I am afraid Mom might say she has somewhere to go. Mom has never heard me say this much all at once. Usually she interrupts me.

"Where did you learn all that about how they're treated?" Mom asks, squirming and fiddling with her lipstick case.

"There was a girl at camp who worked in the kitchen. Her name was Molly and we became friends. She's colored. I want her to come visit me. She told me about her life and her family. Also the porter on the train, James, told me about his life. We had some great talks. Prejudice is the word colored people use when people aren't treating them right. White people don't like colored people because of their skin color, but God didn't make our eyes or skin different colors to hurt people. Otherwise He wouldn't have made flowers and animals and everything in nature thousands of colors." I am trying to hold my emotions but I feel so angry because I know Mom doesn't care about this at all.

"Well, honey," she says, "I think you are learning more about people that are important to you. Dad and I always treat all people the same and we try to teach you to do this too." She's speaking so matter-of-factly as she gets up out of the chair. "I have to go to my meeting, darling, but we will continue this when I get home. Dad should join our conversation, too. I want to hear more about Molly and James. How does that sound to you?"

"Fine," I say, pretending not to be angry.

I get upstairs. I'm learning to fake it, just like Mom.

Everything is always interrupted by a meeting, a lunch, a dinner or a phone call. Everything in her life comes before me. I want her to change and care about me more.

I tell Peggy about Ruby and Molly and about how much I miss Ruby and want to visit her. When we talk about Molly, I realize my concern for her isn't as frantic.

Peggy isn't surprised that Molly was fired for making out with a white boy. She wants to send Molly some clothes. She says her mom won't even know they're missing because Peggy's family is very rich from publishing all the comic books everyone reads. She understands right away why I'm worried without having to explain every detail. Peggy tells me she doesn't have the kind of closeness with her maids that I have with mine because her parents are always around doing things together and talking together. She says even though she's never met Molly, she wants to help me make some money to give Ruby and Molly. We decide to sell lemonade. The last time we sold lemonade together we were ten years old. Even though we agree we're old to sell lemonade, we don't care how it looks or even if other kids make fun of us

Bill walks with Peggy and me to "the island" to sell lemonade. The island, about half the size of a tennis court, is a triangle where three streets meet. It has a large sycamore tree that shades us from the sticky August day with a luscious, grassy area beneath it.

Bill is the silent type. He doesn't like to talk and it kind of feels like he's not friendly way. I wouldn't ask him questions like I asked James the porter, about his life or what he does in his time away from our home. I know he wouldn't feel that it was right for him to be personal with me or anyone in the family.

Bill is tall and very skinny. His hands are large and slender. Sometimes, when he is lifting something heavy, I can see the muscles and veins in his arms. His short hair is getting grey. Bill looks serious and I don't think I have ever seen him smile. He always calls me Miss Rachael, just like he calls Miss Jessy, Miss Annie, and Master Rusty. I like Bill because I feel in my heart that he is an honest man.

Bill brings the table, chairs, and ice bucket. Peggy and I march like silly soldiers giggling behind Bill with the lemonade, glasses, and money holder. Bill turns around and smiles at our silliness. Finally, I know why he doesn't smile often; he is missing a bunch of teeth. We stay for three hours and sell a dollars worth of five cent glasses of lemonade. Bill stands there the whole time just making sure we are safe on our island. I notice a bible sticking out of his pocket and I think that he probably reads it when nothing else is happening.

I decide I will ask Bill questions about his life when no one is stopping by. I am more nervous than when I asked James on the train, because James had a more open face. His expressions were talking to me before he said anything. Even his eyebrows were like a silent movie.

"Bill, do you and Bernice have any children?" I ask, as Peggy turns all the way around in the chair to look at me and then Bill.

"Yes, we do, Miss Rachael," Bill answers without looking surprised that I am asking him.

"How old are they?"

"Miss Rachael, they is growed. One is nineteen and the twins are twenty-one. All boys. They sure do grow up fast, jus' like you are, Miss Rachael."

Bill takes the bible out of his pocket now. He turns to a page marked by an empty, flattened Pall Mall cigarette package. He looks at the page.

I don't want to interrupt his reading. But I wish he'd ask me a question next. Maybe when we are together out on the island again he will. I like him because he's private and serious. All the times I've been with Bernice in the laundry room, I only talk about myself. I didn't even know she and Bill had children. Who took care of them when they were younger and they stayed overnight in the basement, I wonder?

One of my mom's friends, Aunt Selma, drives by, stops and gives Bill a horrible look. She asks where Mom is and doesn't even buy any lemonade. Her hair and car match— silver. The Cadillac looks like a boat and I've heard kids who aren't Jewish call it a "Jew Canoe" because all the Jewish people drive them. Peggy and I talk about Aunt Selma's disgusted holier–than–thou look she gave Bill. She isn't even really my aunt, but, for some reason, we've always called all of Mom and Dad's closest friends Aunt and Uncle.

Later, when we go home, we trudge behind Bill with our stuff, marching a slow step but feeling proud that we made some money. After dropping off everything in the kitchen, Peggy and I go to the backyard and sit in lawn chairs facing the birdbath to decide our next plan of action.

The birdbath is mirrored in silver. We can see our images as we discuss new ideas. We look like silver mermaids. This is my favorite place in the yard because when I'm alone I can talk out and a shape looks back and listens from the mirror. The mirror subtly reflects movement among shades of green and blue in the summer. Sometimes when I talk I imagine a whole audience listening where the seams of the mirror pieces come together. In autumn, the orange and brown leaves fall like rain in the birdbath and it gets all clogged and mucky until Bill cleans it. In the winter, the white and grey colors in the mirror are like shadows whispering back to me.

As Peggy and I talk about plans for the next lemonade stand and what we can do to bring in more money, Mom walks urgently toward us, stopping abruptly in front of us like she is going to make a speech to all the bushes, flowers, and trees.

"Girls, I know you had a great day selling lemonade—with Bill helping you,"

Mom categorically states. "When Selma saw you today, she was appalled because Bill was with you. I happen to agree; he shouldn't be helping you. Bill is a Negro man and it isn't proper. You are old enough not to have anyone stay with you while you sell lemonade in our own neighborhood. If you need help, June can carry things. Next time I will get you paper cups so Ethel won't have to wash the glasses."

I interrupt her, "Mom, just because Selma told you she thought it was awful doesn't mean she's right. Bill has always watched us playing in the yard. It's because he's a Negro, not because he's a man, right?"

"No, dear, it's because he's a man and sometimes men do things to girls even if the family has hired them. I will not have it anymore. I will talk to Bill about this with Dad. Peggy, would you like some cookies Ethel baked?"

"No, thank you. I need to go home," Peggy says looking at me with empathetic eyes. She gives me a look of disappointment, says goodbye to Mom and me, and runs off.

"Rachael, I know you are angry about Bill," Mom says. "He is our help and we respect what he does for us. Of course none of us think he would ever do anything to you or anyone else, but every day in the paper and on the news there are bad things happening to girls your age. I have my rules and reasons for things to run smoothly."

"I have my own opinion about Bill, Mom. He's family to me and I'll trust him always. He takes care of our home, our things and us almost every day. I want to go inside."

I walk away from Mom fast with tears in my eyes. I hear her walking behind me, her car keys jingling in her purse. I wish she'd stay in the backyard and think about what she hastily decides about people's lives.

If Selma hadn't driven by, Mom would never be concerned about this. She cares more about Selma's opinion than Bill's feelings. I'm scared he'll leave, too, like Ruby. Then Bernice will leave, since they're married. Mom probably got rid of Ruby and no one's telling me the truth, not even Ethel. If Ruby left on her own, she'd have written me a note and left it somewhere in my room—unless she hid it so no one would know what she wrote. I'm going to look in all my secret places.

I enter through the back door. Ethel is making dinner.

"What's wrong with you, chil'?" Ethel asks.

Seconds later, Mom opens the back door from the yard to take the back stairs that lead to up Nana's room. Mom never takes this way upstairs. I know Mom is uncomfortable seeing Ethel and me talking, because first she comes into the kitchen and stands there listening to us. But we don't say anything and we just stare at each other until Mom leaves to go upstairs.

"Rachael, you told me June is mean and ugly. Did you done think that, or did you jes' say it 'fore you knew her?" She gives me a knowing look. "You din't even give her a chance, ain't that right, Rachael? I saw the look on yo' face and heard you when you seen her through the door. You need to learn to know someone first 'fore you judge them, jes' like people do to Bill and me. Jes' 'cause you think only colored care for you, that don't mean white help won't care for you. Now, June has been telling me you not nice to her, Rachael. You had better be nice to her or I's gonna tell your Mama on you. I don't care if you miss Ruby or not. June needs this job—she needs the money—you never think that 'cause she white and you never seen po' white folks. I has. You don't know what it's like to be without work and goes hungry and I's hope you never know.

"Now, school starts in a few weeks and I have been talkin' to yo' Mama about you coming to my home to sleep over and to go by Ruby's home to see her. She decided that you could stay one night. But I's goin' to tell on you if you don't start right now being fair to June all the time. And if I tell, your Mama will not let you stay over."

"Oh, Ethel, I am a stupid girl. June is not a bad person, even if she smells, but I don't want her here because she isn't Ruby." I know I'm pouting, but I can't seem to help it. "Ruby would have been watching Peggy and me on the island and the thing with Bill wouldn't have even come up. If June was colored I would have given her a chance to see if I would get along with her because she would remind me of Ruby a little. I know I talk real short to her, like each word cost me money to say. Every time she asks to help me with my hair or run my bath, I say no—not even no, thank you."

Ethel and I have a marked silence.

"Rachael," Ethel says, "it is not too late to change."

"It is. She's going to get fired, Ethel. I did something awful," I mumble looking at my bare feet.

"What'd you go do, girl?" Ethel almost barks in surprise.

"I told Mom she'd been drinking liquor from Dad's closet—that I saw her do it. But…....." I have to confess to Ethel. I can't lie to her. "…it was me. I poured the Scotch out in their bathroom sink." I feel my throat tighten up and my nose sting.

"Girl, you didn't! I's shamed at you. You go tell your Mama you lied. You go tell her right now or I's telling her." Ethel looks straight into my eyes which are now spilling over with tears.

"Please don't be mad at me, Ethel. I want June to leave so much and I want Ruby back. I am so unhappy without her. I cry a lot when you don't see me. Mom may have fired her already anyway. I told her yesterday after I cleaned up the sink. Maybe she's talking to her right now." My voice sounding squeaky.

I drag my feet, walking away from the kitchen as Ethel says, "I hopes you's going up there now to tell your Mama what'cha done."

Mom's bedroom is door closed and June is cleaning up Rusty's room, so she hasn't fired her yet. She's probably talking to Dad on the phone about what to do about June right now. I knock on the bedroom door.

"Come in, dear."

We sit on Mom's side of the bed—she against the pillows and me, by the foot of the bed. "Mom, did you talk to June yet about drinking the liquor?"

"No, dear."

"Mom, I made it up. I can't stop thinking about Ruby not being here and I miss her and June isn't Ruby. June is clumsy when she walks and the way she cleans and does my hair. She twitches and moves like she's nervous. Are you mad at me?"

"Rachael, Dad and I were disappointed you were in trouble at camp. Now you tell me you're lying to us. We don't recognize the Rachael we know." She shakes her head, then gives me a small smile. "Thank you for telling me truth now Rachael. June will stay for now. Give her a chance to reveal herself to you and the family before you make a snap judgment. She already likes you. I won't tell her that you lied about her to me."

"Okay, Mom. I will try to like her. I'm sorry I lied to you." I am ashamed, too. I realize that I'm being prejudiced, just like so many people are about coloreds.

"I need to make some calls now, Rachael."

"Okay, Mom. I scoot out of her bedroom and close the door louder than usual.

# 7
# HOUSES

The next day I pick up the telephone when it rings and I hear laughing.

"Who is this?"

"It's me. You got kicked out of camp," Tommy laughs.

"Where did you hear?"

"Tell me what happened," Tommy chuckles more.

That is the only reason he called. He loves a scandal or maybe now I'm more interesting.

"Maybe later, not now," I say like I mean it.

He wants me to go to a movie with him and a bunch of kids tonight. I say I'll go but I don't really want to that much because with a bunch of other kids around I can't talk to him about what's important in my life. Now that I have real things to talk about I'm afraid to show him the serious side of me. I doubt he would even care about what's happening to the Negroes and how they're treated. I want him to still like me for who I used to be and who I am now. All of it. But I think Tommy only likes me for my silliness and the way I laugh at his jokes. But that's not enough.

Anyway, I decide I'm going to just have fun with him and the other kids and forget about what I care about for one night. Besides, I still want to see if I feel like I used to about him.

Bill drives me to the Shady Oaks Theater. Tommy meets me under the marquee to see *South Pacific*. He looks so handsome and tan from the summer but I don't have the same jolt in my heart when I see him. Other kids join us and talk about what they've done this summer. Girls form a group and talk about clothes, hair, and boys. While I pretend to listen to them talk about who likes who, I'm really thinking of how I can help others. Ruby and Molly are like lightning bugs perched on each of my shoulders reminding me not forget about them—even for one night.

When Bloody Mary shows up in the movie, I whisper to Tommy, "The same actress played that part on Broadway in 1950. She won the Tony Award—that's the highest award there is for stage actors. And she was the first Negro to ever win it."

Tommy puts his arm around me without comment. I have waited for this moment. Just kiss him to see what it is like, I tell myself. Don't wait for him to do it. He looks at me many times but I just stare straight ahead.

Tommy whispers in my ear, "Soon I will give you my I.D. bracelet and ask you to go steady."

I tell him, "I don't want you to give it to me."

Even though this is what I dreamed of, I feel like I'm not talking to him. Am I saying these words? He laughs a nervous laugh and says he will keep asking until I say yes. I still like him, but not like I used to. He's cute, but I don't want to care about him more than as a friend right now I think. And we'll be in different schools this year so I won't see him every day like last year.

For the first time in my life I don't want to let others decide what is important to do with my time. I feel that every moment is precious now—and meaningful.

Today Jessy is coming home from camp—finally. I want to tell her the whole story about Tommy. I'm never sure whether Jessy will keep a secret I tell her. but now I'm not afraid of her embarrassing me in front of Tommy or her friends since my feelings for him have changed.

Mom and I pick her up at Union Station. Dad can't come because of a meeting. I run up to a colored man in the train station and tap him on the back. When he turns around, I say, "Sorry. I thought you were James." Every tall colored man looks like James because of my anguished desire to talk to him again. Deep down I know I'll never see him again.

Jessy liked her new camp better than Camp Hiawatha, but is not real excited to go back. Mom and I tell Jessy about Ruby not being our maid anymore. Mom says how great June is and I roll my eyes. I know Jessy isn't that upset about Ruby because she right away starts talking about camp and what she's going to do for the last weeks of summer. I can't wait to tell her about Molly, but I don't want Mom around when I do. And I want to tell her about my upcoming visit to see Ruby. I tell Jessy that Peggy and I have been selling lemonade on the island to make money. Jessy is surprised we would want to sell lemonade in the August humidity, and at my age. I tell her it's worth it because I'm saving money for something important. Maybe I'll tell her about why later, but not in front of Mom.

Of course, Mom isn't listening when I say I'm saving it for something important—or she pretends not to hear, because she doesn't comment. Instead she says,

"Jessy, I have found two dresses you can wear for the rehearsal dinner. You can try them both on and pick one you like. One is robin's egg blue—that will bring out your beautiful dark brown hair. The other is navy blue with white trim. It looks crisp and tailored."

"Okay, Mom," Jessy says as though she's bored.

"It will be the first time Rachael will be wearing heels so my two young girls and I can finally go to the same shoe department together."

"Okay, Mom," Jessy says, still uninterested.

Mom is very focused on the wedding of Annie and Donald, which will be here before you know it. Her eyes are deeply focused when she's talking to Jessy about the clothes and shoes but they flit all around when we talk about anything else.

At night I lie in bed and think about what I want to talk about with Bernice in the morning, since Ruby isn't here and Ethel can't talk much when she's cooking.

"Hi, Bernice," I say as I bounce into the laundry room in the morning. She's behind sheets hanging on the line. In the summer, they usually dry outside, but since it's been raining Bernice is hanging them on the inside line. I think

Bernice likes it when she can hide behind the sheets, like it's her way of having some privacy from the people going in and out of the laundry room all day.

"Whaddya gonna do today?" Bernice asks, not even coming out from behind the sheets. She has set her ironing board behind them, and is smoothing out the wrinkles in the startlingly white sheets. I don't know why sheets need to be ironed when as soon as I get into bed they get wrinkled, but I would miss Bernice's sharp crisp creases in my sheets if she didn't.

"I'm going to help you fold and maybe do some ironing. Then Jessy and I are going to see if the kids in the neighborhood are around to play with."

"How come you never come down here and just bring a book and read, or maybe read something to me?" Bernice asks in a stern manner, like she's upset.

"I don't like to read except what I have to in school."

"Your sisters and even Rusty read books. Sometimes when I'm upstairs bringin' up ironing or laundry, I see them on a chair or in bed readin' a book and they doesn't even know I came into their room. All I ever seen you do with your books is make trails around the house and walk on 'em with your feet. Those are valuable treasures, girl—they aren't toys. Do you mind if I tell you somethin' 'bout books, honey chil'?"

"I'm listening, Bernice."

Bernice stops ironing and looks up at me, the sheet in one hand and the other hand still on the iron. It feels like time stands still when her ironing stops.

"Millions of slaves—less than a hundred years ago—

were forbidden by law to read or write. If they was caught readin' or writin', they was whipped and chained. Rachael, can you imagine? And do you know why they wasn't allowed to read? Their owners were afraid that if they were educated they'd find ways to escape or learn about what was really happening in the world around them. So there was this organization that got formed called The Underground Railroad. Mainly it was the slaves in the South that could read that got it started. An' they helped the slaves escape to the free North. It wasn't a real railroad but more like a trail to freedom.

"There were Southern families—white ones, too— who'd help hide slaves in their homes for a while until they could escape to the next house on the way north. The people that hid the slaves were even called 'conductors' 'cause it was like a secret train of houses on the way to destination "Freedom." There was even a minister who hid upwards of two thousand runaway slaves! Imagine that. And do you know, that man died in 1863, the very year President Abraham Lincoln signed that Emancipation Proclamation.

"The big plantation owners in the South went to war 'cause they knowed that if the slaves all ran away they wouldn't have anyone to work in the fields of cotton and tobacco for free. It was all for money and greed. That's what made them afraid to let the slaves learn. They knew that if they were literate and they'd know how to defend theyselves against the white man and wouldn't let them treat them worse than animals any more.

"Now I'm done talking. You go out play."

"Bernice, wait a minute. There are so many books I have outgrown. I'll give some of them away to children who don't have books. Wouldn't that be a good thing?

"I didn't know anything about slaves not reading and writing. They didn't teach us any of that in school. I'm trying to understand everything you just told me. I need to think about it. How can it be true that people even now don't treat each other right when they've had hundreds of years to practice?"

Bernice isn't looking at me now because she's folding sheets.

"Okay, chil', now you go and have a fun time today and don't go thinking about all this. I just wants you to read and learn about the world so when you grown you'll be smart. Don't you go worryin' about my husband. He can take care of hisself."

I didn't even say anything about what happened to Bill at the lemonade stand, but Bernice could probably tell I was going to say something.

"Bernice, I miss Ruby and I want her back. Even if June stays here, I want Ruby back. Do you know why she left? Mom said it was a family problem. And another thing. Mom and Dad aren't talking at dinner time and I don't know why. Maybe it has something to do with Ruby."

"Chil', when I am down here it's like another house. Ruby didn't tell me she was leavin' or why. The only time I see your Daddy is sometimes when he's gettin' out of the car and I'm leavin' through the back door. We say hello and how are you. That's it. I'm sorry, Miss Rachael, but I can't help. You had better be nice to June. I think she's fine for you."

"I don't like June. I just don't. She's nervous and doesn't fit in here."

"Well, honey chil', now do any of us fit in?"

I skip June and change the subject. "Bill told me about your children. I wish I was older when they were young so I could have known to ask you about them. Three boys! Can you bring me pictures of them?"

"Whatcha wantin' pictures fer, Rachael? You don't sound like yo'self and I have work to do now. You can help another day, but today is change linen day and it's not a good day for you helping me. You go on."

"Bernice, I'm not myself. Please bring me pictures," I pleaded. "I'll leave you alone." I go over behind the hanging sheets and hug her hard. It feels like a special secret hug that no one could see.

Later after dinner I hear Mom and Dad arguing. I'm in my room trying to read a Nancy Drew book. The only time I'd ever seen or heard them argue before was once, over some medicine that Rusty was taking. I remember Dad was so mad he threw the nose drops against the window. Now I'm scared. I look over at Jessy who is sound asleep. I sneak to their closed bedroom door to listen.

Mom is saying something about Ruby, but I can't hear. Maybe they're fighting because I want to visit Ruby or because I lied about June to get Ruby back? Then they aren't saying anything, so I tiptoe back in my room. I hear Dad open their door, walk downstairs, leave the house, and drive off. The headlights from his car made scary shadows on my ceiling. I go back to listen at their door again and hear Mom crying. I knock. She tells me to come.

I sit down on the bed.

"I'm surprised you're still up, dear," Mom says,

holding a tissue to her eyes.

I don't say anything. Just sit there with my head down.

"I suppose you heard us squabbling. Sometimes married people have arguments. It's nothing to worry about."

"But he left the house," I say.

"He just wanted to take a ride, to cool off."

"Where did he go?"

Mom doesn't say anything at first, then she says, "I don't know."

I see a tear roll down her check.

"Go to bed, dear. There's nothing to worry about."

"Mom, thanks for letting me go to Ethel's house to try to see Ruby"

I slump back to my room. I stay awake and see the ceiling shadows come back. Jessy slept through the whole fight and everything.

I can hardly wait for morning to call Peggy. Like Ruby, she is closest to my heart. She lives only three minutes away, walking. I wish she was my sister. I'm never afraid she'll hurt me. Besides Ethel, Bernice and Bill, Peggy helps me feel less alone in the world.

"Peggy, Dad was gone for two hours last night after Mom and he had a fight. I think it was about Ruby," I whine into the telephone.

"Rachael, do you want me to come over?"

"No, we have to go to the club soon. Are you going to be there?"

"No, we have to go to a party. Let's talk later."

"I hate the club when you aren't there. No one goes there from my school. And even they did, I'd still want you there."

"I know, Rach, that's 'cause you go to private school and no one there can afford it."

"Bye."

"Bye."

When Jessy finally wakes up I tell her about last night. "Jessy, I'm so worried. Mom and Dad were arguing and then Dad left for two hours. I heard Ruby's name. I have never heard them argue and yell before."

"Don't worry, Rach, even if it was about Ruby. Maybe it was about her leaving and they don't agree about it. People argue. You and I argue. Dad probably went for a ride to think about things. You know his car is like his best friend. We're all going to the club today so Mom and Dad must be okay."

When Ethel takes me to her home to sleep over I'm going to ask her if she knows anything about about Ruby's firing. If I ask her now, she might get mad and say I'm interfering and decide not to take me.

It's another humid, thick as lemon custard summer day. Dad always plays golf on Sunday—that's why we all go to the country club. It sounds like we'll be together as a family but I know better. Rusty and I, dressed in our regulation white tennis clothes and will hit tennis balls. Even my

ponytail ribbon is white because the rules for tennis are
strict. I can't wait to start cutting my hair like Lana Turner
to look older. Mom and Annie will go swimming. Jessy is
going to watch dad play golf.

She asked him on our way to the club if she could
watch. I've never seen Dad play golf. I tell him I want to
watch after playing tennis. Golf takes about three or four
hours. Dad tells us one child is enough at a time to see him
play. I don't know why it matters. He warns us not to giggle
like at the dinner table or he will send us away. Golf is
serious and quiet. I will never play such a serious sport. I
think I'm happy Dad didn't teach me how to play. Mom
didn't even take up golf until she met Dad. But she met him
at midnight practicing at an all night golf range. She was on
a date and was driving home when her date saw Dad on the
golf range from the car. They were friends, her date and
Dad, so he introduced Mom to Dad.

When Dad can't sleep, he hits golf balls. I'll bet that's
where he went last night after the fight.

"Rusty, you're hitting good," I shout over the net.

"I know," Rusty yells back.

"I think you're getting good enough to play a game."

"No, let's just hit—you'll win if we play a real game."

Rusty and I have fun just hitting the ball for an hour
until the next group wants our court. Rusty sees a friend to
go eat lunch with and I go to the golf course to find Dad's
game. I walk the greens which look as if they'd been freshly
painted green this morning. I finally spot Dad and Jessy,
and we wave to each other as I slowly run towards them.
Dad is with the three friends that he plays golf with every

week. I know them as Uncle Jack, Uncle Roy, and Uncle Fred, even though they aren't real uncles.

Jessy runs over to me and whispers, "Dad has been drinking and betting money."

"Really? That doesn't surprise me. Is he drunk?" I reluctantly ask.

"I don't know, but I couldn't wait 'til you got here. I am so bored."

Jessy and I stroll over to Dad and his friends. They all say hi as they get ready to tee off. Dad hugs me in front of his friends. For a second, I am a special daughter. Jessy says goodbye to everyone. I have to be quiet and not say a word as they each hit a ball in turn. Dad is last to go and his ball goes so far and high, I feel pride swelling up in me. We all clap.

The men all joke and laugh and tell me Dad is a great golfer. I know that—Dad has lots of trophies from tournaments on a shelf in the library. Mom has some too. Mom always says Dad should have been a pro golfer.

Dad walks with me down the fairway as the other men walk to their balls. Dad puts his arm around me, like he's happy I'm here. He tells me one day there will be a golf cart to ride around in so walking doesn't take up all the time. He has seen some in magazines. They've just started to be manufactured. But for now, every man has a colored caddy to carry around his heavy bag of clubs. Dad tells me how you aren't supposed to take your eye off the ball when you hit it. That is the most important and hardest part of the game, he says. The men are drinking water not liquor. Jessy said they drank whiskey in the beginning to make a toast to a good game. I don't hear them talking about money either.

We walk to Dad's ball which is in the sand trap.

Dad says, "Sometimes golf is a very hard game. It can be terrible if you land in sand traps a lot, because it always wastes points to get the ball out."

I'm surprised Dad is talking to me. I had thought he would be quiet so he could concentrate. At home, he hardly ever talks to me. Even if he talked about golf at home, it'd make me happy. When I drive with Dad in the car, he doesn't talk. I think maybe he's trying to act like a good Dad now because his best friends are watching. He probably wants them to think he is close to me.

Then he says in a serious voice, "Rachael, no one is perfect—even on the golf course. My scores are better than ninety percent of the men at the club, but I'm not perfect on the golf course or anywhere else. Balls land in sand traps and in the rough a lot. Mistakes help us learn what we can do better. Remember that, always."

I look at Dad, but can't talk. I never remember Dad telling me anything about life or golf. I want to ask Jessy if he said the same thing to her. If golf is helping Dad learn about life, he's getting wisdom every Thursday and Sunday. I once figured out that he spends about four hundred and fifty hours a year playing golf. I added it up one night when I couldn't go to sleep. That's time I could spend with Dad instead of him playing golf. Maybe we could teach each other about life—at least during some of those hours.

The family eats at the Club Grille for dinner. Last time I was here in the evening was for my party at the beginning of summer. Just as the first fall leaf fluttering to the ground changes the landscape, the rooms inside the club feel different as I walk through them for the first time in this new season of my life. We all sit at a long table that is not just for our family and are joined by two other families we know.

Mom and Dad hardly look at or talk to each other. I don't know if anyone else notices, but they were talking to us kids much more before the other families sat down to join us. I don't want them to fight, but I like the attention they give me. Dad asks if I would like to watch him play golf again. Mom comes over, fixes my pony tail ribbon and kisses my cheek, while she whispers in my ear that she talked to Ethel and I can go.

During the next few days, at home, during dinner, Mom and Dad look at each other but they don't say much. Maybe the fight they had about Ruby isn't settled.

Saturday morning, seven a.m., is finally here. I have been packed for days. I am going to see Ruby and sleep at Ethel's for one night. We will take the bus to Ethel's. Mom says goodbye to Ethel and me at the front door. She tells me to call when I get to Ethel's house. She looks sad as we hug but doesn't say anything. She says she will pick me up when it's time to come home, but I want to take the bus back. I think she let me go one way to show that she thinks colored people can certainly make sure I'm safe on a bus. Even if she doesn't think that, she has to show she trusts Ethel.

# 8
# THE OTHER SIDE OF THE TRACKS

Ethel and I walk fast to the bus stop. It is only a block away from the gates to our neighborhood. The only people on the bus are colored except one old white man. Ethel and I sit towards the front—not in the back like I thought we would. Even if the bus were filled up I wouldn't sit in the back with Ethel. The bus driver knows a lot of the riders by name—even Ethel's. Everyone is staring at me like a caged animal in the zoo. What do people think I am going to do different than they would do? I pretend I don't notice, but every time I look up someone is looking at me. I whisper to Ethel that people are looking at me. Ethel says to read my book. She says books are like friends that will never be mean and will always want your attention.

I made sure to pack my Brownie camera and took lots of film so I can take pictures when we get off the bus. I decide not to take them while I ride the bus. I want to talk to Ethel and people may think I'm a newspaper reporter and I don't belong here. Even though I brought my camera to camp and I didn't take a single picture. Camp just wasn't that interesting to me. But I know this one important night at Ethel's may never happen again. As I look out of the window I see many pictures flash by, some that tell whole stories. I know they will be vivid colorful memories in my head—that's better than black and white pictures.

After passing through white neighborhoods, we come to a mix of apartments, small run down houses, and stores grouped together with handmade signs. Then we enter the all colored neighborhoods. It's like Moses parting the Red Sea.

I don't understand why the white people have all the nice houses, stores and cars. The colored people may want to live together, but why do they all have to be poor and have dirty, dingy places to live? Ethel told me that I would see this type of living when we rode into her neighborhood. She said before the Civil War, less than a hundred years ago, there were some very wealthy colored people in St. Louis who had mansions and prominent positions in industry. Then when the war came and they were forced to abandon their homes and lifestyle. Missouri was considered a Northern state in the war, but there were many in southern Missouri who were for slavery so it became a complicated issue.

Finally, after a forty five minute ride, we are off the bus. Ethel and I walk on a street with lots of shops, offices, and vacant buildings. There's trash on the sidewalks and in the street, some of it flying around like paper airplanes and whirly flags. It's still very early so there aren't many people walking around but I see a few young colored men, their white shirts hanging out of their dress pants, and wearing dress shoes. Maybe they work in bars that just closed and are walking home. Rickety old cars fly by once in a while. Some music blasts loudly from someone's apartment window. I see one car that's all shiny and polished and even has shiny hub caps, like it was brand new. The wood trim on the buildings is deteriorated and stained with grimy paint in layers of different colors, like each layer tells another story of history. The concrete sidewalks are splattered with darkened splotches. I take pictures everywhere we walk and Ethel doesn't say anything about it. She keeps hold of my hand the whole way.

We turn onto a residential street of large maple trees mixed with pine.

"This here's my street, honey. See that green house over there? That's mine," Ethel proudly states.

The house is small and in between an apartment building three stories high and another small grey house. It still has the outside light on from last night. Ethel uses her key to walk in with me behind her. Her husband, Louis, is at the front door and greets Ethel with a kiss on the mouth. He shakes my hand and smiles, clearly happy to meet me. He turns the outside light off, like it was supposed to stay on until Ethel came home. Louis says the kids are sleeping.

Louis is medium tall and a little chubby—probably from Ethel's good cooking. He has a mustache and very serious eyes. Ethel has two children—Joseph, thirteen, and Caroline, fifteen. I have never met them. The house is sparkly clean and smells like fresh sheets. Ethel shows me around the rooms: the master bedroom, the bathroom, kitchen, dining area—except the bedroom where Joseph and Caroline are sleeping. They share a room. All the well-worn furniture and knickknacks are placed specifically, like they are introducing themselves to me. There is so much pride in this house—nothing is out of place, just like in our house. How does Ethel have time to keep two houses gleaming?

The backyard is small—mostly grass—with one large chestnut tree and a table and chairs on the patio. Ethel tells me how Louis made the patio out of used concrete pieces interlaced with bricks that he found around. Where there are spaces between the bricks and concrete, Ethel has planted different flowers or groundcover that she calls her miniature garden. In the spring, when the snow is gone, sometimes the plants come back; if they don't, she tries other seeds, so there's always a surprise to see what will grow. Neighbors give her seeds they have left over because everyone is interested in what will pop up. Ethel picks one of the flowers, a long purple one—it may be an iris—and hands it to me in a vase. I am going to sleep on the couch so I put it on the nearest table.

I call Mom to tell her I am safe and sound. She sounds quiet and serious like someone died. Then, before we get off the phone, she forces her voice to be its usual self—but I can tell the difference.

Ethel makes me a hot chocolate and we sit down at the table. I notice Ethel has changed to a crisp white shirt, tan slacks and loafers without socks. At first I thought she was still in her uniform because her shirt is white but then I saw that the slacks and shoes weren't white. I feel more at home now that Ethel looks like a mom and not a maid.

"I done called Ruby the other day. She don't want to see us just yet—maybe in a while, Rachael. I dint tell you 'til now cause I dint want you not to come over. I gots her address. We can drive by if you wants to, but Ruby say not to."

"Oh, Ethel! Why didn't you tell me? I would have still come to your house. Can we drive by Ruby's anyway, just to see where she lives? Maybe she'll change her mind." I slam my hands down on the table in frustration, spilling the hot chocolate, "Why doesn't she want to see me? What did we all do to her? It's my fault. I could have made her stay if I'd been home and not at that stupid camp! Even if Mom or Dad did something to make her angry, Ruby would've talked to me about it before she left. Mom and Dad had a fight about her the other night. I heard them through their bedroom door. And Dad left in the middle of the night in the car. Did you know about that?"

"Now, you mustn' think 'bout that—and no, I don't know 'bout it. Ruby has reasons of her own we don't know. Let's go now afores my chirren gets up and want breakfast."

"Can I take some pictures first?"

"Sho', honey."

I take out my Brownie camera and take flash pictures of the house, Ethel and Louis. Then I go outside and take some pictures of the yard, concentrating on Ethel's miniature gardens. I shoot the front of the house and the houses and apartment buildings you can see from the front yard. This time Ethel watches me and so do some of the neighbors.

When I'm done we get into Ethel's car, a green Buick, roomy in the front seat. It's really the family car that Louis uses for work every day. I keep taking pictures out of the car window as we drive through neighborhoods and streets that are similar in shabbiness, poverty and meagerness. It's not so early now and a lot of families are outside, sitting on porches, children playing in yards, lawns being mowed, and stores opening. The air cracks with a sense of the dawn of the weekend. The only thing that looks familiar to me are the trees—the same type that are in my neighborhood—mature sycamores, maples, oaks, chestnuts, and pines.

After about ten minutes we stop in front of Ruby's house and sit in the parked car. There are some brooms, toys, and a few tires strewn in the front yard, like it was another room in the house. After a couple of moments, I get a surprise as Ethel quietly leads me to walk to the front door and ring the bell. No one answers so I go around to the back. There are two broken windows covered with cardboard and some of the glass is on the dirt below the window. There are two holes in the wood under the broken window and, peering through them, I can see inside the house a little. There are only weeds growing in the yard with a honeysuckle bush like we have at home. The bush has never been trimmed. It is wild and snakes over a chain link fence at the end of the yard. I can see bees surrounding it, foraging for the sweet nectar. Bees treat every plant the same, no matter where they are, and they don't fight amongst themselves, but share. Why can't people treat each other kindly like the bees?

Suddenly Ruby's voice cries out from inside the backdoor. "I told ya'll not to come."

"Ruby, it's me—Rachael. I miss you so much," I yell out.

"Rachael, you's not to be comin' here, honey. Go home and be a good girl. I miss you, too. I have to go now."

"We's goin' now, Ruby," says Ethel as she comes around to the back.

"Wait, Ruby, I want to see you so badly. I miss you more and more!" I shout out loudly so she can hear.

There is no sound. We stand there for five minutes before Ethel says we have to go. Reluctantly, I leave the front porch with its empty paper bags, toys, and dead flowers in flower pots. I start singing and Ethel puts her arm around me as we walk to the car. I look back to see if Ruby is in the window, but I don't see her.

Ethel drives slowly away and I look back at Ruby's house. I wish I never saw her poverty-stricken home. I will send her money from selling lemonade. Now I know her address. She never said she had children, but there were so many toys around. I can send her books and toys now that I know the truth. Mom and I need to talk about this.

Ethel wants to make breakfast for everyone when we get back to her house. I can't wait to meet her children. I am introduced to Caroline. Then Joseph appears from the hallway and we meet. They are friendly and dressed nice, like for church. Caroline puts the vacuum away. Ethel tells me to follow her to the kitchen with Caroline and Joseph. We all stand around while Ethel gets food and dishes out to make eggs and bacon. Caroline is very pretty— Homecoming Queen type— with a flip hair-do about to her shoulders. She has a wide smile to show off her extra white teeth. Her skin color is like milk chocolate not dark chocolate. She is as tall as her dad.

Caroline is busy setting the table and putting milk, butter, and the toaster on the table. Joseph asks me where we were this morning and I tell him about Ruby and taking pictures while Caroline is in and out of the kitchen catching as much of my story as she can. Joseph is skinny, tall, and wears glasses. He looks wiry and strong. I can't decide if he looks studious or comedic. After breakfast, Ethel tells us to go into the living room and she and Louis will clean up.

"Come on, Rachael," says Caroline. "Mom means leave her and Dad alone to clean up. Usually she wants us to help, so let's get out of here."

We all sit down and stare at each other for a moment. It seems like longer than waiting for Tommy to send me a letter at camp.

"Can I take your pictures outside on the porch?" I ask very politely.

Joseph says bluntly in a soft voice, "No, no. Whatcha have to come here for?"

Caroline jumps in in an angry tone, "Yeah, why don't you go back to your mansion?"

"Your house is so pretty and so neat," I say, feeling scared Caroline will come back with something mean to say again.

"Don't be thinking our house is always lookin' like today. Mom made us clean everything perfectly afore you got here. Usually it's a mess 'cause she's always cleaning for ya'll. Mom is so tired when she's done at your house, she has ta cook us fast meals. They okay but we know her good cookin' and it ain't nothin' like that. That's what ya'll get. Most of the time we have to go to the store and get everything ready so she has less to do at the stove."

I don't know what to say. Everything Caroline says is true. My house *is* a mansion compared to hers. I'd like to tell her that I'd give anything to trade places with her, but she'd think I was lying. I want to scream and yell at my parents for all this pent up anger, not at Caroline. But she shows me how much the outside of a house means. But it's what goes on *inside* a house that counts. I'm afraid if I say what's in my heart it will sound insincere or dumb. All I can manage to say is, "Your mom said I could stay one night so we could try and talk to Ruby at her house, that's all."

"Well, can't you just go now that she isn't going to talk to you?" Joseph hisses sarcastically. "You found out, so you can just go on back to Richville."

"And don't take any more pictures of anything around here, either" Caroline warns.

Ethel and Louis walk in.

"Let's go sit on the porch," Ethel suggests to all of us.

"Okay," I say.

"I'm going to make some popcorn and then I'm going out," Caroline says.

"I'll help her," Louis says.

They almost trip over each other as they scramble off.

Ethel, Louis and I sit on the front porch chairs. It's another muggy day and there are no fans here or air-conditioning. Most of the neighbors are sitting on their porches, fanning themselves with newspapers. Some young kids have hoses and are playing in the water in the street. When a car comes, they move over until it passes. The kids, hoses and cars move in and out with the rhythm of a dance while the audience sits on porches. I watch as the neighbors wave to each other and slowly mosey over to talk to one another. I can see that there's some whispering and pointing to our porch. While I feel comfortable with Ethel and Louis, I know if I ventured off the porch and onto the sidewalk alone, my stomach would feel queasy. All those people probably think I am too comfortable in their territory.

Joseph and Caroline haven't come out. They're probably destroying my film. Maybe I'd have done the same if I lived here and some rich girl came to see me. I want them to know how much I love and appreciate their mom, but I don't know how to say what's inside me. My heart fills like a big balloon filled with emptiness. I can sense the closeness Ethel and Louis have with their son and daughter, even when they aren't talking. I wish it was like that at home with all of us.

Some neighbors start coming by to see Ethel and Louis.

"Well, hello, Herb. I'd like you to meet Rachael. I work for her family," Ethel says to one neighbor.

"Uh, huh," is all Herb says and moves on.

"Hi, Dorothy, this is Rachael. I work for her family," Ethel offers again.

"Well, hello, dear," Dorothy says.

Most of the rest are polite but they don't seem sincere, except the small kids that ride by on their bikes and yell out, "Hi, Rachael!"

The word is out that white Rachael is on the porch with Ethel and Louis. I feel like I'm on display. I want to go inside.

Caroline and Joseph walk out the screen door onto the porch with popcorn and ask their parents if they can go visit some friends down the block for a while. Ethel says fine, then asks me if I would like to take a ride with her. I cannot wait to get off the porch and I say yes. Louis walks off to talk to the neighbors. I go inside and find my camera in the living room. I check to make sure the film is okay; it is. I go back and get into the car with Ethel.

We slowly drive down her street. When people see me the images from my window are like photographs of faces staring blankly with expressions of confusion, arousal, and curiosity.

I can't stop thinking about Ruby. "That Ruby's not in my life is the worst thing that has ever happened to me," I tell Ethel. "I can't believe she wouldn't even talk to me. I miss her so much."

"You know that heartache is because you loves her, Rachael. But you got to stop this. There're some things we got to live with inside of ourself. When someone's gone— even if they's livin', they's still inside us. A piece of them's takes the place o' the piece of us that's missin' them." Ethel looks away from the road and straight into my eyes as she says this.

"Okay, I say, hugging Ethel, trying to understand what the words mean. I hope I can remember some of them when I want to cry for Ruby.

We drive silently for about ten minutes until we are out of Ethel's neighborhood into a more rundown area where there are apartment houses, duplexes, some small homes, and a few businesses. Everything looks abandoned—not like her street. There are a few families out on the porches or playing in the street, but it isn't a whole neighborhood feeling like on Ethel's street. The wind is blowing trash swirling into gutters and onto sidewalks. Ethel doesn't have air conditioning in the car so we have all the windows rolled down to get the breeze on our sweaty necks and arms.

"Ethel, please show me everything. I don't understand why there are so many poorer colored than whites. It's not fair that everyone can't have the same ways to get the same things. I know important stuff doesn't cost anything—stuff

127

like love and family and friends—but we all want other things that cost money, too. Did you ever tell your kids that my mom and dad don't do a lot of things with my sisters and brother? Or that my mom doesn't bake with us or teach me how to cook?"

"No, I din't ever do that, honey."

"Well, please tell them so they won't be thinking that I have everything and they have nothing. Will you do that, please?"

"Okay, dear, I will."

"What else don't you tell me about how it is different here, Ethel? I want to know the good and the bad. I'm not a little girl anymore. I'm growing up and I care about knowing. Mom and Dad aren't preparing me for the world by only letting me see how rich people live. I don't even know how to cook or iron or sew on a button. Your kids know a lot that they probably don't even realize they know. I think maybe they're mad that they know horrible things— and I'm mad that I don't know anything."

"Okay, Rachael. I's gonna show you somethin' they mad about."

Ethel drives up a country road arched with the branches and sparkling leaves of mature trees. We drive off the road to an old oak tree about a half a football field from the road. Ethel stops the car in the baking sun and we both look at the dust kicked up by the tires and breeze. Ethel puts her head on the steering wheel like it is a pillow.

"Rachael, see that branch hanging down from the others in that tree? A boy named Willie was hanged there. A twelve year old boy from my street that felt like he's family to our whole street-- that was Willie. A sweet, gentle boy. He was hanged there because he was Negro. Last April— only a few months ago. There was two white boys arrested by the police for it and they in jail now. Someone saw them driving on a Negro street and reported their car details after Willie was found. Those boys are sixteen. I sees Willie every night before I can sleep. Then I imagine he's resting in a peaceful place with birds an' butterflies an' fish all around glowing with golden rays from the sun. Only then can I fall asleep."

I can hardly believe my ears. "Oh, Ethel, that's much worse than Ruby not being with me." I want to comfort her but I don't know how.

"Rachael, there was a boy named Emmett Till that died a similar way at fourteen in Mississippi. Din't you hear of him?"

"No, I didn't. What happened?"

"Negros far and wide knows about Emmett, but whites never do." Ethel says with a wry smile. "Our newspapers are sure different in reportin'. Three years ago, when he was fourteen, Emmett done visited his relatives in Money, Mississippi. Now I don't knows if this part is true or not, but supposedly he whistled at a white women in a grocery store—a whistle like he's flirtatious. Later on that same night, that woman's husband and her half-brother pulled Emmett from his bed in his great uncle's cabin. Later, his body was found in the Tallahatchie River with a bullet in his head and other things too awful to repeat. His mommy had a open casket in Chicago when he went home to rest and fifty thousand people saw his body. For the first time the world sees what is happening to Negros and now even if they knows they don't care exceptin' the Negros. Well, Rachael, Willie is our Emmett."

I ask if I can get out of the car. I want to touch the branch where Willie was hanged. It's the only dead branch on the tree and it has names and initials engraved up and down it for people that have stopped here to look at it. It's too high for me to reach and there's nothing to stand on or I would have put my initials on it. What a horrible, tradgedy to have done to a child. I jump up and touch the branch as if I'm touching Willie's leg. He didn't get to live because whites thought they had the right to kill him and kill his family's happiness. I am ashamed for us.

Ethel doesn't hear me quietly open the door and sit down on the burning hot seat. She looks like she's praying; her head is down and her hands are faced together.

"Ethel, are you okay?" I ask gently.

"Oh, girl, you done scared me. What'cha doin'? Oh, I guess I drifted off. I get so sleepy whenever I see that tree. It knocks me for a loop, like a drug or somethin'."

Ethel sounds different, talking here by the tree—like maybe her old voice when she was a girl in the south.

"We better go 'fore I can't drive from bein' too sleepy," Ethel smiles.

Heading back we drive by Caroline's high school. It's close enough that she can walk to school. It's a brick building with six stories and looks more like a factory than a school because the windows are so little. The grass in front is dried out from the summer heat, but ivy climbs up the walls of the building. Ethel says there are no white kids at the school, but there are some white teachers. When Joseph starts high school in a year, Ethel is thinking about changing to one that is mostly white—farther away— because it's a better school. Ethel wants the children to go to college. She knows they'll have a better chance at getting into one if they go to a high school that's white.

I take many pictures before we are back to Ethel's house again.

Louis and the kids have made peanut butter and jelly sandwiches with potato chips for lunch. We all eat on the porch and some neighbors drop by and bring us cookies and we all dip them in milk. I wish it was my home just for a moment, even if Joseph and Caroline don't like me. Just Ethel and Louis being close to their children makes me see what it looks like to be a real family like my heart and cookies; warm and buttery. Ethel and I tell about our morning in the car but I don't say much because I know the kids hate me for coming here and for being rich.

When Caroline and Joseph go inside to get more milk and cookies, I follow them in.

"Can I tell you something?" I ask when we reach the kitchen.

"What?" Caroline says. I see the anger in her face.

"I want you both to know I know your mom isn't home because she is with us in our home. My mom isn't home, either. She could be because she doesn't have to work. I never see her because she is always doing other things. I miss her, so I know what it's like not to have your mom home. I don't even know if mom knows how to cook. I would rather have warm cookies baked by my mom than a new outfit. Your mom is away and mine is too. It's awful." I'm embarrassed because tears start to swell.

"That isn't true. You're a liar. Your mom isn't gone ten hours a day. You are so lucky, you don't have to worry about buying new clothes or records. Sometimes it's cold here 'cause there's no money even for heat," Caroline lashes out.

"No, you're right. She's not gone ten hours, but when she is home she is not with me. She is on the telephone or taking a nap or doing stuff for the house. At dinner time, our family doesn't laugh together. I'd rather be at school than at the dinner table. My family isn't making any memories that I'd want to capture with my camera.

Joseph is looking at me like he's thinking about what I'm saying. They both seem uncomfortable. Caroline puts her hand on mine for one second, and then yanks it away, like she wasn't thinking when she did that; it was just a reflex action. We all look at each other and then Caroline and Joseph get more milk and cookies. I go out to the porch. Caroline and Joseph come out a few minutes later. I wonder what they said to each other about me in the kitchen.

Ethel asks Caroline and me to help make a caramel cake and get dinner started. Caroline hands me the flour and sugar to put on the table instead of walking around me to do it herself. At least she doesn't avoid eye contact like she did before.

I don't know if Mom and Dad made up about Ruby or if Ruby will come back to my home. I don't know if I will ever like another boy like I did Tommy. I don't even know how much longer I can stand June. But I'm hoping Caroline and Joseph will think about what I told them. And maybe they'll come to visit me at my house.

I don't know a lot of things. But for the moment, at least, I am on the right side of the tracks. And I have pictures that tell the truth.

# 9
# HERE COMES THE BRIDE

It's the day before Annie's wedding—the first I'll ever have been to. Mom doesn't know what to do first. She is spinning around. She and Dad talked to each other at breakfast this morning like they talk to the milkman or Johnny, the head waiter at the club. There's an extra distance between them, like they aren't married. After the wedding tomorrow, Saturday, I think they will be like they were before all the planning. They are in love but, with all the extra duties that go into making the wedding, they are trying not to make each other angry. They never argue or say mean things to each other in front of us kids; maybe they do when they're alone, like that night I heard them squabbling. In fact, they seem like they're on a date all the time—like they just met. I am disturbed by the politeness in their voices.

I'm thinking about my new shoes with one and a half inch heels—my first ever; they match my bridesmaid dress. I have been practicing walking around in them. When I can wear three inch heels, then I will finally feel grown up. My dress looks pretty with my auburn hair. When I tried on the yellow dress, Mom said my hair looked like spun gold.

I was so busy with my clothes, I almost forgot the most important thing. "Mom, I need some film and flashbulbs for my camera for tonight's rehearsal dinner and for the wedding tomorrow."

"I'll ask Bill to go get the rolls, dear," Mom said quickly, fluttering her hand like I was a big bumble bee buzzing in her ear that needed to go away.

"Thanks."

"Dear, what is the lunch menu today?" Dad asks Mom.

He has never asked about what there is to eat.

"We're having ham salad, fried chicken, Jell-O mold, potato salad, and corn muffins. Everything cold. Why, dear, do you ask?"

"I want to make sure Leonard has something he likes, darling. You know how picky he is. Even more than me."

Leonard is Aunt Judy's husband. They are cousins from Chicago who have come for the wedding. They're coming for lunch today with Buddy, their fifteen year old son.

I excuse myself from the breakfast table and go into the library. It is rarely used except for card games that Mom and Dad have with their friends. On Sunday nights we have a buffet supper set out on the heater ledge in here and once in a while Jessy and I play jacks on the cold marble floor. I don't listen to the shelves of 78 rpm records or read the hundreds of books. I have never seen anyone in our family do those things either.

But during the last few weeks, at least once a day I like to go to see the droves of wedding presents that have arrived. Some of the gifts are displayed on the leather covered card table and the built in mahogany shelves. Sterling silver serving pieces, flatware and picture frames are abundant. Glass cut crystal vases and platters sparkle like diamonds. I feel like I'm inside a kaleidoscope—every time I turn my eyes to a different part of the room the separate shapes and colors change into another shimmering design. I don't see how Annie and Donald's newlywed apartment will hold all these riches. I went over there one day to help line shelves. I was shocked to see such a dingy place. Maybe they have a secret fairy castle in the woods where they can keep all these treasures. The beautiful wrappings on gifts not opened could hold jeweled crowns, crystal scepters, illuminated manuscripts, mosaics, and stained glass for their noble castle instead of the old, ugly apartment they're going to live in. I will never move into a cramped dark apartment after my knight in shining armor comes to rescue me— maybe it will be Tommy.

The out of town guests are starting to arrive for lunch. Cousins, aunts, and uncles have been coming to our house for dinner all week. I don't remember meeting any of these relatives from Detroit or Chicago before this and I'll probably never see them again–at least until another wedding or funeral. There are too many guests for lunch in the dining room so we young ones move over to the breakfast room. My Aunt Judy sits with us. Buddy, her 15 year old son, sits with us, too. He's pretty cute and Jessy is talking to him the whole time. I think he likes Jessy, too. I've never known a grownup who could make a bunch of kids laugh the way Aunt Judy does. She stands up on her chair in her low heels and sings show tunes from *Oklahoma* and *My Fair Lady* at the top of her lungs. Maybe Mom will let me take the train to visit her in Chicago. James would be my porter and tell me great stories again. I can tell him what I'm doing to help the colored people. I know it's a dream but Ruby always told me there's no harm in dreaming. I hope Aunt Judy sits with me at the wedding tomorrow night. I can tell she wants the kids to feel special because she chooses to sit with us.

After lunch, I'm in my room lying on the bed thinking about what Jessy said she heard at lunch today—that June was going to come tomorrow to help us get dressed in the hotel room. Mom walks by and I yell out my open door, "Mom, I know you didn't invite Ethel, Ruby, Bernice or Bill to the wedding and I want to know why."

Mom stops and stands in my doorway and puts one hand on her hip.

"Dear, we didn't because we had only so many we could invite. June is coming not as a guest but to help us dress. Now I need to do a million last minute things."

"Mom, that is so sad. They care about Annie and her marriage to Donald. I think you should ask them to the ceremony at least— they don't have to stay for dinner."

Mom just shakes her head.

"Why can't one of them at least help us in the room instead of June?"

Mom starts to move down the hall.

"When I get married, they'll all be invited," I yell. "Just remember that."

I hate them for not having Bernice or Ethel come. June hardly knows us at all. The only time I've talked to June about anything important was about Ruby.

"Rachael, why were ya crying last night? I could hear you when you were supposed to be asleep. I thought it was the wind talking, but I got up and saw your head deep into your pillow moving as the sounds came out. I went over to your bed and almost put my hand on your shoulder, but I didn't want to startle ya. I thought you might shout at me and wake up Jessy. I will work happily today if you please tell me what's making ya cry."

"June, I don't care if you work happily. I miss Ruby so much my heart almost feels like a stomach ache. Maybe Dr. Chet can give me medicine. Please go away and leave me alone."

"Rachael, that is called heartache. There is no medicine for it."

"Please go away, June."

"No pills will cure it, but sometimes we can talk to make it better. I have had heartache too and I know it feels like someone is squeezing your heart and what is left is a dried up brittle heart instead of feeling feathery. I wish you and Ruby could always be together and I will pray to God for that for ya every night."

"Thank you Ruby—I mean June. But go away."

I left the room to go to the bathroom to calm down.

When Mom heard me yell she came back to my doorway. "Honey," she said, "I would have to ask all of them because I don't want one of them to feel left out. Also, we can only fit one in the car."

"So now you hurt all our help. That makes no sense. I'm surprised you even thought about their feelings, anyway. You just want the white one. Isn't that the truth?"

137

"No, honey. June is the upstairs maid. Ruby isn't even here. Now I've made my decision. They've already made their plans to take the day off and go home tonight. Everything is arranged. Now, really, Rachael, I have to run."

"Mom," I say angrily, "I'm not going to the rehearsal tonight. Tell me tomorrow what I am supposed to do at the wedding."

"You have to go," Mom insists. "

"I can go stay with Peggy."

"Dear, I am sorry you're upset about the help. But everything is the way Annie wants it. You don't want to upset your sister by not being there tonight. She's been arguing with Donald's mother about plans for the wedding and it's been making her a nervous wreck. That's why she doesn't eat. I'm so worried about her losing so much weight. If you don't show up tonight, that would make her even more worried. Please, Rachael, try to understand why I can't change the plans for tonight!"

"Okay, Mom. I'll go. But I don't even want to go to the wedding—that's how unhappy I am about our help not being there."

"I know how much you care about them being at the wedding—and I promise they'll be there for your wedding. Now I really have to run."

Later, Jessy and I get ready for the rehearsal dinner together. She makes me laugh pretending to be Peter Pan jumping off her bed in her underwear. The rehearsal dinner is at the same hotel where the wedding is going to be. Why do we have to rehearse? The most thrilling and passionate day of my sister's life should not have a preview like a coming attraction at the movies. All the events—fresh as the first fallen snow or the beach sand before a footprint—is what each moment of a wedding should be. I hope they don't make us rehearse when to cry or laugh.

The family arrives at the hotel and we all walk en masse through the cut crystal doors that beam rainbows into the lobby. The doormen are all Negroes in ornate uniforms—brass buttons and appliqués on their hats and jackets. I expect them to salute us, like we're entering the Naval Academy.

This is my first time in a hotel lobby. I want to hold on to the excitement I feel. I take pictures of every detail; the scenes pop like a 3-D movie. It looks like a busy New York City intersection. Businessmen in suits with attaches rush through while women in high heels, long leather gloves and hats drag their children to follow. The bellmen—in navy blue uniforms and peaked matching caps, carry soft, leather, monogrammed suitcases toward elevators. Waiters in starched white uniforms carry food and cocktails above their heads on stacked trays and loudly say, "Coming through." I feel the whirl of movement and being part of something unexpected. My camera feels like it's taking pictures without my interference. Everywhere I look there's a story I want to take a picture of. If I'm not careful, I'll use up all three rolls of thirty six before the rehearsal dinner even begins. This is the first time in my life I don't feel alone because my camera shows me where to go without being afraid.

The sitting part of the lobby looks inviting. People are playing checkers, reading, and talking in groups, sitting in cushy linin chairs and sofas with colorful iced drinks and neatly arranged snacks on tables. Waiters are taking orders as they stand at attention looking like wind-up soldiers, ready and able. We ride up the lacquered wood and brass elevator manned by another colored man in a starched white uniform, white gloves and hat. We step off and enter an ordinary door on the tenth floor. Our footsteps echo like voices in a chorus. There are stacks of bland chairs in piles and ropes showing where the wedding party will walk. I finish my second roll of film; I hope Bill got some more because I'll need more for the wedding tomorrow.

We all take turns walking down the aisle. While music plays, a man with white hair, red mustache and goatee gives out instructions in a gruff billy goat voice. He looks angry. I would rather get married in the hospital where I had my tonsils out, rather than here. Annie should get married in the warm lobby where there are comfy living room chairs.

Mom is directing—with the billy goat man—who should walk when and with whom. The groomsmen and bridesmaids are here, too. All the bridesmaids are going to be in yellow dresses with shoes to match. If it were my wedding day, Ethel, Ruby and Bernice would be my bridesmaids. Each one of the dresses would be a different color of a precious stone—ruby red, sapphire blue and emerald green. Jessy and Annie would be my flower girls, and Rusty would be my ring bearer.

Annie is getting thinner by the day. It's a good thing the wedding is tomorrow or her dress would be falling off her. Mom said Jessy and I will wear the same dress as Annie is wearing when we get married. She said we will preserve it so it won't turn from ivory white to creamy white. Dad sits on one of the folding chairs way back in the corner of the room looking on. I take the last of my photographs of Dad without him even knowing.

After the rehearsal, dinner is served buffet style in another bland room that adjoins the first. I sit almost facing Aunt Judy. Even though I sit two chairs away, she looks at me a lot when she talks or makes someone laugh. I can't hear what she's talking about exactly, but I like to look at her. Jessy sits next to Buddy and ignores me completely. Rusty is on one side of me and one of Annie's friends is on the other. I don't know her so Rusty and I talk and joke around. I like my little brother, but I feel maybe I'm like an aunt to him since we hardly ever talk or do stuff together. I will always remember tonight for being with Rusty and not being with Annie. I heard Aunt Judy say Donald and the guys are going to a bar to drink and have some fun before he's married tomorrow. Annie had some wedding showers the last few weeks that I had to go to. The women sat around while Annie opened presents. When I get married, I'll have bridal showers, too, get drunk with my girlfriends and with Ruby, Ethel and Bernice.

All the girls and women go to the cozy lobby to talk for a while. I snap photos of Annie with her friends. I think I'll understand her better when I look at photos later. Without Ruby, Ethel and Bernice, a big chunk of joy is missing from this women's group, though no one else seems to care.

Instead of joining in the conversation, I prefer watching the people move about like checkers through the lobby area. They could be from Argentina, Iceland, or Paris. Obedient children are dressed like fashion plates, shadowing their moms or dads. No matter where they're from, children can tell when they have to behave like bellboys, doormen and elevator operators in uniforms.

"Jessy, you keep staring at Annie. Are you jealous of her getting married?" I ask.

"Rach, mind your own business. You are, too. At least I get her room and we don't have to share anymore," Jessy looks like she's going to cry when she says this.

"I'm happy Annie is getting married. I'm not jealous. You just can't wait to get rid of me," I snap back, feeling sad myself.

Jess comes over from her chair and hugs me and I hug her back. "I will never get rid of you, Rachael. You are my sister. We both get our own rooms. So now we can have two rooms to have fun in."

The men come into the lobby from the bar and we all walk out of the castle-like fantasy to ride home. Jewish goodbyes are long and dragged out before we all get in our different cars.

On the ride home I think it is mysterious to get married. I wonder what it's really like. It must feel good and romantic to be in love and have that person feel the exact same way about you. Annie never talks about it to me because we don't talk about anything other than how is school, how is Donald—like you would a friend you hardly see. Sometimes Jessy and I sneak halfway down the front stairs and look in the mirror to see their reflection when they're kissing on the couch and imagine what they're saying to each other. They can't see us. I wish Annie would share what she feels about Donald and the wedding with me. Is it a secret world that has its own language and feelings that only people who are married can understand?

In the morning Mom comes in and checks our dresses and shoes to make sure they look perfect. The pale butter yellow one-and-a-half inch heels match most of the dress. An embroidered trim on the waist—pearls and embroidered blue, pink green and white flowers—is the only part I love.

I feel my heart race as I see June's suitcase by the door. If she's not going to the wedding, why does she have a suitcase? She's only helping us get dressed. I click open the suitcase as soon as Mom leaves the room. Inside is a fancy dress. She's trying to get into our family! Maybe Mom didn't even tell her she's not invited to the wedding. She's so pushy. If there's just one button awry or a scuff on the toe of a shoe, maybe Mom would fire June. I thought about making a tear in my dress before Mom inspected it, but I don't want to lie about June anymore. She annoys me with her accent and her smell, but Ethel would be disappointed in me if I tried to get her fired now that I know how much June needs this job.

As we lie on our beds waiting to leave for the wedding, Jessy and I talk about the events of the day. We always talk about personal things when the table between our beds hides our face. It's easier to say things when we aren't scrutinizing every facial expression—more like we're talking on the telephone. Once in a while one of us looks around the table to see the other's face, but then we go back to hiding.

This will be the last time, after thirteen years, that I talk to Jessy in the bedroom that is ours not just mine. Tonight she'll sleep in her new bedroom.

At the same second we both jump up and hug each other real hard. We're probably both thinking the same thing—that later we will be sad about being alone more. I could cry real hard right now, but I stop myself because then I would have to go into the bathroom and I don't want anyone to see me. I don't want to be alone now.

I've always known Jessy doesn't care about Ruby, Ethel, Bernice and Bill as much as I do, so I don't bring up how angry I am that they aren't invited. I wish Jessy would talk to me about how much I care about them. At least Peggy understands. She'll be at the wedding with her parents.

Peggy knows my mom isn't at home like her mom. Her mom even shops at our store in Warren where my mom works. Sometimes I see Peggy's mom wearing a dress or a blouse exactly like Mom's. I think, now I know why I hate new clothes and want only hand-me-downs. If we didn't have a store that sold clothes, I might like new clothes. But new clothes take Mom away from me. I told Peggy that even when Mom is home, she's on the phone or busy. She told me if her mom was like my mom, she'd be so sad she would have to talk to her maids all the time, too. I know she doesn't feel exactly what it's like in my home, but she listens all the time to what I say about Mom and Ruby, Ethel, Bernice and Bill. Jessy doesn't even try to understand me; if she did, she'd say something back to let me know.

I sit on Jessy's bed and she tells me she has a crush on Aunt Judy's son, Buddy, and she can't wait to see him again at the wedding. I saw Jessy flirting with him last night at the rehearsal dinner. He's fifteen and Jessy is fourteen. I read that in Elizabethan times cousins could get married and maybe they still can, if they aren't first cousins. Buddy is a third cousin. I would love to see Aunt Judy all the time so I hope Buddy and Jessy get married.

Jessy and I pack small suitcases with our underwear and wedding shoes for the hotel where we have a room with Annie and Mom to get dressed in. The dresses will be in clothing bags on hangers. I pack my camera, more film, and more flashbulbs. I know I'll want to show the pictures to Ethel, Bernice, and Bill. The photographs will show a wedding that only rich people could have, but they'll still want to see them. I hope they invite me to their family wedding one day—I don't care if it's in the backyard or a park. I want to be there.

The phone doesn't stop ringing all day. I walk into Mom's dressing room with my camera just as she's just starting to put on her makeup. She's in the slip she will wear under her mother-of-the-bride dress.

"Mom, you look like a bride without any makeup. May I take some pictures of you now, before the hotel? I wish I'd been there to take them when you and Dad got married."

"No, dear. I'm really rushed and I would rather have you take them at the hotel when we are in the room getting ready."

"Mom, I love to look at you just like this. Please!"

"Darling, you are so sweet to say that, but I never have my picture taken without 'my face' on."

I give her a pleading look. She sighs.

"All right. Take one very quickly, and then make sure June has everything for the car, please."

I take one of Mom with the flash. Then I hurriedly take one without the flash because the light is streaming in from the small leaded window. Then I run because Mom looks angry when I take the second one. I have two pictures that I will treasure forever.

With all of us, the dresses, and suitcases, the station wagon is full—like we're going on a vacation. Without Ruby and Ethel going to the wedding, I want to tell Dad to stop the car, take me home and to have June stand in my place and wear my dress.

Everything goes so fast after we get to the hotel room. There are shoes and clothes strewn all over the beds and floor. I dress carefully because I don't want to run my stockings or wrinkle my dress. The garter belt straps flap around in wait for the first stockings that I have ever worn. June puts a little makeup on me—some rouge and lipstick—before I slip the dress over my head. She should have done the makeup last because the lipstick could get on my dress, but she says the dress will stay fresher if it's put on last, after everything else is done. June helps me attach the stockings one fastener at a time. She tells me I can do the last one myself. It's easy! My slip is next and then my petticoat.

I pull the dress over my shimmering hair, tuck in my lips and hold my breath, praying the silk lining doesn't snag on a hook or thread. June's breath is vile, like mustard and gravy mixed together; it may smell up the dress so I walk away from her while I finish slipping it on. Jessy finished dressing without June's help.

Annie and Mom are in the living room of our suite. When I walk in, June is buttoning about fifty teeny pearl luminescent buttons that go down the back of Annie's dress. I've never seen a wedding dress except in a magazine. Before today, it hung in a closed dark garment bag in Annie's room. It's made with lace, pearls, voile, and silk trim. The ivory fabric is the color of elephant tusks. I never knew that a dress could be as pretty as a flower.

Mom helps Annie do her makeup. Mom and Annie had their hair done at the beauty shop earlier. Annie's hair is up in a formal hairdo. It must hurt with all the pins stuck in it to make it stay. I cannot help but hug my sister when I see her in the dress even though she's not finished dressing. She hugs me back real hard. She feels more like an aunt to me because I never really got to know her like a sister.

"Annie, I know you're busy getting ready but if you could help me put the film in my camera, then I can take some pictures of you before the wedding," I ask shyly.

I've never asked Annie to do anything for me that I can remember. She doesn't know I know how to load the camera, but I want her to be a big sister and do something for me before she gets married. I wish I had asked her to do other things for me. I always ask Jessy or one of the maids.

"Sure, honey," Annie says. "Go get your film and camera. I'd love to help you."

I dash out of the room and find my camera and film and bring it to her. Mom is watching as June finishes buttoning the dress.

"That was fast, Rachael."

I watch Annie open the camera and put the film in. She does it a lot quicker than I do.

"Here, Sis." We hug again.

"Thank you…Sis," I say quietly, surprised she called me Sis.

After Annie and I hug, Mom cries, and then wipes her eyes and nose with a lacey handkerchief. After a few minutes, she continues to help Annie get ready. Mom only has to put on her dress because she did her makeup at home. I keep watching Annie and Mom fiddle with the dress and her hair. They are quietly talking about Donald, Dad, and all the other relatives and friends. June is helping, too.

The dress has a big train that has to be held until we get to the wedding room. June will hold the train and follow

Annie until she waits to walk down the aisle. Now, the train is folded neatly and placed on the floor next to the stool Annie is sitting on. Careful not to step on the train, Mom stands behind her, looking at her in a mirror. Maybe they call it a train because it lies on the floor like a train on the tracks.

June is not attending the wedding or the dinner. I asked her and she said her place is to help in the room. I don't think she cares if she goes because she's not part of the family.

As I walk down the yellow and white rose petal-strewn aisle, I see everyone looking at my heels wobbling, holding up my skinny legs like a newborn colt. I want them to see my face and see how pretty I look. I imagine Tommy being there, watching me. I can't stop thinking about him all the way down the aisle. I wish he were here.

All the bridesmaids and groomsmen stand on separate sides of the chuppah while the rabbi leads Annie and Donald in their wedding vows. I don't listen to the words because I'm worried I may cry or laugh if I hear them. I hear "love... cherish... death" and all the words that always make me want to react, so I try to distract myself. I look at the room that is magically transformed into flowery splendor. The ugly chairs and tables are now covered in white cloth, the floor is littered with smells of petals is heavenly. It's like being inside a basket of flowers. After Donald smashes the glass, wrapped in a white damask napkin, on the floor, they kiss; then they smile and cry all at the same time.

The musicians play the wedding song as the couples skip back up the aisle. Everyone in the wedding party has a partner this time. Mine is Jay, Donald's friend, who is handsome and nice. I just want to keep holding on to him until it's time to go home. After we get to the end of the aisle I have to go into a reception line to hear everyone say something nice. Peggy is the only one in line I can't wait to see. I tell her I will be able to talk more later.

Aunt Judy is sitting at a table and waves for me. She gives me her glass filled with champagne and motions for me to take some sips. Oh my gosh, sips of champagne! She is so fun. I take three or four sips and thank her with a big hug. I didn't even taste it because I was sipping so fast but now it tastes like honeysuckle sap. I just need to get to the powder room to see if I look silly or drunk. She is laughing as I rush off on my unsteady heels. Mom is waving at me to come back in line, but I turn around and keep going. My Dad looks drunk and laughs with everyone. I have never seen him drunk but his smile looks like it was scotch-taped on. He is flirting with Annie's girlfriend and I wonder if anyone else notices. I don't want a picture to remind me of this moment. Mom looks like she just got married because she is the most beautiful woman here—or anywhere we go. Annie and Donald do look in love while they say hello to everyone. After I come out of the powder room stall, the colored girl taking care of the cleanliness says I can sit on the velvet padded bench if I want to and rest a minute. I am tired from all the emotions tearing at me—my dad is drunk and acting like a teenager, Ruby isn't here, Jessy won't be sharing my room tonight, I haven't been able to talk to Peggy yet because I had to be in the reception line. I feel very much alone and yet there are many people I'm supposed to still talk to. I lean my head against the wall while I sit on the bench, feeling safe here. My head is throbbing like a very bad headache.

"You just sit here and rest, chil'."

"What's your name?" I ask.

"Missy."

"I'm Rachael and I'm not a child anymore."

Missy goes into a little storage room to get me something for my head and I hear her rustle around with cleaning supplies and tissues. And then Ruby comes out of the storage room!

"Hi, Rachael. What you doin', not at the weddin'?"

"Ruby!" I scream.

Ruby and I hug like we haven't seen each other for years. I cry in her arms. "What are you doing here? How did you know I was here?"

"I knows it from people that knows you and I wants to see you, honey."

I say, "Ruby, you cannot know how much I miss you every day."

"I miss you, honey, too. You knows I do."

"Wait, I have my camera, and I want to take a picture of you."

"Oh, chil', I do look terrible. Well, okay."

I take the flash and attach it. I snap it twice to make sure I get it.

"Okay, now you know I miss you, but you must go back to that weddin'."

"I want to stay here with you. I cry every day for you."

"I will find a way to come back."

"Ruby, why did you leave?"

"Rachael, that is a grown-up thing, but I will come back."

I feel dizzy and close my eyes. When I open them, I can hardly breathe. Missy is rubbing my shoulders as I sit on the bench. I must have fallen asleep and dreamed about Ruby because now I look at Missy's tearful eyes. My camera is in my hand. I go in a stall and cry as softly as I can because women are coming in. I remember the last time I was crying in a stall—my thirteenth birthday party at the club when Tommy wasn't paying any attention to me. I yearn for Ruby.

I leave Missy and the powder room. I run into Aunt Judy who's on her way in looking for me. She says Mom sent her to see what happened to me. Aunt Judy and I laugh at our bubbly secret. She asks me if I am okay and I say yes, fine. I feel different going back to the wedding because I still feel a little dizzy from the champagne.

Somehow I am going to find out the truth about Ruby. I know the truth already about Mom: she only cares about her guests and not enough to even look for me herself. All her life is based on what everyone thinks of her—everyone but her children—otherwise Ruby would still be in our family. Whatever it was that made Ruby leave must have been something that looked so bad to my mom's world, it was more important to her than my happiness.

When I come back into the reception, I see Dad dancing with Peggy's mom while Peggy watches. She is almost prettier than Mom. Dad looks so drunk, trying to dance without falling over. I make my way over to Peggy and we talk about my dream and Ruby. I tell Peggy she is the only reason I'm happy to be here. We laugh and talk until dinner. I take fast pictures of Peggy—one of her twirling in her dress. It will be blurry but her smile is like an angel's. I leave her to sit at the wedding table, but I tell her to join me after dinner.

I stare at the food. I kick off my shoes and scoot them under the table. Quickly before anyone tells me to stop, I take pictures of the food on the wedding table, the flowers, the family sitting at the table, and the waiters serving the drinks and food. Everyone is getting used to my picture-taking and not making the usual comments like, "What are you doing, do you know how to take pictures? Why are you taking picture when there's a photographer?" I wave to Aunt Judy from my table but everyone else fades into the background of band music and the low flow and ebb of voices.

After the main course, Dad asks me to dance. We dance awkwardly because Dad is still drunk, but I'm happy to dance with him for the only time I can remember. Donald's friend Jay asks me to dance as soon as the song ends. I have had my shoes off so it's easy to follow his steps. He's flirting with me while we dance, which makes me feel quite grown up. Not just because he's twenty-one but because Tommy acts like such a child compared to Jay. Eight years from now, I will be all grown up like Annie, Donald, and Jay.

As soon as the dance ends I feel nervous about what to do, so I say that I have to get my camera and take some pictures. Peggy is busy talking with other people so I decide to go to our hotel room for a break. I use the key to go into the room. June is watching television. She is still in her uniform and never changed to her nice dress for the wedding.

"What's ya doin' here, Rachael?"

"I'm tired from dancing and want to lie down."

"Ya can't be too tired. Ya too young."

I'm feeling alone in a big celebration. I don't want to cry in front of June but it just streams out like a rain cloud bursting.

June comes over to the bed and hugs me. "What's the matter, Rachael?"

Her arms smell like cooked steak but they feel like June. I push her away and say, "I have to go back downstairs."

"Ya, it is your older sister's day and not yours. You must be grown-up today for her. Wash your face and I'll fix your hair. Sometimes when we pretend we are having a pleasant time, we do. You don't want anyone feeling sorry for ya. Dance with Rusty or Jessy and don't have a glum face or ya will get people noticing an' asking lots of questions about what is wrong." She gives me a warm smile. "If you have to, come up here again, but try to stay. It is only a few more hours and everyone will go home, Rachael. Then ya will have some happy memories to start filling up those creases in your heart."

I walk to the bathroom and wash my face and put on some rouge and lipstick.

"Okay, let's fix that handsome silky hair of yours."

As soon as I go back to the wedding party I see Aunt Judy waving to me again.

"Rachael, where have you been? I can't tell my best jokes unless you are in my audience and I have been upside down looking for you under the tables and chairs. Whoa, is it dusty under there—and some of those old shoes don't smell good. I was going to look in the kitchen if you didn't come back."

"Oh, Aunt Judy, I had to get more film for my camera in the room. Did I miss anything?"

"Yes, honey. Annie threw the bouquet and Marilyn caught it, you know— Annie's best friend. Not exciting enough to worry about, I promise. There's cake left. Annie and Donald fed each other the cake. Annie pushed it all over Donald's face but he didn't dare do that to her. You must have just missed Annie. She went up to change into her honeymoon outfit so they could leave for the hotel. Your mom is looking for you. She was going to send Jessy up to the room to find you but the cake came and she had to organize that event. Sit down here and let's wait until they come down so we can throw rice together."

I wish I cared that I missed my first wedding cake and first flower throwing, but the only time Annie acknowledged I was her sister was when I hugged her after the wedding ceremony. She's been busy with all the other guests. Even if we have known each other my whole life, I don't feel sad she's leaving home. If I get really lonely, Jessy said she'll sleep with me in my room or I can come to hers.

"Aunt Judy, can I come visit you sometime? I could take the train. They have porters that watch children traveling alone."

"I know, dear. Your mom told me about the camp vacation that was cut short and your train trip. I know you didn't have a long wait in Chicago or I would have come to the station to see you."

"Aunt Judy, now I'm embarrassed. I did get into trouble and was sent home. I bet that never happened to you."

"Honey, you do need to visit so I can tell you about your wild Aunt Judy. We really are related."

I laugh. "I can't wait. Maybe Mom will let me come during spring break."

I throw rice at Annie and Donald with everyone else and they leave the hotel in Donald's dented, scratched and dingy painted Studebaker. Cans have been tied to the back bumper and they screech along the pavement as they drive away. I say goodbye to relatives and family friends. Aunt Judy and I hug like bears. Mom and Jessy and I go up to pack our stuff in the hotel room, though June has already done most of it.

All of a sudden I realize I do miss Annie. Spending the hours with her in this room was a close feeling that is now gone forever. It feels empty without her. We finish packing and meet Rusty and Dad in the lobby with our suitcases.

The valet brings the station wagon round and I sit next to Jessy, who puts her head on my shoulder, like she is sad Annie is gone. Mom and Dad are talking about the wedding. I can hardly hear what they're saying because some of the windows are partly open and the breeze and traffic muffle their voices. I hear snatches——how perfectly lovely everything turned out, how beautiful Annie and our family looked, how everyone had a "simply wonderful time." Mostly Mom is talking and Dad is nodding his head, agreeing. Then Mom says that Dad danced with Lilly—Peggy's mom—too many times. Dad says he's sorry if he did but he was too drunk to even remember. Mom gets quiet after that. Dad didn't try to make her talk anymore and the whole car is still.

As I fall asleep, my room smells of Jessy so I feel she is still sharing the room with me.

# 10
# WHIRLIGIG

As soon as I get all my pictures back, I show them to Ethel. The chairs are right next to each other and our legs touch under the kitchen table.

"Why, dear, youse look so pretty dancing with yo' Daddy," Ethel says. Peggy took this one of me with my camera. "Oh, look at dat table all dressed up, too. There's Jessy in that one. She's having a good ol' time. Your Mommy is one movie star lookin' lady, now, ain't she, Rachael? Oh, I love these of Annie and Donald. They look so in love—like two birds. Oh, is that Peggy? Isn't she a dream? You's the most beautiful of them all, Rachael, you know that?"

"Oh, Ethel, I love you," I say surprising myself. I have never said that to anyone—not Mom, Dad, Ruby, Jessy—anyone!

Ethel gives me a big hug and then gathers up the pictures and puts them in a straight pile.

"I'm going to find Bill and see if he can come down to the laundry room to see the pictures with Bernice," I say to Ethel.

"Ok, dear, you go right along."

I find Bill in the garage looking for something on a shelf. The air is muggy and heavy with the smell of dried oil and paint and the sun is streaking into the open garage door.

"Bill, I want to show you and Bernice the wedding pictures. Can you see them now?"

"Yes I can, Miss Rachael, as soon as I find some car polish your Daddy just had me buy last week. I put it in a real special place," Bill says smiling at me. "I'll meet you there in a few minutes."

I go downstairs to the laundry room as fast as I can. Showing the pictures to Ethel, and now to Bernice and Bill, is more exciting than the wedding.

"Bernice, Bill is coming down so I can show you both the wedding pictures,"

I say cheerfully.

Bernice turns around from getting some clothes out of the washing machine. There is sweat dripping from her narrow dark chocolate face and her white uniform is marked with large circles of wetness under her plump short arms. No air-conditioning in the basement makes the laundry room feel balmy, like when I can't wait for a cool dip in the pool. All the windows are open but it doesn't help the sticky stale air mixed with hot metallic iron smells.

"Well, if you can stand it down here, honey, I'd love to

see those weddin' pictures, but be quick. I got lots to do, honey," Bernice replies with a tired sounding voice.

I'm standing close to Bernice and take note that I'm almost as tall as she is. She's shorter than Ethel and Ruby, so I'll reach her height first. She sees me checking out my height next to her.

"Soon, my little girl, you will be there. Don't rush too fast to grow up," Bernice laughs as she sits down in the folding chair ready for the show. I pull up another chair folded against the wall to be right next to her while we wait for Bill.

"I'm coming." We hear Bill's quick footsteps coming down from the garage.

Bill stands behind me as I show the pictures one by one and hand them to Bernice to hold. He looks over our shoulders and breathes in the hot moist air in loud breaths. His light blue shirt is dark where sweat has stained it, like a modern painting design. His umber colored face is streaked with small rivulets running into the creases of his neck. The sweat is mixed with a perfume smell, probably men's cologne.

"Oh, lordy, look at Annie and ya'll dressed like kings and queens!" Bernice says, enjoying herself. "Mighty fancy weddin' I say, Miss Rachael."

Bernice never called me Miss Rachael before. I like her calling me that. Like I'm special to her.

"Oh, look at yo' Daddy and Rusty dressed like they was…" Bill doesn't finish the sentence. "Rachael, you look so growed up—and Jessy, too. I guess Jessy'll be the next bride. Hope we'll still be around."

"Don't say that like you'll be somewhere else, Bill. I want you here always."

We look together at each and every picture with a lot of "uh-huhs and "oh mys" and laughing. Our picture break ends too fast.

# 11
# SCHOOL

Tommy and Jessy are in high school now. This is the first time I won't see them at school every day. Jane, my best school friend, is in my English and math classes. We don't have the same lunch period, though. Some of my other good friends are in my other classes, but I miss Jessy and the hope of seeing Tommy pass in the hallway.

The first week I find guy friends more interesting and fun to talk to than my girlfriends. All my girlfriends talk about is hair, clothes, and boys—just like I used to—but I soon tire of those topics now. Boys can talk sports in detail and they like to kid each other. They're more honest and don't try to manipulate their friends to get what they want. They say what they think and don't mind arguing or disagreeing. Girls hide things they don't like and it comes out in jealousy or anger.

Boys were central to my existence before this past summer, but since making friends with Molly, meeting James, and with Ruby gone, everything's changed for me.

161

At least boys still make me laugh. I hope one of my guy friends will be interested in the same things I am now.

In English, my assignment, is to write an essay on what we did all summer. I told the teacher, Mrs. Werner I wanted to do photos with descriptions instead. She said that was fine, as long as it included some writing. All the photos are developed from my stay with Ethel. For each picture I write what it's about and where it was shot. I had one picture blown up to five-by-seven inches—the one of the tree where Willie was hanged. I wrote a whole page about Willie and Emmett Till. The others photos are of Ethel's neighborhood, her family, her neighbors, and the other neighborhoods Ethel and I drove through.

I know Ethel is busy getting dinner on the table but I want her to see my report before I hand it in. I run downstairs, grab her hand, and tell her it will only take one minute. Ethel turns off the burners and checks the roast in the oven. We run upstairs together laughing. I don't tell Ethel how different she looks without her white uniform. She always looks pretty, but with regular clothes on–like in the pictures–she looks even more beautiful. "Ethel, this is my report for English class," I say, pointing to everything spread out on the floor.

Ethel looks over everything. "Oo-wee, girl, you done a lot of work. Uh-huh, oh, gosh, well, I see." Her brow furrows and she turns to me and says, "Oh, Rachael. I don't want you worrying about me and my family. You just thirteen. Let me worry about you, now. But this is good, Rachael. You sure do surprise me." Ethel has tears in her eyes as she speaks. She picks up the photograph of her husband, Louis, and reads the description aloud: *This is Louis, my cook's husband. He told me he wanted to be a pilot when he grew up but colored people weren't allowed to be pilots on commercial airlines so he joined the Army and got to be one of the first*

*Negroes to fly in the Tuskegee Airmen, an all Negro Army unit stationed in Alabama. The Navy wasn't allowed to have colored pilots or he would have joined the Navy. Now Louis is a barber; when the war was over there were still that prevented him from becoming a commercial pilot.*

Ethel says she has to go quick and leaves the room.

I am still standing with the photographs and descriptions spread out when Mom comes in my room. She probably heard Ethel and me talking and wondered what Ethel was doing here when dinner is about to be served. Mom has seen me working on the project, but now she is looking at it again closely. She picks up the same description of Louis that Ethel read, then, after a moment, walks out without a comment. Maybe she's angry about my project, but if she is, I don't care.

"Mom, can you come back, please?"

Mom comes and stands at the door with a look of disapproval on her tired face. "What, dear?"

She probably expects me to talk about the project. "Mom, I have something I have to ask you before dinner. I need to know why Ruby left and if you don't know, then I want you to find out." I demand in a tone of voice I did not know I had.

"I know how much you miss Ruby. Dad and I did not agree on her leaving. Dad knew Ruby was drinking every day from his bottle of Scotch and he ignored it for years, but finally he confronted her one day about her stealing the liquor. She lied to his face and then told us the next day that she needed to leave. Ruby would not tell the truth. We would have kept her if she had not lied. We would have helped her to stop drinking on the job, Rachael. Maybe she couldn't stop and she knew it. I hope someday she will ask to come back after she is sober. Dad and I didn't want to tell you because we know how highly you think of her. If you knew she drank and lied you may have felt angry at her for not being the kind of person you thought she was. We wanted you to always remember her as special to you, not a liar. But you deserve to know the truth, honey."

"Thanks, Mom. I wish you'd told me before. Then I wouldn't have been wondering all this time why she left. And I wouldn't have been wondering why you and Dad seemed so angry with each other. Now I understand, you didn't agree about Ruby leaving."

I wish I knew Ruby better. Maybe she feels I shouldn't know the parts of her that might scare me. I don't know why she drinks but she's still the same person to me. I hope she'll be able to tell a good friend or her mom and get some help. I know she shouldn't drink in our home, but if she can't wait until she gets home I think she must be in a lot of pain about her life.

Mom hugs me and says, "Come on to dinner, dear. You'll feel better after you eat." She starts to walk out, then turns at the door and says, "Your project looks good, Rachael, really good. And sweetie, I'm happy you notice when Dad and I are not our normal selves with each other. You notice more than we think you do. Planning a wedding and having it turn out like we want has been very stressful. Remember, it's our first time. When you and Jessy get married, we'll be old hands at it."

"Mom, I want to stay here for a little while. I'll be down soon." What I really want to say is, *Mom, I want you to stay here with me and tell me the parts of my project you like and why you like them. Your opinion is really special to me. I'd love to go over everything with you.* But I don't say it because I'm scared Mom would say she's too busy.

She starts to walk out again and, again, turns in the doorway.

"Rachael, Uncle Russ wanted to be a doctor but he couldn't get into any medical schools because there was a quota of how many Jews were allowed. He knew that even if he finished medical school, many hospitals had Jewish quotas on admitting physicians. One of his friends could not get hired by any hospital—even after all his training. Jews have a hard time, too."

We share an intense look and I nod, then she goes downstairs. Now I know Mom likes my report because she can relate it to Jewish people.

I run to Mrs. Werner's English class early to put my assignment up on the bulletin board. Mrs. Werner is in the room watching me as I pin the photographs and descriptions standing on a stepstool. I wonder what she thinks of it. She's a nice middle-aged, married woman with a sweet disposition that makes her popular with everyone. If she were like Miss Jackson, a gruff, manly, hot-tempered woman, the discomfort of not knowing her reaction to my project would cause me to rethink what I'm doing. Mrs. Werner slowly goes back to working without saying a word. This project will be seen by all of her English classes before I present it in the fourth period.

At lunch, no one says anything about my project. Maybe the kids didn't even see it on the bulletin board. I can't stop thinking about how excited I am about telling my English class what I have learned. I leave lunch early to make sure everything is in place on the bulletin board.

Mrs. Werner is sitting at her desk and says hello to me.

I look over to the board and see a few of the pictures are hanging from one tack—like someone hanging from a tree— instead of the four I put in each corner. Someone has done this on purpose. I say nothing to Mrs. Werner but I rearrange the thumbtacks project. I wonder if Mrs. Werner herself did this to show her discomfort or disapproval. I don't care who did it; I'm not letting it affect my report. I need to tell my classmates things they don't know, important things.

The whole class is here now and Mrs. Werner asks for everyone to face their desks toward the bulletin board with my pictures and explanations. I stand in front of everyone and speak loudly, louder than I ordinarily would because I feel so strongly about all this.

*These are pictures of my cook's house and her family. Her name is Ethel. She lives here with her husband and her two children. Their daughter is fifteen, and their son who is thirteen years old. The schools they go to—only for colored children—aren't good, so Ethel is trying to get them into integrated schools close to where she lives. In the school they go to now there are many discipline problems; there aren't enough books or even desks for the children; and they have no art or music classes. Many of the teachers don't stay long as teachers because the kids there don't care about learning. A lot of the parents have to work so hard that they don't have time to be involved in what their children are doing at school, so many of these children don't care what kind of grades they get.*

*Ethel's house is small but inviting and clean. Ethel has to take care of our cooking five days a week and then go home and cook and clean for her family. The kids and husband help her a lot.*

*These are pictures of their neighbors and their homes. As you can see, the neighbors are coming over with food and greeting me. Every weekend neighbors get together on porches or front yards and share food and talk as the children play. Their front yards and porches are gathering places for relaxing and getting together, instead of public pools, country clubs or parks which they don't have. They really watch closely over each other's families like they are one big family. They fix their own plumbing, roofs, and anything that goes wrong with their houses.*

*These are pictures of the neighborhood streets where stores are. As you can see, most of the buildings are boarded up because of crime or not having anyone rent the buildings. The ones that are open need paint and repairs. They don't have a corner drugstore where kids hang out because no one can afford to buy cokes and milkshakes or many things drugstores carry. Ethel told me there was a drugstore, it got robbed and the owners could no longer afford to pay the rent.*

*This picture is of the high school that Caroline, Ethel's daughter, attends. It is not air-conditioned and the heat doesn't always work. It hasn't been painted in many years. There is a football field but the grass is brown and the seats are not secure. They don't have a scoreboard that is big so everyone cannot see it. Sometimes the teachers have to use text books twenty years old because the school cannot afford new ones. Colored schools don't get very much money for their teachers and students.*

*This picture isn't just any tree; it is a very sad tree. A colored teenager was hanged on this tree because white people didn't like the color of his skin. All the neighbors knew the boy. He was a sweet boy and did not do anything wrong. Three years ago another teenager was killed named Emmett Till. He was fourteen and supposedly whistled at a white woman in a grocery store. The woman's husband and brother beat him, put a bullet in his head, and threw him in a river. Fifty thousand people walked by his open casket in Chicago and finally people from all over could see what happened to an innocent colored boy. Hardly anyone knew about the lynching of innocent colored people until Emmett Till's funeral. It was in newspapers all over the country. I never heard about this because it wasn't discussed at my dinner table. Was it discussed at yours?*

*All people, white or colored, should have the same opportunities in jobs, schools, buses, and neighborhoods. When you care about people like I do, you realize skin color should not determine fairness.*

*These are pictures of my sister's wedding the week before last:*

*The cost of all this extravagance would probably pay for many poor people to eat for a year. I haven't added it all up, but what I want to tell you is that most of the students in this room don't even think about having enough money for food or a house or clothes. I didn't either until this summer when I made friends with a colored girl at camp, a porter on a train, and saw where my colored maid lives.*

Thank you for listening, I say. I don't really know if anyone did listen. I can feel my face getting red but I walk straight to my desk, even though I can't feel my feet stepping because my legs feel numb. Everyone is looking at me except Mrs. Werner. She asks for any questions or comments.

"My parents say the Negroes are much better off now than during slavery," Alan says after he is called on.

"Alan, slavery ended over a hundred years ago. Changes are taking too long," I say strongly.

"I think our schools are fine the colored schools should be just as good. No one wants to leave their neighborhood and travel to a different school," Betsy states.

"Well, we would have to get studies of all of the schools before conclusions can be made," Mrs. Werner interrupts before I can answer.

"I think the colored people have it so hard and I think it's good, Rachael, that you made us all think about it. We all just think about our own problems; at least I do—I'm pretty selfish," Margie says and everyone laughs because they are thinking the same about themselves.

"Negroes are not as smart as white people. They're lazy and stupid," Walter states. I see other kids nodding their heads and smiling, almost laughing, in approval of Walter's comment.

"I think that will conclude our questions and comments," Mrs. Werner says abruptly before I can respond.

The other reports are about trips kids took, camps they went to, or summer family traditions, so Mrs. Werner probably feels I just hit her a fast ball.

When class is over I walk out of the classroom and I know the truth has come out—like a glowing sun—about what I care about. It's a start, I hope, that there are larger concerns than clothes and boys.

"Rachael, I hear you love colored people," Phil, a boy I have never talked to yells out as I walk by.

"Yes, and what about it?" I answer.

Phil shrugs his shoulders and walks off. I'm sure he thought I would try to defend myself. All the other comments today are a mix of "good job, bad subject."

Kids comment on my project—kids whose names I don't even know. They say nice and mean things to me in the same breath. "Good report," they'll say, "great pictures. But who cares about the Negroes—no one but you." They say I don't know what I'm talking about. They say, "Write to your Congressmen—don't tell us your problems."

Jane, my best friend since kindergarten, doesn't talk to me about my report. She only cares about boys, makeup, clothes and parties. My concerns are for the whole world, making unfair things fair, and getting Ruby back. Next year, by the time we go to high school, we will be many steps onto our separate paths. We will just pass each other in the hall and say hi and that's all there'll be except the memories of our nine-year friendship. I will always cherish the years we have been best friends.

The telephone rings just as I enter the house after school. When the telephone rings at my house anyone can answer it. In my house, there are no rules about who can pick up the phone or who can sit in the living room. Our furniture never has plastic covers on it. Our phone is never just for Mom, Dad, or the help to answer. So I answer the phone. It's Mom.

"Dear, the school secretary called me at work and Dad and I set up an appointment to come in and see the principal about your report today. The secretary didn't give me details so please, dear, tell me what happened!"

"Mom, I gave my report about Ethel's house and neighborhood and what is happening to the colored people in her community. You saw my report. That's all." I say with conviction.

"Well, dear, we will see what's wrong with that at the meeting. You are to be there also, this Friday at eight in the morning. See you for dinner. Bye."

I hang up without saying goodbye. I want to talk to someone other than Peggy about this because I know Peggy will say I'm doing something I believe in and should stand up and be strong no matter what. I want someone outside of my family to give me feedback on my report—even if it's negative—so I can figure out what's wrong with what I'm saying. I want to call Tommy to see what he thinks. He's always honest. But he'd have to go and see my report on the bulletin board before having an opinion of it.

I dial his number and hang up several times. I'm afraid if I hear his voice I'll ask him if he still likes me instead of asking him about my report.

I go to my room and lie on my bed with my shoes on. I feel so tired from today. Jessy steps into the room.

"What is it with you that you so pity the colored people? Why don't you worry about poor people that are white? Even plenty of our friends aren't very rich and they could probably use money," Jessy says snidely.

"They might need money, but the colored people need more than money. They need fairness in schools, jobs, voting rights, sitting on buses. You haven't heard or seen what I have this summer."

Jessy walks out of my room.

I sit up, put my hands over my face and my head in my lap.

Next thing I know, Mom is waking me to go to school. She said I slept through dinner and she just left me sleeping because she thought I needed the sleep. Today is the meeting with Mom and Dad and Mr. Langford, the principal. We leave the house in time to get to school, park, and sit in the waiting room. He comes in and nods, goes into his office, and shuts the door. His secretary comes out to tell us to go in. What is this, a meeting with the FBI? So much formality, like I committed a crime punishable by death. After we sit down Mr. Langford comes out from behind his desk and stands to talk.

"Rachael, you have been a good student since

kindergarten and I know your entire family well. Your mom and dad are proud of you. I am proud of you. School is a place to learn about ourselves, the community, and the world. Your report brought a different light to the current affairs of our community that the school does not condemn, but also does not encourage. We want you to be aware of what's going on in different places in the world, however, we believe that some of this knowledge can be dangerous and disruptive to our school. Your opinion matter but does not make it factual. To know exactly what is occurring in our community and government, even in our little town, one must read newspapers, go to City Council meetings, and talk to many people."

He pauses and stares at me.

"I applaud you for trying to find out the inequities and unfairness among certain races and classes within the community. However, unless and until you are fully qualified to assess the facts, we cannot have this type of superficial reporting in our classrooms. There are parents and children with whom I have talked about your report who are quite concerned about what you may have brought to light about the colored community. Your report may have some truths, but until you are old enough to delve into this much deeper, we must insist this is not a part of our curriculum, and will have to expel you if you do it again."

"Mr. Langford..." I start to speak, but Mom interrupts me.

"Mr. Langford, Harold and I agree with your school's policy and Rachael will abide by all your rules, as she has always done."

"Rachael, what were you going to say?" Mr. Langford asks.

"Just because I don't know each and every fact, there are some things that have been in the newspapers that could be discussed in class because they are fact. Like Emmett Till's murder. Then the class could have discussions about what different opinions there are about what happened. I think the school should discuss current events, not just what's in our history books. This is history being made and it affects everyone in our city and the whole country. School is where we can learn about what's happening now. Some of our books are twenty years old."

"Rachael, we certainly do discuss current events in our school and if you want to bring in articles that concern you, you may do so, but you must have something from a substantial newspaper or magazine to start this discussion. I will speak to the English teachers about guidelines for this. Now, if you will excuse me. I need to start my day. Thank you for coming."

I kiss Mom and Dad goodbye. I'm already planning my own research about racial discrimination. No one is going to help me. And I know I'd never learn the truth from the "white" newspapers and magazines. I'm going to delve deeper to find what is real and what is not real—in my family, too.

# 12

# DOLLHOUSE

The stockings are hung over the fireplace and we have a huge tree that touches the ceiling. Nana doesn't approve. We are Jewish, but every year we celebrate Christmas, and not Hanukkah—but not the Jesus birthday stuff, because Jews believe that Jesus was a Prophet, not the son of God. I know Christians blame the Jews not the Romans for crucifying Jesus so I feel a little uncomfortable celebrating a holiday that reminds us of a murder that some people still believe my people are guilty of. But it's still fun. It's three days before Christmas and we're out of school. I always get a warm feeling a few days before Christmas and it's always over too fast. Very little decorations—snow bulbs, miniature sleds, small Santas, decorative reindeers—are on end tables, coffee tables, the piano, and fireplace mantle

Even though we're older, Mom and Dad still hide the tree and all the presents in the garage and decorate the tree and put the gifts under it while we are sleeping. It would be fun to decorate as a family and see all the wrapped gifts pile up one by one as the days go by before Christmas. Maybe

they think it is more Jewish to do it in one swoop, even
though I don't know anyone else whose family does the
tree and presents our way. Even the streets and stores have
decorations and twinkling lights way before Christmas; it
makes your memories of this time weave together like a
cherished colored quilt like a covering on your heart to keep
it protected from anything bad that could happen.

The stockings were handmade by one of Mom's
friends. Each of our names is embroidered on the red,
white and green felt that has worn craggily fur topping.
We've had them a long time and some of the letters are
coming loose but no one bothers make them look
presentable.

I outline my name on the stocking with my finger and
my heart bounces like it's on a trampoline with anticipation.
I trace Jessy, Rusty, Annie, and Donald's names, too—
Mom embroidered a new one for him when he and Annie
got engaged so he wouldn't feel left out. I know this is the
only time in the year I can taste what a real family feels
like—when my parents and the kids share a tradition. This
is what I want more of. I don't want just one lick of a
lollipop; I want the whole thing.

Ethel startles me when she says, "Rachael, aren't them
pretty as can be?"

"Ethel, how long were you there? I didn't even hear
you."

"Just now, honey."

I know she's fibbing because she looks down at the
floor when she answers me. "I treasure these old worn out
stockings," I say, figuring she's been watching me trace the
names. "I'm out of school for two weeks. Hooray! I hope it

snows for Christmas."

"I knows it, honey. Your Mama's gone to work already. Daddy is bringing home the bow machine for the customer's gifts and Mama wants you to help after dinner—she aks me to tell you. Jessy, too. Before Jessy's Christmas party starts tonight. Come eat breakfast, darlin'."

Just when I was about to follow Ethel into the kitchen, Nana arrives.

"Good morning, dear. I see you were admiring the decorations," she says with a look like she just tasted rotten meat.

"Hi, Nana. Yes, I love them."

"You know we don't believe in Christmas, but my son and your mother like to pretend we do." Nana says, looking at the stockings.

"I know, but it's just for the holiday fun and spirit, not the religious part," I say examining her wrinkly profile.

"Well, dear, maybe someday you will understand what I'm trying to say. Hopefully when you have your own family you will celebrate only Hanukah and leave Christmas to the Christians. You can come in my room and see the Chanukah lights. Tonight at sundown I will light the fifth candle and there are only three more after that," Nana says with a look of disgust.

"I know, Nana. You light them every year and I always remember to come in your room at least once to see the lights. I will this year, too, I promise," I say cheerfully, trying to make her feel better.

"Okay, darling. I remember you do. But I wish you

came every day at sundown for the eight days," Nana says looking much happier.

She walks out of the living room towards the stairs to her room, near the kitchen.

I go into the kitchen where my Rice Krispies, cantaloupe, and orange juice are on the kitchen table. Ethel is cooking something and gives me a warm smile when I sit down.

While I'm eating breakfast, Ethel bakes cookies for Jessy's Christmas party tonight. They're for Jessy's friends but I eat some.

All of Jessy's parties are in our basement. She has one or two a year. Mom and Dad are fine with any of us giving parties, as long as they're in the basement, but neither Rusty nor I have given one yet. I never want a party unless it's my birthday because I always think no one will come or it won't be good. Jess has more confidence than me. There is a room that is only for ping pong, parties, or just playing music—some kids call it a rathskeller but our family calls it the basement. Once I saw Bill and Bernice bring a tiny little burner in there that they cooked dinner on. Sometimes Dad uses the ping pong table to build stuff on.

"Maybe I'll go down to the basement to bring the cookies," I say.

"You better not, Rachy." Ethel says seriously. Ethel calls me Rachy when she wants to make her point.

"I know. When I give parties down there next year, she can't come."

"Now why you startin' in on that now, dear? Where you going tonight so you won't be tempted to go down there?"

"Maybe Peggy's? I don't know." I stir my Rice Krispies. "You know, I like a boy in Jessy's class and he is coming tonight."

"That don't matter. Stay away," she says as she busies herself at the stove. Then she turns to me and asks, "Who is it?"

"Tommy. The one that likes me sometimes that I told you about. I never see him since he's in high school this year. Ethel, I...ah...I hate school because nothing changes and I keep expecting it to. I don't want to complain but I'd be pretending if I didn't tell you. Oh, Ethel, I pretend to so many people and I can't to you." My eyes get watery and I try to hide it with my napkin.

"Why, honey? 'Cause a' that report you did? Is that the problem? You think you's goin' change things with one report?"

"No...but my friends only talk about stupid stuff I used to care about—boys and hair. They don't think about anything but themselves. So I'm faking who I am at school when I sit and listen. But I'm quiet. I used to be happy talking to them about boys and hair. Now, I just want to make things good for you." I push away my bowl of cereal. "Nothing makes sense anymore."

"Chil', enough o' mopin' around. Now, you go call one o' ya friends for tonight—or I will."

I give Ethel a hug and run upstairs to my room. Even though shedoesn't talk about sad or gloomy stuff to me, I feel comfortable telling her stuff that isn't happy about my life. I'm never embarrassed with Ethel.

June is packing a dreary, brown suitcase that's lying on her bed. We both stare at each other.

"I'm going home to Denmark for Christmas."

"Oh, I didn't know."

"Mommy didn't tell ya?" June says wearily.

"No. When are you leaving?" I say, smiling without meaning to.

"Tomorrow. I miss my family. But I will miss all of ya, too. Here is something I made especially for you. Don't open it 'til Christmas, okay?"

"Sure, thanks."

It's probably something ugly and useless. I wish she was packing to leave forever. I can't stop smiling. I don't like it when I think mean things about June because she does nice things for me and another maid could be even worse. She isn't a bad person—she just isn't Ruby and I feel nothing for her. If Ruby had never existed, then probably I would like June, but I wouldn't love her, not like I do Ruby.

I sit on the edge of her bed and make sure no one is coming into my room, "June, I can't go to the party tonight, but I want to ask you to find a boy and give him something from me. I'll give it to you later. Will you?"

"Okay, dear. You know I would do anything for ya as long as it won't get me in trouble."

"I know and thank you for your kindness."

I go into my room and write Tommy a letter using my best stationery. It has my three monogramed initials on it in red fancy script and the ragweed linen paper is ivory like the color of Annie's wedding dress. I've been saving this stationery since my birthday; it was a gift from Annie. The letters I wrote at camp and never sent had a duck on the paper like mom would buy me when I was six years old.

*Dear Tommy,*

*I wish I could see you tonight at Jessy's party. When I don't see you at school it makes me think about you more. Don't dance too much tonight.*

*Rachael*

I read it over and think: every time he thinks I like him, he doesn't call me or pay attention to me. I can't send this one. I try again.

*Tommy,*

*Remember camp when we danced? Please don't forget me.*

Still no good.

*Tommy,*

*Can you call me? I have something to tell you.*

*Rachael*

And another one.

*Tommy,*

*Meet me at the drugstore for a coke. Can you?*

*Rachael*

Yet another.

*Dear Tommy,*

*I can't come to the party. I hate school. Do you like High School?
Do you like Rock 'n Roll music? I love it. Have fun tonight.
Here's a gift for Christmas or Hanukkah—I am not sure what
you celebrate.*

*Rachael*

I tear up all the bad ones and toss them in my
wastebasket. I give June the letter with a package of baseball
cards and bubble gum. I know Tommy loves the St. Louis
Cardinals. My handwriting looks sloppy—maybe from my
hand being tired from writing so much. Maybe that shows I
don't care.

I call Peggy to see what she's doing tonight. Her maid
answers. Elsie is colored, like most maids. She is sweet but
distant—not like a family member. Her voice is all business,
stiff and dry like she has a stomach ache.

"Hi, Peggy. Jessy is having a party tonight and I don't
want to be in my room all night alone. Do you want to
come over?"

"Come here instead and sleep over. We can go to the
stables to ride the horses and brush them tomorrow. I really
want you to meet my horse Ginny."

"I'll ask."

I call Mom at the store but have to wait a long while
until she finishes up with a customer. She says I can go to
Peggy's to sleep over and to the stables tomorrow. She tells
me that she and Dad are going to a Christmas party too.
She sounds happy I have something to do—in fact she had
already called Annie to see if I could spend some time with
her and Donald tonight because she didn't want me to be

alone in the house just with June. This is a first. I have never heard her concerned about what I'm doing when I'm alone with the maids. Rusty is going to a friend's to sleep over. I'm happy I won't even have to hear the party music and wonder who Tommy is dancing or laughing with.

I walk to Peggy's house cutting through the neighbors' yards. Her father opens the door and greets me without a hug or kiss. He is scarier than my father even when he says hello—like his perfectly tanned face forgets how to smile. He and Dad probably have a contest to see who will be the most tan in the winter. After Peggy and I hug, I join the family at the dinner table. They're eating early because it's Saturday night. Even though Peggy's parents are going out for dinner with friends, they sit at the table and talk to Peggy, her brother, Eugene and her sister, Barbie, while they eat. Everyone talks and laughs about things that happened in the day. It's like a party—a family party. I listen with wonderment.

Once we're excused from the table we fly up the stairs where the banister is trimmed in green garlands with silver bells and luscious pink and white bows, which match my pink overnight suitcase.

Peggy's room is all pink and plush. The bedclothes are extra soft and comfortable and every chair and table seems to be saying, "Stay forever." From the door, her dollhouse is facing me in full view as if the room were built just for it. After putting my stuff on the bed, Peggy and I automatically stand looking at the dollhouse. It's two stories with a basement and an attic, just like our houses. It sits on a round table covered with a quilted tablecloth that's adorned with tiny pink and red roses, like it's the garden around the dollhouse.

Peggy and I don't really play with the dolls anymore but

we stand and look over every detail of the dollhouse. Some of the fabrics for the curtains and upholstery match with her real living room and dining room.

I tell her about Tommy and the note I wrote. Peggy says it's good I didn't send the other notes. We are silent for a minute while I look at all the tiny dolls in each room. For some reason, the dolls look sad and I want to find a way to make the house happy, like I used to feel when I played with it. Am I changing or did I just never notice this? I look more closely at the kitchen where there are no dolls at all— no help, nobody. I look closely at each white faced doll.

"They should make colored dolls to buy. Maybe they do in the stores around where they live." I get an idea. "Peggy, can we color some of the dolls with marker so their skin is dark and put them in the kitchen and laundry room?"

"Rach, do you want them to be maids just in the kitchen or part of the family?"

"I think they should be maids first and then see if your Mom doesn't care and maybe next time we can add some other colored family into the house."

"Why, Rach?"

"I don't want to get you in trouble. Your mom will probably understand if the colored dolls are maids, like in your house."

Peggy and I decide brown shoe polish should work. We've seen "black face" entertainers with shoe polish on their faces which always bothered me but this is different because we're not trying to make fun of anybody. Peggy sneaks into her parents' room and goes into her dad's closet

183

for the polish while I keep a lookout at the door and listen for her parents. She has the polish in her hand and she scoots back to her room, giggling softly and hunched over to move quietly.

Peggy and I go into her bathroom and use our fingers to apply the polish to four of the dolls' faces. The smell is like Dad getting ready for work in my parents' bedroom. Dad seems to love shining his shoes—almost as much as polishing his car. Sometimes I happen to be there watching and a hollow in my throat forms and I find myself holding back tears while he shines his shoes to leave. I want him to stay home and really be with me, just me, alone.

Peggy and I talk while putting on the polish. We don't talk on the phone much, like I do with my other friends. We prefer to talk in person. Sometimes, when we don't see each other for a few weeks, I am bursting to talk to her, but just like with Jessy, I only feel like telling her about my private life when I can see her face.

"I don't care about parties and boys—except for Tommy, who I hardly see. Who do you like now?"

"No one special. Since my school is an all-girls school, it makes it easier not to think about having a boyfriend."

"I wish I went to your school with you."

"Me, too. I miss you every day. Let's pinky promise we will be best friends no matter what."

We lock pinkies and hug. We put the dolls in the laundry room, kitchen, and maid's room and Peggy walks away from the dollhouse.

"Come here," she calls from her walk-in closet.

I go over and see the riding boots Peggy is holding.

"Nice. Can I try them on?" "Sure."

I put them up to my nose. "They smell good like mom's leather trunk."

I put them on and walk around bow legged, like I've seen cowboys do on TV. We giggle. Why haven't I ever even seen these boots before?

"Why do you wear these?"

"Because when you ride your legs would get scratched from the horse. Also you get a better grip with your legs against the horse's body so he can feel your signals from your legs. If you want to go fast, you must hold tight with your legs so you won't fall off—then the horse knows you're in control.

After putting on our pj's we sit on Peggy's high comfy bed. Her mom and Dad come in to say goodnight. They hug and kiss us both. I think her dad doesn't want me to feel left out but his smile is still locked up.

"What's that smell, Peggy?" her dad asks.

Peggy and I look at each other with scared faces.

"Well, please don't be mad. Dad. We used your shoe polish to color some of the dolls' faces brown for the dollhouse," Peggy says in her sweet voice.

"It's okay, girls. But was it that important to take the shoe polish secretly? You should have asked. The part that disappoints me is that I've taught you to talk to us, as your parents, before doing something you know is wrong. Mom and I have to go out now but we will talk about this further.

Rachael, I will have to tell your parents tomorrow. Goodnight now."

After they leave, I tell Peggy how sorry I am. "It was my idea because my maids are family to me. They talk to me about my life and worry about me like I want Mom and Dad to do. I spend a lot of time with them, time that I wish for every day from Mom and Dad. I'm gonna take all the blame tomorrow."

We hug goodnight and I get on my bed. The luscious covers soothe my anxious body.

"We both decided to do it, Rachael," Peggy whispers in the dark. "Stealing. I'm always such a goody-two-shoes. It's okay, Rachael. Let's go to sleep."

"Yeah. I'm not even thinking about the stealing. I'm thinking about Jessy's party and Tommy. Maybe he's kissing someone right now."

"Go to sleep, Rachael."

"Goodnight."

"Goodnight."

# 13
# TOMMY AND ACER

In the morning Peggy's mom calls my mom before we leave for the stables. Peggy and I are in the room when she talks to Mom so I hear her explain in detail what Peggy and I did to the dolls last night. I'm surprised when she tells us we have to clean the dolls' faces before we leave. Mom wants to talk to me.

"Mom, I'm sorry we took the polish and put it on the dolls' faces," I say sadly.

"I'm disappointed in you. Dad will be, too. As soon as you get home today, I want you to compose a letter telling Peggy's parents how this is truly wrong, not only to steal but to disfigure toys that are not yours nor did you have permission to do so. I'm letting you go to the stables so as not to upset everyone's plans. Behave and think about what you have done," Mom says like a strict teacher.

Peggy and I get nail polish remover and soap and water to remove the shoe polish. But even after all the scrubbing it doesn't change the skin from brown to pink; it comes out light brown. We look at each other and smile because we are both happy that perfect pink skin will never be on the dolls we colored and we will always know which ones they are.

I hand the phone back to Peggy's mom and they continue to talk about today's activities. Finally, we all get in the station wagon to head to the stables. As we enter the stable grounds a winter mist rises from the ground. The car bounces in and out of potholes on the muddy road. In the winter Peggy comes here once every few weeks to see her horse. She doesn't ride much when it's cold or icy or snowy, but she wants me to meet Ginny, her horse. When we drive through the gates I see a lot of horses crammed into an outdoor space surrounded by a beat-up looking, grey wooden fence. There must be twenty-five horses in the corral that are practically stepping on each other and their heads dip up and down as if they are saying yes to each other. They are all the colors of fall leaves: brown, sable, rust, cream, and titian-red, like my hair color. Peggy and I go into the gate to find Ginny.

Up close I am scared to death of all the horses because I don't know if one will kick me or knock me over, but I follow Peggy without saying a word, like maybe if I'm silent they won't notice me. And I don't want Peggy to wish she had never brought me here, so I don't let on how scared I am. We twist in and out of the horses heads, legs and swishing tails like we are playing hide and seek. The smell is strong, like Mom's leather purse mixed with mud.

"Here she is, Rachael. Isn't Ginny beautiful? I love her. She's a palomino, which is a type of horse that originally came from Arabia. Not Ginny. She was born here. Acer, my best friend here, was her peeler." Peggy sees the look of puzzlement on my face. "Oh, that means he trained Ginny so I could ride her. She was pretty wild before training. Some horses are only for roaming and they are called broomtails," Peggy tells me. "I'm sorry you're getting dirty out here. I have to bring her out of this pen to brush her and put her saddle and bridle on."

Peggy hugs another horse. "Oh, hi, Sampson, you're looking good." She turns to me to explain, "Sampson just became a gelding; he was castrated. That means a veterinarian cut off his testicles so he wouldn't make babies because he wasn't a prime horse. He doesn't have the qualities the owners look for in a stud horse. Rachael, stay close by me. Are you okay?"

"Yeah," I say, feeling somewhat bewildered by all these terms as well as a bit terrified.

"I was scared, too, the first time I was surrounded by all these horses, but they never bother you unless you do something to them. Come on, let's lead her out and get outta here." Peggy says determined.

"Yeah, good idea."

"You are so funny," Peggy teases me, laughing, as we lead Ginny out of the corral. "When I take anyone here the first time they don't admit being scared but I'm glad you did."

"I didn't…"

"Yes, you did. Your face did. It's like a ghost."

Laughing, too, I said, "Do we have to go back in there?"

"No, I just open the gate to the pen to get her back to her friends."

We tie Ginny up on a fence a little distance from the pen. Peggy's mom has been talking to the stable helpers this whole time. I can see her from where we are. Everyone in Peggy's family rides horses. All these new words I hear from Peggy make me feel like I don't know her and she has a secret world away from me. I feel left out.

"Hi Peggy, glad to see ya'."

"Hi Acer, this is Rachael."

Acer, Ginny's peeler is a colored boy about eighteen. He wears riding boots and jeans and a cowboy hat. This is my first time seeing a Negro cowboy. He looks handsome in the outfit.

"Hi, Acer," I say shaking hands.

"Acer is my cowboy," Peggy tells me, then turns to him. "How has she been?"

"Getting fat for the cold. Runnin' her when it's not too bad out."

Peggy and Acer talk about supplies and food for Ginny while I listen. I didn't know how much Peggy loved her horse. She never talks about riding to me in any detail—just that she went riding or she's going to ride. She is so sweet to everyone and now I see she's sweet to all animals, not only her family dog.

Peggy and Acer start brushing Ginny with strong wire brushes. Ginny lifts first one leg, then the other as they groom her. Her tail is swaying to brush some flies away. Neighing and snorting noises come from her mouth and nose, giving the whole process a rhythmic feeling, like a dance. Peggy says she may even train Ginny to be a racehorse, but she doesn't like how racehorses are treated.

Sometimes they run them so hard and they even drop dead on the racetrack.

Acer says he has to do something and runs off. Peggy hands me Acer's brush and shows me how to brush Ginny. Then she shows me how she adds horse gel— gooey stuff that comes out of a giant tube—to her mane to make it shine. The feel of the horse's coarse hair and hard muscles makes the nerves inside my hands feel like lightning just hit them. The giant wall of Ginny's caramel colored body frightens me at first. But slowly I'm getting used to the strange feel, tremendous size, and dusty smell of Ginny. I kiss the side of her face to feel closer to her. Peggy shows me how to pick up her leg and clean her horseshoe with a tool that takes all the dirt out of the crevices. I don't want to do this because I may miss and dig into her foot and hurt her.

I see Acer a little ways off putting a saddle on a horse that's bucking.

Peggy notices and says, "Oh, Smokey's a rough string buck. That means every time he's saddled, he bucks. I think Acer is showing off for us to see if he can saddle him while we're looking," Peggy says.

"Acer looks cute trying to do that," I say blushing.

"Rachael, I'm surprised. He isn't usually a showoff. I think he's doing it to impress you."

"Me, too. I've never seen a guy our age do anything except sports at school. This is much more interesting to watch. Wow! He got the saddle on."

Acer mounts Smokey and rides over to the girls.

"Okay, we saw your show," Peggy smiles.

"Acer, I liked it. Is there a double feature?" I say kidding.

Acer laughs. "No, girls. Finish brushing and meet me in the ring after saddling her." He rides off.

"Hi, girls, looks like you're giving Ginny a good brushing," says Peggy's mom.

I didn't even see her walking up to us. I hope she didn't hear me saying that I think Acer is cute. If she did, she'll tell Mom, and then Mom will want to know about the Negro I like at the stable.

"Do you want to ride with me, Rachael?" Peggy asks sweetly as she saddles Ginny with heavy leather stirrups, a bit for her mouth, leather reins and a caramel- colored saddle. She's doing it like she could do it blindfolded. Ginny stamps her feet like she's getting impatient to ride. I hug her neck and kiss her face some more, like I do with my stuffed animals. In the sunlight her coat looks like an expensive full length mink coat. All the tail and mane hairs are brushed and oiled perfectly, like she went to the beauty shop.

"Okay, but I'm a little scared. I've never ridden before—well, maybe a pony when I was really little."

"We'll just ride in the ring a little. Mom wants to leave soon."

We walk over to the ring where Acer is. Peggy and Acer talk about what horse I'm going to ride. Acer says I should ride Downie, the horse for beginners, but he might have just come in from another ride. He goes to check with the stable hand.

"Peggy," he yells. "Come here."

Peggy goes over to the stable where Acer is. They talk but I can't hear what they're saying. Peggy runs over to me.

"I'm sorry, Rach, but Downie just got in from a ride and needs to rest. We'll have to do it another time. There aren't any other horses for beginners."

"It's okay. Maybe I'll ride next time."

"I'm going in the ring with Ginny to get some lessons from Acer. A rider never stops learning, but I won't be long. You can watch me or groom another horse, but I think...uh...you want to watch Acer."

"I want to watch you, Peggy—but I don't mind getting another look at Acer, either."

Peggy mounts Ginny and rides into the ring where Acer stands dead center. He gives verbal and hand signals to Ginny and the horse obeys. Peggy stops Ginny in the exact spot Acer tells her to; they stopped so fast, there's dust everywhere. She gets Ginny to back up and makes her walk between small wooden stakes in a very specific pattern. Ginny neighs and rears up, her two legs high off the ground, and then prances around like she's dancing. Peggy looks happy and excited—not at all scared. It's so cold, both the horse's and Peggy's breaths show, like smoke rising, giving a mysterious air to the show. If Ginny were my horse, I would miss her every day.

Acer seems more like a man than a boy. He isn't afraid of anything. If I sent him a sweet note, he wouldn't run away like Tommy, afraid of someone liking him. After Tommy gets my note he'll probably ignore me for a while because he'll know I'm thinking of him. I think he really does like me, but every time I show him I like him, he gets uncomfortable. I wish I knew why. I'm starting to think it isn't me but that he's afraid of his feelings. I think a girl really hurt him badly and he thinks all girls are alike. I don't know. But I want to know and I'll never find out unless he tells me. It'd be good for him to learn to train a horse and know what it is to be really scared to death of something that could hurt more than his pride.

Peggy gallops around the ring a few times before dismounting. Then we walk Ginny back to the pen where she joins all her pals. Some of them trot over to see her all fixed up and smelling fresh, neighing their welcome.

Before we all say goodbye, Peggy gives Acer a hug and a Christmas gift. He opens it. It's a blanket for his horse, Smokey, for the cold. He thanks her and says it's the warmest and handsomest blanket he has ever had.

On the way home in the car, Peggy tells her mom how happy she is that Acer loved the blanket they picked out together when they shopped for everyone's Christmas presents last week. I can feel the sting of unwanted tears threatening like a leaky roof. I have never shopped with Mom for anyone's presents.

When I get home I go upstairs and notice Jessy sitting on her bed in her room.

"Hi, Jess, how was your party?"

"Hi, Rach. Okay." She sounds dispirited.

I love when Jessy calls me Rach. It sounds like she loves me. "What happened?" I ask her, 'cause I could tell it wasn't great.

"In the middle of everything, Nana stormed down to the basement, turning on all the lights, and shut down the music."

"Oh, no!"

"Then she shouted at everyone, 'Out!' We weren't doing anything wrong. I asked her why, but she wouldn't say. Everyone left early."

"Do Mom and Dad know?"

"Yeah. They don't care. They said Nana's in charge if they're out."

"I'm never giving a party here, Jess. I would die of embarrassment if she did that at my party. I'm so sorry."

Jessy nodded her head, then looked and me with a wry smile. "I know who you still like because I saw all the other letters to Tommy you threw away in your wastebasket. I saw him reading the one June gave him. I didn't know it was from you until I saw the others."

"That wasn't right," I said angrily. "Why did you snoop in my wastebasket?"

"I went to your room to see if you were home yet this morning and—I saw bunches of crumpled papers on that good stationery  Annie gave us—so I looked at them. What's the big deal?"

"Okay, fine. From here on, I'll look at what you throw away anytime I want to."

"Sometimes things that aren't in wastebaskets still get treated like trash and thrown on the floor," Jessy says sarcastically, like she knows something I want to know.

"What are you talking about?"

"Well, did you give Tommy any baseball cards that look

like this?"

Jessy hands me the baseball cards I gave him. They're unwrapped. The gum is missing.

"Where did you get these?"

"On the floor after the party."

I can't believe Tommy just threw my gift away like it meant nothing to him. But I'm not going to show Jessy that it matters to me.

"My private life is none of your beeswax," I say defiantly. Then, on an entirely different note, "What are we going to do about Nana?"

"Nothing. After all these years, she's not gonna change. Aren't you used to it by now? Nana told me Mom and Dad trust her with us. I'm never talking to her again. She yelled at me in front of my friends that the party was just for making out and dancing close. After everyone left, I cried in my room." Tears are welling up in Jessy's eyes now as she tells me this awful story. "She came in and said I wasn't a nice girl," she continued, "that we live nicely—that it costs money to live like this—that she helps pay for how we live and I better behave nicely if I want to live nicely. She kept saying nicely and nice over and over. I wanted to push her out of my room! I'd rather not live so 'nicely' and have her out of our house. She doesn't want us to celebrate Christmas—the one holiday we all love the best." Jessy is almost shouting now, like she doesn't care who's listening.

"Did you tell Mom everything she said?" I ask.

"Everything except the part about the money. Anyway, if it's true," now her voice lowers to a whisper, "Mom knows already. And Mom and Dad will never get rid of her if they need her money to live like this—never!"

"Yeah, you're right. All she ever does is cover me up when I'm sleeping, except then I'm not 'cause it always wakes me up. She isn't in my way—yet—as far as boys go. Not the way she is with you."

"Tommy laughed at Nana when she was yelling and she got even madder when he wished her a happy, fifth night of Hanukkah. He ran out of the party with all the boys like the house was on fire."

"Sounds like him—always with the jokes." I don't look at Jessy when I say, "I miss his jokes. He threw away my gift and I still miss him? What is wrong with me?"

Jessy doesn't answer my questions or ask me anything about the horses. Maybe she doesn't even know where I've been. I like having some things that are all mine and I don't have to share. She always thinks Peggy is her closest neighborhood friend because they're the same age but I know she's my closest so I don't argue about it. Jessy wants to argue about everything lately. I can't talk to her about Tommy and how I still like him. She'd probably say something to him or tell me he has another girl he likes, just to make me feel bad. Maybe I will talk to her about it another day. Her showing me the cards he left was enough torture for one day.

Jessy says, "Rach, there is a boy I really like and his name is Bret. Don't tell Mom and Dad, but I'm meeting him somewhere. Please? If anyone asks, say I'm going down the street to see my friends Jenny and Jill. I'd do it for you," Jessy says in a begging voice.

"Okay, but why can't you just tell them you're going to meet a boy in your class?"

"He isn't the type Mom and Dad would like. He's not Jewish and he's from a poor family. He's new in school and we have so much fun in class and he asked me to meet him today just to walk around and talk."

"Okay, but remember this when I ask you to do something for me," I say smiling.

"I will, don't worry," Jess says convincingly.

I run downstairs to talk to Ethel but then I remember it's Sunday and all the help are off. I still miss Ruby so much. She'd tell me what to do about Tommy. With Acer there's really nothing to talk about to Ethel; she'd just be short and to the point. Anyway, I won't see him much and it's just a crush. Ruby and I used to talk for hours about every little detail until I felt better. I would tell her how I was afraid to speak up if something a friend did to me wasn't nice, how boys would tease me and I wouldn't know what to say to them, when I would get scared in my bed at night for no reason, how I felt lonely when Mom wasn't home, when Jessy was mean to me—things like that. Bernice and I don't talk about personal things when I help her with the laundry, but we sing to the music. I like being with her, not even discussing anything. If I put Ethel, Bernice, and Ruby in one room with me I would get to be myself three different ways and feel like I'm loved each way. Now that I'm getting to know them better, it feels like there's more of them that I can love back.

# 14
# PEGGY

It's snowing all day on Christmas Eve. I can't believe
we're really having a white Christmas. I have waited all year
for this night. Tonight, after dinner, Mom and Dad's best
friends, the ones we all call Uncle and Aunt, arrive for
cocktails and dessert. I hope the carolers come this year.
Some years they go to other neighborhoods to sing. After
we kids go to bed Mom and Dad and their friends will trim
the tree. We have no say in this tradition, as much as I want
to help them.

There'll be presents in the morning, but the only
present I want is for Ruby to come back. I took a special
picture for each maid and made a cardboard frame with a
hook glued to the back so they could hang them up. Dad
gave me the hooks from his toolbox. For Bill, I took a
picture of him washing Daddy's car; Bernice is ironing;
Ethel is icing a cake. I even made June a picture of her
combing her hair. Jessy took a picture of me for Ruby; the
card that goes with it says, "I miss you." My card to June
doesn't say that. It says: "Have fun in Demark." Ethel

promises to take Ruby's present to her. I wrapped each of them in the paper I saved in my closet from my birthday. I don't care about the paper anymore now that I have my camera to take memories.

The snow continues to fall through dinner. I can hardly eat. I get the same feeling when snow falls on Christmas Eve as when I see Tommy: a hint that something wonderful is about to happen, but that the magical happiness doesn't last very long. This feels like the love I have for Peggy, Jessy, Ruby, Ethel, Bernice, Bill and sometimes Tommy. I love the snow melting on a warm sunlit winter day and my crush on Acer, but both are short lived.

Mom and Dad's friends are sitting in the living room with their drinks and desserts while Jessy, Rusty and I run in and out to say hello and watch for the Christmas carolers. Rusty still believes in Santa Claus, so Ethel pours him a glass of milk to go along with her recently baked cookies to leave for the jolly elf. He writes Santa a letter that he is a good boy and to please leave him a new bike, sled and log cabin set. I write a letter, too, so Rusty thinks I believe Santa is real, too. Jessy says she doesn't want to write a letter that helps Rusty's ignorance. She doesn't care if Rusty finds out about Santa.

*Dear Santa,*

*I have been good to my parents, friends, and the help, so please leave me money for all the poor people. Also, some cameras so they can take pictures of their families growing up and have memories of fun times together.*

*Thank you and enjoy the cookies and milk.*

*Shalom, (I am Jewish but I still believe in you!)*

*Rachael*

The carolers have come and are singing on our snow covered lawn. We all race to the front door to listen. They wear old fashioned velvet clothes and hats—like from the early 1900s—that are the color of jewels—rubies, sapphires, and emeralds. I've seen pictures of my great grandmothers and grandfathers in similar clothes. The snow is pretty deep and sparkles in the front door lights. They sing "Silent Night," "Santa Claus Coming to Town," and "Frosty the Snowman." I want it to last forever—the snow, the feeling of family and friends standing together clapping and smiling, Dad's arm around me and Mom standing next to Dad. Jessy and Rusty hug each other after the music stops and the Christmas tree lights shining in windows across the street and the houses next door leave me stunningly happy.

Mom says many of the Reform Jewish people have trees and celebrate Christmas so we don't stand out as being different. She explains Jewish immigrants who came from Europe before us wanted to fit in with other Americans so badly they started celebrating Christian holidays. She says in a few generations, when they feel more American, Jewish people will probably not celebrate Christian holidays as much. Some of the old folks, like Nana and Grandma, don't care about assimilation—one of my recent vocabulary words I learned at school—into Christian culture and hate the fact that we celebrate Christmas. I will always celebrate Christmas with my children for the overwhelming good feelings I want to share with them.

We say goodnight to Mom and Dad and their friends. Jessy and I go into her room to talk. I sit at her dressing table, which makes me feel very grown up. It has perfume bottles, lipsticks and powder. The mirror has light settings for day and night to show how makeup will change in different lights. Jessy is only allowed to use powder and lipstick for parties, not school. I wonder if I will feel different inside when I see my face change as I put on makeup. Jessy already wears a bigger bra than I do and gets to put on stockings for dress up.

"Who do you like now?" I ask Jessy. It seems to me Jessy changes who she likes every other day. I try to keep up but I know I can't.

"No one and if I did, I wouldn't tell you."

"Did you kiss anyone with your tongue last night before Nana broke up the fun?" I ask confidentially.

"You're such a little brat, asking me personal questions."

"Let's make up—it's Christmas Eve."

"You're right. Come here and give me a hug, Rach— then go to bed."

I get up and give her a hug and she hugs me back hard. We laugh. We both stare out the window and see Bill shoveling the walkway and scattering salt on it so no one will slip leaving the house. His coat looks tattered and he doesn't have gloves on. I wonder if he even owns any.

"I hope you get what you want tomorrow," I say with looking sad.

"Why are you so sad, Sis?" Jessy asks.

"Because I don't want anything except to help certain people."

"What people?" Jessy asks.

"You'll make fun of me if I tell you," I say rubbing my nose dribbles with my hand.

"No, I won't. Promise. Cross my heart and hope to die."

"Just look outside the window and you can see Bill's hands turning blue because he can't afford gloves. Dad has at least ten pairs in his drawer right now. Is that fair?"

"I know. I read your report and saw your pictures for school. So you want to give money to our help and other colored or poor people. Jesus!" Jessy smiles sarcastically determined to make her point.

"Yes, so why did you ask me?"

"Because we never talk about it."

"I know, because you make fun of everything I do and say lately."

"I'm sorry. I'll try not to. I feel sorry for them, too— our help. But I still want presents."

"We are different, Jessy."

"I know. Good night, Sis."

"Good night."

I go to my room, but I can't sleep unless I ask Dad right now for a pair of gloves for Bill. I creep down the stairs as quietly as I can. In the hall mirror I can see the company in the living room with Mom and Dad. They haven't brought the tree in yet because it has only been a little while since Jessy, Rusty and I went upstairs. I step down the last stair and everyone stares at me.

"Uh, Dad, can I talk to you a minute?" I say in a slightly wobbly voice.

"Sure, Snooky," Dad says smiling and walks over to me at the entrance to the living room. Whenever he drinks he smiles a lot and calls Jessy, Annie, and me Snooky.

"Dad," I say in a soft voice, "Bill is outside shoveling the fresh snow and ice up and down the walkway so the company won't slip when they leave. He doesn't have gloves and his hands are like blueberries. Do you have an old pair I can give him?"

"Sure, Snooky. Go in my dresser drawer, the last drawer, and pick one out for Bill." He kisses my cheek and walks back to the company.

"Thanks, Dad."

I run upstairs. I am so excited. I'll bet Dad wouldn't have done this so readily if company wasn't here. He likes to impress his friends. Even though they couldn't hear our conversation, if he had said no, he knows I would have looked sad or started crying. I reach into the drawer and find a lined pair of black leather gloves that look worn. Suddenly I'm reminded of taking Peggy's dad's shoe polish and my hands start to shake, like I am stealing again. But I'm not! I run downstairs and open the front door. The walk is almost done, but Bill is nowhere to be seen. Maybe he went to warm up. I put the gloves on the biggest mound of snow by the front door so the light gleams on them.

I run upstairs to Jessy's room, careful to be quiet since she's already fallen asleep, and look out the window. The gloves are gone and Bill is way down the walkway, starting where he left off, and—he's wearing the gloves. My heart is as full as I have ever felt.

In the morning, Rusty comes in my room very early. I get up and together we go get Jessy. We all run downstairs. The tree is all lit up with it seems like thousands of beautifully wrapped presents covering almost the whole living room. There are names on each present and some, to Jessy and me, are from Marlon Brando, Paul Newman, and Gregory Peck. We are allowed to open one each before Mom and Dad come down. Jessy opens a sweater set. Rusty opens an erector set. I open a Hummel figure. Mom knows I love them. Red, silver, gold and green paper and ribbons are jumbled all over the room like they're having a wild party. When Annie and Donald get here they'll open their presents and add to the mess.

I run up to get my camera and take pictures of the room. Mom and Dad come down in their pajamas. Dad has his movie camera and records us opening presents. He's with us, but he's watching us through a lens, like looking at a good movie show at the Shady Oak, our local theater. When I watch home movies, I know I'm in them, but then I feel like really an outsider. I snuggle with Mister while Dad makes sure our dog gets in the pictures, too. I've decided I'm going to show Mister more attention, like Peggy does with animals.

Annie and Donald arrive and open their presents. Dad always opens his presents last. Mom takes movies of Dad while he opens all his gifts. I just realize I never think about buying anything for Mom or Dad with the gift money I save. Maybe next year I will feel like making them something.

While Mom takes the movies I stare outside at all the white beauty still coming down. I want to go out and play in the snowflakes. I go to the front door and open it just to see what it looks like. Someone built a snowman facing our door; it wasn't there last night. It isn't very big but it is so cute and it has Poinsettia flowers for eyes, one red eye and one white. I go outside in my pajamas and slippers. At first the snow feels like prickly pine needles on my face and fingers, then a wet cold drop from the window. There are notes hanging on the flowers. I pull the Poinsettias out of each eye. One of the notes says Jessy and one says Rachael. Despite the cold air I feel a little warm spot inside me when I see my name. I say goodbye to my snowman and run inside, careful not to slip.

"Jessy," I call, "Come here quick!"

Jessy comes in from the library where she had been looking at Rusty's toys with him.

"Jess, look what we got!" I say excitedly as I show her the flowers and the cards. "They were on a snowman outside—one that must have been made while we were sleeping.

"Oh, wow! Let's open them!"

My jaw drops as I read mine.

*"Dear Rachael. Have a good Christmas, From Tommy and Mr. Snowman."*

Jessy grabs my card so I grab hers and read it.

*"Hi Jessy. Mr. Snowman says Merry Christmas and me, too. Tommy."*

"Rach, isn't that sweet from Tommy? Let's go see Mr. Snowman."

"I already did. You go," I say sadly. I wish Tommy had written something romantic to me. He treated me and Jess just the same.

Dad goes into the kitchen to make his famous French pancakes and I follow him. When he sees me, he knows I am there to watch him cook. French pancakes are thin and small, rolled with grape jelly and sprinkled with powdered sugar. I think they look like snow fell on them. They are special because Dad only cooks them on Christmas morning.

"Dad, can I help roll the pancakes?" I ask

"No, this is my special treat. I'll teach you one day"

"Okay," I say, thinking about my visit to Ethel's and how we all helped with food. But Dad wants to finish the pancakes fast.

I take pictures of Dad cooking. He's smiling at the pancakes in the pan, like he's creating a masterpiece of art. He doesn't like having his picture taken but I ignore what he says because I know he won't be angry at me on this special morning. Mom comes in to help Dad make bacon and put out dishes in the breakfast room. Mom is never in the kitchen. I'm surprised she knows where the dishes are.

Nana comes down for breakfast and hands Jessy, Rusty, Annie and me each an envelope and then disappears up the back stairs that lead to her room, not wanting to join in any of the Christmas festivities. I know her gift is Hanukkah gelt—gold wrapped silver dollars—because it's what she always gives us. I'll open mine later and share them with Ethel, Bernice, and Ruby.

We are all cozily squished around the breakfast table that is too small for our whole family. I know these magnificent few minutes will seep like liquid gold into my memory bank to be cherished, but I wish someone else in my family would believe that this is what families do every day, not just once a year. Dad gets up and at first I think he is leaving the table, but he's just getting more pancakes to pass around.

He sits down and raises his glass of orange juice. "Mom"—that's what Dad calls Mom sometimes when he wants to emphasize that she is The Mom—"look at this family—we have a lot to be thankful for on this holiday, even if it isn't Thanksgiving. Our kids are beautiful and growing, our daughter just got married, and we have more weddings to look forward to. Let's raise our glasses and drink to health, wealth, and happiness." We all raise our glasses and drink.

I feel guilty going along with this charade, like all of a sudden he's proud of the family he borrows once in a while to show off, like for a television commercial. I look at Jessy and I know she sees Dad as her hero; I can tell by the way she looks at him. She doesn't feel the same way I do, I know—even though we've never talked about it. I'm scared to tell Jessy what I think about Dad because she and I aren't best friends anymore and she won't listen or care. If she says anything she will say I'm wrong about Dad not caring about all of us equally or that I'm too sensitive—that she knows Dad and I want too much attention. But I can tell Peggy next time I sleep over.

After breakfast, I bring all my gifts upstairs and put them on the floor of my walk-in closet. There are sweaters, slacks, and shirts, a pink clock radio, and the game *Sorry*. I put all the clothes in a bag for Ethel, Ruby and Bernice. They're my clothes and I can give them to whomever I want. I will not ask Mom's permission to give them away. I was surprised I also got some furniture I had wanted for Peggy's dollhouse and it is from Peggy—a washing machine, a dryer and an ironing board. Now the colored dolls have something to do.

Suddenly I hear Mom calling me and Jessy into her bedroom in a voice I've never heard before. She sounds like she just saw a rat running across the carpet, with more to come. Her frightened whisper is almost inaudible, a scratchy hoarse voice that has been hidden until now.

Jessy and I arrive at the same time, almost bumping into each other in the doorway. Mom's face is screwed up something awful and it's all blotchy.

"Girls, I am going to tell you something that is the most horrible thing you have ever heard." Her voice wavers, like she's about to cry. I've never seen her like this. "Oh, girls, I am so sorry to tell you this."

Jessy and I hug each other, frightened. "What, Mom, tell us?" I say frantically, thinking it must be that Nana has died.

"Peggy was out riding her horse this morning. She was thrown and...and...she died. I just got a phone call."

Shattered glass is exploding into twisted shards that stick out of my skin. I cannot breathe. I don't even know what death means. There has never in my life been a time that the word has had a meaning. First I have to figure out that I will never again see or talk to or walk with or touch Peggy. Disbelief streams through every part of me. My head is stuffed with a mass of feelings completely foreign to me. In order to make any sense out of them, I have to separate them one by one. But I can't. I can't. I scream. Jessy howls. We hold each other and cry hysterically.

"No, Mom, please say this isn't true. Please say she's only hurt. I can't live without Peggy. I love her!" I'm shouting out loud, not even knowing it's me forming the words.

"Mom, I can't believe it. I love her, too. Mom, please hold me," Jessy cries and melts into Mom's arms. I move with her and we all fall over on the bed in a lump, holding, hugging, and crying.

The rest of the day I run back and forth from Mom's room to Jessy, then sit alone on the stairs staring. Rusty returns from a friend's house and finds out. He starts crying when he sees all of us sobbing and out of our wits.

No one can calm me and I don't calm anyone. I scream in the backyard over and over; just screams and cries like a wild wolf in wracking pain. Mom comes outside to tell me the details of what happened. Acer had telephoned Peggy to come and get a Christmas present he had for her family and they decided to ride the horses when she got there. Peggy and Acer were riding Ginny and Smokey when a slick spot from melting ice on the ground caused Ginny to rear up when she stepped in it. Peggy was thrown off the horse and struck her neck on a high electric wire breaking her neck.

I suddenly feel sick to my stomach. I go to the bathroom and throw up. I want to die and be with Peggy. I want to ask Mom more questions. I never ever want to be here in this house; in this world. I keep running all over the house. Once I get a hug from whomever I run to, I run somewhere else. I can't seem to stay in one place very long. Sometimes I run to my room and sob on the bed. The day is a cloud of dark vapor behind my mist covered eyes. I move through space in an envelope of confusion until, finally, I fall asleep on my bed, fully dressed.

~~~~~~~~~~~~~~~~~~~~~~~~~~~~~~~~~~

The funeral is today. Mom and Dad are dressed in black. They walk into the kitchen where Jessy and I are eating cereal at the table. They tell me and Jessy we are not going. It is only for adults. I don't care anyway. I've never been to a funeral and I don't even know what it is. Mom looks awful. I have never seen her when she didn't look beautiful. Her eyes have dark smudges under them. I don't know if it is makeup rubbed from her mascara or in her skin. But Dad looks the same; handsome as always, like a movie star. They both hug us like they need the hugs. I stop eating and just stare into the heaviness of the air in the kitchen.

Each day that passes I spend either crying, sleeping, and frequently throwing up. Mom keeps Jessy and me home from school when it starts again after the Christmas break. She says we can stay home another week to mourn Peggy. Mom tells us that mourning is when you miss a person you loved so much that concentrating on anything else is impossible. Mom says in time we won't be as sad.

Later in the week Jessy and I visit Peggy's family. We stay for dinner.

"Girls, would you mind sleeping over?" Peggy's mom asks, looking back and forth at us with bloodshot eyes that have dark smoke colored circles under them. "Your mom says it's okay. Some of Peggy's friends have been taking turns sleeping over because we think Peggy would have liked that. To be honest, Peggy's dad and I get comfort from having girls in the house."

"Sure," Jessy and I say at the same time.

"I have to get something from home. I'll be right back," I say looking at Mrs. Shapiro.

I tell Jessy I'm going to get the dollhouse furniture Peggy gave me for Christmas and run out the door. I see that Jessy looks scared to be alone without me when I turn back to close the door—like I might not come back. I would not want to sleep in Peggy's room alone either. It would be scary, like her ghost might come and appear before me. The word ghost was never frightening until now.

Mom is home and I explain I am getting my dollhouse furniture gifts to put in Peggy's dollhouse. She says she understands and that we are helping her parents through this horrible time and that she is very proud of us.

I hurry back carrying the package.

Peggy's mom and I open the dollhouse washer, dryer and ironing board while Jessy watches in silence.

We all go upstairs and the smell and look of her room makes me gasp. I can't comprehend that she isn't here anymore. The dollhouse even has the greyish faced dolls that we painted black, but they are outside the house lying down in a lump. I place the new miniatures in the laundry room with some of them. But we painted more dolls than I remember so I put some of them at the table eating with the white family, like they were friends too, not just maids. Peggy would want this; I know she would. The dollhouse should be like a real house. Jessy watches me as I place them.

"Rachael, why are you doing that?"

"This is where colored people should sit. White and colored can be maids, right—and they can be friends too. Peggy and I talked about it," I say sadly, "and we wanted the colored dolls to be part of the whole dollhouse and not just be maids anymore."

"Okay, Rach, now that Peggy's gone I'll try to

understand—the way she did," Jessy says quietly.

I don't know if Jessy means it or is just saying it so I'll feel better. But I hope she means it.

Jessy and I get into the twin beds. I let Jessy sleep in Peggy's bed because I don't want to argue about who should sleep where. And besides, I don't think I want to sleep in Peggy's bed. My mind is driving me crazy. I want to transform into Peggy so her parents and everyone will go back to the way it was and I can disappear. I can't get that thought out of my head. I can't sleep.

"Jess," I speak softly, just in case she's fallen asleep, "I'm scared. It's creepy to sleep here without Peggy, like we're being punished for her dying."

"I know. The room feels like it *is* Peggy—the whole room."

"Do you think her ghost will come and talk to us?"

"Maybe."

"Can I sleep with you?"

"Okay."

"Thank you," I whisper as I snuggle in close to my sister.

In the morning Peggy's mom, Lily, wakes us up. She tries to smile. Her eyes are so red, it's like blood is oozing out of them. Her hands are shaking. The circles under her eyes look even deeper than they did last night and they're almost grass-green. I feel angry at Lily when I look at her. I want everything the same and she's making it different. I hate her right now for asking us to sleep in this room, like that's going to help. Nothing is going to help. My life will never be the same and I want it to be.

"Girls, Elsie has breakfast for you."

"Okay," we say together.

After breakfast, we tell Peggy's mom that we'll always visit and sleep over. We hug goodbye. The house feels cold without Peggy; my lips quiver. Now her house feels more like my home always feels. Not warm and homey, like it used to when Peggy was here. I want to take Peggy's memory home with me to warm up my house and my heart.

We walk home and open the back door. And there's Ruby, standing in the kitchen.

"Ruby!" I scream her name. We all hug and jump up and down holding each other, carrying on "Ruby, I can't believe it." "Are you really here?" "Yes, it's me." "Please tell me you're not just visiting." "I'm not just visiting. I'm back."

I feel better and more cheerful than I've felt since Christmas. Ruby is back. We hug again and Jessy brings Ethel over to join in the hugs.

"Come on, girls, let's go up to *my* room," Ruby says. "I have something for ya'll. My, you've grown up," she notes as we climb the stairs.

We go into Ruby's room and everything is neat, like she never left. The smell of Ruby surrounds us. She tells us while she was away she learned how to sew, like her mother, who has a machine and made all of her clothes when she was growing up.

"I made you each somethin'."

Jessy and I unwrap the packages she hands us and discover beautiful navy blue skirts made of cotton.

"Oh, Ruby, I love it," I tell her. "I can wear it to school and show everyone." I'm smiling as I speak and it feels like it's been a long time since I smiled. I feel certain Mom brought Ruby back because Peggy died. Ruby doesn't make up for Peggy, but I feel so much better having her here, at home.

Mom told me Acer got fired as Ginny's trainer. In fact, her parents sold the horse. I feel sorry for Acer and Ginny. Blaming them will not bring Peggy back, but at least they don't have to go to those stables and breathe the same air where it happened.

Ruby runs into my room announcing, "Rachael, Peggy's mom is in the front hall asking for you."

I run downstairs and see a giant box, big enough to hold a television, with Peggy's mom standing next to it. "Hello, Mrs. Shapiro."

"Hello, Rachael. I've brought you something I'm sure Peggy would want you to have." There are tears in her red eyes.

I go over to the box and open the lid. "Oh, no, not her dollhouse!" Now tears are rolling down my face, too. "Oh, Mrs. Shapiro, I don't know. I mean, I'll treasure this forever, but…are you sure you don't want it in Peggy's room?" I ask.

"Dear, I've thought about it a lot. You know, I've heard you and Peggy playing with the dollhouse since you were both so small." She stoops and puts her hand down to the height of a three year old and smiles wanly at me. "I know how much she loved playing dollhouse with you. Oh, sure, her other little girlfriends would play too, but not like you and Peggy. You would play for hours and giggle and scream with delight at the fun you were making. I want you to have those precious memories by having this," Mrs. Shapiro says and I can hear in her voice that it gives her pleasure for me to have it. "Now I have to go."

"I don't know what to say, but my heart and soul say thank you. I will treasure it forever, like my Peggy," I say.

We hug each other goodbye and we both cry as I snuggle into her arms.

I'm going to ask Bill to move the dollhouse into my room and I'm going to put all the colored dolls eating at the dining table with the white dolls.

THREE YEARS LATER, 1962...

# 15
# LIFESAVER

Today is my first day at work ever because it is summer so I'm going to work in Dad's store. I am excited to start; now I can earn money to give to Ruby, Ethel and Bernice. Mom says one dollar an hour is okay for an almost sixteen year old, these days. Dad opened his second store a few years ago nearer to our house. I'm going to do inventory or clean up the dressing rooms after the rich ladies toss the clothes they don't buy on the floor or crumpled up on the chair. I have to admit I throw clothes on my rug at home, but I think it's not proper for customers to do it in a store.

Now Mom works some days in the store closer to where we live; not the one I work in. Nana used to work at the one Mom works in now. Mom tolerates Nana at home but not in the store. If they said one thing to each other that wasn't nice, Mom would storm out—and then Dad would be angry. Mom will do anything not to make Dad mad. I'm not sure why Mom is working more now than she used to.

I like this store, but it feels different going there today

than when I went in it just to look at clothes or visit with Mom. It's in a busy part of town right across from Saks Fifth Avenue, the most elite store in St. Louis. There are a lot of apartment buildings mixed in with big mansions and expensive stores, like ours, mainly on two streets near some fancy hotels and restaurants. It's more like a city than our quiet suburb. It isn't downtown St. Louis, where my grandfathers used to work, but it is where a lot of people moved when they left downtown twenty or thirty years ago. Most of them moved to get more land, and they kept moving further and further out into the suburbs— like to Warren, where we live now.

I get to drive in with Dad, whizzing around in his pale green Jaguar with the top down. With his sports car cap, he looks dashing in his grey linen suit and blue striped tie with a perfectly pressed white shirt to match his flawlessly coiffed, slick and suave black hair. He looks so out of place in St. Louis, more like a movie star who got lost on his way to Hollywood. He catches me gawking at him, like a fan or something.

"First day," I say, feeling like an idiot. My hair is getting blown by the wind and I am sure I look like a deranged Raggedy Ann doll.

"Yes, Snooks. I'm sure you'll find it challenging and sometimes even fun," Dad says, smiling.

For some reason, he loves to call me Snooks or Snookie when he's in his car. Why can't he say, *I'm so happy to have you work with me?* Or, *"I'll take you to lunch to show you off to all my buddies?*

The rest of the drive is in silence, which is the normal way we are in his car. I think of all the ways our seemingly traditional family are so strange.

I'm embarrassed to be in a car so different from everyone else's. In some ways, I want to be like my friends, even if I don't like the fact that they don't think about how the colored people are treated. None of my friends' families have a sports car, so they gather around the Jaguar when my mom picks me up at school, like it's a living dinosaur. And I'm ashamed of having more money than most of my friends.

Jessy and Annie give me their old clothes—hand-me-downs. They know I would rather wear them than the spanking new cashmere or cotton outfits from the store that Mom lays on my bed for me as a surprise every few months in the winter and summer. There are fresh new skirts, dresses and Capri outfits hung in my closet for the country club or parties. But not this summer, because Mom didn't go to New York with Dad to buy clothes for the store last spring; that's when she picks up some new outfits for Jessy and me. On those buying trips, Mom shops while Dad is working. Nothing was said why she didn't go this time.

It's weird that she didn't go this time because I know Mom loves to go to New York with Dad the few times a year he goes on his buying trips. She adores seeing a Broadway show, stopping by the Russian Tea Room. I don't know if that is in an embassy building or what because I only hear her drop the name, and dining at Sardi's, famous for dining before and after the theater, a place that "everyone goes to." Normally Mom shops on 5th Avenue while Dad buys new clothes on 7th Avenue, where the clothing manufacturers are.

Dad showed us a picture postcard once of the street. You can see racks of clothes being wheeled around the middle of the street while the taxis and automobiles try not to hit the people and racks. It looks exciting; with the bustling people stopping to chat about business, balancing their racks for a few minute chat. This should have been the summer I saw all the sights of New York with Dad. Annie went when she was sixteen. Jessy was going to go with me this year waiting so we could go together. Annie told Jessy how boring the nights were when Dad had meetings; she watched TV and ordered room service. At least Jessy and I would have had each other for company. I wish I knew why we didn't go to New York.

I'm not supposed to notice what Mom and Dad do with money. But I'm not deaf, dumb and blind. I sense something, and I feel scared about an unidentifiable, ruffled calm—like the spooky quiet before the tornado when I was eleven, and we sheltered in the basement.

When I walk into the store with Dad, all the sales clerks greet me warmly, like I'm the President's daughter. I have met most of them before when I visited with Mom or Dad. They are in a messy receiving line that wasn't planned. I shake hands with them and smile shyly because I do feel kind of scared. I've never worked before today and I feel alone and very nervous. They're probably not sincere, but feel they have to be pleasant because I'm the boss's daughter. Maybe they think I'm a spy for Dad. I wish Mom worked in this store.

I don't know where to go or what to do when Dad starts walking away. He turns his head back and says generally to the five salesladies to keep me busy and he will be in his office.

Elaine takes me by the elbow to show me how the clothes are organized. Elaine has grey hair which she wears in a bun. Her blue eyes are sparkling and she doesn't stop smiling, as if teaching me is the best job she has ever had. She's paunchy with white hairs growing on her chin and above her upper lip. If she didn't wear nice clothes from the store, she would look ungroomed. Dad makes everyone wear the clothes he sells. Elaine tells me that first the clothes are organized by color, then size. Even though I have been to the store several times, I'd never noticed the organization of what I'm now learning to call stock, like it was cattle. Dad is lucky to have Elaine work for him because she's friendly and easygoing.

Already I'm bored just looking at the clothes hanging there, like lonely women sitting at a dance without partners. There are some men's clothes, too—just shirts, ties, and silk handkerchiefs—all displayed on shiny, dark brown wood shelves, neat and color assorted. If a customer wants a suit to go with the men's accessories, Elaine tells me to recommend Saks Fifth Avenue—and always with a smile. Dad's store is small and has only four hanging areas for women's clothes along with some shelves. Drawers hold extra gloves, scarves, and jewelry if ladies want to see more than what is displayed. On the men's side there are only two areas where sport shirts, a few dress shirts, and nice casual pants are hung. In drawers are ties, handkerchiefs, socks and cufflinks. Maybe if I worked in Saks I wouldn't be as bored because there is more to look at there.

I don't know how to act in here. I feel like I should stand against a wall all day with my arms down at my sides and, when someone walks in, salute at attention like a toy soldier waiting for orders.

When Peggy was alive she taught me how to treat others by the way she acted; I heard her talk to people and I saw how she listened to me and to everyone else. But I'm shy. I guess I just don't have much confidence; I never know what is appropriate to say, which Mom tells me is very important. When I'm around kids I don't know so well, most of the time I just sit and don't say a word. Or if

I do say something, I say it so quietly no one can even hear me. Other times I say something at the wrong time or too loudly. My timing is so off, like a bad comedian. I'd rather hide in a trunk until a ventriloquist takes me out and talks for me. Nothing comes out naturally unless I'm talking to my very close friends. I think most kids learn from watching their parents interact with family and friends. How could I learn from parents when they're never around? And even when they are, they barely notice my existence. I wanted Peggy to always teach me because I loved her and wanted to be like her. The hardest thing I have to tackle on my own is how to fit into the world without Peggy.

Now I'm alone, trying to figure out how to be in the store, around customers, around the salesladies, and around people I know who may come in. It terrifies me. Maybe I should try out different personalities to see what feels like the real me, like when you try on a new outfit to see if it looks like you Just figuring that out feels like a full time job. Suddenly I realize I don't really want to be here, even though I'd like to earn some money for the people I love. Let's face it, Dad doesn't really care if I'm here or not and the salesladies would rather I wasn't here. Just like home.

Walking by his office to go to the ladies' room, I hear Dad talking on the phone. He looks more serious than I have ever seen him; he's talking about money. He yells something about "thirty days" and "sending back clothes." When I come out of the bathroom, Dad is talking to Mom; I can tell by the way his voice is. They're arguing, but his voice isn't angry—it just isn't happy. At home I've overheard Mom when she talks on the phone to Dad at work lots of times. But today sounds worse. What could it be? Nothing makes sense. And why is Mom working in the other store almost every day now when she used to only come in either store whenever she felt like it?

I feel sorry for Dad. There are millions of papers all over his desk with orders and numbers. It looks like homework. His face is wrinkled like a paper napkin. When he holds the phone with his neck, it makes him look ninety years old. He doesn't even ask me how I'm doing on my first day as I walk by.

Marjorie is a young saleslady. She has a blonde pageboy, white teeth, and blue eyes that smile when she isn't smiling. Everyone working here looks Jewish but her. The others all have dark hair, olive skin, wide hips and noses too big for their faces. Maybe the other salesladies aren't Jewish but they don't look Gentile like Marjorie.

Pretending a woman looks good in an outfit that you actually can't stand, making sure everything is neat and tidy, and hoping people won't return what they buy are forms of torture to me. But then Marjorie gives me some clothes to move to the window. Window displays are like art. I could use my imagination. Maybe, if Marjorie is going to dress the mannequins, she will let me help.

The mannequins are all white, like in Peggy's dollhouse. I see a nice colored lady walk by and look in the window and I want to smash through the window and apologize to her. Dad better not go outside to tell her this place is for white people only. If he did, I would take the bus home, make sure to sit in the back, and never speak to him again.

The colored lady stops walking. She is probably going to catch a bus home after working all night as a maid at Saks Fifth Avenue. Oh, she is tying her shoe. The shoe may be too tight and she may have a blister. She trips while tying her shoe. I run out to offer her a Band-Aid but as I get to her side she looks at me suspiciously, like maybe she thinks

I'm trying to chase her away from the store. She hurries away and I feel so bad. I want to run and tell her I just wanted to help, but she is almost running now and I know I shouldn't go after her.

I go back in the store. Marjorie was in the back while this happened so she didn't see any of it. She's coming toward me with more clothes for the window. I don't say anything about the colored lady. It will take too long to explain. Marjorie probably wouldn't care or listen anyway.

She starts to dress the windows and I ask if I can help. She lets me. Together we spend a few hours dressing the naked, white dummies in shoes, hats, and clothes. Mostly we are silent while dressing the big, stiff dolls.

"Rachael, do you want to take over your Dad's store one day?" she asks. "Maybe you'll run one and Jessy will have the other."

"No, I want to do something completely different," I say, adjusting a hat on one of the mannequins.

"What do you want to do?"

"Something to help less advantaged people. The colored people, the poor. I'm not sure yet, but I will find out."

"That is very grown up of you," Marjorie says with a questioning look in her eyes. She is not like Mom and Dad and may understand what I am all about.

Dad comes out of his office and says he'll be back in a while. He doesn't ask how I am doing.

I wonder if Dad drinks during the work day and not just at home before dinner. If I were a full-time spy, I'd

225

follow him. But I'm trapped here until five except lunch time.

Looking out the display window, I see Mitch Gordon and his mother walking toward the entrance. Did he know I started work here? Jessy might have told Tommy, and Tommy must have told Mitch? Maybe his mom is buying him something. I quickly check my hair in the reflection of the window, in case Tommy is following behind Mitch and his mom. I know it seems hopeless, but I can't help it—I still have a crush on him.

Mitch is Tommy's best friend. Mitch and I met on the playground when I was in first grade and he was in second. He ran by me as I was playing second baseman and said, "Don't you know you don't stand *on* the base while you try to get an out—just stand close to it." That was the first time anyone who I didn't know already ever talked to me at school—especially an older boy. All the way through sixth grade, every time we passed each other by, we would say hello. Once every so often we would see each other at the drugstore and he would joke with me about why I need to have another Pez container when I probably have enough already or why don't I try a chocolate phosphate instead of strawberry because no one gets strawberry.

In seventh grade, Mitch went to Country Day, an all-boys school, so I never ran into him anymore. The next time I saw him was at a Halloween party when he was in the eighth grade. We talked and joked about how he didn't wear a costume because his new fat was his disguise. I don't remember my costume—maybe he does. There was nowhere to sit, the place was so crowded so, without even thinking if he would want me to, I sat on his lap; he didn't seem to mind at all and I knew then that he would always be my close friend. He isn't distant and scary, like some boys. We have the same sense of humor. And his eyes are always warm, like melting syrup. I feel like he's a lifesaver, coming here now, on my first day. It will make me feel so much more comfortable.

I step out of the window display and approach him.

"Hi, Mitch, what are you doing here?"

At seventeen, Mitch is a roly-poly guy—baby fat that stayed too long. He has light brown hair worn in a crew cut and a round face. When he walks, he waddles like a duck. He was over just last week—we played some 45s in the library together. Sometimes I think I could like him as more than a friend but it kind of scares me. I should tell Mitch about when I'm nervous around him. Then maybe we could laugh about it. After we listened to music, Mitch taught me how to play bridge and Ethel made us a snack. Mitch chomped on a fried drumstick that greased up his face and left little bits of crust hanging off his chin. I think he tests me to see if I will have him around when his shirt is untucked and disheveled, just the opposite of Dad, who is always neatly pressed and tucked. Mitch isn't trying to impress anyone with what he says or by his looks. I think Mitch likes everything I say or do.

I need to talk to him about the changes that are going on at home and at work. The new car Dad loves to buy every year did not happen; no new clothes for me after Dad went to New York this year; and what I overheard at work. Since I have never heard Dad talk at work, maybe this is the normal kind of thing that comes up. Also Mom may *want* to work more and Dad could still come home with a new car. Or maybe we're all in trouble. Or maybe my imagination is just a bad Humpty Dumpty fairytale that will end with all the pieces fitting together again. I need to talk to Mitch about all this and see what he thinks.

"Rachael? Hi! What are you doing in the window?"

"I'm playing with dolls. Big, creepy dolls."

When Mitch belly laughs, I know he has a crush on me, which at this moment makes me feel like the most beautiful girl in St. Louis. I told him when I would start working. I bet he told his mom to come to Dad's store. Funny, Mitch's dad is in the clothing business, too. But not retail; he has a factory manufacturing children's clothes, which, of course, Mitch used to wear when he was little.

Across the store, his mom is signaling with her eyes to walk over to the shirts. I see him shaking his head no. Maybe he knows he's too chubby to fit into any of them.

"Okay, see you when you leave, if I'm still dressing the dolls."

"Yeah, okay." He waddles off.

I turn toward Marjorie and she is smiling like she thinks she knows something about Mitch and me—like maybe he's my boyfriend. But I look away so she knows I don't feel like talking to her about personal things and she goes back to the mannequins. She dresses the display with *Life* magazines, books, slippers, tennis shoes, tennis racquets and balls looking like they just rolled out of the can, places sunglasses on a throw rug under the dolls' feet. The scene makes no sense. The mannequins are all standing dressed in nice cruise clothes and heels. No one is relaxing or in tennis clothes. But Marjorie doesn't ask my opinion.

If she did, I would also add *Ebony Magazines* and colored mannequins. I would have both white and colored ladies, some with cigarettes in their hands, some with purses; gloves would be partially on and off some ladies;

some would be wearing shorts and T-shirts. The clothes would be color-coordinated to blend in with each other. They would be putting on makeup and accessorized in eye-popping detail, like they were discussing a charity event or a seating chart for a dinner party. I'd place some small tables around with scattered pictures of table and flower layouts, drawings of the room, pictures of entertainment bands, and charity accounting numbers. Everyone happy together in one window would be an excellent start for the rest of the world to see, even if only in a window display.

About twenty minutes go by and I see Mitch and his mom walking toward the exit.

"Hi, Mrs. Gordon. Did Mitch get a nice shirt or tie?"

"Hello, Rachael. He did get both and they are lovely. Good to see you."

"Bye, Mitch, see you."

He walks up to me and whispers in my ear, "I picked the first shirt and tie so it wouldn't take forever—I don't even like them." "Bye," he says out loud. We both laugh.

He doesn't know that I saw him say no to some of the shirts. I don't want him to leave the store. He saves me from the rest of the difficult day. I wish Tommy could see me here working, like I am moving on to becoming a woman, not just Jessy's little sister.

I wonder if Mitch talks to his mom about what girls he likes. She looks like she's really interested in his life. I bet they don't have many secrets. I bet they have fun family dinners and inside jokes about each other and that they talk about what they're going to do together as a family on the weekend. They probably discuss news events or even go

229

around the table to tell jokes. The family might have so many memories they say, "Remember when we slid down the hill together in sleds that were garbage can tops? Remember when we sang Christmas songs together around the piano and Mom sang off key so loudly she woke Grandma?"

What memories are Mom and Dad going to tell about us when we are grown up?

Marjorie must feel sorry for me because it's my first day and Dad didn't even ask me to go to lunch.

"Rachael, I brought my lunch but there's a small café two doors down. Do you have your own money?"

"I do," I lie.

First I smell the cigarette butts on dad's desk—at least fifteen—piled up in an ashtray like miniature buoys in dirty sand. I decide to see if Dad has money in his desk drawer. I find three dollars. Then I see a folder on top of his desk that is blank on the front. I steal it and take it into the bathroom. I open the folder. There is a name—Joan Sather—and a phone number with all kinds of math numbers, too. I copy the number and put it in my purse. I put the folder back, but then Marjorie walks by and sees me at Dad's desk.

Awkwardly I say, "I didn't have enough money for lunch after all so I found some in Dad's desk drawer." I'm holding the money in my hand.

"Okay. See you after lunch," Marjorie says looking somewhat askance.

I walk into the café a block down. This is the first time in my life I have eaten alone. I would rather be here by myself than in the store. I feel grownup ordering, eating alone and paying. I walk back to the store and Dad is staring out the front door like he's waiting for me.

"Hi, Snooky. Did you have a good lunch?"

"Dad, I took three dollars from your desk drawer. I had no money.

I went to eat at the café down the street. It was good."

"Good, Snooky. I'll be sure to give you money next time. Sorry, your dad should have asked you about that." He walks to the back into his office and shuts the door.

Marjorie and I finish the mannequins and the window. It looks like every other window I have ever seen in my life. There is nothing different about it. I go into the dressing rooms and pick up all the clothes that the rich ladies threw around and hang them up.

Dad comes out of the back and walks around the store, inspecting everything quickly. He sees the window and says we did a beautiful job and now it's time to go home.

On the road, in the Jaguar, he doesn't say anything. He looks like he is worried. Then finally asks, "Did you like work, Snooks?"

"It was okay. I liked doing the window the best."

"Okay. I'll remember that so you can do them again."

"Thanks, Dad."

The rest is silence, which hurts every second. I don't know why it hurts so much. I think if he hit me, it wouldn't hurt as much.

The next morning, Ruby comes into my bedroom to open the curtains and let the light shine in. She obviously thinks I should be up by now. I squint and yawn. I should be annoyed I guess, but when I see her smiling face I feel happy, until I realize I have to go to work again today. My stomach starts to hurt.

"Come on, honey, don't you waste a second of the most gorgeous day that you and I ever seen," Ruby says sweetly but firmly.

"Good morning, Ruby. I want to ask you something. Have you noticed something different in the house? I don't know what it is exactly. Like a heavy feeling? Like a sadness? Have you?"

"Sadness, my child, is a part of life, all our lives—even as a child. Some days gets more syrup than others. You know, honey, the sweetness is not all equal but God divvies it up later to make it equal. We don't know when, but He does know."

Not buying all this sugar coating, I question, "What's going on?"

"Everything is fine. Now get up, chil', and get dressed for your job with Daddy."

"Okay, but first I have to tell you my secret. I dreamed last night that I told you my discovery."

"Okay, chil', but get out of bed, go to the bathroom, and then put these clothes on I picked for ya and then we will talk about yo' 'covery."

"Okay. You promise?"

"Oh, chil', stop that promising all the time. Rise and shine."

I go and do what she says so fast that I'm ready to talk in what seems like a minute. I find Ruby in Rusty's room, making the bed.

"Okay, come here," I say sweetly.

Ruby and I walk back to my room. I close the door. We sit on my bed facing each other.

"Ruby, I…" I hug her and she hugs back. "I can't ever leave you. You are really my mom. You are the person who cares about me. How did I live without you when you were gone?" I say softly.

"Honey, now you listen to me. Of course I loves ya and cares for ya, but I cannot be your mama. Your mama loves you even more than I does. She jes' shows it different than me. I know she do. If yo' Mommy and Daddy is having problems, you shouldn't be worryin' 'bout it. They's the adults and they's be fixin' them problems. Just be a chil' while you can, sugar. You got to have faith and believe. When I thinks nothing'll be able to get me through, I believe in the faith. Do you knows what I mean?"

"No, I don't, Ruby. I don't. Tell me some more."

"Wells, chil', I can't. It has to be in there." Ruby points to my heart.

"It isn't, Ruby. It isn't in there. I'm Jewish."

"Well, didn't they teach you faith?"

"No, they didn't. I disliked Sunday school. The only thing it taught me was that I didn't want to go there."

"Chil', maybe I's gonna show you my church if yo' mommy will let you someday, so you sees how people can live with the faith and get through and know God loves each 'n everyone of them."

"Okay. But how can I ever go with you?"

"Well, maybe yo' momma will drive us there when I goes some Sunday. I will aks her in a very nice way. I will tell her you need to see how to believe that someone is helpin' you go through things that are scary an' then maybe you'll see likes you can too."

"Oh, Ruby, that'd be so great. Please talk to Mom today about us going. She'll probably think we're crazy, but I don't care."

I'm pushing my egg and toast around with my fork, taking a few bites in the breakfast room when I see Dad walking past the picture window. I get up and watch him examine the outside of the house like he's never seen it before. He touches the wood around the windows like he's memorizing every inch. He looks very worried. A secret is under the floorboards in this house and it feels like something is breathing smoke through the crevices and every day I can see and smell it more.

The second day at work is practically the same as yesterday. Dad is silent in the car. Marjorie and I do the mannequins in the other window. It's another boring window. All day Dad is in his office talking on the phone or to the salesladies so I don't have a moment to go in and see anything on his desk.

I know what I have to do now and the reason I'm here to work. Ruby told me there is a reason in everything you do that is more important than you know. She said when you really don't like something you have to do, do it anyway, because there is a bigger reason why you have to do things.

Mom gave me lunch money so I go to the café. Today I sit at a sidewalk table outside and watch people bustling by. A few buses stop in front of the café to let people off and on. I see the colored people in the back of the bus getting off the bus. The colored women are dressed in nice, crisp clean clothes or maid's uniforms. The dressed up women could be going to a funeral or to a party. Some colored men are in uniforms like a bellman's uniform or dressed in work clothes like Bill wears at home. They could be going to someone's home to work or cleaning toilets in a hotel. I want to know more about their lives.

After a long day doing the windows and straightening clothes, Dad and I drive home.

"Snooks, how was your day?"

"Good, Dad."

"Did you eat at the café?"

"Yes, it was nice. Where did you eat?"

"I ate with some men at the Men's Club."

"What is a Men's Club?"

"It's a restaurant where women aren't allowed."

"Like where Negroes aren't allowed in some restaurants and other places?"

No answer from Dad. Just a stare like he doesn't want to be bothered. The ride is taking forever.

# 16
# NEW HOME

I appreciate the privacy of my room where I can be alone with my thoughts. Before I started working I didn't think having my own room was so important, but now I do.

Right now I'm looking at all the Christmas presents I've gotten during the last three years. They were in bags in the corner of the closet but are now spread out on my bed. Instead of buying Ruby, Ethel, Bill and Bernice presents, I wanted to give these gifts to them. They wouldn't take them, so I saved them in case they changed their minds— but they didn't. They all said the same thing; Mom and Dad wouldn't like them taking my clothes. I know they mean they were afraid to lose their jobs. I'm going to bring them to the country club this summer and give them to the colored help there. Dad doesn't pay me enough to buy nice gifts for everyone.

Mom comes into my room and finds me looking at the

haul. She asks me why I've never worn any of the clothes I got for Christmas every year and I tell her the truth.

"I just don't need them, Mom. I can use whatever Jessy and Annie don't wear anymore."

Mom gives me a long look. "Well, dear, they're yours— you can do whatever you wish with them."

It's obvious to me, though, that she doesn't approve of my decision.

"Honey," she goes on, "I have the list to send out for your sweet sixteen party with all your girlfriends. Grandma is going to be making you the sweet sugars."

Mom's mother makes bouquets of sugar cubes tied with pink satin ribbon and lace for her granddaughters who've turned sixteen. You're supposed to hang them in your bedroom for good luck the whole year—then throw it out before the bees and mosquitoes start finding the sugar through a hole in a screen.

"But Mom, I don't want a sweet sixteen party!"

"Well, why not, darling? This will be a big day in the life of my daughter. I want to have a party at our home to celebrate. It will be so lovely."

Jessy and Annie had theirs at the club.

"I don't know. I just want a quiet birthday. Go swimming at the Casey's with Jessy and Jane. I'm not sure about the evening," I say, hanging my head.

"Darling, do you want a boy-girl party? You don't have to have a luncheon with all girls." Mom puts her hand on mine, like she really cares, but I know she wants the party because it's the proper thing to do to maintain her standing with her friends, even if it is at home.

"No, Mom. I don't want a party. Please don't buy me clothes, either. I'll only give them away." I leave my hand under hers because I like the feel of her always warm hands.

"Okay, dear. I understand." without looking understanding. "Maybe a little tea or something not complicated with a few of your best girlfriends?"

I lift my head up. "The thing is, Mom, I don't want anything to do with parties, presents or sugars. With all the inequality in the world, a fancy party feels wrong." I take my hand away before she does.

"Alright, dear," Mom says, resigned to losing the argument.

I don't feel guilty for not being a typical sweet sixteen year old. I am supposed to love my parents, but I don't most of the time—I do feel guilty about that.

"The only present I want is for you to drive me and Ruby to her church."

Mom stands up abruptly and says, "Rachael, Ruby asked me if I could drive you and her to church on a Sunday, which struck me as odd since you only go to temple when we go as a family for the high holidays. She said you needed some extra spoonfuls of faith and you want to see how she gets hers. That it would help you. Help you do what?" Mom says all in a rush.

"Things seem different around here. I can't explain it. Just different," I say warily.

I lie to Mom. Even though things seem different the

real reason I want to go to church with Ruby is to be with her alone so I can learn more about her and her ways. I know Ruby cares about me—and I need to feel her caring any way I can. Maybe getting older has helped me become more aware of how one really *shows* caring. It can't just be with words—it has to be with actions.

Mom probably still feels guilty for not taking me to Peggy's funeral and she feels she can make up for it by driving me to Ruby's church. She agrees too easily, like she doesn't want my struggles to get in her way. If she really cared, she'd talk to me about what I think is "different." But it's easier for her to let Ruby take care of me. She walks out calling Jessy's name and heading to Jessy's room. Jessy went to see Bret and told me if anyone asked where she was to tell them she went down the street to see her friends Jill and Jenny.

"Honey, do you know where your sister is?"

"She's down at Jill or Jenny's house. Why?"

"I need to talk to her about something."

I hate lying for Jess when she goes to see Bret. I do it so she will like me more.

I dial Mitch's number. He answers.

"Hi, Mitch. It was fun to see you at my dad's store the other day. I want to talk to you about something."

"Okay. Talk."

"No, not now. Can we get together tonight?"

"Where?"

"At Steak 'n Shake. Mom can probably drop me off for dinner after she gets home from work. I'm not working today.

"Okay. I am working today, at Dad's factory, so I'd have to go home first to change and get ready. Six?"

The way he slops his clothes on his body, how would I know the difference? It's like me wearing hand-me-downs instead of perfectly matched brand new outfits in the latest in fashion.

"Okay. I'll ask Mom for sure and call you back."

Mom says it's okay and I call Mitch back and we make the date. Steak 'n Shake is one of the hangouts in Warren. I hope we can talk privately without a lot of kids we know coming over to the table.

During the ride to Steak 'n Shake I'm thinking of making Mitch my assistant detective. He can call the company phone number I took off Dad's folder and maybe find out what's going on in my family. It may just be a clothing manufacturer's phone number and have nothing to do with anything about my family. But I am curious. After all, it was in a folder all by itself without anything written about the store or clothes. And I know something is going on. Mitch will do this for me; I know he will. I spot him in a booth.

"Hi, Mitch."

"Hi, Rachael. Let's order before I faint." Mitch laughs. "I always say that to girls because they want to talk instead of eat."

"Okay."

We order.

"Mitch, what if you really needed to tell someone something that you couldn't say to anyone except your best friend, even if it was your best boyfriend? Would you do it?"

"Sure, why not?"

"Do you want me to tell you?"

"Am I your best friend?"

"Since Peggy died, you are."

Mitch's smile is about three feet wide. "Go ahead and tell me, then, before my mouth is so stuffed with food I can't talk. But first, what do you mean 'boyfriend'?"

"I mean you are my best *boy* friend, not like a boyfriend. Get it?"

"I guess." Mitch says as his smile fades.

"Okay. I have a phone number to call that might give me some answers. Dad is angry at work—on the phone with Mom and with other people. Mom is working longer hours and almost every day—and we didn't get a new car this year like we always do. I'm worried that money is not falling off of trees like my folks are used to and they're nervous. I'm scared something bad is going on and I don't know what it is. I didn't want to call the phone number alone, in case Mom or Dad or both are in trouble with the police or something. My imagination is wild with bad thoughts. Will you come with me to the phone booth before the food comes?

"Sure," Mitch says like he isn't really worried about

how I go on and on. I probably sound slightly hysterical about nothing.

Mitch and I both squeeze into the phone booth in the back of the restaurant. I have never been this close to him before. It feels good to me, like we're brother and sister. Maybe to him it feels good to be close to a girl he has a crush on. He smells like crayons and silly putty mixed together with dirt and sweat, from nervousness, except his breath smells like dusty shelves in an antique store. He already has lots of coins in his hand to give me. I dial with the sweaty coins.

A voice answers, "Wells Realty. May I help you?"

I hang up the phone and hang down my head.

"What's wrong, Rachael?"

"It's a realty company, Mitch. Dad always looks at the house now like he's inspecting it. I think we're selling our house. It all makes sense now!" I say opening the door to the phone booth. We are so squished; as we get out we accidentally touch more places of each other than intended. We keep apologizing and excusing ourselves to one another.

"Rachael," Mitch says, once we're back in a booth, "talk to your parents. Tell them you think you know what's going on. Maybe you'll find out they want to move to a nicer house. I'm not saying your house isn't great, but with your Dad having two stores now, maybe he wants to spend some of his money on a bigger house. You don't really know what's going on."

"Everything they do is about saving money. Dad didn't buy a new car this year. Mom didn't go to New York, and

Ruby told me Bernice and Bill are only coming five days a week instead of six. I hate them for not sharing things that affect the family. They think everything they do is only about them. I haven't talked to Jessy about this because she would say not to worry, that Mom and Dad will tell us stuff when they want to. All Jess cares about is her boyfriend. She even makes me lie about where she is sometimes."

The food arrives.

"Wow, this sounds really hard, Rach. If my mom or dad hid these things from me, I'd be upset, too. This requires some real thought," he says as he shovels a mouthful of food in.

I stare at the burger and fries in front of me. I keep thinking about tomorrow and calling the realty company and trying to figure out where I'll call from and what I'll say.

"Mitch, you eat. I need to think. I can't eat. Want my burger?"

Mitch lifts it off my plate with a grin. Just to sit and be with him makes me feel sparkly and shiny, like a clear, crystal ball I can see the future in. It's so weird, because on the outside he appears dusty, murky, and filmy. There are no hidden nooks and crannies I have to figure out. He is all present. I hope he'll always be my friend. When Ruby left and then Peggy died, I realized anyone can leave me anytime without warning—even Mitch or Ethel. It scares me that no one will stay.

As Mitch polishes off the burgers and fries, I start to think about tomorrow and going to church with Ruby. Sometimes I think I like him more than just a friend but I don't dream about seeing him or wish I were with him. I am more excited about Ruby's church than I am about

Mitch.

He drives me home and I hop out and thank him for the ride. I want to thank him for his friendship but it isn't the way we talk and he would just stare at me and say, "Huh?"

The special Sunday—church Sunday—is finally here and I wake very early, even before Ruby. I think about Mom being quieter and more serious looking of late. I lie in bed trying to imagine what she is going through, if we are moving away from St. Louis. She was born here, grew up here, and has lived here with Dad for twenty five years. All her friends and family are here. She knows where to go for every little thing in the neighborhood. Like Dad, Mom lives a certain way and she's used to things the way they are.

It's time to get going. What should I wear? I don't want to wear something fancy, like those white lace Communion dresses I see little girls in at Easter. The priest or minister may think I want to convert to Christianity. I put on a yellow skirt and white blouse with short sleeves and a black patent leather belt with flats to match. My white short cotton gloves are the icing that makes me feel proper. When I come downstairs Mom looks me up and down without saying anything, but her eyes are disapproving. It's not about the clothes I'm wearing because she bought them for me.

Mom, Ruby and I get into the station wagon and drive to Ruby's church. I concentrate on the roads that look familiar—same ones we took to Ethel's and Ruby's houses. I am happy to be going back to where they live. I brought my camera and take pictures whenever we're stopped.

Finally, I see a large sign that says "Baptist Church of Jesus." It's a small brown wooden building—like a house—

tucked among mature trees. There are cars parked on the weeds and grass in front and on the sides of the church. The big cross on the roof is rusty and leans toward the ground like a tornado hit it. My two inch heels sink into the muddy ground when I get out of the car. Ruby gets out of the backseat. Mom stays in the driver's seat watching us go in. I notice a book on the front: *Marjorie Morningstar.* I guess she's going to read till we come out.

I can hear singing, loud and clear and fast. I spot a large colored family all dressed in fancy outfits: suits, ties, and hats for the men and boys, dresses, blouses, and white gloves just like mine for the women and girls. Children point at me because they can see I'm in a place where I don't belong. The preacher holds the door for us. He tips his hat to Ruby and Ruby says hello. The large family all look at me with suspicion but the mom smiles and the dad tips his hat to me twice, like we approve of you being here, so don't you worry about a thing, now.

The backless benches are worn, wooden, and narrow. Ruby takes my hand, nodding to people as we walk to our seats in the third row. I see everyone look at me. They nod at me more than Ruby. I feel at home with Ruby in her church.

The minister is singing with the congregation. He wears a black robe that hangs down to the ground, its skirt grazing the floor. The tattered bottom part of the robe goes up and down when he intermittently jumps during the song. As soon as one song ends, another one begins; it's like there's a program that everyone knows—including Ruby—without looking at words on a page. When colored slaves weren't allowed to learn to read, they had to learn their music by heart.

Some of the people shake tambourines and wave their

arms in wide swoops above their heads. Children are in the aisles dancing with their whole bodies, not just their feet. They don't have partners, but just move to the music with their heads, arms, and legs. Soon the minister points to a few people, inviting them up on the stage, which is only one step up from the floor. At my parents' temple, the rabbi and cantor are several steps above the people, but here the adults and children are on the stage singing and dancing together. One or two songs seem sad, like slaves might have sung in the fields. The charismatic minister motions for the singing to stop and everyone to listen.

The minister talks loudly and melodically, almost like he's singing: "God works his powers through songs and gives us positive power to fulfill the American dream of freedom. We will all receive equal, just, and fair treatment in all our ways throughout our daily lives. Songs are emotional releases and courageous ways to join the movement that is God-inspired. He will take care of us. In the book of Esther it tells how God saved the Israelite nation through Esther. Women in our churches are inspired by Esther. Our Exodus is traveling from fear to peace and joy and equality in our land."

He goes to the people up on the stage and blesses them with his hands and asks them to shout out their fervent prayers.

They shout, "Freedom. Power. Peace. Love. Health for my granddaughter. Joy for my brother and wife. God is everywhere. Our souls are alive in Heaven forever." There are many things being called out but I cannot differentiate because everyone is shouting together.

After they shout, songs start again, even louder than before with more children in the aisles. Some women hold their babies and dance slowly and steadily with their eyes closed. I keep looking at Ruby to see what she does. When she sings, I hum. When she stands, I stand. When she moves her body, I move mine.

Sometimes I see her glance at me when I am looking at everyone and I know what she is thinking—she is proud of me, but she doesn't want the responsibility of trying to make me happy even though she knows what it takes to make a child happy. I think Ruby wants to shake my mom and scream at her about how easy it is to love me if Mom would just spend time with me. Oh, maybe Ruby isn't thinking this at all, but I wish she was. I have no idea really what Ruby is thinking. For all I know she could want to get out of here and have a drink of whiskey, just like I think Dad wants his drink when things get difficult.

The people leave by moving and singing after the minister leaves. When we go out of the church, we shake hands with the minister and Ruby nods, shakes hands and hugs a lot of people. Some of them even hug and shake my hand. She looks so relaxed and comfortable in her movements and her voice. She has so much confidence. I want to be like her someday.

We get in Mom's car. I help Ruby into the backseat and sit beside her. I know this makes Mom and Ruby uncomfortable. Mom turns and gives me a look that could kill. Then I look at Ruby before I close the door. Her eyes say, *why do this when Mom let you go with me to church?* I feel good in the back for a few minutes with Ruby. Then I open the back door and get in the front.

"Well, dear, how did you like it?" Mom asks with some slight sarcasm.

"I loved it, Mom. It was fun, joyous, and warm; like a party." I tell her, not caring if the truth hurts her feelings.

The rest of the drive is quiet so I hum the church songs. Mom looks at me with a disapproving look and shakes her head, but I still hum. When we reach Ruby's house, I don't ask to go in because I am grateful I got to experience Ruby's church and Mom's look tells me I should just let Ruby out of the car. Ruby and I hug goodbye from my window. Mom's tires screech as she drives away quickly. The car talks for Mom.

"Rachael, I'm glad you liked the service. I hope it made you see that synagogue is where you belong—with your own people," Mom states coldly.

"I want to think about how I feel about all of that and not say where I belong just yet." I take a deep breath, then ask fearlessly, "Mom, why are you working almost every day?"

"Well, dear, sometimes, when Dad gets busy in the other store, he needs me to help more than usual. Don't worry, dear, it's nothing for you to concern yourself with. I love working in our store. Are you enjoying it?"

"It's okay. Clothes are not my favorite things to be around. It'd be more fun if Dad owned a bowling alley or a skating rink."

"I know, dear. I'm sure you would like that more," Mom says with sadness in her voice.

I hope she understands I'm confused about where I belong. For the first time she actually brought me somewhere I wanted to go—to church with Ruby.

When we get out of the car at home, I hug Mom—first time I hugged her first that I can remember.

"Thank you, Mom, for taking me today." A stray tear

escapes my eye and rolls down my cheek.

"Okay, dear," Mom says drying my wet cheek with her white gloved hand, not even caring if it gets smudgy. My mom wears gloves just to drive the car.

We go into the back door, past the empty kitchen—it's Ethel's day off—and up the stairs together. I stop at the phone desk in the hall to pick up the ringing phone.

"Hi, Rachael." It's Mitch. I know his voice. "Want to go to a movie next Saturday night?"

"Um. That's my birthday." No response. "Mitch, what's wrong?"

"So, want to go?"

"How did you know?"

"A little peacock told me."

"Sixteen is a big deal for girls. I already told Mom I didn't want any kind of party, luncheon or presents so let me check with her to make sure she didn't plan a family dinner. I'll call you back, Mitchey." I like the sound of "ey" at the end of his name. "Oh, wait! I want to call that realty company. Can you figure out a way for me to call again? I don't know where to call from without someone hearing me. Can you call for me and just ask if our house is going up for sale? You can say you heard it was and you may be interested in buying it. Just act and sound like a grown-up, please," I say desperately.

"Can we talk business in person when I see you?"

"Okay," I laugh thinking how funny he is.

Every night during the summer I hear Dad's car in the driveway. It's the only time of the year my windows are open all day and night, even if the air conditioner is on so I can listen for Dad's car. The sound of the car tonight is different. I look out my window and see it: a bright new red convertible. I know it's an MG because the MG plate is huge on the front of the car and it stands out in black and white capitals, with the regular Missouri plate on the back. My heart pounds in my throat. A new car! We're not moving and our money is okay! I run into Jessy's room and tell her to hurry outside with me to see the new car. Mom is already sitting in the car when Rusty, Jessy and I get there.

"Dad, red! This is the coolest car a kid can have!" shouts Rusty.

"A kid. Well, yes. I am a kid," Dad laughs.

"Nice, Dad," I say puzzled and happy at the same time.

"Yeah, Dad, nice," Jessy says unfazed.

"Yeah, girls."

Mom is smiling constantly, like really old people do about nothing. She looks at all of us and then at Dad and the car, and then at us again. She does this over and over. She has this confused look staring into the backyard and then over at the car with a stupid smile.

"Your Mom and I are going for a spin," Dad announces.

I hope the "spin" isn't to talk about the money Dad shouldn't have spent on the car. Mom looks worried and excited about the car. I think Mom would like to go back in time, when Dad was picking her up for a date, showing off his new car.

They take off. Jessy and I run upstairs to her room.

"Jess, what does this mean? I think Mom and Dad are in trouble money-wise and we have to move to a new house—a smaller one—but now Dad buys a new car. When Mom didn't go to New York and then I discovered Dad is phoning real estate agents at work. I know that money—the unspeakable word around here—was probably the reason. Add that to the fact that you and I aren't going on the trip with Dad to New York for our birthdays. Isn't it obvious that it's a money issue? I didn't talk to you about this before because all you really care about is your boyfriend. But with the new MG, it looks like everything is back to normal."

"Rach, you worry too much. They'd tell us if we were moving. We've been here sixteen years and nothing is going to change. Now excuse me, I have to use the phone."

"Fine," I say, angry, and slam Jessy's door. She never talks to me about important stuff. If I told her I was going to kill myself she would probably say, "I have to get ready for my date."

I go into my room and lie on the bed thinking about the people at Ruby's church. Their happiness doesn't come from money—if it did, they would never be happy. Our family's happiness shouldn't be from money either. I'm embarrassed that Ethel, Bernice and Bill will see the red car in the morning when they come to work. Just what they need to be reminded of—another thing they can't ever afford.

Ruby comes into my room the next morning, "Honey, yo' daddy just got himself a new shiny car. Don't that make you happy?"

"Honestly, Ruby, that's a joke. If he got ten new cars I

wouldn't care."

"Okay, whatcha wanna talk 'bout?"

"Ruby, I'm almost sixteen and I feel like sixty."

"Honey, I knows what you mean."

"You mean at sixteen you felt old?"

"I felt old at five."

"Ruby," I can feel my face turn into a frown, "we may move. I hear things and feel things. I don't care as long as you come with us." Now I start to pout. "No one talks about anything around here except 'pass the butter.' Maybe Dad got a new car because when we move he wants to have something nice because the next house will not be as nice." Why did you feel old at five?"

"Honey, don't go askin' me about five. When you done growed up, then we will talk about me. Don't you knows a house is straw and bricks, not love and sweet times? Now get up off that bed and see what you's doin' tonight."

"Jane wants me to go to the movies. But I just want to lie here and be with you. Can I borrow some of your magazines and hair cream?"

"For what?"

"Just to play. Please?"

"No-- now Rachael, honey, please get off that bed and call Jane—or I will."

"Okay, but let me just think for a minute with you sitting here. I just like to sit with you and know you are here."

Ruby puts her hand on my head like she is blessing me. We don't talk and our eyes sometimes meet and we smile. Ruby takes my hand in hers for a moment and then stands up and gives me a pull so I get up. I follow her to the back staircase and watch her skip down the stairs. I wait a minute until she disappears. I can hear Nana on the phone in her room but she can't see me on the back stairs. She talks loud, like she's getting deaf. She is talking about where she will live and she sounds worried. She says she hasn't lived alone for so long. I wait to hear more but she hangs up.

I run to the telephone to call Jane. But when I get to the phone I don't dial her number. I don't want to tell her about moving away yet. It feels so confusing to be thinking that we are moving away from the home I have always known. I take a deep breath and finally call Jane. When she answers, we just talk about the movie we're going to see. Everything I really want to tell her I keep inside. She says Ruth, her older sister, is driving us and picking us up, so I get ready.

It was fun pretending everything is the same and the movie, *Seven Brides for Seven Brothers,* took my worries away. Sometimes I can't even tell a close friend what's important to talk about.

Even though today is Monday, Dad doesn't go to work and he tells me not to go. He says we're going somewhere. We all get into the station wagon. Dad drives past the club. We all start asking him where he's taking us. He doesn't answer. Mom just says they have a surprise to show us. We drive for another ten minutes and park in front of a house.

"Kids, this is your new house. Let's get out," Dad says, his voice filled with excitement.

"What?" Jessy says, shocked.

"Mom, I don't want to move." Rusty holds onto Mom as he cries.

"Told you," I whisper to Jessy.

We all climb out of the car and stand on the curb looking at the house. No one steps onto the sidewalk: it's like it's a magnetic wall pulling us away from moving forward with our lives.

"Let's go in," Dad says as he walks toward the front door.

A one story—wood house painted light brown with dark brown trim, it sits on top of a hill steep enough to offer a great sled ride. The two brown colors remind me of Ruby, Ethel, Bernice and Bill. The trees are sparse and not fully grown, like Jessy, Rusty and me.

"Wait, Dad. Why are we moving? I want to know before we go in."

Dad turns around and faces all of us.

"Look, kids, here are the facts: your Dad can't make enough money to stay where we are. This new house will allow us to enjoy our lives. I need to close one of the stores. It costs too much to keep both and St. Louis doesn't have enough customers for two stores. This house is smaller but we won't need as much room. Your grandmother will have her own place. The neighborhood is nice and we will meet new neighbors and feel more like we belong here." Dad says all this like a prepared speech that doesn't take into account that each of us has feelings about change.

I can't move. My feet are embedded in the sidewalk.

Jessy hugs me and pulls me up the endless front walk and into the front door after everyone is already inside. A woman is standing at the front door welcoming me, like I am entering an airplane. An attic smell comes at me from a darkness seems to cover my skin. If there are any windows, they are covered in green heavy cloth that drags on the grass colored carpet. I hear footsteps echoing all around, like the kind I hear going upstairs in my house when only the maids and I are home. Jessy drags me away from the front hall to the kitchen where the source of footsteps comes from.

Dad, Mom, and Rusty are looking at the stove like it is a mysterious rocket ship. If Ethel doesn't work for us anymore, Mom will have to learn to cook. Ethel knows how to work the stove so everything tastes magnificent. Mom will be lost in this wilderness called "kitchen." While Mom and Dad look inside the stove and cabinets, I hope a mouse or spider jumps out at them. I'm already so frightened, it wouldn't even bother me.

"Rachael, maybe we can fit the table from our kitchen in here. Would you like that?" Mom knows I spend a lot of time at the kitchen table with Ethel and she thinks the table will make me feel good.

"Sure, Mom. Fine," I say in a dream state.

"Okay, let's go to the bedrooms." Mom leads everyone out.

"Oh, great. We get to share again," Jess states, furious and annoyed. She runs out of the room down the hall, leaving me standing there in our new bedroom.

"Where's Ruby's room? Where's Bernice and Bill's room?" I shout into the echoing hall. But I know, with money problems and all of us kids growing up, there won't be any help living here. But that's not why we need them, I yell inside my head. I need them because they are my best friends. Where will Ruby work? And Bernice, Bill and Ethel? I have to find them jobs.

No one answers.

"We won't need the help." I say this out loud but quietly as I sink to my knees.

No one had to answer. I know. My heart is gone without them. I suddenly remember the story asking if, when a tree falls in the woods, there is any noise if no one is in the woods to hear it. I am that tree. There is no heart to feel inside me if they are gone.

Jessy bounces back into our bedroom and points to the drapes—the same puke green drapes that are everywhere. I pull open the drapes. The windows are grimy and thick with cobwebs, spider webs, and black and brown goo. No wonder they're covered up. The window stretches across the wall of the room with wood frames that were once painted brown but are now gooey as car grease with few remaining flecks of paint. I gag and run to the bathroom. Jessy runs after me.

"Jessy, I don't care what the house looks like or how small it is. I only care about being with Ruby, Ethel, Bernice and Bill. You know I love them so much," I say nervously.

Jessy doesn't say anything back. I think about Ethel's house, small but warm with love. Mom and Dad can fix the floors, carpets, drapes, dirt and scum but they will be able to never fix the hole in my heart from missing my real family. I sit on the pink dirty tile floor with my head over the toilet while Jessy calls Mom. I don't want her to see me.

Jessy holds my head. I gag some more but I don't throw up.
I go out to the backyard with Jessy. Mom and Dad are
there, too.

Other than the birds chirping in the tall trees, the yard
is silent. If I was six I would like the yard. It has bushes
around a nice grassy lawn. There are some dirty swings and
a dilapidated playhouse. We all circle around like horses
going back to the barn. Mom and Dad have blank looks
that match mine.

When Mom or Dad says something about fixing the
house up I can't hear the exact words. I don't care what
they want to do to it.

We leave the house and drive to the club. I spend all
my time in the pool, mostly under the water. Jessy jumps in
with her friends to splash, talk, and see if I am okay or if I
want to eat. Sometimes I see Mom dangling her legs over
the side of the pool with a cigarette, hat shading her from
the sun, a drink in hand, talking to her friends. Her hands
always move when she talks. I see her look at me, but she
doesn't see me wave. I drink frosty Cokes all day and listen
to the screams and laughter of young kids playing. I hold in
my screams.

# 17
# SWEET SIXTEEN

My birthday is tomorrow, Saturday. I can't wait. Sixteen is so grown up. I love my birthday because each year I get to start from scratch, like a clean wet blackboard, and I can hope everything will be different with my family. I will be treasured and loved like I want and Mom and Dad will realize how special I am. This birthday will be the one I hope will start a fair world where everyone is treated the same and I will have Ruby, Ethel, Bernice and Bill every day.

I wake up in the morning with Ruby standing over me singing "Happy Birthday" in a sweet voice, like an angel. My mind starts thinking of her not being here.

"Thanks, Ruby." I hug her and she hugs back like sugar falling all over.

"Get up chil' and get goin'. You only sixteen once."

"I know. After breakfast I'm going swimming at the

Casey's with a bunch of kids. Want to come?"

"Who, me, chil'? No. I has to work and make yo' special day nice. Now get on down to breakfast. Ethel made you something nice. Mommy and Daddy already left for work. Rusty is at camp and Jessy is still sleeping. She goin' with you to swim."

I wake Jessy and we bound down the stairs. Ethel has birthday candles in the waffles. Bernice, Bill, Ethel, Ruby, and Jessy sing to me. I smell a cake in the oven. I see the caramel frosting in a bowl on the counter as it is every birthday. Caramel is happiness in a bowl. We walk to the Casey's. I remember how three years ago my neck got a rope burn and I wasn't allowed to wear a two piece bathing suit. The past three years have been the hardest in my life: I learned to live without Peggy; I learned to care more about other people—all the Negroes who are treated so unfairly; I learned to care for those who sincerely show appreciable caring for me—not Mom and Dad, but Mitch, the help, and a few girlfriends.

The day is going by fast; swimming, talking, and playing cards with neighbors and Jane. Jane surprises me by coming. She says she doesn't want to be left out of my birthday. I don't expect Tommy to show up or even know it's my birthday.

Jane gives me a bra with lace trim and underpants to match in bright pink. My face is the color of the fabric when I look up and see the neighborhood boys looking. I wish I had invited Mitch. He's always there to save me; he'd tell me it's alright to be embarrassed—that's life, he'd say. He always gives me a look or says just what I need.

The pool party is over by late afternoon and Jessy and I skip happily back home, like we are three and four-year-olds. I know this feeling of Jess being close to me is contradicting the awful dread of moving. If only she would be this way with me all the time.

Later that day, when I'm upstairs in my room, Ruby tells me that Mitch is at the door.

Before I go downstairs, I put on the new bra and underpants Jane gave me and slip on a yellow linen dress. My shoes are espadrilles that have a wedge heel. Ruby hurriedly fixes my hair in a twist. Jessy says I look grown up and I feel grown up. We hug goodbye. I knock on Mom and Dad's door to say goodbye hug.

Ruby fooled me. Ruby, Ethel, Bernice and Bill are in the kitchen with caramel cupcakes spread over the whole kitchen table—there must be twelve of them. They each have one or two candles in them and they sing "Happy Birthday." My heart is beaming. I hug Ruby first and then the others. The warmth comes off their bodies and heats the room. I am loved. I can feel their love and I love them. Each one has a gift for me. I open Ruby's first. It's a picture of her whole family with a calendar of the month of June drawn below the picture. Ethel's is the recipe for caramel cake so I can make it someday for my own family. Bernice and Bill's is some colored thread and needles so I can sew my own rips. I'm overwhelmed and can't find words to say how I feel. I hear the doorbell. It is Mitch, my lifesaver.

When we get in the car, he tells me Ruby called to tell him to be a few minutes late because she had a surprise for me. Ruby plans everything that is precious to me.

First we drive to Steak 'N Shake to eat. We sit at a table in a corner.

"Mitch, I saw the new house I'm going to be moving

to. Forget calling the realty company. No secret anymore. You wouldn't believe the charm it has," I sarcastically say.

"What?" Mitch's been looking at the menu like he's never seen it before.

"Oh, didn't you hear what I said?"

"Sure. You said you're moving to a haunted house?" Mitch jokes and I hear his stomach growling.

"Sort of. It's the color of throw-up everywhere," I joke back.

"What color would you want it to be?"

"Maybe boogers."

We both laugh.

"Rachael, your parents will fix it up. Don't worry—it's your birthday."

He gives me a present; from Saks Fifth Avenue. I open the box. It's a scarf and pin. My mouth is shaped like an O, ready to say "Oh, Mitch, I really like the gift," when some kids from school come over to our table. While we are talking to them, I look over at the door and see Tommy coming in with some other kids from school.

In walks the pretty blonde girl that everyone talks about plus two guys I know and two other girls. That means they are in twos, a triple date. The other girls look like they are fifteen. One has the shiniest brown hair I've ever seen; it's so long; down to her butt. She walks on her toes like she's dancing and she's laughing with her girlfriend who has short black curly hair and wears bright red lipstick. I can't see her face.

My heart is in my throat. I pretend I don't see Tommy, but he walks toward our table.

"Hi, Rachael, happy sixteenth. Where's the birthday party?"

"No party so I didn't invite you," I say quickly. I sense a little jealousy from him, seeing me with Mitch. and it feels indulgent.

Tommy leans over and kisses me on the lips with his cherry red lips. Maybe he has red lipstick leftover from the girl with the short black hair. The kiss is long. He smells like a tropical ocean breeze. My heart is beating and my face is burning. As soon as he pulls away, Mitch kisses me on the lips—longer than Tommy. My heart is beating even harder and I don't know if it's for Mitch or Tommy. I see him grimace as Mitch kisses me; then he walks away and sits at the table with his friends, putting his arm around the red-lipped girl. If he does have her lipstick on it is now mixed with mine.

"Okay, Mitch, sixteen and kissed by two guys!"

"Okay, let's order," Mitch says. His face is as red as a sunburn.

The waitress comes over to take our order. I order a Coke and French fries. Mitch orders five or six things—I don't even listen, it might make me feel sick. I look around to see if Tommy still has his arm around red-lip girl. I see some colored kids being led to a corner table that is surrounded by empty tables and is far away from everyone else. My stomach cramps, like it's screaming at the unfairness these kids must be feeling. My head automatically goes down, like I'm praying in Ruby's church.

"Rachael, what's wrong? Don't be sad on your birthday."

"Mitch, I have to do something tonight. Remember the store window I was fixing up when you came into Dad's shop with your mom?"

"Yeah, I do. They were big naked dolls until you dressed them."

"I have to go there tonight and do something. I need some brown make up, *Ebony* magazines and colored hair products. Ruby has all of the stuff I need in her room. I have to go there and get it. I am going to paint one of the faces brown with the makeup and put the magazines and hair stuff in the window to show that colored people are welcome at the store. I know I will get punished for it, but I don't care."

"Rachael, I can't. I'll get in trouble. Why do you have to do this?"

"Because colored people can't even get their music on the radio. Did you know they call colored music "Race Music" and they have white singers on the radio to sing the songs the colored talented writers worked hard on because if the DJ's play the recordings by colored people they'll get fired? Colored people would make more money if they could get the same jobs white people have or could sing their own songs. I can't sit back and not even let them in my dad's store to shop. If they see the colored face and their magazines and products, they'll know we think they're welcome. Please do this with me, Mitch. You'll feel good about it.

"This is not the kind of stuff I like to do, Rach. Let's go bowling or to a movie—you know, normal stuff."

"Okay, don't do it with me," I say, feeling let down. "I'll do it alone. Just drive me home to get the stuff from Ruby's room and wait in the car. I'll be really fast. Then we'll drive to the store. I'll put it in the window myself— you don't have to do a thing. Just drive me there."

"Wait, you want me to be an accomplice to this?"

"Yes! It's the only thing I want to do tonight. Please!" I'm begging, but it's so important to me.

"Okay, but if we go to jail, we'll have a record and never get into college."

"Mitch, sometimes you have to take risks if you believe in something."

"But I don't believe in what you are doing. You're like a Freedom Rider."

"How do you know about the Freedom Riders?"

"How do you know?" Mitch asks.

"Ruby showed me the colored newspaper the other day and I read all about it—I read it three times. I excitidly say.

"I was playing basketball in Shaw Park with some colored boys and they kept talking about it. I asked to tell me what the Freedom Riders were. It's shocking." Mitch said, looking at me intently.

"Mitch, no one even knows about it in our town. It probably was in a tiny article in the paper. Mom and Dad never mentioned it. But this is what I know: last month, in May, a bunch of college kids took buses from the Northern states to the Southern states to test the anti-discrimination laws that were passed years ago. The separate waiting rooms for white and colored in train stations and bus stations are still in existence. There were white and colored drinking fountains and colored people couldn't sit at white counters in drugstores or even ride buses, unless they sat in the back.

"The Ku Klux Klan burned one of the Freedom Riders' buses and the kids were beaten up. Many of them landed in jail. President Kennedy didn't want to deal with all these civil rights issues because he's worried about Russia and the Cold War. But finally there were so many Freedom Riders coming to Montgomery, Alabama, and so many of them had been thrown in this one jail, the President had to send in the National Guard to help free them and get new laws passed. Hoover, the head of the FBI, didn't even stop the KKK. This just happened a few weeks ago."

Mitch just sat there in silence, staring off into space.

"Mitch, did you hear me?"

He shook himself. "I did and it is frieghtening that we don't even know what's happening because if everyone knew…whew, if I knew, I'd be on the bus with the Freedom Riders, Rach."

My heart swells with joy as my friend says those words. He can't possibly know how much it means to me that we see eye to eye on this.

The food comes. I drink my Coke and eat a few fries while Mitch consumes a hamburger, milkshake, fries, salad, and apple pie. We are quiet. I think he wants to help me but he doesn't want to get in trouble with my parents or his. I understand because he isn't close to his help like I am. I don't know anyone who feels about their help the way I do Mitch hasn't heard how Ruby or any of the help at my home talk to me. It's hard for him or anyone to understand our relationship.

"When I learned all that," I break the silence, "I cried thinking, if I were only a few years older I would have been a Freedom Rider on a bus testing those laws too. The one thing that the Freedom Riders did that no one expected was they were peaceful. They didn't fight back when they were beaten up. They showed the world they just wanted what all people deserve—for colored people to have the same rights that white people get." I felt the blood rise in my neck to my cheeks. "I probably sound like a history teacher. But there is this one colored leader who's been written about a lot; Martin Luther King, Jr. Have you heard about him?"

Mitch shakes his head no.

"He helped the Freedom Rider keep going by telling them not to give up. They were in a church and he was talking to them about being peaceful and to continue protesting until they got what they deserved. They were all afraid the KKK would try to burn the church down.

Mitch sat there in silence again for a long moment. Then he spoke up. "Want to go, Rach?"

"Thanks for dinner, Mitch. Even though you aren't going to help me, I want you to know I appreciate you talking to me about what I am so upset about."

"I can't turn you down, Rach."

"What did you say?"

"Okay. Just let's do it before I think too much and change my mind."

Mitch and I go into my house. In the living room I see plates, glasses, napkins and a balloon tied onto the leg of the coffee table. Ruby probably put it there before she left. We tiptoe upstairs—in case Rusty is home and grab the stuff I need from Ruby's room and run outside. I go in Mom and Dad's room and get brown shoe polish and rags from Dad's shoe kit. I take the extra house key because I know it will fit the store. It's the only other key on Dad's keychain when he drives. I am sweating like I ran three miles. I throw it in the car and get in.

Mitch and I drive silently to the store. As we approach, I see Saks Fifth Avenue and think of Mom shopping there in New York and the broken promise of Dad taking me there for this birthday. I wish he wanted to show me off.

The streets are pretty deserted, like they always are here on weekends. Mitch finds parking real close to the store. I get the key out and open the door. I go back to the car and get the rest of the stuff. I turn on the lights and put the stuff in the window. My hands are shaking but I don't care.

I put the magazines out on the floor of the window and arrange the cosmetics nearby. I spread newspaper out on the floor and put Ruby's jar of brown liquid make-up on it mixed with Dad's shoe polish. It's a little lighter brown than Ruby's skin. Ethel; Bernice, Bill, and Ruby are all different shades of brown. I pour some on a rag and begin applying it to the face of one of the mannequins. It looks splotchy and uneven. I keep going over it until the face color is as even as I can make it. The arms are covered with cream colored gloves up to the elbow so the face is the only part I have to color. I wish I had brown face powder to smooth out the color. I wish I had more of a story—books, records, colored newspapers.

I look out the window and see Mitch sitting in the car. He is staring straight ahead-- looking to see if any cops are around. He keeps the car running the whole time. Even though I am doing this alone, I feel Peggy and Ruby with me. For a moment, I think of taking it all down and rubbing the face clean before it dries. I go outside and look at the window, looking proud at my reflection. I am now a part of the window and the story. I go over to Mitch's car and knock on the passenger side window, snapping him out of his trance.

"Are you okay?" I ask.

"Yes, Rachael, let's go. I don't like this."

I get into the car with the shoe polish and rags and look back at the window. I am sixteen and all grown up. If I never do another great thing in my life I will always know I have helped an enduring problem.

Mitch lets me off at my front walk. It's 11:45 at night. He doesn't even get out to open my door. I think he just wants this day to end.

"Bye, Mitch. Thanks for the best birthday ever," I kiss him on the cheek. He looks surprised.

"Bye, Rachael. And you're welcome."

He zooms off, leaving a rubber smell.

Tomorrow is Sunday so the store will be closed. Dad won't see it until Monday. I want Mitch to drive me past the store and see if anyone is looking at the window—maybe around one o'clock after church and lunch is over.

In the house, Mom, Dad, Jessy and Rusty are waiting for me in the living room. They sing "Happy Birthday" as I walk in and I see presents. It's late and but I can tell that Mom, Dad, and Jessy probably just got home from an evening of socializing. They must have awakened Rusty to join the party.

I can smell the shoe polish on my hands. I tell them I have to go to the bathroom. I wash all the shoe polish off my hands and hide the paper bag with the polish and rags behind the shower curtain.

A dark caramel cake—the same color as the few leftover polish smudges on my fingers—is on the coffee table with seventeen candles. Mom lights the candles. They sing again and I blow out the candles in one breath. My wish is that I will always be true to myself no matter what anyone says.

I open Dad's present first. It's a fishing pole with some fishing gadgets. I've never even said I wanted to go fishing but maybe he would like to take me fishing. I kiss Dad on the cheek—it feels soggy and cold. Everyone is too tired to question this gift or even care—although Rusty and Jessy look both puzzled and intrigued.

"Slim, I want to take you fishing with me."

"Thanks, Dad, let's do that." At sixteen I thought he knew that I have no interest in cars, fishing, golf, or poker. Maybe he could have interested me in these things earlier in my life, but it's too late.

"Okay," Dad says with a gleam in his eye and a smile. He never shows his teeth when he smiles. I know he's trying to make up for making us move. But a gleam and smile—and a fishing pole—won't do.

Mom's hands me a small box. It's wrapped beautifully.

"Mom, I said I didn't want presents."

"I know dear, but we had already bought this for you

before you said that."

Mom's eyes are watering. She knows nothing will help make me feel better about moving.

I open the box. It is a string of white cultured pearls with a gold clasp. They are lustrous.

"Oh, instead of my add-a-pearls?" I say.

"Yes, these are the grown up kind. You can give your add-a-pearls to your own little girl someday."

I loved getting a pearl each birthday for my add-a-pearl necklace. It is the one thing Mom and Dad gave me that I treasure because I watched the necklace grow with me.

I open Rusty and Jessy's present— a new Brownie camera. The one I have is four years old and this one has a better flash attachment and a bigger viewing area. I'm so excited—this is one present I want. I wish I had brought my camera to the store tonight so that I could have photographed the window. I know it's possible that it will all be taken down before I see it again.

"Thank you so much. I love it." I hug Jessy real hard and Rusty warmly. They hug back like they love me.

We all eat caramel cake and drink milk.

"Where did Mitch take you?" Jessy asks.

"We went to Steak 'n' Shake and just stayed there until I came home. There were kids there from school."

"All this time?" Mom asks. Then she lowers her voice. "Please, children, don't mention to the help about moving. I will tell them in due course."

"What, why is it a secret?" I ask.

"Who was there?" Jessy asks, as if she didn't hear Mom.

"I'll tell you tomorrow. I'm tired right now," I say to my sister.

"Girls and Rusty, please do as I say. It is best not to tell them yet. I don't want them to know until we can give them an exact time we are moving, and we don't know when that is yet." Mom is glaring at me as she speaks.

Jessy gives me a look like there is something else going on and it's not about not telling the maids. She might think Mitch and I made out in his car after dinner or did something other than stay at Steak 'n Shake all night. I always cover for her when she isn't home on time so she knows not to push me to give answers right now.

We all say goodnight and hug each other like we always do.

In bed, I can't stop thinking about what I did tonight. I don't think I can sleep and I don't care. I wish Ruby were here and I could talk everything over with her. I don't think she'd like what I did because she's afraid now to do rebellious things. She would not be sympathetic and bawl me out. She would say, "Shame on you," and make a sucking sound with her tongue against her gums about five times in a row. Grandma and Nana do this when they don't approve of what someone has done. I think Ruby learned it from them.

Somehow I fall asleep but in the morning I have a nightmare that wakes me up with a start. I don't remember what it was about. I call Mitch.

"Please, Mitch, please just drive me by the store around

one o'clock. I want to see if anyone is looking in the window or maybe the cops took it down," I say in a pleading voice.

"Okay, I'll pick you up," Mitch says right away. I think he's curious now too.

We sit in the car in front of the store. There is a colored family looking in the window for a while. They look happy when they walk away. Some white adults walk by and point and shake their heads. They are angry. Then white and colored families are standing looking together. Most of these folks probably came from one of the churches down the street, or out taking a Sunday stroll.

I wish I could hear what they're saying. The white woman is looking at the colored woman and then at the window. The white adults leave first, whispering to each other. Maybe they will at least talk about some things that are usually forbidden. I'm so thrilled; I'm cheering silently as I turn to Mitch.

"Mitch, I'm going to clean it all up before Dad sees it tomorrow. I already feel better about doing the window and I want to tell Mom and Dad what I did and reactions to people walking by. Dad will never leave it like this, but maybe he'll think about it." I can take pictures so Mom and Dad will believe me."

Mitch listens and nods his head in agreement. He actually pushes me out of the car. He can't get any words out, but he sighs with relief.

I get out of the car and take pictures of the people, colored and white looking at the window too. I shoot all angles. The people watch me. I open the store and take pictures of the people looking at the window from inside. I take more shots of the window display from the inside. As soon as this group of people leave, I start cleaning up. Gathering the magazines and other props is easy. The hardest part is removing the brown shoe polish. I've wet a cloth and I rub and I rub, but I can't get it all off. When I explain everything to Mom and Dad tonight I will tell them there are a few smudges I couldn't remove. I hope Dad will let the smudges stay.

After dinner, when Mom and Dad are in their bedroom, I knock and say I have something I need to tell them. Mom pats the side of the bed, inviting me to sit down.

"Mitch drove me to the store Saturday night and I went inside with your key, Dad. I…I changed the windows." I kind of blurt this out, uncertain of how to explain myself.

"What do you mean, you changed the windows?"

I can tell that Dad is going to be angry. But I don't care. "Well," I say in a strong voice, "I wanted the store to be for everyone; not just rich white people, so I used some shoe polish to make some of the mannequins look like Negros."

"Shoe polish! What on earth are you telling us?" Mom says harshly.

"I put some *Ebony* magazines on the floor of the window display, and I took pictures of everything in the window and even of the people walking by looking. When they're developed I'll show them to you. I cleaned everything up this morning, so don't worry, okay?"

"Rachael," Dad says, shaking his head, "I'm very disappointed in you. You surprise Mom and me with your rebelliousness. And dragging Mitch in on it. If I pressed criminal charges, he would be guilty, too, just for driving you."

"I'm sorry I had to bring Mitch into it but I just had to do something on my birthday for the Negro people." The silence in the room shakes me. I know I have to tell them everything. "There are still some smudges on the mannequins that didn't come off. Maybe Bill has something that will clean them up better." I'm nervous about what Mom and Dad will do to me.

"You know, Rachael, I'm not going to do anything to punish you," Dad says. A whoosh of relief escapes me. "You came and told us," he goes on, "and if nothing is ruined permanently, then so be it. I think the upcoming move has brought out some resentment toward Mom and me because you don't want to leave your home. Your concern for people with less than us is honorable. I want to forget about it, and I'm sure your mother does as well. We have too much else on our minds," Dad says looking over at Mom as he speaks.

I hug them both fiercely. "Thank you for not punishing me." I have never before felt such understanding from Mom and Dad.

# 18
# RUNAWAY

Every day Ruby and Bill help Mom pack. They started in the attic last week and are still at it; there's so much stuff up here. It's Saturday and I'm up with them to see what they're doing. The smell of mothballs and wool mixed with dust and musty papers brings back my entire childhood in one whiff. I don't go up here much but when I do every breath is mixed with sadness, joy, and regret. I'm not sure where one feeling starts and the other stops. It's like a mixing bowl of ingredients together; it all blends in one finger lick. It's sad to see faded old toys in their original boxes from all four of us at different ages haphazardly piled on wooden shelves. I don't remember giving my toys enough time to be sent off to the attic like a prison sentence. I wish I could recall the times I spent with them and could remember if I was happy.

As I was on my way upstairs to the attic I passed Mom coming down.

"Hi, Mom. I'm coming up to help you."

"Okay. Ruby's in the closet, getting things sorted. You can help her. I'll be back in a few moments after I make a phone call."

"Hi, child. What you doin' up here?" Ruby calls warmly from the closet. I go over to her and we hug like she hadn't just seen me this morning at breakfast.

I walk into the closet, which is a big room.

"Ruby, I want to be with you. I don't care what I have to do just to be with you more before we move. I can't stand thinking about leaving you and not seeing you every day for the rest of my life. I'm so worried that you don't have a job now. Or do you?"

"Now, girl, you quit yo' worryin'. Bill told me about a place where he and Bernice is thinking of working. They need a housekeeper and I's gonna meet the people the same time they's goin' to, so don't you go worryin' yo' little head, okay?"

"Okay. But what will I do without you to look after me?"

"Rachael, you old enough to look after yo'self. You gonna be fine," Ruby says, hanging up a coat that fell on the floor.

"I don't care if I'm a hundred. I want you to be with me." I hear Mom coming back and we stop talking about leaving.

As they go through the clothes, I guess that Ruby is thinking of how much money each cost while Mom is reminiscing about which party she wore them to. I wonder if Mom thinks romantically about the times she wore them, hanging on Dad's arm, walking into a party or dinner, just the two of them—with us four at home.

Mom's furs are stored in beautiful brown cotton clothing bags. Each bag has a tag noting the type of fur. There are seven or eight of these hanging in the back of the closet. Mom won't be wearing these as much in her new life. Maybe no one will invite Mom and Dad to fancy parties since they won't have the exquisite house or two stores—only the one by Saks Fifth Avenue. I feel sorry for them having to go from popular Queen and King to just middle class. I want them to be happy, even if they don't notice whether or not I am. I'd like to take these furs and give them to Ruby, Ethel, and Bernice; they could sell them and the money would help until they found new jobs.

Nana's clothes are all in a back corner section of the closet where the lighting isn't as good. I see her furs hanging together, some with fox heads that she wore around her neck like a trophy. The fox heads are still scary They have teeth in their open mouths and real eyeballs staring at me. I wanted to scream at Nana, *how could you think that is pretty when the fox is dead?* I won't miss Nana covering me up at night when she thinks I'm sleeping, since it seems okay to her to ignore me when I'm awake.

Dad's tuxedos and Mom's gowns are the next in importance in the closet. You can tell because they are placed in stunning clothing bags shiny, like black taffeta, with padded hangers. Some bags have tiny clear windows. I remember each dress just by the swatch of material and color but I don't remember my dresses and where I wore them. Mom's gowns remind me of all the nights I saw her twirl, her dress clinging to her body and some swinging out at the bottom, the sound of her high heels hitting steping toward the front hall and out the front door to waiting friends. I'd run up to Jessy's room and watch from her window, Mom's party dress still swirling until the car door shuts.

I open the bags and smell the dresses. Her perfume lingers on some and makes me sad because I reminince how much I didn't want Mom and Dad to leave. Dad's tuxedos have tags hanging on the top of the hanger that read "black tux," "white tux," "tails," "morning coat": they look like the toe tags on cadavers. There are no windows to see through his bags. I imagine ghosts coming out at night to try on the formal clothes and dance.

The hat boxes are stacked on the shelves by size. Each box has a store name or hat designer name written over wallpaper-like floral prints. When I was little—seven or eight—Ruby and I came up here and took down all the hat boxes. She dusted the boxes and set them back on the shelves. She knew I would ask to see what was in each one. She would carefully unwrap the tissue paper and show me the hat. We both took turns trying them on and looked at ourselves in the full length mirror—and laughed until we were rolling on the floor. Ruby never did end up dusting every box because she was afraid we would be caught playing up there so long. I wish we had gone up there again to finish our antics. She and I are looking at the boxes now and we give each other knowing smiles behind Mom's back. I hope Mom keeps all her hats and boxes in the new house so I can see them and laugh while I tell her what we did.

Mom and I eat in the breakfast room while the maids eat in the kitchen with Bill. We all eat the same exact thing but in separate places. I eat in silence because I am angry I am away from warmth and coziness I could have in the kitchen one of the last times. But I don't want Mom to eat alone. It may hurt her.

After lunch, Mom asks if I'm going back to the attic to help. I tell her I may but first I want to go see if Jessy is going to work at the store or wants to help pack.

She's still sleeping. Lately, she acts so much older, like almost being a senior in high school makes her a snob to anyone younger.

"Hi, Jess. Are you working today?" I rub her back to gently waken her.

"Hi, Rach." Jessy rubs her eyes, sits up and, still halfway under the covers, leans against pillows on the wall side of the bed.

"Are you okay, Jess?"

"No." She falls back into bed.

"What's wrong?"

"I don't know," she whispers with her eyes shut.

"Should I tell Mom you're sick? She's up in the attic packing."

"No. Were you up there?"

"Yeah. I was helping Bill and Ruby. I feel sad packing."

"Me, too. At least we have each other. Rusty is alone." She lies there silently for a moment and then, in a quiet voice, says, "I'm not going with you."

"Where? Up to pack?"

"No, to our new house."

"You can't stay," I say quietly, suppressing my desire to shout.

"I'm going to stay at Aunt Alice's and finish my senior year at our school."

"Who says?" I ask, like a brat.

"I say," Jessy says, like a brat back.

"No, Jess. I can't go without you."

"You have to."

"Why? So you can be with your friends and boyfriend? Aren't I important too?"

"Well, sort of."

"What do you mean?"

"I don't want to tell you."

"Tell me."

"I can't."

"You have to Jess, I can't move without you."

"Okay, if I tell you, you promise not to tell the help? You're so close with them. And I…." Suddenly Jessy runs to the bathroom, holding her stomach. I hear her making gagging noises. I run in after her and hold her head while she throws up in the toilet. I reach out and slam the door shut.

"I don't want to say it out loud," Jessy says, catching her breath. "I'm so ashamed and mad—and I feel so stupid. But I'm happy, too."

"What are you talking about?"

"Oh, Rachael, I'm pregnant," she blurts out.

"Jessy, you're not! I don't believe you! You did *IT*? Oh, my god. I am in shock. Did you tell anyone else? What are you going to do? Oh, my God."

We are both sobbing while she intermittently throws up. I'm so afraid for her. We look at each other. Her eyes are red and streaks of tears mar her face. Mine mirrors hers exactly. Holding her stomach, Jessy walks slowly back to bed as I support her with my arm, worried she might fall down from all the emotion.

"I had a blood test at Bret's doctor's office last week— his Mom took us—and the results came in last Friday." She looks at me with fire in her eyes. "It's your fault, Rach."

"What are you talking about? Are you crazy?"

"All those times you covered for me and told Mom I was studying at friends' houses. Why did you do that and get me in trouble with Bret? You should have told me to come home and not sneak off with him."

"Ever since you lost your virginity," I shout at her, "You have been so mean and awful. You were so much nicer before. I am not staying here to listen to this. You deserve to be pregnant and be married at seventeen and not have a normal life. I don't even care what happens to you!" I run out and slam Jessy's door.

If I hadn't covered up and lied about where Jess was all the times she was with Bret maybe she would not have gotten pregnant. Maybe it is my fault. I don't want to go back to the attic and help Mom pack. I don't know where to go. I run down to the basement to see Bernice. She looks at me as I sit and put my head down.

"What's wrong, chil'?"

"I hate my sister."

"Now, what is goin' on?"

"I can't tell you, Bernice, but I think she is mean and awful and I don't care if I ever see her again. I don't want to leave you and not be able to talk to you when I want to anymore. I will miss you terribly. See, I can tell you I hate my sister. I don't want to leave. Will you miss me?"

"Of course. Why don't you help me fold some clothes and get your mind somewhere else?"

I start folding dish towels that are smooth and soft like diapers and wish I wasn't thinking about Jessy's baby. She's mad at herself and has to blame me for it. I like seeing Bernice concentrating on folding and then switch to ironing.

"What do you think about when you work?" I ask her.

"Now, honey, that's an bewildering question. I think about the lake where we go in the summer to swim with the family and picnic and how the little ones run in the damp grass in they's bare feet 'til the sun licks them dry later. I think that's why I like laundry, because I can be quiet enough to make the daydreams."

"I think it's wonderful you make your work pleasant."

"Someone is calling you and it sounds like Jessy."

"What do you want?" I yell back.

"She sounds frantic. You go, chil'."

I climb the basement stairs slowly and see Jessy at the top.

"Oh, Rach, I am so sorry. I can't believe this is happening. It's none of your fault. It's just that…I'm so scared."

We both  go into her bedroom.

"Rach, I'm going to have a baby and get married," Jessy whispers.

"Oh, my god, you are. I knew you weren't a virgin anymore. I saw your face change ever since you did it. You did it first at your Junior Prom in May, right? You looked different since that night. Like a woman—but not like Mom—like a fast woman. Sorry. Oh, Jessy, Bret's not even Jewish."

"What else can I do?" Jessy ignores both the Jewish and when she did it first comments.

"You can have an abortion."

"I will not. I want to have this baby and get married."

"You aren't even eighteen. How do you know Bret will marry you? And, besides, you can't do it without permission from Mom and Dad. You're still considered a child by law."

"I'm going back to bed," Jessy says angrily.

Okay. I hope Dad will give you money to live on. You know I'll back you up in front of Mom and Dad, even if I don't agree with you. I'm scared for you, Jess. I don't even care that we're leaving our house. Ethel's house is small but her family is happy so maybe we will be happier in our little house."

I run to the phone in the hall and call Mitch. "Mitch, I have to see you."

"Okay, when?"

"Meet me at Baskin-Robbins at six tonight."

"I'll go straight there from work."

I feel so nervous. I feel like I'm Jessy and what would I do. I keep unwrapping the straws in the holder. Then I see Mitch sitting where I couldn't see him.

"Hi, Rach."

"You were here before me," I say sounding exhausted before I even start telling him what's going on.

"Yeah. I told my dad I had to meet a beautiful woman after work. He had a glint in his eye, like he remembered the 'days'."

"Who's the woman?"

"Someday you—or, if you go away, someone else."

"What do you kids want?" the waitress asks as she takes a pencil out from behind her ear. I feel nauseous thinking her ear is dirty because her clothes have food stains and even her face and fingernails are grimy, so the pencil must be filthy.

"I'll have number seventeen," Mitch says pointing at the menu where it lists all the concoctions. Number seventeen is caramel and marshmallow sauce on two scoops of blueberry ice cream in a dish.

"I don't want anything except a spoon to taste his," I

say. When the waiter leaves, I lean towards Mitch and says, conspiratorially, "Mitch, I hate Jessy."

"So what? I hate my brothers."

"No. She is doing something to ruin my life for good."

"Yeah, by being older."

"No, she is going to…"

"What, going to kill herself?"

"No. She's going to have a baby!"

"She just said that to get attention. You girls are all virgins until some cute dope marries you."

"That's nice. You don't believe me."

"Are you mad because I said a dope would marry you?" Mitch asks.

The order comes and the tan, white and blue don't look good together so I pass on dipping my spoon in the goop. Mitch takes big spoonfuls quickly and soon the sauce and ice cream look like a liquid bruise.

"Just like Jessy to be the only Jewish girl going with a gentile, not a nice Jewish boy who waits for marriage," Mitch says, shoveling it in.

"That is so prejudiced. Maybe because he looks like a movie star and she wants to have babies that aren't "Jewish looking. I don't like some of "the Jewish features. Guess I'm prejudiced too." I admit.

"I'm sorry, Rach. I know this moving is hard for you. I will hold your hand, so to speak, always," Mitch says with a gleam in his eye.

"I know. But what do I do? Tell her to have the baby or to get an abortion? She wants to have the baby and get married."

"Tell her not to marry that jerk. Just 'cause he's cute. I know he's not that nice and she should do what has to be done and grow up."

"I don't know him that well. What did he do that's not nice?" Before Mitch can speak, I hold up my hand. "Don't tell me. I don't care. She needs to wait and be older. At least nineteen or twenty. She won't listen to me."

"He stands on the sidelines waiting for the girls to drool all over him and then they do—just like they do with me."

I laugh. I think Mitch won't let me go home until he makes me laugh. That's how he shows he cares.

"How can you eat all that? Oh, Mitch, I am sad to move away from you."

"Rach, the telephone was invented along with the automobile. You are moving about five miles away—I measured it already."

"Yeah, I guess you're right. I keep thinking about Jessy and her problems, not mine, but when I miss you, will you hop in the car and come see me?"

"Uh-huh. Let's go. I'm hungry for dinner. I told my parents I'd be home for dinner."

"How can you think of dinner after all that?"

"'Cause I'm hungry. Let's go!"

"Do you have a date?" I ask hesitantly.

"What? What are you talking about?"

"I want to know. I think I'm jealous. When I think of moving away I think of you finding someone to be with."

"Want to talk later?"

"Okay."

I kiss Mitch on the cheek but close to his mouth. His face turns red.

Mitch walks me home on the secret trail and leaves me at the curb in front of our soon not to be house. I hate when he leaves me. I feel alone. The secret trail goes from Baskin Robbins to the back of our neighborhood through a dusty, dirt walkway that only a few people know about. Mitch, Tommy, Jessy and I took it many times to get ice cream. Jessy talked about making out. I listened and learned. Jessy had no idea at the time that I was crazy about Tommy and embarrassed at the talk. She told them who she had made out with, asked them who they made out with, and then talked about what a good kiss is. She'd tell them how the boys would try to unhook a girl's bra with one hand quickly before the girl can say wait. I laughed, but I was dying inside because Tommy named girls he kissed, girls he went to second base with, and girls he wanted to go further with. This was over the last two years of walking the trail. Every time I became jealous. I will never know if it was true or if he was lying to make me or Jessy jealous or to sound cool in front of Mitch, who had far fewer girls to talk about. I will miss those dusty walks.

Tonight we eat dinner in the library because it's Sunday

and Ethel isn't here. We have the traditional deli and spaghetti served on the knotty pine ledge that covers the heating vents and matches the rest of the paneled library. Jess and I eat on the cold marble floor, which reminds me of tombstones and also where we sat to play jacks when we were little. We stare at each other.

We all watch The Disneyland Show on TV, like we do every Sunday night. Walt Disney narrates while showing the different places in Disneyland before a cartoon comes on. Tonight it's part of the movie *Lady and the Tramp*. When it's over, Dad turns off the TV and announces we're going to have a family meeting after dessert.

Thinking about moving, I don't even hear Mom clearing the plates and food until Jess nudges me to help. We all put the food away and rinse the dishes. They will be washed tomorrow by Ethel.

Rusty, Jess, and I sit on the green living room rug with the bumpy pattern. Mom and Dad bring chairs in from the library and face us, like we're in class.

"Kids," Dad clears his throat, "Mom and I want you to be the first to know—our plans have changed. Uncle Jack has offered me a very good position in San Jose, California. I can do much better there than I can keeping only one store open here. I want my family to do as well as I can provide, so instead of moving to the house we found here, we will be moving to California this fall."

It's as though Dad's words were coming from somewhere else. I see his mouth moving and I hear his words but they seem like two different things. I feel like I just fell into a deep well. Jess and I put our hands to our mouths and gasp. Rusty's tears run down his soft cheeks. I don't think he knows if he's scared or excited. Jess runs out of the room and up the stairs to her room so I run after her.

"Why are you running?" I ask.

"Because I don't want to listen. My life feels over," Jess explains.

I whisper to her, "You didn't tell them about the baby, did you? Are they doing this because of the baby?"

"Not yet. I can't"

"You have to tell them. I can't stand it!"

"Then they'd make Bret and me move away from each other so they don't have to be ashamed in front of their friends. They'll have me as an excuse to run away and hide from the fact that Dad isn't wealthy. And then they'll make me get rid of the baby."

"You have to tell them," I repeated.

"But I'm so scared. Come with me please," she says, hugging me.

"You're only nice to me when you need me."

"You are my best friend, honest."

"I hear them coming up the stairs!"

We both get up slowly, like we are going to our death sentence. I push Jess ahead of me. She walks into their bedroom first.

"We need to talk," Jess says.

"Okay," Dad says with a vampire look in his eyes.

I want to scream and run out of there and never come back. I pull Jess aside and we tell Mom and Dad we have to go to Jess's room first.

"Jess, Dad's eyes looked like he wanted to kill you. Did you see them?"

"I know, but I want to get it over with. First you tell me to, then you stop me. Why?"

"Because I wanted Dad to maybe get kinder before you tell him. I got scared for you," I say nicely.

I hear Mom on the phone so we lay down on the beds and wait for a while without talking. Finally, we go back into their bedroom.

Mom and Dad tell us they already know everything. Bret told his Mom. So Bret's mom called mom and dad. Dad knew about the possibility of the California move but only decided to take it after hearing of Jessy's pregnancy, believing it was a better opportunity for the family. So it's Jessy's fault we're moving away. I hate her for everything. I stayed while she talked to Mom and Dad just to support her because I knew she needed me. Mom, Jessy and I hug while Dad remains staunch like a starched shirt. No wonder he drinks—since he can't laugh or cry, he gets drunk instead.

# 19
# THE MOVE

All the items on the dining room table are for sale. I didn't know we had these beautiful antiques because most of them were stashed away, probably in the attic. There are price tags on them and lots of strangers are milling about in our living room. Mom is running around talking about items like they are precious stones that are millions of years old. I don't see Nana anywhere. I know she buys things at auctions so maybe these are all her great buys. Mom and Dad must need the money or they wouldn't sell all this stuff. I want to steal a few things and give them to the help. No one would even notice. Ruby could go to a pawnbroker and get cash for something. I've heard about pawnbrokers from watching *Dragnet* on TV. But I don't know if I can steal especially from my parents. But since it's for Ethel and Ruby and Bernice and Bill, I do it. I take the smallest items, hide them in my cupped hands, and walk quickly upstairs. I don't even know what they are, I took them so quickly. No one saw me. Oh, my God. I am a liar and a thief. I don't care. Jessy lies, Mom and Dad lie, and now I lie and steal.

Upstairs, I look at what I took. One is a small china bird. One is a teeny gold box. Maybe it's real solid gold. There's a tiny kangaroo, a silver charm and a gold ring with a red stone.

Maybe someone saw me take the stuff. I'm not sure who was there when I took it. Mom could have been near or Ethel. They may have seen me looking guilty. How do people do this and sleep at night? I haven't stolen candy or a piece of gum in my life. Now I am part of this broken house and the broken people in it. Everyone is acting different: Mom and Dad argue a lot, even if it's not in front of us. I can hear them in the hall when I pass their room. I feel like I'm their prisoner so I might as well do something to deserve my sentence.

I wish they would take Bill to the club to play golf with them. The only colored people allowed on the golf course at the club are the caddies for white players. And colored players aren't allowed to play in national tournaments.

Jessy is so sad about having to leave Bret. She sleeps a lot or talks on the phone to Bret endlessly until someone else needs to use it. Bret never comes over; Dad said he'd shoot him if he ever saw him again.

Nana doesn't even talk to Jessy or me anymore; she treats us like we're being sold along with her auction items. Mom says Nana is worried because she doesn't know where she will live. There are friends of Nana's that live in apartments—not the lifestyle Nana is used to. Dinners are very quiet with Mom and Dad and Jessy and me not laughing.

The atlas shows San Jose as a tiny speck fifty miles south of San Francisco. The Britannica says the population is two hundred thousand and it is mostly agricultural land

and industrial businesses. St. Louis is seven hundred and fifty thousand people. I am going to be a hick and my closest neighbors will live a mile away on their rural farm. I will learn how to drive a tractor and walk barefoot in the dirt and avoid stepping in cow dung on the way to a school up a mountain. I could be friends with Tab Hunter or Paul Newman soon because Hollywood is not far and forget all about Tommy.

I will take pictures of Ruby, Ethel, Bernice and Bill in the weeks to come. No one will ever take away my pictures.

Today I tell Bill I want to work with him to remember more about the home I grew up in. Bill is suspicious to have me working alongside him. In the driveway, we fill up the bucket from the garage with car soap and water. With thick sponges we spread the soap suds all over the MG and Bill's eyes gleam with pride, like it's his car, or President Eisenhower's. When I look at him, he gives me a wink to tell me I'm doing a good job. His forehead has a few drops of sweat starting to descend onto his blue button-down shirt from swishing the sponge fast and hard. After rinsing the car with the hose, he shows me how to start drying it from the top with the chamoise. We dry every nook and cranny so the car won't get streaks from the sun. I'm so happy just to be with Bill and smile the entire time. He makes me feel like his best friend. I'm soaked with soap, water, and grease.

"Rachael, you shouldn't have worn good clothes," Bill says, looking at me.

"The only clothes I have are good clothes."

We both laugh at the inside joke.

Next we water the flowers, lawn, and trees in the front

and back yards. Afterwards, Bill shows me how to turn on the metal sprinklers around the yard to soak the ground before the sun gets too strong. He explains that if you water in the morning, mildew may kill the grass. I never even thought of how to use a hose other than having water fights or running through the sprinklers.

When we're done, we go into the kitchen where Ethel is cleaning up from everyone's breakfast. I wait until Ethel has a free minute to hug me. She finds food in the icebox and breadbox for Bill and me to eat; butter, jelly, cinnamon rolls, juice, milk, fresh oranges, and coffee for Bill. Bill and I sit at the kitchen table like good friends. We talk about what's next on the list of tasks. Bill tells me the fireplace in the living room needs some work for the cold weather. He wants to know how I like the day so far.

"Oh, Bill, I feel like my house is an old friend that I never really knew. Now that I know it better, I will miss it even more. I'll miss you, too. Where will you and Bernice work? Do you know yet?"

"Now, Rachael, don't you go worryin' 'bout us. We already have a few offers in your neighborhood and we'll see what we like best. There's one with four children, like you have, and one without children, so Bernice and I are taking a little time to decide in few days and we'll be all set."

"Oh, I'm so relieved. I do worry and want you and Bernice happy. Now when I think about you every day I'll know you're fine and dandy. I hope you take the job with the children because it'll be too quiet without all the noise you're used to." I can feel my cheeks get hot. I press my lips together hard to hold tears back.

"Before I came to work for your Daddy, I was a Pullman porter. A friend of mine said that President of the

Southern Pacific built and lived in your house before your family so when I got the job here I wrote that President that I was now helping in the house he built. And you know what, Rachael? He wrote me back."

"Bill, I would love to see that letter. My favorite part of camp was the train ride on the railroad."

"Is that why you cried when you came home—because the train rides were over for another year?"

"No, I cried because I didn't want to go home but I didn't want to stay at camp."

Ethel comes over to clear our food and dishes. Bill doesn't ask me why I didn't want to come home. He says we have to get going. Other than the porter on the train, I've never talked to a man so much in my life as Bill—even Dad. I don't even remember eating anything because I was so enthralled to be talking to Bill. Even though I didn't say very much, he really listened to me, looking me in the eye and smiling. I know he could read between the lines of what I was saying so I didn't have to talk a lot.

Bill tells me to meet him in the living room. He comes in with wire brushes, rags, cleaning bottles, and hand brooms. We take out the black andirons and grate from the fireplace and put them on a large rag. He shows me how to sweep the ashes out inside the fireplace. Then we sprinkle on powdered cleaning material and sweep inside again. He tells me he has to clean the chimney once a year so soot won't build up, otherwise Santa won't come down. We laugh. We take the andirons down to the basement and put them into the deep cement sink to thoroughly wash them until they look perfectly clean. Bill and I talk about the brass andirons on the outside of the fireplace. He says another day he will shine them until he can see his black face in them.

When everything is back in place in the fireplace we get into the pale yellow Ford he uses to come to work and drive to the paint store to buy paint for Nana's bathroom. Drops of sweat slowly run down the lines in his face, like light rain on the cracks in a sidewalk.

We talk about the friends I've had for my whole life that I now have to leave. I tell him I cannot imagine not seeing them almost every day. They're the only faces and names I've ever known. I don't know what kids are like in San Jose. Maybe they go hunting or fishing or surfing all the time. Maybe their houses are made of wood instead of bricks and they eat fresh fish a lot with oranges and lemons they pick off their trees. I may never see snow again. I tell him I like a boy and may never see him again. I start thinking about Tommy getting married. In the moving car it seems easier to talk because we aren't face to face.

"Bill," I blurt out, "when I get to California I hope I see that the colored people and the white people are treated the same."

He doesn't respond.

I tell Bill I don't think I'll miss my friends, even my closest ones, as much as I'll miss him, Bernice, Ethel, and Ruby. I say I would have missed Peggy for sure but the others don't feel the same to me—except Mitch—no matter how long I've known them.

Bill gives me a look like he doesn't think I know about missing friends yet, that I'm too young to know how much people mean.

This is the first time I've ridden in his car. It smells like his work clothes, like a car that's not kept washed and polished. I want to ask him if that's something he thinks about—not having a car all spiffed up, but I don't.

After the paint store, Bill and I touch up Nana's bathroom and then clean up the mess it makes. I tell Bill it's the first time I've ever painted anything that wasn't on paper in art class. I watch him fix a toilet in the guest bathroom, oil the lawnmower, and then I help him wash windows. We meet Bernice in the kitchen for a late lunch that Ethel made. Ethel sits down with us and Bill and I tell Bernice and Ethel about our day. We laugh and joke like old friends. They are the center of my life. What will life be like without them?

Tonight all my girlfriends are giving me a dinner party at Jane's house and then dessert at Pamela's, another friend. I'm surprised they're doing this, but no one we know has ever left before, so it's a big deal. Tommy called me this week to say he would come over to say goodbye to Jessy and me. I wish he would take me out instead. Mitch is coming over the morning we leave this Sunday.

My friend Sara honks and I run out and get in her dad's car; she's driving now. I have known her since kindergarten, as I have every other girl and boy in my class. She isn't close to me but she is in my group of friends. We talk about my leaving. Her black eye makeup starts to run from the tears forming as we talk. I didn't know she cared about my moving. I want to say thank you for crying about me but it wouldn't sound like me. I never talk like that to friends.

At Jane's there are fourteen of my girl friends. They're all hugging me. They all smell like Prell shampoo. I wonder if they have Prell in California. We never hugged much before so I didn't realize we all smell the same. We have a buffet supper and eat outside on card tables. Jane's mom and dad are talking to all of us. They seem interested in my move and in all of our lives.

Jane's mom asks me a question with a smile. "Are you getting all ready for the move, dear?"

"Yes, almost everything is packed except the furniture," I say. I want to kiss her; she is so sweet and loving.

"Jane will miss you so much. I will too, you know."

I talk to everyone about California, driving, moving. I like my girlfriends but I don't think I'll miss them—it's their families I will miss; the feeling I get when I go to their apartments and houses. Their homes are calming, like gentle waves on a tiny lake—or maybe the ocean, though I have never seen it. There is unspoken caring and wondering about each other. Each family is different but I feel the warmth in almost every one of my girlfriends' houses. I want to find that in California with my own family in our own home.

We all pile into cars and drive over to Pamela's house for dessert. We have sundaes with cookies. Pamela's mom never talks, she yells—even when she isn't mad. Her dad is in the kitchen helping to bring in the food. I've never seen a father help in the kitchen except when my dad makes French pancakes and chocolate sodas on Sundays. I feel like I'm in another country, seeing her dad help do little chores that moms or maids do. Pamela and her mom argue about how many plates they'll need.

All of a sudden, Sara yells, "Pamela, there are peeping Toms in the window!"

We all scream when we see dark eyes looking at us through the living room window. Pamela's dad goes out the front door to see what's going on. He has a baseball bat in his hand. We all huddle together with our arms around each other, feeling scared. Pamela's dad comes in with four guys from our class—Jimmy, Roy, Carl, and Paul. They were looking in to see what was going on and are crashing our party. They are so cute—like little brothers. I'm happy they came over to say goodbye but they should have knocked on the door. Pamela's father told them next time they peer in the window he'll call the police and they'll find themselves in jail for criminal behavior. Pamela's dad is a lawyer so they listen.

"Rachael, what will you do when all the guys go surfing? Join them?" asks Roy.

"Of course, in my bikini, hanging ten," I joke back.

"Don't forget about the sharks," laughs, Jimmy.

"There are plenty around here I've learned from," I tease.

On moving day I wake up early. I get dressed, comb, smooth and hairspray my hair, put on a headband and lipstick. Today we leave and I want to look nice if any of my friends or Jess's friends come over. I hear people running around upstairs in the attic, maybe doing last minute packing. When I come out of my room and look down the stairs I see Mom, Dad, Jessy and Rusty flitting around in different directions. I bump into Ruby on the stairs and we hug. Then she is gone somewhere.

The front door is open. Mitch and Tommy walk into the sparse-looking living room. When I see Tommy, I feel my cheeks flush; he runs upstairs. Mitch and I lie on the floor on the bumpy green rug and I look around as memories jump around in a jumble of chaotic images.

"Hey, listen, I'll write and maybe I'll get to visit," Mitch stammers. Then he thrusts out his hand. "I brought you something." It is an unwrapped Ike and Tina Turner record. He remembered I saw them perform in East St. Louis. "You'll remember they started here—their hometown. I hope you'll remember me as much as you remember them," Mitch laughs.

"Thanks, Mitch. I will never forget you." I reach out to hug him and stop as Tommy is coming down the stairs.

"Okay, let's go," he gestures to Mitch. "I don't like long goodbyes so...goodbye, Rachael."

"Well, you said more to Jessy than that," I say sarcastically.

"Yeah, well, I shouldn't have."

"Shouldn't have what?" asks Mitch.

"Shouldn't have... nothing. This house looks haunted. I want to go."

Mitch and I stand up. Tommy and I hug. Mitch and I hug. I walk them to their car. Tommy secretly hands me an envelope when Mitch isn't looking. I watch them get in and drive away and we all wave. My eyes fill with tears.

As I walk up the stone path I look at the envelope. It has "Rachael" written in script on the outside—Tommy's script; of course I recognize it. I open the envelope. The one piece of paper says: *Hi Rachael, I didn't know what to say to you so I wrote this. I hope you have fun in California. I will miss you, Tommy.* Did he give Jessy the same note? What did he talk about to Jessy? At least he says he'll miss me. I'll miss Mitch for his unwavering friendship. He made me laugh more than anyone ever has. But I won't miss Tommy for making me wonder how he feels about me every time I see him. I will probably never know.

There's nothing more to say, nothing more to do except say goodbye to the help. I slowly walk into the house. Everyone is moving every which way. I go up to my room which is now emptied of every last piece of my life. I walk into Ruby's room and call out "Ruby" one last time. The room echoes with emptiness. Maybe this is what it feels like to die. Everything you have ever known is gone and you just stop going on.

Jessy is in the hallway on the phone, whispering. I'm sure she's talking to Bret. She will probably keep on talking to him until we leave. She's sobbing softly into the receiver. I hear Nana talking to someone in her room. She's moving to an apartment in St. Louis where a few of her friends live. I won't miss her—I can cover myself up at night—that's all she ever did for me.

I look out the window in Jessy's room and see our station wagon all shiny. There are a few droplets that Bill missed when he was drying it. To me they seem like tears the car is shedding. Dad's car will be driven out to California.

I don't know where to go now. I feel lost in these last minutes in my home. I want to find Ruby and feel her arms around me until we shove off. I slowly walk past Jessy, still sobbing, on the phone. I walk downstairs for the final time. I always thought I would descend these stairs on my wedding day. I would be wearing the most beautiful, lacy satin dress, and the whole wedding party would watch me descend then slowly walk down a pink rose-petal sprinkled aisle to my future husband. Maybe my future husband is in California and that is why I have to move.

Ruby is looking up at me as I raise my head on the last step. Her hand is outstretched and I take it. We hug hard. Soon Bill, Bernice, and Ethel are surrounding me spontaneously hugging. I have never felt so much love. I can't leave this love. I look up with tear-stained eyes and laugh because they are all smiling. No one says anything but they know what I feel.

The last thing I do is take the stolen items from the sale on the dining table, which I hid behind the house in a shrub, and put them in my purse.

Getting into the car feels as if a force from the love I feel is moving me. I may tell Mom and Dad what I did. We have a long ride and even if they're angry, I don't know how they could punish me on the trip. Then again, I may sell my stolen objects at a pawn shop when we get to California and send the money to Ruby to distribute to herself and Ethel, Bernice, and Bill.

There they are—standing on the front yard waving. Rusty, Mom, and Dad do not cry, but Jessy and I sob in each other's arms as we drive away.

## 20
## HOME


"Rach, I'm going to San Francisco tomorrow for the baby thing."

"What? Why didn't you tell me sooner?"

"I just found out Mom made an appointment. I told her I was going to run away and get married to Bret and have the baby. We had a terrible row. She went and made the appointment."

"So, are you going to get rid of it?"

"I don't want to. I hate myself." Jessy burst into tears. "I'm so miserable."

I move over to her bed and stroke her back while she cries into her pillow.

"Jess, I'll help you run away if you want to. I'll go with you and we can take a train to St. Louis and you can be with

Bret," I say holding her.

The mention of his name sends Jessy into another round of tears. "Rach, every time I talk to Bret on the phone he sounds like he doesn't love me anymore. It's like he's trying to be nice but he doesn't really want me to come back or get married. At first, before we left, he said he wanted to, but since we got here, he sounds far away, like maybe he likes someone else. I still want to go there and be with him and have this baby, but maybe when I get there he won't want to have anything to do with me." She sits up, angry now. "I think his mother told him to not have the baby."

"Oh, Jess, I don't know what I would do if I were in your shoes. I think at seventeen it's too hard to think about all this. I guess that's why Mom waited till she was twenty to marry, and Annie, too. Can't you marry him when you're twenty and then have a baby?" I ask, still holding her.

Fighting to control her tears, Jess turns over and looks at me. "But that's three years from now. What if he finds someone else by then? I'll never love anyone else, Rach. Ever! I know that. I hate my life and I hate California."

"Then let's sneak out tonight," I say adamantly. "We have enough money to take the train. Let's pack!" I want to help Jess more than anyone right now. And besides, I want to go home, too.

"Rach, I can't," Jess moans.

"What do you mean 'you can't'?"

"I can't move out. I can't do anything. I'm too depressed. I can't pack and sneak out and get a train—or maybe I really don't want to," Jess says with a shudder, looking down at the covers where her stomach is.

"Do you want me to come with you and Mom tomorrow?" I ask a voice so sweet I don't recognize it as mine.

"That is so sweet, Rachael. Thank you. But I just want to be with Mom. I don't want to even think of you having to go through anymore of this." She sits up and looks at me earnestly. "Just don't do this to yourself, Rach, no matter how much you love a boy. Just wait until you're twenty and get married first. Promise?"

I feel the tears threatening to spill out of my eyes. "I promise. I do. I love you, Jess. I'll sleep in the bed with you tonight if you want. I can put my head at the other end so we aren't crowded." It is the first time in a long time that Jess and I sleep in the same bed. It makes me feel so close to her, almost like Ruby and me. Maybe we will be closer out here. I remember how many times I hoped we'd be closer in St. Louis. But Jessy isn't steady like Ruby and I have to keep reminding myself of that. I lie there and think about tomorrow and worry about how she will be, and if Mom will be nice to her. Thoughts of the baby, Jess and Ruby, float through my head before I go to sleep.

In the morning Jess and I hug hard and she tells me she'll be home tonight after dinner.

All day all I can think about is Jessy up in San Francisco with Mom. I hate the idea of a baby that should be here but is not going to be. We could have raised it—all of us. I don't think marriage with Bret would be right at seventeen but Mom and Dad, Rusty, Jessy, the baby and I would be a family. Maybe people would gossip about the baby, but a baby is more important than what people think. Mom and Dad could say it was their baby. What would be the difference if they hid another truth?

The abortion is a secret, too. I know no one in the family would agree with me so I keep my idea to myself. I have heard about girls getting abortions and then they can never have babies again, and sometimes they even die. They aren't legal in the United States, so quack doctors have to do them in dusty, dirty backrooms. They only take cash and there's no medical record of it. Mitch told me about dirty abortions. I'm so scared for Jessy every minute today. I sit down to write to Mitch because I can't concentrate on anything else.

*Dear Mitch,*

*I wish you were here right now. I am so scared for Jessy. She went to get an A. I am not going to spell it out but you told me all about them. I am going to tell you what we have been doing because all I can concentrate on is writing to you and I don't want to say any more about the above.*

*We stopped in Las Vegas on our way out here and stayed in a fancy hotel with mahogany writing desks so I have plenty of this pretty stationery from the hotel. I was so sick of our smelly, trash strewn car; I didn't care where we stopped. I wanted Disneyland where there is something for kids to do but I got out-voted. In Las Vegas you have to be twenty-one to step over the line painted on the floor in the casinos—even to watch gambling.*

*The whole trip was an awful seven days of driving Route 66 through small towns that are boring and mostly all truck stops for gigantic eight-wheelers going or coming who knows where. There were some big cities like Oklahoma City, Tulsa, and Albuquerque, but mostly we just passed the main part of these cities and stayed in a dingy motel on the outskirts.*

*At night I'd hear the door to the room open and see Dad creeping out to go to a bar. Whenever he came back, he smelled like Scotch and cigarettes. I figured he was probably drinking from worrying about money.*

*The car always smelled of smoke but I was used to that because our house always did, too, with Mom and Dad smoking Kents all the time. At least back home I could go into my room, but in the car there was nowhere to escape. Even though I learned to smoke at camp last year it never smelled so bad because I was outdoors. I hope I never smoke indoors and smell everything up.*

*In the car, Mom and Dad talked a little but I couldn't hear what they said because they whispered, like they were sharing secrets. Mostly they just seemed upset and hardly ever smiled or laughed with each other or us. When they talked to us it was only to tell us to stop laughing so loud or stop arguing.*

*Even on this trip, Mom and Dad always dressed like they were going to the country club for lunch. Maybe they thought they'd run into someone they knew and had to look perfect.*

*I saw something I am ashamed to write about. In St. Louis, Mitch, we are so unaccustomed to how the world treats colored people unless we are aware—like I did when I went to Ruby's house. It didn't matter if we were in Oklahoma, Texas, or New Mexico; in every hamburger stand I saw two drinking fountains, one that said "Colored" and the other "White." I always drank from the colored fountain to shock Mom and Dad. The first time I did that Mom told me that it was meant for colored people. I told her I knew that but I wanted to drink from their fountain to show it was the same exact water. She shook her head from side to side to show she disapproved; Dad did the same. I just shrugged my shoulders and took another sip.*

*One day I'm going to go back to St. Louis the same way we came, on Route 66, and tear all those signs down one by one.*

*One thing Dad did that I will remember the rest of my life: he saw this colored boy selling newspapers when we stopped at a Foster's Freeze and he bought every single one of the papers so the boy could have the money fast and not have to stand in the sizzling sun all day. The boy was so stunned he gave my dad a bright smile and a handshake, like he was getting a high school diploma.*

*When we went to the Grand Canyon and the Painted Desert in Arizona, Jessy stayed in the car and sulked, probably about her situation. Rusty and I followed Mom and Dad around to see the sights. Everything was spectacular. The colors were more brilliant than anything I had ever seen in my life, especially the Grand Canyon. At the National Petrified Forest I touched a log and it felt hard, more, like concrete than wood. I guess that's why they call it "petrified." It was like the forest died but it still looked like living wood. Rusty's expression was like we were on Mars.*

*When we crossed the Rocky Mountains and saw the Pacific Ocean, it was my turn to feel like we were on Mars.. I've never seen anything so huge. It made me uncomfortable, like the ocean or the mountains could swallow me up. They seem like beautiful monsters that defy the imagination. It was weird, but I felt scared and calmed by them at the same time. I can see how the enormity of nature can change people's lives.*

*It was such a contrast, being in a small car with my family, especially when compared to being in our big old house. But it still seemed like we each had our separate rooms.*

*Once we got to our destination; San Jose, we all stayed at a motel for a whole month before we found a house; it was one room with two double beds and a rollaway for Rusty.*

*I bought you something in Shamrock, Texas so you would really know I am thinking about you. I'm putting it in the mail soon. I hope your summer is not boring like our drive was. Maybe you can visit soon.*

Then I write to Ruby.

*Rachael, 1962, Summer*

*Dear Ruby,*

*I mailed you a postcard from every town we stopped in to sleep: Tulsa, Oklahoma; Shamrock, Texas; Amarillo, Texas; Gallup, New Mexico; Flagstaff, Arizona; Kingman, Arizona; Las Vegas, Nevada, and now here, from our new town, Spartina. Did you get all my postcards? Someday you can show me all of them so I will believe that I was really in all those places.*

*This whole trip feels like it has happened to someone else, not me. Have you ever had that feeling? I miss you every second of every day. Some nights I cry myself to sleep. I am worried about Mom and Dad adjusting to a new life. Mom lived in St. Louis for forty-six years and Dad fifty-one. I think that is harder than me leaving after sixteen.*

*Some nights my parents go to San Francisco to socialize with new friends. Our cousins live there so Mom and Dad are invited to all the parties our cousins go to. I haven't met them yet, but I hope they are nice since we don't have any other family here.*

*Ruby, I hope you are working with a nice family and that you have a room that you like, if you sleep there. Please tell me all about your family and the family you work for.*

*Love, Rachael*

I wish we had never left. I feel so lonely and afraid. But when I look around the house it does kind of feel like home. It has all our furniture from St. Louis. I see all the familiar ashtrays, knick-knacks, and pictures around me; all the same lamps, tables, dishes, chairs, sofa. The floors look strange, however. The front hall has wood floors, rather than the stone we had back home. The carpets are shag, not flat like before, and they are gray not green. We only have one story—no stairwells. The outside walls are made of wood siding, not brick like we used to have, and it's painted brown. There are so many lush plants around, I feel like California is on another planet. Almost every plant has color—even weeds! I don't care that the house has only three bedrooms instead of six and two bathrooms instead of five. We don't have a library, a basement, or a room we called a porch in St. Louis. I like the coziness of fewer rooms.

I hear Jessy and Mom walk in the front door late tonight. I've been so concerned and frightened for my sister. I run to greet them.

"Hi. How are you?" I say, giving Jessy a hug.

"Fine," she says lightly, like sprinkled, powdered sugar on French toast.

Jessy and I walk arm in arm into our room. Mom follows us. Jessy lies down on the yellow sun-streaked bedspread and closes her eyes. Mom feels her head. I watch, sitting on my bed. Mom walks out of the room without saying a word.

"Jess, are you all right?" I go to her bed and lean over her.

"Yes, it was fine. I'm sad, but I am fine. I wish we were Catholic. They can't have abortions. The doctor told me that. He wanted to make sure I wasn't Catholic. Maybe the church would arrest him. If this happens to me again, I am going to become Catholic.

"Was it a real doctor?"

"Yes. Maybe. I dunno."

"Was it clean and nice? Did it hurt? How long did it take? Were you awake?" I pray in my heart the answers will be good as I pepper her with questions.

"No, it didn't hurt," Jessy says, closing her eyes again.

I know she's tired. I watch her sleep and then listen to my clock radio, which I keep at a very low volume, until I fall asleep. I hear Mom come in during the night to feel her head and put the covers over her.

Jessy wakes me up early.

"Hi, Jess. Are you okay?"

"Yeah. It was fine. Mom and I had lunch in Union Square wearing white gloves like everyone walking around the square and then we went to the doctor. It wasn't in a back alley. It was a regular doctor's office. He had white doctor's gloves on, too. I feel okay. You know Bret and I write letters. I can't call him because Mom and Dad hate him and they wouldn't pay for a call. Can you mail a letter for me today after I write it, Rachael? I know he wants to know how I am after today. I miss him so much. I still love him. They can't make me not love him."

"I know, Jess. I wish I knew what it feels like to love a boy and have him love me back and not be able to see him. It must be so hard.

As I begin my new life as a California teenager in a new school, I feel like I don't know who I am. Did I only make friends with Ruby, Ethel, Bernice and Bill just to get love? And what about the colored porter on the train and the colored girl at camp who got pregnant? And the trouble I started redoing the windows in Dad's store? Do I really care about other people? If there are no colored kids in my new school that need help, will I be just another teenager who likes boys, parties, and clothes—all the stuff I thought was mindless? If Mom and Dad are too poor to go out much, will they show me more love and attention or just be around the house and ignore me? I feel like I just don't fit in anymore. I haven't started school so I have no idea if I'll feel good there. I used to know my place in the family. Until a few years ago, I was the silent one, the one with no opinions, the one that never got in trouble. But that sure has changed. I've gotten in more trouble in the last couple of years than I have in my whole life before that. I guess now I'm more like Jess. Except Jessy is only nice when she wants something. My older sister Annie really never knew me. And Rusty is too young for me to be close to. Nana and Grandma always thought I was the *extra* girl, that I should have been a boy. I know that Ruby, Ethel, Bernice and Bill loved me for exactly who I was and would do anything for me.

It's the first day of the new school semester. From the outside I look at my new school: Spartina High. It looks like an expanded house, not a sterile brick school. There are several different size rectangular buildings, each two stories high. There's a caramel colored stucco brick front with several levels of roof lines that make it look very modern. It's only four years old, so Jessy will be in the first graduating class. The lawns, flowers, shrubs and trees are spread in a natural landscapping manner not formal. The many windows are massive, so the rooms are probably bright with sunlight. In St. Louis, the windows at Warren High School were small with nothing to see except another outside wall or the sky and the rooms were dark unless the lights were on. It wasn't a warm, inviting place of learning.

Mom, Jessy, and I walk into the school office. Mom has already been here to tell them we will be attending this year.

Next year Jessy will be gone, off to college, so she won't be around to talk to and argue with. Mitch isn't here to show me I'm accepted no matter what I say or do. He's the one who always made me laugh. Who will now? Tommy isn't here to like. Who will I have a crush on? Will my new girlfriends care about the world or just getting a tan? Will they care about studying or college or will I?

Jessy is angry today because of her abortion last week and having to leave Bret. I see a girl that looks my age sitting with her mom also waiting to see someone in the school office. She has straight, shiny, brown-black hair that touches her shoulders, a turned up nose, olive skin and two different colored eyes: one is brown and the other is hazel. She looks just like her mom, who is very pretty. She doesn't look nervous because she and her mom are talking in low voices and smiling, like they are happy to be here.

Finally, Mom, Jessy, and I are called into the principal's office. He smiles, welcoming us nicely. Mom already signed all the papers last week so he's just making sure we feel comfortable. He seems very kind. After we're done talking about the school and our schedules he walks us out of his office. He introduces us to the girl sitting with her mom. Her name is Florence and she is also new and in eleventh grade. I think how great it would be if Florence became my best friend so I wouldn't have to search for one.

She goes with her mom to put her things in her locker but keeps looking back at me. She looks like an Ivy league type, like me. Mom walks us to Jess's locker. Jessy throws her stuff agrily—notebooks, papers we got in the office, and extra pencils—into her locker in a messy pile with papers torn and creasing. We walk to my locker and I see that Florence's is in the same row as mine and she is putting her stuff away neatly, like I am. Our moms look at each other and it seems to me their eyes say they are ready to let us go into this new experience.

Florence and I look at each other's written schedules. We have gym class together for our last period. We say goodbye and we will see each other later. But I have a sinking feeling in my stomach: she is not Peggy—I hope for someone like Peggy. I want to shout out, *"You are not Peggy! I am only kidding myself that you will take her place. You don't even come close to my Peggy. I can tell right away. I want Peggy, not you!"*

Mom leaves Jessy and me with warm hugs and says she'll pick us up today but starting tomorrow we will take the bus. Jess walks off without saying anything to me, like her awful life is my fault.

I'm still nervous and excited about my classes. In every class I'm introduced by the teacher, which I hate because I don't like to be the center of attention. I have a lump in my throat all day, just like I had at the club in St. Louis or any time with new people. I was hoping that personality trait would stay in St. Louis, but it didn't! Once in a while someone will introduce herself to me as we leave to go to the next class. And I can't wait until gym to see Florence. Today I saw two colored boys who look athletic and had a lot of kids around them, so they are probably popular. I want to meet them. They must be from a rich family, since this not a poor area, or maybe their parents work for someone important. We didn't have any colored kids at all at Warren High.

I see Florence entering the gym and I call out to her a little too loudly. I hope I don't sound desperate to see her.

"Hey, Florence."

"Hi, Rachael, how was your day?" Florence asks quietly.

"Okay. I was sort of nervous," I admit.

"Let's talk later, okay?" she suggests as we walk to our gym lockers to get our uniforms.

I ate alone because Florence said she had to go clear some things up in the office. No one talked to me. I saw the colored boys and I would have eaten with them or Jessy but the seniors eat at their own tables nearby. I ended up going to the bathroom after quickly gobbling down my food.

On the second day, Florence motioned for me to sit next to her. We ended up eating lunch together almost every day. She has no one else to eat with either. I can tell she doesn't care I'm sitting with her because she hardly looks at me while we eat and talk.

It isn't hard to spot the popular kids because they're all attractive, spunky and act like they own the school. All the juniors eat at the same time in tables set together. I like this because I can see who is in what grade.

Everyone eats outside in a courtyard on picnic tables surrounded by lush plants. How different to eat outside in the open air looking at mountains and hills all around, like we're on a picnic. I can tell I would like the popular group of girls by how they look, talk and laugh. They look wholesome, not phony; they don't wear any makeup except a little lipstick. They look scrubbed and clean. The sun has imbued them with a golden tan and sunlight has set streaks in their hair. They seem like they are having fun and have a magnetic energy that makes me want to know them.

Florence tries too hard to make the popular kids like her. Still, I think it'll be easier for me to get into that crowd with Florence rather than trying alone. So I'm happy she's here with me.

The boys in the popular group barely stay seated at a table near the girls. Mostly they are hanging around, squirming nervously whether they're sitting or standing. They are cute, clean-cut, tanned, and athletic looking. They all wear their hair medium short with pomade to slick it down. Some of them dawdle over by the girls and hang around with their sandwich or apple in hand while they flirt. At Warren High you couldn't wander around while you ate lunch.

The boys stare at Florence and me and point. We laugh at them like they are silly. None of them are brave enough to saunter over to us.

There are some couples who sit together and touch each other on the face or hand as they talk close and whisper. It looks like fun to be a couple. I want a boyfriend this year. Badly. I wish I could wipe Tommy from my memory. I think about him and wonder if he misses me. I will never write him unless he writes first. He would look sickly and pale here with all the leftover summer tans. And Mitch would look like an ashen-faced misplaced Ivy Leaguer with his partially untucked shirt and dirty khakis.

All the boys here wear pants that look like jeans, but they're thin and don't have cuffs and belts in the loops and they're in different colors. Instead of polo shirts and Oxford shirts with collars, they wear T-shirts in lots of different colors. There are no loafers with pennies in them here; only slip-on canvas shoes or basketball shoes.

On the bus there are two girls who talk to me, but they're not in the popular group.

"Hi, Rachael. I'm in your typing class. Elaine." She holds out her hand. "What do you think of school?" she asks.

She has long blonde hair that looks like she streaked it with a bottle of peroxide or maybe lemon juice; it doesn't look natural like the popular girls. She has very full boobs and her shirt is unbuttoned so I can see the start of them and where her tan line ends. Her eyes are very blue and searching like she wants to know me fast. She has a skirt that looks too short for school; it shows her heavy legs. I read the school dress code that Mom put on my bed. The rules say if your skirt is more than one inch above the knees or if you wear patent leather shoes, because supposedly it reflects your underpants, they will call a parent to take you home to change. I think that bit about the patent leather shoes is something an old maid made up. At Warren High your skirt had to touch your knees, but Elaine's is about two inches above her knees.

"Hi, Rachael, I'm Cindy." She didn't even let me answer Elaine's question. "Welcome to Spartina. Where'd you come from?"

Cindy is also blonde but it looks natural with a lot of brown in it. The top looks bleached from the sun. Cindy is short and skinny. Her tan is so dark, I wonder if she sits in the sun every day. She's wearing sunglasses so I can't tell if she's looking right at me—but her breath smells like smoke. Her voice is raspy, maybe from smoking, and she taps her foot constantly like she is bored with the bus ride and wants to get going.

"I like it. I'm from St. Louis, Missouri," I tell them.

"I can tell you're not from here. You have a bitchin' accent," says Cindy.

"I didn't know that it sounds like a bitch," I say, my voice squeaking because now I feel self-conscious. I must sound mousy.

"No," Cindy laughs, "bitchin' means great, a great accent, not a bitch accent. Haven't you ever heard the word bitchin' in St. Louis?"

"No. Thanks for clearing that up," I say smiling.

Cindy and Elaine turn toward each other and talk quietly until I get off.

Every day on the bus they say hello and talk to me a little. The day after I met them, when I went to typing class, I said hi to Elaine and she smiled so broadly I could tell she wanted to be my friend.

At lunch Elaine and Cindy sit with girls who wear risqué clothes. Their blouses are partially see-through or have low necklines. They wear much heavier makeup than I do, especially their lipstick, and they all wear nail polish that's bright red. When I do wear nail polish, it's pale pink.

Today is Wednesday and I am going to my first All School Assembly. I'm excited to see the whole high school at once. We sit with our Homeroom class. In Homeroom we meet for fifteen minutes to hear announcements for the week, stuff like club meetings, sports events, parent events, and schedule changes. The assembly is held in the gym. We sit on bleachers.

I watch everyone file in. The ninth and tenth graders are already sitting down. Our class is coming in and now I see some people I hadn't noticed before. When the twelfth grade class arrives, I gasp silently as I watch the two colored boys come in. They are very tall and stand straight, like soldiers. They have on nice clothes and are talking and laughing to the other kids in line with them. I can't wait to meet them. I want to be friends with them because they remind me of Ruby, Ethel, Bernice and Bill. They look warm and friendly. My eyes are so glued to them; I don't even hear anything the speakers are saying—like it's just me and the two colored boys in the gym by ourselves. I feel nervous sitting there, watching everyone else talk to each other and laugh. I feel so left out.

On Friday on the bus Elaine asks if I want to go to the beach after school. I tell her I'll call my mom from school and see. Elaine says she has an extra towel and a bathing suit that would fit me and I can borrow them.

On the phone Mom asks who I'm going with and when I'll be home. She says I can go but to be careful in the ocean—that the waves can kill you. She starts telling me about Dad in Florida, when the waves brought him far out and a lifeguard had to rescue him because he couldn't get back to shore. I don't understand any of this since I have never been in an ocean and the pictures I have seen show a serene, magical place where people are swimming or wading in the turquoise water somewhere in Hawaii or the Caribbean. Drowning and dying never entered my mind when imagining the Pacific Ocean.

# 21
# OVER THE HILL

Kids call it "The Beach Over the Hill." The girls tell me they watch surfers there and I tell them I've never seen surfing or even the ocean. They laugh like I must be joking. They seem fascinated by me. It makes me feel so happy that they're taking me in so quickly, like I was their long lost cousin. I don't know them well, but so far they seem bitchin' and sort of wild.

After classes are over, we change in the school bathroom and put the towels around us. I feel naked in the bikini Elaine lent me; it's my first time wearing one so below the waist. I can't help thinking that boys will be looking at me.

I get into the car with Cindy, Elaine, and two other girls I haven't met before—Laura and Peggy. Laura has a movie star face—the kind you can stare at all day because it is so beautiful—aqua eyes and curly blonde hair that flows down her back like a golden cape. She seems quiet. Peggy has green eyes and wavy brown hair with some red in it that looks like she brushed it a thousand times, it's so shiny—like a doll's hair. Her teeth are extra big and she lisps when she talks. Since she has the same name as my Peggy I want to know her.

Elaine drives very fast on a windy road the girls refer to as "over the hill to Santa Cruz," a half hour away. I sway in the back seat as we swerve around curves and my body parts stick to Cindy and Laura. We are all giggling. I feel embarrassed to have my body touch theirs. I don't even know them, but it already feels like we are close friends.

Elaine's bikini fits me well and makes me feel like a sophisticated teenager. The wind, sun, and sound of cars whizzing by makes me feel lightheaded, like I'm drunk with life. Elaine's driving is so reckless, I think maybe I'll die my first week at school, if not in the car then in the ocean. I am speechless and trembling with excitement about going to a real ocean.

Elaine honks the horn to avoid crashing; like a wave hitting the shore.

We finally arrive, park, and swiftly run down to the shore where we find a spot on the sand to put our stuff. It's close to where the surfers drip salty shimmers of water like liquid diamonds.

I drop my towel and purse and, alone, walk bravely to the ocean's edge, mesmerized. It feels like a best friend I have not seen for many years. It goes on forever. This is why the word infinity was made up—to describe the ocean. I have never seen anything so big, restless, scary and beautiful in my life. Like it contains every human emotion. I thought it would be like a giant lake or the Gulf of Mexico that Mom and Dad took us to on vacation. But it's nothing like that.

I stare at the waves. Each one is a different shape, size, and color. There are light and inky shades of colbalt, aqua and navy blue mixed with greens, purples, and yellows, like tubes of oil paint spilling out their colors. How can any child be denied the ecstasy of seeing, smelling, feeling the ocean? Parents should be in jail for life if they deny the ocean experience to a child. Even if I never love my new house, school, or classmates, I will always have the ocean. I can cry with it, talk to it, and laugh at it. It feels so personal, like it's all mine. It's weird but the ocean gives me reassurance, makes me feel I'm worthy of being alive; like it's Mitch, Ruby, Ethel, Bernice, Bill, and Peggy giving me all the love I want in one swoop. I know it can hurt me if I'm not careful, just like people I love can, but I will treasure it and respect it. The ocean is endless, like my life at sixteen. I am in awe as I silently walk back to my new girlfriends.

"Rachael, what do you think?" Elaine asks.

"It is unreal and beautiful."

"Do you want to go in the water and feel it?" She asks.

I nod, eagerly. Elaine and I run barefoot on the damp hard sand. We stop where the sea meets the sand—but this time is different than a few minutes ago because this time I'm going to feel the ocean all around me like a big hug.

There are a lot of surfers—only guys—in colorful Hawaiian print bathing suits. Some are in the ocean and others carry their boards, talking and laughing.

The other girls I'm here with are dug into the sand on wrinkly towels. They're probably watching to see how I'll react as I put my feet into the ocean for the first time. The fishy, salty, fresh smell leads me out into its grasp. I gasp as the freezing water cuffs my ankles. The last time I swam I was in the chlorine-scented lukewarm water at the country club. I never knew how free the ocean and a bikini could feel.

"Is it always this cold?" I ask Elaine as I splash the water like I'm whipping cream.

"Pretty much. But once you get in, it's fine."

"My toes and ankles got in. I think that's it for today," I say.

"We'll see. Maybe a cute surfer will initiate you by dragging you all the way into the Pacific," she adds mischievously.

The way she says *all the way* makes it sound like my first time doing *it*.

"I am fine just being introduced to *it*," I say, smiling at Elaine like we both get the joke.

The rest of the afternoon, the girls talk about the surfer guys and school. Elaine talks about going to beauty college after high school but Cindy, Peggy, and Laura say they are going right to work after graduating; they say they never want to study or take tests again.

Some of the guys they know come over and talk in between surfing. They all have coffee colored tans, long blond or brown hair with blond streaks and strong looking arms and legs. They are all pretty cute.

I'm uncomfortable just sitting here waiting until a guy comes over and notices me. I would rather just be by myself looking at the ocean and thinking about it. I cannot believe these girls do this all the time—watch and wait for surfers to flirt with them. I don't want to be a surfer girl. It looks empty watching the girls try so hard, their eyes full of hope that someone will pay attention to them.

I'm sitting on a towel next to Laura while the other girls are in the water trying to catch some waves—body surfing. It looks scary.

"Laura, where do the colored kids go to the beach? I don't see any here," I ask.

"Oh, I don't know. I never see any on this beach. Steven and Marcus—the colored ones at school—they probably know. Ask them," Laura says, watching the surfers.

"I don't know them," I say.

"You will. Everyone knows them. They are top football players and are cousins. I like them. Everyone does."

Sitting on the beach, I think about the week: how I will get to meet Steven and Marcus next week; how the teachers are not as distant as I am used to; the homework is easier. There is casualness in the classrooms that I felt the very first day from the teachers. When a student walks in late, the teacher ignores the tardiness but will talk to the student after class, privately. At Warren High a late student would be embarrassed in front of the whole class by a comment from the teacher. The teachers here want the students to succeed—they've already shown they care about me. Teachers at Warren didn't notice whether I needed help or was doing well.

A new exciting idiosyncrasy about California hits me. I am more aware of the sounds and smells of nature. The light is golden, not watered down; the deep and rich light of cloudless skies turns the blue into iridescent gold that shines on the leaves and grass. The air smells like fresh cut flowers with the backdrop of green hills and rainbow colored mountains and it widens my appreciation. No bugs hamper outside dining or walking anywhere. My feet are getting calluses from going barefoot all the time. The fruit orchards grow right around my neighborhood in multitudes of straight rows laden with peaches, plums, lemons and oranges. One story houses made of wood painted in muted colors are surrounded by fences low enough to talk to neighbors. Cars carry surfboards on top ready to dash to the beach.

Dad set up a workshop in the garage and tinkers around the house fixing things that are broken. He spends hours alone in the yard planting and trimming. I didn't know he liked gardening. Maybe I can partake of his hobbies and be closer to him. But I'm scared he'll say he doesn't want me to be with him while he gardens or tinkers--so different than his old life at the country club. Now that golf doesn't take him away every weekend, I see Dad more often.

Dad works in a store that has the cheapest stuff you can buy like at J. C. Pennys or Sears Roebuck, except it is all on one very large level. They even sell groceries and toiletries. Dad owns and runs all the clothing departments: men's, women's, and children's. When you buy something, the merchandise is put in a paper bag—no hangers, no wrapping, and no tissue. I'll shop there because I don't care if I don't wear expensive clothes. I never have cared about that.

Mom cooks every meal, and after dinner Jessy, Rusty, and I help with the dishes. My heart beats faster when Mom is in the kitchen. I want to shout and yell: *I can't believe you're in the kitchen like other moms. I love that you are cooking and feeding us like you care. I know you have no choice because we have less money but it looks like you are enjoying it. I feel like I am in a sweet, luscious dream that tastes like home cooking. When I set the table and clean up I don't even know I am helping you because I feel so much joy. Even though you are still distant from me when you look or talk to me, I feel love on your face when you are in the kitchen.*

"Mom, when did you learn to cook?" I ask while going in and out of the kitchen, setting the table.

"Your grandma would cook all day at home when I was growing up and I watched many, many times. She never had a cookbook—just did what she thought would be tasty. It was a labor of love to make everything from scratch. There were no frozen foods, no canned foods and very little refrigeration. Only a hunk of ice in a small wooden box that we called an icebox. Because the icebox wasn't very big and the large pieces of ice took up most of the room, you had to decide what was really important to keep cold. It's funny, but I forgot how much I do like to cook. I cooked for your dad a little when we were first married, but when Annie came along, we hired a cook because I was too busy with her," Mom says. She looks kind of surprised with herself for having revealed more than she thought she would.

"Mom, I want to learn by watching you," I say, scared she'll say nothing back or something not encouraging.

"Okay, dear. You can," Mom says, distracted while looking into the refrigerator, not at me.

"Mom, why doesn't Erna, our new maid stay and help us with dinner?"

"Dad and I are watching every penny here and we can't have her more than once a week and only during the

327

daytime."

"Okay, I say," having heard this talk about money several times since we moved into the house. I think Mom is having a hard time. I know we moved because Dad lost his stores, but I didn't know we had to watch every penny, especially since Mom and Dad still dress up and go out a lot in San Francisco with their new rich friends. They pretend like they're still rich.

I think Mom feels guilty she didn't get to cook for us until now and that's why she can't look at me. Maybe she'd have preferred having a more homey life, like the one she had growing up. I hope so. I want to experience what the cozy life feels like, even if it's just for a few years before I leave for college.

I've seen Mom and Dad more in the few weeks we've been in our new house than in all the years I can remember in our big house in St. Louis. This place has only one story and fewer rooms. No extra bedrooms—only three, because Jess and I still share. The only T.V. is in the living room so we all have to sit together to watch. There is no attic, basement, library, breakfast room or sunroom. All the frills of the house I grew up in are gone.

Erna, the maid, is from Latvia and is not even trying to be friends with me. Even though she is a smelly, white, fat maid with an accent that sounds like a Russian spy, I care about her. She just cleans and doesn't smile or talk, like she just wants to get done and go home. I don't know why we can't find a colored maid. If she were colored, I would probably try to see if she could be "my Ruby."

I have been reading the newspaper everyday and listening to the news to find out more about discrimination of colored people. I cut out articles in the paper so I can figure out what to do next. Maybe I will see something about people from Latvia being treated horribly and then I would want to help Erna. The whole world is learning about the treatment of colored people in the newspapers. The University of Mississippi and the University of Alabama are going to desegregate soon. There are demonstrations in front of the universities with colored people marching for desegregation and white people marching against it. I thought the Civil War was over long ago. Governor Wallace of Alabama doesn't want to desegregate the University but I hope he will have to. I'm sure there are many troubles that don't even get printed in magazines and newspapers, things the whole world should be aware of. At least during the Civil War everyone knew what was going on. It was out in the open. This undeclared war doesn't affect white students in high schools in California, maybe, except me.

Mitch hasn't written yet but I know he will soon. I miss his sense of humor and laughing with him and the comfort of his company. Someone told me for every friend I have in St. Louis I will seek a similar type of friend in California. I haven't found a Mitch yet. In fact, I don't know the boys at all. Florence isn't like anyone at home. I still think of St. Louis as home. I want to find a Mitch, Tommy, Jane and Peggy—then I would be happy. Maybe.

Do you want come with me to Florence's today? She invited me over. I want to be with you if you'd like come?" I say to Jess.

"No, please, go. I just want to stay here in bed and sleep." She sounds so sad.

After breakfast Mom drives me to Florence's. She and I have decided to try out for cheerleading next week and we have to do it in front of the whole school, so we are going to practice. Florence lives with her mother who works in a bank. Her parents are divorced and she is an only child. She told me her dad lives in Sacramento and he only sees her at Christmas and in the summer. She doesn't like him because he doesn't give any child support money to her mom so they can't afford a lot of extra things. I want to give her money because I feel sorry for her having a mom who works all the time to help Florence have a nice life—unlike my mom, who worked because she wanted to be with Dad. I have never known a mom who had to work except colored moms. Maybe that's why Florence so often seems distracted—she is probably worried all the time about money.

As I step in the door to Florence's house, I can see immediately that they are poor. The furniture and carpeting are shabby. I think of Ruby's house, ragged like Florence's. I meet her mom who I saw at school, who looks like an older version of Florence. I can tell Florence and her mom are close. They speak more with their eyes and not so many words and they understand each other. I am sad for Florence not having a father around. We get some lemonade and go out to the backyard. After we practice cheerleading moves, we go into Florence's bedroom. There is nothing extra to make it cozy and girl-like; only a bed with a tattered blue blanket, one pillow with a dusty yellow pillowcase; a wooden chest of drawers with a picture of Jesus in a frame above it, a brush and comb set and a bottle of perfume on it; a round multi-colored rug that slides over the wood floor when you step on it; one poster of Tab Hunter on the wall; and a wooden cross with Jesus hanging from a nail over the bed.

"You are so much better than me, Florence," I say. "You can do cartwheels and jump higher." I feel like I'm being phony nice to make up for her being poor.

"I know, Rachael, but it is a popularity contest, too. Since we are both new it going to be hard for both of us to win," Florence says with confidence, like she knows everything.

"I am happy just to try out. It's fun having a new experience with you," I reply. "In my old high school I didn't care about much except getting passing grades and having friends—no extracurricular activities. My friends only cared about boys and clothes—not the world. I did have fun but I was more concerned about the colored people being treated fairly because we had a lot of colored people working for our family."

"Rachael, that sounds so cool to have all that help. I would love that."

"I know it sounds good, but you're close with your mom. I would love that." I didn't give her a chance to respond; it was the most intimate thing I have ever said to a new person in California. I start a new subject on purpose because I don't know her well enough to talk about me and my mother and how we are not close.

"Florence, don't you think it's weird that there are only two colored boys in our school? I saw them at the school assembly on Wednesday and walking around the school before that. First I thought there were four boys, but it turned out they were the same ones. Why aren't there more colored kids at school?"

"Rachael, I haven't given that one thought. I heard the cousins are really popular and nice and they do have a sister in our school. Why do you care so much about how many colored kids we have?" Florence asks sounding puzzled.

"First of all," I begin, "do you know it's illegal to marry

outside your race in fifteen states? Why should the government say colored kids can come to our schools but you cannot marry a white person if you fall in love with them? That is so awful. I hate that they are treated like they are less than us. There are so many things colored people are denied that most people our age don't even know or care about." I talk without stopping to breathe before Florence can say anything to change the subject.

"Rachael, are you Jewish?" Florence asks, looking brave about asking the question and ignoring what I just said about colored people.

"Yes, why?"

"Someone at school said they thought you were Jewish. I have never met a Jew. There are only two others in our school and people are talking about it— that you and your sister are Jews and what they think Jews are like. They said Jews are loud, cheap and have hook-shaped noses but that you and Jessy aren't like that. The other two Jews in the school are boys. One is Sam in our class and he isn't like that either and the other is a freshman named Roy. He does have a hooked nose but he isn't loud. They're also telling bad jokes about Jews—just to warn you if you hear one."

"Have you met my sister Jessy?" I ask.

"I saw her. Someone pointed her out to me."

"Some Jewish people *are* loud and have large noses, of course," I say, "like my dad's nose—even though he still looks handsome with it. But some Christians are loud and have big noses, too. Some Jewish people are cheap and some Gentiles, ah, Christians, are too. What religion are you?"

"Catholic. Have you ever met a Catholic?"

I think she will never have an abortion. Lucky her. Catholics are forbidden to. I wish I were Catholic. I don't say that, though. Instead, I say, "I have heard the expression, *He Jewed him down.* That is not nice and it isn't true because other people try to get things cheap, too, but maybe Jews are better at it. Also, in biblical times they were the money lenders, so the rumor may have started two thousand years ago. Do you want to know about the Civil Rights Act?" I want to change the subject.

"I'm sorry, Rachael, if that hurts your feelings. If I hear it again I will stick up for you and say it isn't true," Florence says.

I don't believe her, but at least she knows I am bothered by what was said. I don't trust her yet. I hope when I get to know her better, I feel differently.

"I do want to know about civil rights," she says, to my surprise. "Actually, in college I want to study American Politics and International Policy so I can be a diplomat." Then she jumps up. "Let's practice some more."

Even though she doesn't ask anything about Civil Rights I am so excited I have a new friend who might be interested in it that I don't even care that much about cheerleading. But we practice a lot and laugh and have fun and I'm happy because Florence must clearly think about the world if she wants to be a diplomat. Funny, but having a new friend makes me miss Peggy more.

Peggy always looked out for me; but we grew up together. I wish so much to fill the hole in my heart that still misses Peggy. I hope a new friend will help heal it. It will not be Florence, though, because even though she's sometimes outgoing, pretty, wholesome, and fairly friendly, she isn't pure sweetness like my Peggy.

When I get home, I see Rusty in the kitchen cutting string beans. He doesn't even look up when I come in the kitchen.

"What'cha doing with the beans?" I don't want him to know I'm shocked to see him working in the kitchen. "Where's Mom? What's she doing?"

" Mom burned herself on the barbeque, but don't tell her I told you. She's outside trying to figure out how to make it not so hot for the chicken. It's her first time using a barbeque."

"Oh, no. Dad should be barbequing, not Mom. I always see dads in pictures doing that. What'cha making besides chicken and string beans?"

"Corn on the cob, and salad."

"I hope it tastes better than last night's roast. I took one bite and didn't say anything. It was awful. Mom doesn't know how to cook like Ethel.

"That's for sure."

"Rusty, do you like your new school?"

"Yeah, do you?"

"I do. Do you miss your friends?"

I'm trying to get closer to Rusty than I was in St. Louis by showing I care about what he's experiencing in our new town. I want him to know I realize it is hard for him to be in a new place. In St. Louis we were in our own worlds and hardly even talked to each other.

"Yeah, do you?"

"Yes, I'm going to like it here. I don't miss my best friends as much as Ruby, Ethel, Bernice and Bill. Do you like helping Mom?"

"I sure do! Why do you miss the maids more than your friends?" Rusty asks with more animation than I've seen him display since we moved here.

"I felt they were part of our family. They were there every day and knew me and I knew them. But I can't wait to eat *your* cooking." I smile.

Rusty smiles back like he got the joke and wants to please me by being nice. I hope he stays sweet during this changing time for him.

Mom took Rusty to temple last Friday night. Since neither has brought up what happened, I would rather ask Rusty first. Since he will be thirteen in January maybe he has decided to have a Bar Mitzvah.

Rusty is getting a chubby, pimply look and it probably bothers him. I see him more around the house now since the house is like an open book. He always looks happy. I don't know if he's all of a sudden interested in cooking or will do anything to be near Mom. I hope Dad will be with Rusty more than he was in St. Louis. I remember a friend of Mom and Dad's, named Jack, who used to take his son, Rusty and Mom miniature golfing on Sundays when Dad was at the club playing golf.

"So, how was temple?" I ask sort of matter-of-factly.

"Okay. I liked it because a kid was on the bema doing

part of the service because he's getting Bar Mitzvah'd. Mom introduced me to his family afterwards; they're Mom and Dad's new friends in San Francisco. I may do that, too," Rusty says.

"Do what?"

"Get Bar Mitzvah'd. Probably to get a lot of presents, but also Mom wants me to. She says all of her new friends' sons are doing it. She didn't care in St. Louis because our temple didn't even have Bar Mitzvahs. Almost all temples do but ours didn't, which is so weird."

I feel so easy talking to him, like he really wants to be closer to me.

"Yeah, I know. So Reform. Don't you have to learn Hebrew before you are thirteen?"

"Yeah, I would need to start soon and maybe get Bar Mitzvah'd at thirteen and a half."

"That would be great, Russ," I say, never having called him Russ before. The phone starts ringing. "Let's talk more later," I say, running for the phone.

"Shalom," Rusty says laughing.

"Shalom," I say back, smiling at his gleaming face.

I know I have the surfer girls as friends if I want them. They're so friendly in the halls and in classes and when we go to the beach. It's like I was in their group already. This is only the second week of school and Elaine asks me to sit with her and her friends at lunch. I thank her but tell her I sit with Florence, a new girl. I can tell by the look on her face that she's disappointed. But I know my closest girl friends will be more like me. I'm not like the surfer girls.

They look cheap and only care about flirting with boys.

Florence and I still sit together at lunch—alone. Right away I want to tell her about what I know from the paper and radio and TV about civil rights.

"Florence, there are so many injustices right now as we sit here. Have you ever heard of Martin Luther King Jr. and Rosa Parks?" This is my second try and I'm hoping she is interested in what is going on.

"I have heard their names but I don't really know what they do. I know they're colored," Florence says, looking around at the boys, not me.

I want to tell her about the Jim Crow laws, Rosa Parks, Martin Luther King Jr. and desegregation so she and I can figure out what we can do to help. But I can see she's distracted now. I hope we will talk about it later but now and at cheerleading practice at her house she has not wanted to know about specifics. I guess Florence has more pressing things to think about—like money, her dad, and her mom working all the time. I don't know what coming from a family like hers is like.

Some of the boys have been coming over to say hello to us—just a quick "how are you"; a few of the girls from the group I want to be in tag along with the boys. Ray, one of the guys, is always the one to head up coming over. He's always smiling and joking with me and Florence, but Florence doesn't laugh. I don't know if she doesn't get his humor or is worried about other things, but Ray sees me laughing.

"Where's your Southern drawl, Rachael?" Ray asks.

"I'm not from Southern Missouri," I laugh

"Well, why did Northern Missouri let you go? I know your parents gave you no choice but to drag you here to California."

"Yeah, I was dragged all the way behind the car." We laugh together. Laughing at the same time is very bonding. I feel Ray and I have a similar sense of humor and enjoy kidding each other. Florence doesn't know how to do this but I want her to learn so she won't feel like an outsider.

By the end of this second week I feel more and more comfortable. I really like all the kids in this group. We joke around when they drop over longer. They all talk about the same things—clothes, parties, boys, funny stories, family, homework, exams, college, grades, but they are sweeter, nicer and have a lust for life I didn't see with my friends back home. I study the way they talk to each other and learn more considerate ways of treating each other than I was accustomed to in St. Louis. They use friendlier gestures, like putting their arm around each other, looking into each other's eyes more, and laughing more. If they were anti-Semitic they wouldn't be as friendly or nice to me.

Florence thinks I should like Ray as a boyfriend. I think she wants me to like anyone that will help her stay in the popular crowd. Everyone thinks we have to do everything together. When I talk to the kids in the group, Florence doesn't join in on the conversation—she just stares at me like she doesn't want me to talk to anyone. She waits for someone to talk to her before acting friendly.

We are both shy in different ways. I am shy, except when I can tell someone wants to be friendly, then I can be myself. Florence is shy even if someone is friendly; she doesn't laugh even when something is funny; she just stares at the person who's saying the funny thing. Once she did laugh—and it was so loud everyone turned around and stared at her.

Frankie is coming over to us. He is a few pounds overweight, has blue eyes, is short, and either has a very serious, worried expression or is smiling. He's been going steady with Bobbi for a long time.

"Hey, do you want to come to my party Friday night?"

There is a long silence as we sit there a moment taken aback—I can't believe he's asking us. Since I know Florence isn't going to respond, I say, blushing, "I, ah, we would love to. Thanks, Frankie."

"Okay, good," Frankie says, walking away quickly like he said a dirty word or he is embarrassed.

He asked probably because Bobbi and her identical twin sister Natalie and I talk at lunch more and more as well as in our classes together.

Bobbi and Natalie are fun, pretty, and love to laugh. They are both cheerleaders. Today they've invited me over to their house after school. Their parents are warm and love that I came over. They have a huge, new home that has giant glass windows in the living room called picture windows that go from the ceiling to the floor. I think it looks like the futuristic homes described in science fiction books. They have two more sisters who are also beautiful, so there are tons of boys over all the time. Natalie is going steady with the only other Jewish kid in my class—Sam. I haven't talked to Sam yet except to say hi. He is never alone when I see him. Also I don't want to talk to him just because I know he's Jewish. That would make me uncomfortable, like I was just trying to be friendly for that reason.

At the twins' house we spend a lot of time fixing our hair and makeup in the bathroom or we sit in the living room and listen to music and play games. They start teaching me to sew muumus on their sewing machine. Most of my new girlfriends change into muumus after school when the weather is warm.

I feel closer to Bobbi than Natalie. She has a more than beautiful look you can stare at all day. And Bobbi has a more giggly personality than Natalie. They are both about my height, have medium brown hair with blonde highlights, beautiful skin, blue sparkling eyes and figures that are like models in *Seventeen* magazine. They smile and joke all the time. Maybe Bobbi could be my Peggy. Bobbi and Natalie are so much sweeter than Florence.

"Are you a virgin?" Natalie asks while we fix our hair in the bathroom.

"What?" I laugh taken by surprise. "Yes, I am!" I look down as I answer, embarrassed at even having the subject brought up. Then I look back up at my red face in the mirror.

Natalie peers in the mirror at me and says, "Well, let's talk about it more when you have a serious boyfriend."

I like that she's talking to me about sex, but I know I will never go all the way until I'm married. I don't want to get pregnant like Jessy.

# 22
# CHEERLEADING

Today, Monday, the third week, all the girls that want to be cheerleaders have to try out first in front of Mrs. Carter, the P.E. teacher. Mom signed a paper that I could try out but she didn't ask me any questions about trying out.

After the top ten are chosen by Mrs. Carter, they try out Friday in front of the whole school. Five are chosen to join the other cheerleaders that are from last year, which includes Natalie and Bobbi. There are around thirty girls trying out. My stomach jumps when I see a colored girl trying out. I've never seen her before.

"Florence, do you know the colored girl's name?" I whisper.

"Yeah, Gloria. She's a senior."

I watch as she practices. She is way beyond the talent of anyone else. Cartwheels, spins, splits, dance moves. Everyone is staring at her. I have to meet her. I leave

Florence to walk over to meet her.

"Hi, I'm Rachael."

"Hi, I'm Gloria."

"Good to meet you. You are so talented."

"Thank you."

"That's Florence," I point to Florence.

"Hi," Gloria yells across the room.

"Hi," Florence yells back and keeps on practicing by herself.

"Good luck, Gloria."

"Thanks, Rachael."

I watch Gloria in awe. She must hear music in her head because her moves are graceful, like a ballet dancer. Her jumps and arms coordinate like she is on ice skates not a wooden floor. She glides like a swan and looks elegant and relaxed.

Everyone takes turns trying out and the top ten names are called. Florence and I make it but not Gloria. I am so angry. Florence goes off to class. I find Mrs. Carter talking to some of the girls and I wait until she is finished.

"Mrs. Carter, I am so happy I made top ten but I know in the popular vote on Friday, I won't win because I'm so new to the school. I'd like Gloria to try out instead of me. She's better than any of the girls. Can you please tell me why she didn't make it?"

"Gloria didn't display what we are looking for in our

cheerleaders," Mrs. Carter says not looking at me.

"What are you looking for?"

"We have guidelines, Rachael," Mrs. Carter says staring right into my eyes.

"What are the guidelines?"

"Those are between the school administrators," she says, dismissing me by turning around and walking away.

I walk out and run into Florence.

"Florence, we have to do something. Gloria should have won."

"Rachael, that's up to Mrs. Carter," Florence says with a mean look in her eyes.

"No, Florence. Now it's up to us."

"Rachael, I don't want to start trouble. We just got to this school," Florence says so fast without having a moment to think about it first.

Now I understand Florence so much more. She wants to be my friend but doesn't care about injustice. She is a hypocrite, saying she wants to be a diplomat after college. She's doesn't want to be a fair diplomat.

During the day I make sure to see all the other girls who made top ten. Seven girls agree not to try out in front of the school on Wednesday unless Gloria is part of the group. The only ones who don't agree are Florence and another girl, Veronica, from the senior class. They understand how unfair it is and they all thank me for letting Gloria take my place.

After school I go to see Mr. Woodman, the principal. Even though my heart beats fast when I walk to his office and open door, I'm not scared; it's strength not fear that quickens my pulse. I wait until Louise, the receptionist, tells me I can go in.

As soon as we greet each other, I say, "Mr. Woodman, seven of the top ten cheerleaders are not going to try out for the popular vote in Friday's assembly."

"Why, Rachael?"

"Gloria should have made top ten. She is better than any of us and she didn't make it. I want to have Gloria take my place. I made top ten but I don't want to try out Friday. I think she didn't make it because she's colored. That has to be the only reason."

"We treat everyone the same here. Let me talk to Mrs. Carter. I'll get back to you tomorrow. Come to my office in the morning before school. Rachael, I admire your independence and standing up for what you believe is right." Mr. Woodman speaks so calmly. I feel that he wants to agree with me but he has to do the right thing by first asking Mrs. Carter what this is all about.

"Mr. Woodman, since I'm new here and don't know many kids, I want to ask you about Gloria. Is she Steven or Marcus's sister? I haven't seen her around school until today."

"No, well, she is Steven's sister, actually his twin, and also Marcus's girlfriend. They aren't cousins like some think. They have wonderful families. I hope you will get to know them."

"Thank you," I say looking down at the floor and

stopping myself from blurting out my whole story about wanting to help anyone who is treated unfairly, especially the colored people. He's busy and I can tell now is not the right time to tell him.

The next morning I wake up early to get ready for my meeting with the principal.

Jess rolls her eyes when I tell her what I'm doing. "Why are you doing this? We're new here. Do you just want to get noticed?"

"No, I want to be fair to those who are discriminated against."

"Okay, fine, but Jews are discriminated against, too. Why don't you fight for them as much as you do colored people? I heard someone telling a bad Jew joke when they thought I couldn't hear."

"Then say something, Jess."

"I don't want to start trouble like you do. I'm already in enough trouble with Mom and Dad."

When I told Mom and Dad last night about my meeting with the principal they were okay with what I was doing but said they would feel better if the school agrees with me and I'm not causing trouble. Mom drives Jessy and me to school early instead of taking the bus.

When I get to school that morning, Gloria is waiting by my locker when I go to put my books away.

"Rachael, I appreciate what you're doing. Everyone knows. It's all over the school. I don't want you to get into trouble," Gloria says looking very serious.

"Gloria, I have to go to the principal now. I have to find out what he decided. Can you wait for me here?"

"Okay."

I run off.

"Rachael," Mr. Woodman states, "I have talked to Mrs. Carter and we agree with what you want to do. That is all I am going to say on the matter." I have the feeling he wishes he could tell me more.

"Oh, thank you so much! I'm so happy. Thank you."

I run to my locker to tell Gloria. We both hug. Even though I don't know her I like her so much.

"I don't know what to say because no one has ever done anything like this to help me. The kids in school are nice but this is more than nice. Thank you for standing up for me when you didn't have to. But, why are you doing this, Rachael?" Gloria asks with tears still in her eyes.

"It's a very long story and I want to tell you, but it will wait. The main thing is, I think you're so talented and deserve the chance to be a cheerleader," I say eagerly, determined to make this one thing fair.

"Hey, Rachael, maybe after all this is over you can come to my house for dinner. Also, I have a twin brother who is pretty cute," she says smiling.

"Okay! I've seen your brother and he is cute, so please keep that a promise!" I say smiling back.

The tryouts are in the gym with the whole school watching as each girl does a whole cheer routine. Gloria is outstanding and far above the other nine. Afterwards, everyone in the school is given a ballot; it's a blind vote and the ballots are collected before we leave the gym.

If Gloria wins I would think everything I have ever thought or done in the way of fighting discrimination would be worth it. If she doesn't, I want to go to another school and start over. This school would not feel right for me. I'll move back to St. Louis and live with Aunt Alice and see Ruby every day. I daydream about doing that because I know I will hate it here if she doesn't win.

Every minute waiting to see who's going to win seems like hours. I want to yell, have a drink, pace up and down the halls. My stomach hurts. I want to go to the nurse.

Finally, the winners are announced over the class speaker in my third period English class. Gloria didn't win.

I am so heavy with sadness I put my head down on my desk. It feels like a joke—I can't believe it. Florence is not in my class. I wonder if she would have clapped. Florence was one of the winners. I am also jealous because she is new and won the popular vote and maybe I could have won, too. The rest of the day I can't concentrate in my classes and when I eat lunch, even though I sit with my group, I hardly talk or look up.

Elaine, my surfer beach girlfriend, comes over and whispers in my ear, "I'm sorry Gloria lost and I want you to know I voted for her."

"Thanks, Elaine." I look at her and smile.

When I look up I see Florence sitting at our group's table but as far away from me as she can get. She is looking at me smiling and I look down again at my food. She's probably smiling because she won, not because Gloria lost,

I think to myself.

No one else says anything to me about Gloria. I thought maybe Bobbi or Natalie, would say they were sorry. I hope they will get to know me better but I know that takes time, just like wiping away prejudice takes time. Maybe another day some of my new friends will say something about Gloria losing the popular vote; I hope so. I thought Ray would know I was sad and at least come over and put his arm around me so I would know he knew how I feel.

After school, Jess and I talk about the cheerleading tryouts.

"What did you think of the tryouts?" I ask.

"I was mad that you gave up your spot. I wasn't mad that you gave it to Gloria, though," Jess says quickly, like she wants to get that last part in before I interrupt her.

"Really?"

"Yeah, really. Gloria is so good and should have been a cheerleader. But I wanted my baby sister to be a cheerleader, too."

"Thanks, but I wouldn't have made it anyway, Jess. The popular vote has a lot to do with who you know and, besides, I'm not that good."

"Then why did your best friend, Florence, win? She's new."

"She isn't my best friend anymore. Maybe because she can do cartwheels and I can't, for one reason."

"Why isn't she your best friend?"

"Because she didn't stand up for Gloria!"

"Okay. Geez, good thing I did or maybe you'd hate me."

"Maybe I would!" I feel strong saying this, like I'm finally standing up for something and not hiding it.

This school is not the place I want to be. No one cares, just like in St. Louis. I don't want to go to any high school. Maybe I'll drop out and never finish.

"So you think you can just get everyone to care about colored people like you do just because you think it is right? Rach, it's 1962 and colored people can't use the same bathrooms as us, can't sit at counters with us, can't go to our schools, and a lot of folks still try to keep them from voting. But Rachael, this is happening in the South and other places but not in California so most kids aren't aware of it. Since it doesn't affect them they don't care. If we didn't come from St. Louis where we had a lot of Negro help we probably wouldn't even know about all this. God, I sound like you," Jess sighed, rolling her eyes. "Why do you think you can change people? They don't even like Jews. I pretend I don't hear the "kike" jokes kids tell, or I walk away. The kids like Gloria-- they like you, they like me—but that doesn't mean when they get to do something secret, like vote, they are going to change their prejudices."

"Yeah, I know, you're right, Jess," I nod sadly. "Their parents are in their heads and they hear *Negro people aren't as good as white people. They are stupid and lazy.* It means a lot to me, Jess, that you've noticed what I want for Gloria and all Negro people. I know you may even not care about them the way I do, but at least you care about me by talking to me about why she didn't win."

On the weekend some boys come over, including Ray. Dad jokes around with them. This makes me feel proud because Dad cares about my friends enough to kid with them and take time away from washing the car or tending the putting green. Since Dad doesn't play golf twice a week anymore, he put in his own putting green so he can practice. The guys think Dad is so suave and cool with his Jaguar and his talk about golf and his movie star looks.

Dad still plays golf, but only about once a month with his rich friends in San Francisco. But he talks a good game with anyone who will listen, and all the boys love to hear his golf stories.

Ray comes over to me. "Hey, Rachael, if you go to the party with me tonight I'll tell you a little secret."

"Tell me now."

"Nope. You have to go tonight. It's not what you think."

It's probably not about Gloria even though that's all I think about. Maybe he'll say he wants to be my boyfriend, but I don't like him that much. I don't care about what it is. I feel I failed Gloria and nothing else matters much.

Still, I am thinking about the party at Frankie's house tonight. His parents will be out of town. Maybe I'll get to make out with one of the guys—just as a friend—because there's no one I really want as a boyfriend yet. But I'd like to kiss and hug Ray to see what it feels like. Maybe then I'd know if I can like him enough to be a boyfriend. His lips are like smooth pillows that I think I could melt into.

Most of the kids who are going to be at Frankie's house tonight are going to be from our group, but there'll be some other kids I don't know and even some kids from other high schools. I know there'll be alcohol, but I hate the taste of it. I usually drink Coke mixed with rum because it tastes like liquid candy.

At the party, Ray motions for me to sit on his lap. I'm kind of scared to like him or anyone at school because then I will have to see them every day. I wish Ray went to a different school. That way, if we broke up, I wouldn't have to see him. I wish I wasn't still so frightened about a boy hurting me.

Ray still has adolescent pudginess, but not like Mitch's. Ray's rolly-polliness looks temporary, like it could disappear tomorrow if he lifted a few barbells. He has a round face and tan complexion, aqua blue eyes with long dark eyelashes, white teeth that glow in the dark, a beginning mustache with light hairs that are fine as those on a baby's head, and a constant smile like he is drunk all the time. All this more than makes up for his chubbiness.

He's on his third straight scotch, and kisses me gently. I like his kiss. He kisses me more deeply with his tongue first touching my tongue, then circling around it. We hug each other's bodies but he doesn't try to feel me up. I have never made out before. I am now fully a sixteen year old girl who can feel my body responding to him.

I spot Frankie, the one giving the party. "Hey, Frankie, great party. Are all the guys on the football team invited?"

"Hi, Rachael. I'm not sure who's coming. Word just spreads. No one is really invited.

"Okay, just wondered how to find out about these parties in my new hometown."

But I am distracted, thinking, what if Steven and Marcus show up? What would I do? Would I pop off Ray's lap? Would I be embarrassed and Ray would want to know why?

Ray tries to kiss me again but I start getting fidgety. My legs are shaking a little. I keep looking at the front door to see if Steven and Marcus are coming in. Ray guides my head to his and doesn't say anything about me looking away from him every few minutes whenever I hear the door open.

Even though I've never even spoken to Steven or Marcus, I don't want them to think Ray is my boyfriend. If I liked Ray more I wouldn't even be imagining this. I won't even think about Marcus since he's Gloria's boyfriend. When those guys walked into the assembly I felt drawn to them, even though I was sitting far away. Maybe it's only because I still miss Ruby, Ethel, Bill and Bernice so much but I want to get to know Steven and Marcus more than anything right now.

"Rachael, you need a few lessons." Ray interrupts my reverie.

"Lessons in what?"

"Kissing."

"Okay. But first tell me the secret—or did you forget?"

"I'm half Jewish, on my dad's side. Can you tell? Look at my nostrils—totally Jewish," Ray laughs.

"I don't really believe you but I will still let you teach me to kiss better," I say laughing.

It's getting late. Clearly, Steven and Marcus aren't coming. I go back to making out with Ray so when I kiss a real boyfriend I will know how.

# 23
# FRIENDS

Mom doesn't wake me today because it's Saturday and she knows I got home late from the party. When I wake up, I'm not sad anymore about Gloria; I'm angry! I get the paper from Mom and Dad's bathroom and bring it to the breakfast table and read it. I know Mom and Dad are finished with the paper, so I get a scissors from the kitchen drawer and start cutting out articles I want to save.

"What are you cutting from the paper, Rachael?" Mom asks.

"There are peaceful protests everywhere in the South and the police are using dogs and fire hoses on colored kids to break them up, just like they did in Birmingham. And this is about the Woolworth's lunch counter in North Carolina last year. Some colored kids from the Agricultural and Technical College couldn't get served. And there were sit-ins at the counters, protests so they couldn't serve anyone, by a lot of college kids in Maryland, Virginia, South Carolina, Georgia, Florida, Tennessee, Louisiana, and

354

Texas. Mom, they're finally starting to serve colored people at lunch counters now because of the protests. Even in Sacramento, protesters occupied the Capitol's second floor rotunda between the two legislative chambers for weeks to end racial discrimination in housing. Governor Brown wants to end housing discrimination but legislators on both sides are still fighting it. The students slept there, Mom!" I said enthusiastically. "I wish I had been there."

"That's great, honey. But what can we do? We aren't there," Mom says, sounding disinterested.

"Mom, I'm going to figure out what to do to help. I'm gathering material so I can do something when school's out this summer. Maybe I can go to the South this summer and be a Freedom Rider." I try to say this very calmly even though I want to scream. But if I'm emotional Mom will never say yes. As it is, I'm sure she's going to have a conniption fit, hearing my request.

"A sixteen or seventeen year old girl alone in the midst of that mess is not a safe or smart way to help," Mom says sharply.

Without a second's thought she says exactly what any parent would say instead of she thinks it's wonderful that I'm the kind of person who cares about others in this world. She doesn't care about what being involved means to me.

"Mom, if we could send money to Ruby, Ethel, Bernice and Bill for their families every month, then I would feel we are doing something. But I know we can't. I know we're having our own money difficulties now. But I want to at least see them this summer." Maybe this more personal approach is better than the civil rights approach.

"Honey," Mom says looking confused, "let's talk to Dad about all this later." I think she just wants to get off the subject as fast as she can.

It's Saturday and there's a football game tonight. I feel part of the school because now I know enough kids to sit with and talk to. I don't know at all what is going on in the game but when we make a touchdown, we all stand up and cheer. Gloria and I spot each other. She's wearing Marcus's football letter jacket. "Hi, Gloria, sit here," I motion her over.

"Hi, Rachael, thanks." She smiles.

"Cool jacket. When did you get it?" I ask jealously.

"Last summer. He wants me to be warm at the games."

Steven, Marcus and Ray are on the team. Whenever they're on the field, my eyes stick to their uniforms. I clap loud and stand up longer than anyone when Steven makes a touchdown. I think everyone notices but I don't care.

The party tonight after the game is just a group of cars that park up in the hills. The road is supposedly a secret; we think no one outside of our school knows about it. We go in and out of the cars drinking, smoking and talking. If it gets cold we sit inside the cars and use the heater to warm up for a while.

Steven, Marcus and Gloria come to the party. They look happy we won, confident and proud. But seeing them, I find I'm shaking inside and feeling nervous. Even more so because I know they all know I helped Gloria. I walk over to them to introduce myself. But Marcus speaks first.

"Hi. You must be the Rachael Gloria keeps talking about," Marcus says.

"We've been wanting to meet you," Steven chimes in.

"Hope she said some good things," I say nervously, glancing at Gloria, because right away I am attracted to Steven. My legs are quivering like the strings on a bow. I feel like if I don't lie down right now my legs will be too weak to hold me up. I never felt this with Ray. Or even Tommy.

Steven's friendly eyes twinkle. His long eyelashes and sparkling brown eyes go well with his coffee with cream, smooth as marshmallow skin. His smile makes me melt like a sweet dish of ice cream. His arm muscles, which show through his sweater and his Sequoia tree size neck, hold my attention an embarrassing length of time. His brown-black curly hair matches his skin. His voice is warm and soothing.

Marcus's skin tone is rich chocolate and his small warm eyes light up like fireflies. His oval face is smaller than Steven's round face but his smile is also inviting. His arms are wiry, like the frames on his distinguished glasses. His long sideburns and hair make him look older and more serious than Steven.

Ray comes over.

"Hey, are you two making time with my new girl?" Ray says. "Well, as long as you're in the Classics, it's okay," Ray clarifies laughing.

Ray didn't say girlfriend.

"We are 'The Classics'," Marcus says, his sparkly eyes focused on my shy eyes.

'The Classics' are a car club that parks together in the school parking lot. The cars are from the 1940s or 1950s and they all have a tag on the back window that says *The*

*Classics.* I don't know what they do other than park together.

"Let me guess. You have a 1954 blue Pontiac," I say joking, looking at Marcus and then Steven.

"Close. A 1943 Mercury, maroon," Steven says. "Well, we have to go."

"What? Didn't you just get here?" I say, feeling crushed.

"Well, we met you—and that's why we came," Marcus says.

"Okay. See you around," I say to all of them, my gaze lingering on Steven longer.

Disappointed as I am, I think maybe they left because they don't feel comfortable socializing with the kids at school. Maybe they never go to parties from school. I will find out.

Gloria sees me walking to class Monday and runs up and hugs me. I hug her back. She is all smiles.

"Can you come over this Friday night? My brother Steven will be there and Marcus, my boyfriend," Gloria asks jumping up and down a little like she cannot wait for an answer.

"You didn't get to be cheerleader and I'm so sorry. You should have been. You were the best. Anyway, I'd love to come over. I'll ask Mom and let you know," I say excitedly.

We walk the same direction for a while and then say goodbye. I like the warmth she sends out when she talks and smiles.

After school I go into the kitchen where Mom is cooking dinner. "Mom, Gloria wants me to come over to dinner tomorrow night after school. She's the one that I tried to help get onto the cheerleading team." I hope I don't sound as pleading as I feel.

"Oh, you mean the colored girl? Rachael, I'm not happy about you going over there. Who knows what kind of place it is or anything about her parents?" Mom says coldly. "Let's talk it over with Dad tonight at dinner, okay?"

"Why are you causing trouble?" Jessy asks after I tell her about the invitation to Gloria's house for dinner.

I don't even tell Jessy about Steven being there because even though Jessy and I are a team, I am never quite sure when she'll decide to be on the opposing team—my parents. I don't trust Jessy like I should be able to trust a sister. If she said "I am so happy for you," even about only seeing Gloria, then I would have shared everything. Maybe it's because Jessy misses all our help more than I think and wishes Gloria was her friend, too, to remind her of them a little.

I don't share my thoughts. All I say is "Don't talk to me about causing trouble." That shut her up.

At dinner we sit silently at first. My stomach hurts because I know Mom and Jess want me to bring up going to Gloria's house for dinner and I know they're dead set against it.

"Okay, Mom, now that Dad's here, can we talk about going to Gloria's house for dinner?" I ask sweetly.

"Well, ask your father," Mom says quietly.

"Dad, can I go to Gloria's house for dinner tomorrow

after school?" I ask, as he butters his roll.

"Who is Gloria?" Dad asks like he's never heard of her.

"Gloria is the girl I helped get into the top ten in cheerleading."

"Is she the colored kid your mom talked to me about?"

"Yes, she is," I say looking right into his eyes.

"Why do you want to go there?"

"Gloria wants to have me over to study and for dinner. Her parents want to thank me for what I did to get her into the top ten."

"Yes, Mom explained that. It reminds me of the windows and mannequins in our store that were ruined because you wanted to help the colored people then. What is this, Rachael? This is not a normal thing a girl your age should be doing—helping the colored people. Not that I have anything against you going over there for dinner. In fact, maybe you should go. See how they live and how they think. Maybe it will cure you of wanting to help them. Go! Be around them. Get it out of your system!" Dad sounded angry.

Everyone eats dinner in silence. I hate Dad for his prejudiced attitude, and I hate Mom for not confronting him. Then I go straight to my room and slam the door. Jess comes in and rubs my back. We don't talk.

At lunch today, even though Florence and I both sit with our group, she sits as far away from me as she can at the table. I see her laughing and having fun and I feel a little jealous that she can have fun and be mad at me at the same time. I think she's jealous of me because now I'm close to

Bobbi and Natalie and she isn't.

Whenever I feel left out this way it makes me miss Ruby so much. Ruby never left me out. Steven, Marcus, and Gloria make me miss her, too. They remind me of her. And I miss Peggy. She never left me out, either. Neither did Mitch. But Tommy left me out.

I try to imagine what Ruby would say to me right now: *"Honey, why you making all this trouble for yourself? You go have a nice life but don't make trouble. Look, your best friend since your first day is mad, your parents are going to be mad, and maybe your other two best friends—Natalie and Bobbi—will be mad if you like a colored boy. You can love all us Negroes but you don't have to make trouble. Yo' Mommy and Daddy have enough trouble moving youse out to a new place, yo' Daddy had to go and get a new job, yo' folks settlin' in with new neighbors, friends, schools and the like. Just be easy on dem. It'd be a whole lot easier to have a white boyfriend. Why you rebellion like dis? You was such an easy chil' here most of the time."*

What would I say back to her if she were here with me? *"Ruby, I am not doing this on purpose, honest. I have feelings for Steven and I can't help it. Tomorrow, when I go to his house for dinner, I will see him with his family and get to know him more. What if your daughter liked a white boy? Would you think she was just making trouble? Ruby, we're all people and all people should be treated the same way, and that's what I care about. I'm treating Steven like I would anyone else I thought was a good person. Do you understand now?".*

# 24
# THE VISIT

After school the next day, I see Steven walking toward his car. I call out, "Hi. I found it: the only maroon car in the parking lot. Where are Gloria and Marcus?" I wonder if Gloria is late on purpose so Steven and I can be alone for a few minutes.

"I didn't see them heading back to their lockers, so they'll probably be right out," Steven says, examining his car to make sure no one dented it during the school day.

"I like your car. It's so shiny and maroon. Is it all yours, or do you share it?" I ask laughing.

"It's all of ours," Steven replies, grinning. "Me, Marcus, and Gloria all went in on it. Marcus and I shine it every weekend."

Just like Dad and his Jaguar— taking care of their car and worrying about it getting a little scratch.

"Hi, Rachael," Gloria shouts.

"Sorry we're late." I sit in front and Steven drives; Marcus sits in the back, legs stretched out like a daddy-longlegs, and Gloria is squeezed into the corner. The car smells like fresh wax and cigarettes. Marcus and Steven light up as soon as the windows open. Gloria doesn't.

"Want one?" asks Marcus.

"Okay." I take it and Steven lights it. We fog up the interior as the streams of smoke flow out of the windows. Gloria motions to me that she'd like to take a drag off my cigarette. I hand it to her. I know Mom and Dad would disapprove of my smoking, but...

"My Dad has a MG; he's had either a Jaguar or MG since 1955. Since we moved out here, he's been polishing the car himself," I say hoping one of them won't ask who used to do it; then I would have to say "the man who lived at our place," like they would know what that meant. No question it would lead around to the man being "colored help." Oh, it would make me feel tense and shy, like I used to be at the dining table when I was growing up. I don't want to ever be that person again. Luckily, no one asks me anything about it. I like that my dad has something in common with them. I probably shouldn't have brought it up, but it seemed a good way to connect.

We drive toward town and turn up a steep incline on Carmelina Road, which is covered with giant redwoods and is near where the party was after the football game. There are small homes scattered along the road. Maybe I should feel frightened, like we are going into an isolated place on the outskirts of Spartina; but I trust the three of them and don't feel at all afraid. We turn off a dirt road and drive the length of a few football fields before we turn up a long dirt driveway. There are several homes scattered along the road, all with long driveways, like the one we drive up to Steven and Gloria's house.

The small ranch house is beige. There are shutters on the exterior windows. The grass is beautifully kept and the driveway is grey stone and concrete. There are a few magnificent redwoods hovering over the house, like they are guarding it, and some potted plants pots scattered around the front of the house holding trees, flowers and shrubs. Bright red geraniums in pots by the front door greet us as we enter.

It's clear to me that they don't live like Ruby and Ethel in broken down houses and neighborhoods that have junk scattered everywhere outside. This is Spartina, situated amidst the beautiful redwoods; very upper middle class. It's a place where kids from all over the United States go to camp.

"Did you help him shine the MG?" Marcus says laughing. "Next time, you can help us."

I'm surprised Marcus picks up on what I said a few minutes ago.

"No, not me," I say.

"Who pray did, then?" Steven asks.

Oh, no! What do I say? Why does this have to come up? Because I started it by bragging about Dad's car. My worst nightmare is Steven and Marcus finding out the only colored people I associated with before were taking care of our family.

"Uh, my dad paid someone to do it," I say sweetly.

The subject doesn't go any further. Thank goodness.

"Welcome," says Steven as we enter the front hall.

We all walk into the kitchen and Steven opens the fridge while Marcus stands behind him to see what's inside. I hang in the center of the kitchen, waiting to see what's going to happen next. It feels like a scene in a play. Gloria disappears for a few minutes and then comes back. Marcus takes out some Cokes, leftover fried chicken and chili. Steven takes out ice, gets plates and glasses, and sets them down on the worn out tile counter.

"Mom always makes enough food for dinner so we have leftovers after school the next day," Marcus explains. "Because dinner is always late, we eat them after football practice,"

Steven and Gloria nod their heads agreeing, while Marcus spoons out some onto plates for each of us.

"Where are your parents?" I ask Gloria trying to act cool but I really want to know.

"They're at work."

"Rachael, do you want yours heated?" Steven offers sweetly. "We just eat everything cold. We're always too hungry to wait to heat up anything."

"No, cold is good. I eat cold spaghetti leftovers for breakfast all the time."

We all eat standing up. I watch Steven gulp down his food. I force myself to look at Marcus and Gloria to be polite, but my gaze is magnetically drawn back to Steven's presence.

Gloria isn't saying much. Maybe she can't think of anything to say to me. I don't want to talk about the cheerleading incident over and over and she probably doesn't either. I can see the living room from where I stand in the kitchen. It is sparsely but comfortably decorated in green, brown and beige with some nice antique chairs and end tables finished in glossy pine; quite beautiful. There is artwork on the walls—mostly large framed original oil paintings, I assume, since the finish is not smooth, as in photographs. I guess they're of family members. The carpet in the living room is spotless and a green-grass color, like a putting green. The floor of the kitchen/breakfast room is linoleum; it's worn out in spots, like the boys played a lot of sports there when they were little, pounding on it. Everything looks really clean. Family pictures are in a corner hutch in the breakfast room. I walk over and look at pictures of the kids when they were probably four or five. I see pictures of their dad and mom in dress up clothes—the kind like Mom and Dad wear.

"What'cha looking at Rachael?" Gloria asks, still munching away.

"Family pictures. Your mom and dad look nice. Where was this taken?"

"Church," Gloria says laughing. "When we finish cleaning up, I want to show you my room."

I notice Steven rinsing the dishes and putting them into the sink as Gloria cleans the counters. He has left my dish out as there is still food in it.

"I can't eat anymore," I tell Steven.

"Girls never eat much around boys I've noticed," Marcus says, smiling.

I help Steven dry and put away the dishes. As we do so, I watch his giant hands and beautifully sculpted fingers grasp everything. I wonder if boys' hands keep growing like their height does until they're twenty-five or so.

While Steven and I finish up, I notice Marcus and Gloria go down the hallway. Guess Gloria forgot about taking me to her room.

I feel both comfortable and excited with Steven. He goes into the living room so I follow. The living room is sparsely furnished. There are a few tchotchkes around— ashtrays, pictures, and lots of books on a shelf. A dog comes bounding in from the back door.

"Hey, Sparkey, how ya doing?" Steven asks.

Wagging his tail, Sparkey puts his two front paws on the sofa and licks Steven's face.

"Hey, Sparkey, this is Rachael."

Sparkey is a cross breed. He's big and has long, soft black, grey and white fur. He has blue eyes like wolves do but they are sweet eyes. I like him right away.

"Hi, Sparkey," I say rubbing his fur along with Steven so our hands touch. I feel sparks from Sparkey to my heart.

"Rachael, do you want to take a walk with Sparkey?" Steven asks.

"That'd be great."

We go out the front door with Sparkey on a leash and walk around the neighborhood. There are some folks out in front of their houses, kids playing, adults watering lawns. Even though it is a white residential area, each family waves to Steven as we pass—all except one. There's an older couple who turns their heads when Steven waves to them, snubbing him.

Anger wells up in me as I wonder how that must make Steven feel. I want to know more about him and Marcus and Gloria. I want to know how they ended up here and not in a colored neighborhood. I hope to find out today. Maybe their parents work for a rich senator or congressman? Maybe they run Macy's in San Francisco or own a hotel in San Jose? Maybe their mom and dad are like Bobbi and Natalie's: their dad is a pilot and their mom is principal of a high school. I have so many questions.

"Rachael, you know Marcus and I date a lot of girls but my parents don't want us dating white girls—they had the 'talk' with us," Steven says kind of shy like. "To be honest, we don't feel comfortable going to parties where we would meet only white girls. Besides, maybe no one really wants us there anyway. It doesn't matter because most of the time we don't show up. We meet colored girls at our church and through my parents' friends." He stops walking and looks into my eyes. "I want to ask you out very much but I know your parents probably feel the same way."

We both look at each other. I think I see the same longing in his eyes as I know there must be in mine.

"I wasn't expecting you to say that, Steven."

We resume walking as Sparkey sniffs everything here and there. I go on. "My parents not only don't want me dating anyone with a different skin color, they want me only dating Jewish guys. We never talked actually talked about that—we hardly ever talk about anything— but I get that sense. Great choice I have at Spartina for dating a Jewish guy," I say joking.

"Guess they didn't think that part out when they moved you here," Steven laughs. "I didn't know your family was Jewish but, yeah, Sam is the only Jewish guy in my class and he's taken for now." He stops again and looks at me, concerned. "I have to tell you, Rachael, I did hear some kids talking about Jews, but I didn't know if they were referring to your family."

I can see he is ashamed to say what he just told me.

"It's just words," I tell him. "Still, it would hurt me to hear people unjustly speaking about Jews, so I understand a teeny bit of what colored people go through. But not really, because I could only do that if I was colored."

"Yeah," is all Steven says. Clearly, he does not want to get into that.

We resume walking.

"How did you guys end up at Spartina? What do your parents do?" I ask, changing the subject so Steven doesn't have to talk about what I just said and I don't want to make him say more than he wants to say.

"Rachael, I like that you are interested in things. I like you. Our parents work at Stanford University. Stanford is doing a study on Spartina High School to see how the colored kids end up after going to a small, suburban white school. I'm not sure of the details, but Stanford wanted us to be here," Steven answers. The look in his eyes is a determined one, like he really wants me to understand.

"What kind of work do your folks do at Stanford?" I ask, hoping he won't say cleaning or doing laundry.

"They're both professors. Dad teaches history and Mom teaches English, and Marcus's dad teaches engineering," Steven says with pride.

"Boy, you sure don't like to brag. Why didn't you say that in the first place instead of they just work there?"

"Because I don't want to be the colored guy who brags to make us seem the same as you. I can't compete in your world and I don't want to even try. We have separate lives, Rachael—except at school and a few parties, my life doesn't overlap yours."

He sounds sad as he says this. I start to respond but stop as Steven pulls me to him under a big tree that hides us from the houses and neighbors and kisses me on the lips. I kiss him back and the kiss lasts for a long time. This kiss goes down my whole body. Ray's kiss just stayed on my lips.

After what seems like forever, we separate ourselves and look at each other.

"See how separate our lives are?" Steven says, laughing.

"No, I don't want to see that," I say, breathless.

"The Jew and the colored boy—what a story!"

We both laugh.

Then Steven looks at me earnestly. "You know, Rachael, maybe we can't have everything, but at least you and I have friends who don't leave us out because we are different. Anyway, you're not so different to the outside world as I am. Your skin is white. You don't know anything about prejudice."

"But I am involved in your story," I say, believing that now Steven is ready to hear me.

"What do you mean?"

"My real family in St. Louis was Ruby, Ethel, Bernice and Bill," I say.

"Okay, who are they?"

"They were the colored help my parents hired—but, oh, so much, much more than that to me. They made me feel safe and loved in a way my parents, my grandmothers, even my older sister and kid brother didn't. I miss them so much. My parents were hardly ever home. When they weren't at work, they were always off socializing with their friends. They didn't do anything with me when they were home."

"So what are you saying? You want more colored folks, like me and Marcus and Gloria, to care about you here like your colored servant that polished your Dad's car?"

Oh, no, I've offended him. How can I explain? "No, that's not what I want," I say sincerely. "I want my parents to be more caring and loving. And I want you and Gloria and Marcus to be my friends. There's no way anyone could replace Ruby, Ethel, Bernice and Bill. I miss them terribly. "

"Rachael," Steven says, shaking his head, "you want a dream world where everyone is treated the same. Don't you think I want that too? But it ain't gonna happen—not in our lifetime."

His eyes smash into mine. Sparkey sits there, looking at us like he knows something serious is going on.

"It may sound like I'm just talking," I say, raising my voice a little, "but I've seen discrimination in St. Louis and at summer camp and I did some things to make people aware of those injustices." I don't want to sound defensive, so I tone it down a little. "Not a lot of people. But I read things about civil rights. I am bothered by all the unfairness. I did some things back there that I got in trouble for. They weren't bad but my parents thought they were." I look into his eyes, hoping he'll understand. "I plan to take greater action this summer. I don't want to say what right now because I'm not sure what it will be." Steven is silent through my entire rant. "Do you hate me now?" I ask.

"Well, you saved my sister from something that was unfair, so I know you have a good heart. No, I don't hate you."

We quietly walk with Sparky back to his house, both of us deep in thought.

Soon after, their parents come in through the back door into the kitchen. Gloria and Marcus join us and Steven introduces me.

"Mom, Dad, this is Rachael. Rachael, these are my parents, Eliza Dunford and Henry Dunford," Steven says politely.

We all shake hands. My throat feels tight, like it does when I'm nervous.

"Hi, Mr. Dunford, Mrs. Dunford." My voice sounds too high and squeaky to my ears.

"Gloria has told us all about you. We hold you in high esteem," says Mrs. Dunford.

"Thank you," I say.

"We are pleased you could come for dinner," says Mr. Dunford.

"I am, too." I feel my head shaking. Oh, no, what is this, a new nervous tic? Even though my head shakes, my body is as stiff as a surfboard. Maybe this is an epileptic seizure. I take a deep breath, let it out, and—the tic is gone. But when I look at Mr. and Mrs. Dunford I know my eyes are jumping around; I can't seem to look at them directly. It's like my eyes are bowling balls rolling all over the lane, trying to settle in one place before it lands in the gutter. I'm a nervous wreck. If I didn't like Steven so much, I'd be okay. It would be just like at a friend's house. But this is different because I know I like him and his parents don't want him liking a white girl. Even though I always say we are all the same, it's a strange feeling that they are a regular family and they are not waiting on me. I feel guilty for even thinking that. I hate myself.

At the dining room table everyone talks about their day. I'm very uncomfortable because now I like Steven more than a friend and I feel guilty about it, like I shouldn't like him. If I only liked him as a friend I wouldn't feel so sweaty and scared. I'd be friendly and somewhat relaxed. I think I am wrong to like him, just like Mom and Dad would think. But if I'm going to stand up against prejudice, I should not be thinking like Mom and Dad. Maybe I'm just nervous because I like him so much and it has nothing to do with Mom and Dad. As I sit here thinking about all this there's a lot of conversation going on and I'm only taking it half in. I should be listening to the others and not worry so much about how I appear to them.

"Rachael, please pass the butter," Mrs. Dunford asks.

My hand shakes as I pass it.

"How long have you been living in Spartina?" Mr. Dunford asks.

"We only came in October. We moved here from St. Louis."

"May I ask what the reason for you to move here was?" Mrs. Dunford asks.

"My Dad closed his clothing shops in St. Louis. He felt there was a better opportunity here." I didn't say he had to close the stores because they failed.

"I love Rachael's clothes," Gloria says looking at her mother. "Do they all come from your dad's store?" she asks me.

"Some of them do but mostly I wear my sister's hand-me-downs."

From the corner of my eye I can see Steven looking at me when I talk wearing a thin pencil-line smile. I hope no one asks me anything else.

I listen to the chatter about a relative coming to visit from Tennessee, the lawn has to be mowed by Steven this weekend, whose turn is it to wash the car next. I hear more respect, love and attentiveness than I do at our family dining table. I do think things are better than in our family than they were in St. Louis, but we have a long way to go.

We all help clear off the table and wash the dishes. I say my goodbyes to Mr. and Mrs. Dunford and Steven drives me home. I don't let him kiss me in the car in case someone is watching. I jump out and run into the house, slamming the front door hard without knowing I did that.

"Jess, come here, I have to talk to you now," I yell happily, hoping she's home.

Jessy comes bounding out of our room. "Rach, what

happened over there? What's with that stupid smile all over your face?"

"Okay, remember when I stuck up for you and made excuses for you when you and Bret were sneaking around? Now it's your turn."

"Everyone was at the Dunfords' house for dinner tonight, Steven, Gloria, their parents, and Marcus. I like Steven so much, Jess—like a boyfriend. We kissed before his parents got home. It was the best kiss I've ever had. I liked him the minute I saw him. I don't want Mom and Dad to know yet. I have to figure out how to tell them," I stopped, breathless.

"Why do you have to pick a colored boy when practically everyone here is white?"

"I didn't pick him—my heart did. So, are you on my side or not?"

"Sure, I am, but this is trouble."

"I will decide what trouble I make. You decided yours," I say confidently.

"Rach, I know you like the wrong boy just like I do. I don't care what color or religion Steven is. Bret is Christian and white. Maybe if Steven was Jewish and colored, Mom and Dad would approve."

We both burst out laughing and hug each other real hard.

Next day, Steven finds me at school and walks me to classes. I don't know how he knows where I will be but it seems like he has every step of my schedule memorized. We are together during each break. Sometimes he puts his arm

around me and some kids stare—out of jealousy or
curiosity or prejudice, I don't know. And I don't care. He
makes me feel like I'm special and cared for. I'm not going
to say I'm in love with him because I don't know yet.

As the days go by, I hope and pray one of my friends
doesn't slip up when they drop by my house and say
something to Mom. It would have been easy to have a
secret boyfriend in St. Louis since Mom was barely home.
But now she's around a lot and wants to be involved in my
life. Just what I've always wanted. Lucky me. This is what is
called irony—a word I learned in English class.

Steven and I spend time together at parties and going
out with other kids after football and basketball games to
get pizza. We only make out in private, usually in his car
when it's parked at Magoo's Pizza. At a house party we
might sneak away to a dark corner. We pass notes to each
other in the hallways at school that say we miss each other.
I draw our initials inside hearts.

I save every note he's given me in a secret box that I
keep under my bed along with a pair of gloves that I love
from Dad's store in St. Louis. They're short white gloves
and feel silky because the linen, Dad told me, is the finest
ever made.

Steven and I are both scared Gloria or Jess will slip up
and say something in front of our parents. We have to be so
secretive. I wish I could spend a whole Saturday for a real
date—maybe even go to the beauty shop to get my hair
done and smell like hairspray. I would let Jess do my
makeup and Mom would say I look pretty. I wish Steven
could pick me up for a date from my home and then, when
he brings me back, we could linger on the steps, kissing
each other goodnight. I wish he could come to our house
for dinner and laugh with me as we share our secret

language in front of Mom and Dad. Mom and Dad would smile at each other, remembering when they did that, and Mom might even blush. Then Mom and Mrs. Dunford would plan a luncheon date to talk about us and pretend they didn't know whether we are serious or not.

Jessy is right: why did I have to pick a colored boy? I will never have any of what I want.

A lot of my group is not really as warm as they seemed before Steven and I got together. What am I supposed to do? Pretend not to like him so I can be popular again? Like a Christian boy? Then Mom and Dad would be cold to me. I can't win.

Steven doesn't call on the phone because he knows it's too hard for me to talk. I don't call him because I don't like to feel I'm chasing him. Jess is mad that I like him even though I'm never mad she still likes Bret. So here I am again—feeling alone, like I did in St. Louis.

There's a New Year's Eve party at Frankie's because his parents are out of town so everyone knows they can drink and smoke. Ray picks me up, even though he knows I would rather go with Steven. It isn't a real date. He's doing it as a friend so I can see Steven and not have to explain anything to my parents. I know Ray likes me, but at least he and I have an understanding: we will both dance with other people when we get there.

Steven, Marcus, and Gloria come late. As soon as I see Steven my heart leaps. He walks over to where I am talking to a bunch of kids. We hug and he asks me to dance.

"Steven, it's a new year—1963. Let's have a real date!" I say, melting in his arms as we dance. "The kind where you come and pick me up from home. I'm not happy with our secret anymore. I want to tell Mom and Dad tonight. Will you do it? I'm ready. Are you?" "Rach, I am so relieved to hear you say that. I feel the same way. I can already picture myself getting ready for a real date with my real girlfriend. My parents will know. When I pick you up we will start our new chapter, my love," Steven whispers in my ear. "Let's make it next Saturday night."

# 25
# THE FIRST DATE

Tonight Steven is taking me on our first real date. He's going to come and pick me up and we're going to a drive-in movie. I am so excited; my face feels hot all day. Jessy helps me get dressed in a cashmere pink sweater set, pearls, and winter white wool slacks. She does my hair in a pageboy. Since Steven became my boyfriend, she's been nice to me most of the time. She told me that maybe now I will understand what it's like to care about a boy.

I have told Mom and Dad I have a date with someone they don't know from school, but they don't know it's with a Negro. Steven has also told his parents he has a date, but he hasn't told them it's with a white girl.

My heart jumps as the doorbell rings. With my bedroom door open, I can hear him say hello to Mom and Dad and hi to Rusty. I don't hear Mom and Dad saying anything. I wish I could see their faces. Now I hear them saying hello, but, unlike Steven, they don't sound friendly; their words sound blurred.

I walk down the hall slowly, dreamlike, like Loretta Young coming down a royal circular staircase. Steven, standing in the hallway, looks at me smiling as I walk toward him. He looks so handsome in his black slacks, V-neck sweater and white dress shirt. We are both way too dressed up for a drive-in movie.

Mom and Dad look very unhappy and Mom's face has turned bright magenta. They look up at me, then down at the floor, then up and down again a few times before I reach Steven. They are doing it almost in sync, as they practiced this odd head dance.

"You look pretty, Rachael," Steven says.

"Thank you," I blush.

I start to say goodbye to everyone. Rusty yells goodbye and runs down the hall. Mom and Dad don't say anything.

Mom whispers, "Rachael, come here." She yanks me into the kitchen. "Why didn't you tell me you were going on a date with a colored boy?"

"You didn't ask me," I reply, keeping my cool.

"Dad and I are not at all pleased with what is taking place in our home."

"What is taking place is that your daughter is delighted with looking forward to going out with a nice boy from school who she likes very much and who happens to be colored. If you think that's not acceptable, then you and Dad should have let me know how you feel about colored people long ago. After all, we've lived with them since I was born. Would you let people live with you that you didn't approve of? I didn't think you would, so I assumed it wouldn't matter to you if some of my friends were colored.

I need to go on now, Mom. Steven is waiting for me."

"Well, Rachael, we will talk about this later."

Mom storms out of the kitchen, pushing the swinging door hard. I follow. I wish I could hear the conversation Dad was having with Steven while Mom and I were in the kitchen.

"Bye," Mom hisses, looking down and stiffly polite.

"Get home on time, ten-thirty!" says Dad.

Eleven-thirty was always my regular time.

"I promise I will get her home safely and on time," Steven says looking right at Dad.

Sitting next to Steven in the car I can feel his body tense, like mine.

"Rach, that was awful. I knew it would be, but imagining it and living it are two different things. I don't ever want to feel that way again in your home." He keeps his eyes on the road as he speaks. "I can just hear them talking about me now: 'who does he think he is, dating our daughter?' Your Dad didn't talk at all so I asked him about his MG's and Jaguars and what he uses to polish them. He answered as if I had asked what underwear he likes. Then I asked him where he goes to have it tuned up. I tried to keep the conversation going, but it was awful."

"Oh, Steven—I'm so sorry. They'll get used to it. They'll have to! I hate that they're prejudiced. They're probably wondering if we dressed up to try to impress on them what good wholesome kids we are." I pinch his side. "I didn't know you were going to dress up too!"

He cracks up and so do I. The bad part of the evening is behind us.

"We think alike, Steven." I lean over to plant a light kiss on his cheek and put my arm around his neck. I feel proud to be sitting next to him.

Our bodies relax a little as we listen to The Beach Boys on the radio and our bodies move to the beat as we drive.

Just before we get to the drive-in, I say,

"Steven, stop the car. I want to hide in the trunk before we go in."

"Really? You really want to get into the trunk? Don't be silly, Rachael. I can pay for you."

"I know, but everyone will see us drive through the gate together. What if there are some real bad people who may react seeing a Negro and a white together. I don't want anything to happen to you or me." I've read so many stories about mixed couples being attacked; it really is scary. "I know no one can tell if I'm rich or Jewish—only the white part. But still…" I put on a sexy, breathy voice, like Marilyn Monroe. "Is there a trunk in this '43 Mercury?"

"Yeah, a small one—only for small rich Jewish girls."

"I was rich—but not anymore. Still white and Jewish, though."

We laugh as Steven helps me very gently and gallantly, helps me into the trunk. Once we're past the gate and he's found a space for us, he acts the knight again as I climb out, making sure my dress stays where it should.

We see *Splendor in the Grass* with Natalie Wood and

Warren Beatty. The title comes from Walt Whitman's poem: *What though the radiance which was once so bright/ Be now for ever taken from my sight,/ Though nothing can bring back the hour/ Of splendour in the grass, of glory in the flower;/ We will grieve not, rather find/ Strength in what remains behind...;* I know I will always remember this movie because I know the same story may happen to Steven and me. The star-crossed lovers cannot be together, despite their deep love. The timing is not right. They are in high school and they end up later with lives that are not what they really wanted.

Steven and I haven't said we love each other but I do feel love for him during the movie. I wonder if the movie is making me feel this love or if I really do feel it.

He kisses me many times during the movie and the windows steam up. It's almost like I'm watching myself in a romance I've read about or seen on TV. It's so unfair that we have to be afraid just because some early humans developed on this planet with darker skin to protect them from the sun. It certainly doesn't protect anyone now to have dark skin.

Steven says he'll be right back. He's going to get me a surprise.

I wait for him to come back for what seems like forever. Then I start to worry. I grab his letter jacket from the back seat and put it on, to protect me from what, I don't know, but his jacket feels like a shield. I can't stand it anymore, so I get out of the car to find him. My stomach is in knots. It's taking way too long.

At the snack bar I see Steven inside with what looks like ketchup all over his arm and wrist talking to a policeman and another guy—a white guy. Steven sees me and his face drops. He motions for me not to come near him. I can't hear anything but the three of them are talking, standing in a tight circle, and everyone at the snack bar is staring at them. There are some people from school that I know standing close and trying to listen.

Finally Steven walks over to me and takes my arm. He is angry. He practically drags me to the car, opens my door and I get inside while he goes around to the driver's seat. He turns on the ignition and heads out of the drive-in.

"Please, tell me what happened. Why is there blood everywhere? Are you okay? Oh, my God!" I'm sobbing as I take a tissue out of my purse to wipe off the blood—because that's what it is, of course. Not ketchup.

After about ten minutes, he pulls the car over. I can see his jaw tensing in and out.

"Rachael, I told you to wait in the car. Why didn't you listen? You could have been hurt. This is not good," he whispers, wiping the blood off his hand and nose. "I can't do this to you. I'm a bad guy for taking you here or anywhere. I saw kids from our school in the snack bar. Some of them who are friendly enough at school did not look friendly tonight. I was in line to get popcorn and drinks and the white guy you saw talking to the police hauls off and hits me—so I hit him back. After I hit him, he yelled, 'You nigger, what are you doing with a whitey? I seen you smooching with your big fat brown lips. Those are our girls so stay away. There are more of us than you—understand?' Even the kids I knew from school didn't do anything. What could they do anyway—get in a fight?

"Rachael, I wanted to kill him. Kill him for me, for you, for every colored man, woman, and child. I can't be free to be with you," Steven slurps the saliva collecting in his mouth and nose while he wipes everything with tissues. "I didn't do what Martin Luther King, Jr. said. I hit him back. It was an impulse. I want to protest peacefully. I'm so ashamed."

I put my hand on his shoulder, "I understand it was a knee-jerk reaction any man or woman would have. It's okay. Nothing will stop me from being with you, Steven. It is dangerous for us right now and I'm losing friends already but it won't always be. Things will change eventually. Why did the police let you both go?"

"The police weren't there when the guy socked me out of the blue. One policeman stuck up for me—that's a change. Maybe he's a mulatto. I was sure I was going to have to spend the night in jail and have a felony record. I was so scared—more scared than I have been in my whole life, knowing I'd be disappointing my parents and you." He takes a couple of deep breaths.

"I like you more than ever—that you can almost cry and still be a man. I wish I saw my dad cry in front of me just once. Then I would think he's human."

Steven is still angry, but he's calmer now. He starts up the car and we park in front of my house earlier than my curfew. Steven goes around to open my door and we walk up to the front door. We kiss gently and I go in. I hear Steven run to his car and start it up as I close the front door.

I see Mom in the living room, ready to pounce the minute she sees me. I bend down to take off my flats in the hallway so my back is to Mom, then turn around to face her.

"Rachael, come here this instant!"

"Coming, Mom."

"What is that on your sweater? Is that blood? Oh, my God, why do you have blood on you?"

Oh, dear. I wish Steven or I had seen the blood before I came in the door.

"You have some explaining to do, young lady, and you'd better start right now."

"Mom, some white guys hit Steven because they saw him with me. He was in the snack bar getting popcorn. The police were there and let him go. He didn't start it. I guess some of the blood on Steven got on my sweater. I wasn't there in the snack bar when it happened. I'm telling the truth. Can I please go to bed and we can talk more in the morning? Please?

"All right. But you'll have to talk to your Dad, too, and explain more than you are now. You can never go out with him again, do you understand?"

"Mom, just let me go to bed." I run to my room and slam the door shut, waking up Jessy.

"What's going on, Rach?" she asks, groggy with sleep.

"Nothing. Go back to sleep." I try to keep quiet.

"Told you it would be difficult to go outside Mom and Dad's little rule book," Jess says sarcastically.

"You were right." I get into my pajamas quickly, before Jess can see the blood and ask me a thousand questions. "Okay, I want to tell you. Someone hit Steven at the snack bar when he was in line to get drinks because he was with a white girl. Steven hit back. The police came and let them both go, even though the white guy started it. Steven's face was all bloody and some of it got on my sweater. Mom saw it and wanted to know how it got there. I told her the truth. Of course, she wants to know every single little detail in the morning with Dad there, too. What should I do, Jess? I hate my life. I hate everything."

"Oh, Rach, I'm so sorry. Do you want to talk about it?"

"Let's talk in the morning. I am so tired," I say, more exhausted than I have ever felt.

The only thing I can see when I close my eyes is me getting on the Freedom Ride this summer.

In the morning, as I walk out of my room, Mom walks over and puts her arm around me and pats me. I hate when she pats me, like I'm a dog. Why doesn't she just hold me like she loves me. At that moment Dad walks out of their bedroom and joins us in the hallway.

"You and Steven aren't going out again, right? I'm sure you got that out of your system after last night." Dad drills his eyes into mine.

"Can you just get to know him first?" I plead. "Have him over and then decide. He's the same as white boys— it's just a skin color. And he cares about me and we have fun." I'm holding onto Mom.

"I don't mind if you're friends. But I cannot stomach you being with him for a boyfriend!" Dad looks at Mom to get her approval.

"Look, dear," Mom says still holding me, "let's just make this easier on all of us and go back to being his friend."

"Yeah, sure okay," I say. I'm lying, but all I want to do is go to my room. I know I can't do what they say.

Steven telephones me the next day.

"Hi, darling girl."

"Hi. I've been worried about you. How is your nose and hand?"

"Fine. Don't you worry about me. What did your parents say when you came home?"

"They had 'the talk' with me about not dating you and us just being friends."

"I understand. My parents gave me 'the talk', too. I had to explain the bloody nose so I told them about the fight and the police. They said it's too complicated. They don't want us dating either." Steven's voice gets really soft and he says, "Rachael, I really want to be with you all the time, but I can't go against my parents at this time. I hope you understand."

"Yeah, I guess so. I hate my parents. I would go against them if you would, but not alone. I have to go now, Steven. See you at school." I run to my room and sob into my pillow. I feel like Ruby just left me again. I miss her and my old life so much. I want to go backward. Forward is too hard.

At school, when I put my books away in my locker for lunch period, Steven is nearby. He comes over after I slam the locker shut and we start walking toward the lunch area. He takes my hand for a few seconds; I squeeze his back— and then he goes off to sit with his lunch group.

Are we breaking up, never going out on a date again, or

sneaking around again? It is so confusing.

# 26
# JESSY

I'm happy to see Rusty when I came home from school because he is so sweet and I know he doesn't have a racist bone in his body. Jessy is being the same to me— sometimes in my corner, sometimes sarcastic and wanting to argue. I'm sick of trying to figure her out. If Steven's dad was president of the United States, Mom and Dad would still be prejudiced. Steven's parents think being with a white girl is an extra difficulty their son doesn't need—not that they don't like white people. My Mom and Dad just see black and white. I wish they were blind—then they wouldn't know his skin color.

If Ruby were here she would tell me exactly what to do. I sit on the bed with my stationery and best ballpoint pen.

*Dear Ruby,*

*I am sorry you haven't written to me but I know you would if you could. I hope it's not that you are sick, but that you just haven't had time to write. Ruby, when I visit I will call you and we will talk in person about everything. I just want you to be happy and not worry about money and I want you to be treated nicely by everyone.*

*I have a special boy I really like but Mom and Dad don't like him. You would like him, I know. He is my first real boyfriend and he is colored. I don't like him because he is colored. I just like him. I want to know what you would say about this. He is a senior and is going to college in the fall.*

*I don't want to tell you everything in a letter. I will explain it all to you when I see you again.*

*I think Mom and Dad like it here but they don't tell me that. I am reading their minds like I have always done. I wish I could figure out my problems so I liked it here. I miss you every day. No one will ever be like Peggy or you—ever. I think about you every day.*

*Love,*

*Rachael*

I will mail it later today at the mailbox on the corner.

Steven and I only talk at school now. He doesn't call and he doesn't ask me out. He told me he would if he could, but he can't ruin his relationship with his parents.

Our parents are running our lives.

Maybe it would be even harder if we had gone out more than once, but I still like him and when I see him at school I yearn for him and his kisses. I want to feel his body close to mine, like at the drive-in, but I know it's impossible with not only our parents against us, but the whole world.

This is what must feel like to be colored every day—
that the whole world is against you and you have to fight
for everything and people stare at you and don't want you
to sit at a stupid drugstore counter. I can't feel like the
colored people do but I feel what it's like not getting to
have Steven be my boyfriend when we both want it.

It's spring now. I've been having a better time now
that I don't see Steven as a boyfriend. Mom and Dad aren't
angry. My friends are warm and fun. Inside I'm still
disappointed at the world, but I put that aside until I get
into bed at night. Ray, Bobbie and Natalie are still my
closest friends. I go to all the parties and have fun after
school or on the phone with them. My self-confidence has
grown just knowing my friends care about me and want to
be with me.

I have some dates with guy-friends and I get a crush on
a senior guy—Michael—but he dates Bobbi. Sometimes,
when Bobbi and Natalie go to Hawaii to visit their Dad, he
takes me out. Bobbi doesn't care because she isn't in love
with him. I find out he's half-Jewish like Ray even though
he doesn't say so. I like the attention and flirtation, but I
still miss Steven.

Steven, Marcus, and Gloria all get into Stanford. In the
South, when colored kids get into all white schools, the
National Guard has to be called in to get them in the door.
Crowds of people block the entrances, yelling that they
can't go to the school because of their color, even though
they were accepted. But it's not the same struggle at the
universities and colleges in California, thank heavens.

Without Steven, Marcus, and Gloria here for my senior
year, I don't know who I will talk to about civil rights.

Jessy will be leaving soon—either going to college

or…somewhere. She and I talk tonight before we go to sleep like we do every night, but this time Jessy starts the conversation I've wanted to have for a long time.

"Rach, I'm not staying here after I graduate. You will go to college, maybe Stanford, just to be with Steven. Maybe I'll go away to college or do something, but not here. I have to get out of here."

She sounds so desperate. I understand because I kind of feel that way myself .

"I don't really want to study anything in college," Jessy goes on. "If I go it'd be just because I had nothing else to do. I only think about Bret and wish we could be married. Mom never finished college. She quit to marry Dad." She whispers, "Don't tell anyone but I've been taking money from Dad's valet stand little by little to save enough to go back to St. Louis. Yesterday I tried to call Bret but no one was home. Marrying Bret and living in St. Louis is what I want—it's all I want."

"Where would you stay?" I ask, worried. Then the thought of my living here without Jessy hits me. "You can't. I would be too lonely without you."

"I'm sorry, Rach, but I have to get away from all the rules. Mom and Dad watch me like a hawk, as if I'll get pregnant again if I touch a guy. I think they listen in on my telephone calls. They ask me so many questions about where I'm going, who am I going with, when will I come home, and on and on. I hate it here!"

I would never get pregnant like Jessy. I will never "go all the way" until I'm married. There are some things that *are* black and white

"I know how you feel, Jess." I decide to tell her my plan before I tell Mom and Dad. "Do you know about The Freedom Riders? This spring and summer they are taking buses into the South from northern cities to make sure the Jim Crow laws, prejudicial laws against colored people, are not permitted. Not just colored people are going—a lot of white college-aged kids are going. Have you ever seen drugstore counters that won't allow colored folks to eat there? I hope we never see that. A lot of white people in the South are still upholding the Jim Crow Laws. I'm going to be one of the Freedom Riders!"

Jessy sits up in surprise, shaking her head.

"Just think, Jess, I'm asking Mom and Dad to let me celebrate my seventeenth birthday in St. Louis, but I will be on the bus doing something for others, not just myself. Maybe Steven wants to be a Freedom Rider too and we can go together."

"You'll never get Mom and Dad to say okay to visit St. Louis."

"Why wouldn't they? I'm not asking for the whole summer—and I'll pay them back for the airplane ticket by working the rest of the summer. Don't you dare tell them about my going on the Freedom Ride!"

"What is it anyway?" asks Jess.

I'm thrilled that she seems interested. "It's mostly college-age kids who are showing support for civil rights— stuff like voting rights for Negroes, and integrating schools, lunch counters, public places, and housing. If everyone stays home because their parents won't let them go, nothing will change, even with President Kennedy on our side."

"I won't tell, but don't ask me to go because I'm not interested," Jess states.

"I know." I'm not surprised.

At school, Steven and I still sometimes meet by my locker in the morning just to say hi. This is one of those mornings.

"Hi, Rachael. What's wrong?" he asks as I put my books away. "I can tell it's something. I know you so well."

I look at him with all the longing still in my heart—for Steven, for my desire to participate in a movement. I confess, "I want to be a Freedom Rider this summer—and I want to go with you, Steven." I say this in a soft voice so no one can hear.

"Rachael, Rachael," he says, his eyes softening. "We can talk about this, but not now. School starts in a few minutes."

"I know. But will you go? Just say yes and I'll feel better."

"I can't tell you now, Rach. We have to talk about it first."

"Okay, let's talk later."

We walk off in opposite directions.

At lunch Steven and I sit together with some of his classmates and some of mine. Since there are only two weeks of school left, we juniors can sit with the seniors.

There's so much chatter and noise about, no one can hear Steven when he starts "The Conversation" with me.

"Okay, Rach—where did you come up with this idea?"

"I've been reading the papers. It's all over the news. All the older high school and college kids on the buses already going to the South. If it weren't for them, civil rights issues wouldn't have already moved along as far as they have. Kids are going to colleges and other public places to integrate, and voting rights legislation is making it easier for colored people to vote. You can go to Stanford because it's already integrated. We don't live in the South."

"Rach, you sound like President Kennedy."

"I want to join in—this is happening now. And I want you to come with me."

"I can't do that. I talked to my parents about the Freedom Riders already. Marcus and I were ready to go and they said if I went they wouldn't help me with college.

"Oh, I'm glad you had already asked," I say knowing Steven had more to say.

"They said just going to Spartina High was all they could handle right now—and all they felt I could handle. They knew it would be difficult for me to be at this school, that I'd maybe be harassed or left out of parties and groups of kids that form cliques. Look what happened at the drive-in!"

I drop my eyes, knowing he's been through stuff I cant imagine. But I'd be so sad to go without him.

"Rach, I can tell you aren't happy with the answer but you know Stanford is studying how Marcus, Gloria, and I get along in a white school," he goes on. "My parents have to answer a lot of questions."

"I know you would go with me if you could," I say.

He puts his hands on my shoulders and says, "Besides, my sweet, kids have been killed and burned by the KKK in those freedom buses. You can't do it, Rachel. You could get killed!"

"So leave it to everyone else? No! I have lived all my life for this opportunity to do something I believe in. I want to do it more than my life!"

"This is so strange," Steven says, shaking his head and looking down at his feet. "The white girl telling the colored boy to stand up for his rights."

I don't want Steven or anyone else to see me. "I have to go," I say and run to the bathroom.

Jessy sees me run off and follows me inside. "Rachael, hold up. What is wrong?"

"He won't go with me," I say with watery eyes.

"Go with you where? To the Prom?"

"No! On the Freedom Ride this summer."

"So?"

Jessy still doesn't understand how important this is, even though I told her. She doesn't care about the Freedom Riders. But she does care about helping me do what I want.

"Jess, I want Steven to go, too. I'm…" I feel ashamed to say this but I have to. "I'm afraid to go alone."

"You want Steven along to protect you?"

"Yeah, I guess so. But I also want him to stand up for

his own people!"

"Rach, no one can protect you or me or Steven, no matter where we go—Freedom Ride or here at school. You must know that."

I look at my sister and realize what a wise thing she just said. "You're right, Jess. I'm scared for him every day." I sniff, and suddenly remember, "Dad gave me a compass for my birthday once. I thought then it was just an instrument to figure out where I was if I was lost, but I wish it meant he would be there someday to lead me in the right direction—wish he was my true North—like all of a sudden and at last he'd be there to protect me. But he never was, never will be. I have to be my own compass."

"God, Rach, you think anyone protected me when I had the abortion? You sound like you had a philosophy class. It's just a stupid compass."

"I see what you mean. What a horrible thing—to have only ourselves. It's too scary to live."

"Well, do re mi. Welcome to the world. So what? We can all be scared together. No one is not scared." She takes hold of my shoulders. "Do what you have to Rach. Don't let anyone stop you from getting on that bus—not even Mr. or Mrs. Fear."

"Yeah, you're right. When did you get so smart?"

"I'm not, really. I just want you to be who you are without needing approval from me, Mom, Dad, or Steven. Who gives a hoot what they think?"

"Mom has leaned on Dad all her life, but I think she's still scared."

"Yeah—and Dad is too, probably. I don't know," Jess shrugs. "I'm making this all up as I talk."

"Pretty good make-up lines, Jess. They make sense to me—at least now, anyway."

We give each other a hug and walk out of the bathroom. Almost immediately, Steven comes up to us, like he's been waiting behind the bushes to appear at a defining moment. My heart gives an extra beat.

"Hi, sisters."

Jess runs off, saying, "I'm leaving—I have to get a book."

"I'm going on the Freedom Ride alone. I need to go."

"If you go, Rach, you'll be going for me, Gloria, Maurice, Ruby, Ethel, Bernice, Bill, the girl at camp, the conductor on the train, and millions of us who aren't going—because we can't, or we choose not to, or are too afraid. You know your parents will never approve, but I will—and I do." He leans down and gives me a tender kiss on the cheek, then walks away.

After school today Mom picks Jessy and me up for dental appointments. Afterwards, since Dad is working late, the three of us head to a nice place for dinner. When we get out of the car, out of the corner of my eye, I see a car that looks like Steven's drive by. There's a colored girl next to him and her arm is around his shoulders. My stomach turns flip-flops. I want to believe that I'm imagining this scene from a movie. Of course, he's free to have a girlfriend. I can't stop him. But my hands are shaking. As we walk into the restaurant, I grab Jessy.

"What are you doing, Rachael?"

I whisper in her ear. "I just saw Steven drive by with a colored girl and she had her arm around him."

"Oh, Rach, I am so sorry."

"Girls, what are you whispering about?" Mom asks.

"Something about school," Jess says.

Mom excuses herself to go to the bathroom.

"Jess, I can't believe it. I know he likes me still but he already has someone else. I knew he would eventually—but I'm so jealous. I love him."

Mom comes back and I look at the menu not really reading it. I'm not at all hungry. I make up a fib. "Mom, I can't eat. My teeth hurt too much from the dentist."

Mom and Jess order, eat, and we talk about classes and Dad. Nothing important, like college, relationships, or civil rights.

The following night at dinner I get up the nerve to talk about the summer. "I want to ask you if I can visit my friends and relatives in St. Louis when school gets out. I want to celebrate my seventeenth birthday there." In my mind my fingers are crossed.

"Actually, Rachael, Mom and I want you to work this summer," Dad says.

"I want to, too. But first I'd really like to go home to see everyone—just for a little while. When I get back, I'll work in your store, Dad, and pay for the whole trip." I try to make this sound like it's the most important thing in my whole life—and it is, but they don't know the real reason why.

I know I am lying because, after visiting in St. Louis, I may be a Freedom Rider the rest of the summer and won't get home until right before school starts. But if I tell them the truth, they'll never let me go.

Mom and Dad murmur to each other and I can't hear what they are saying. Finally, Dad speaks.

"Rachael, you're a good student. You haven't been any trouble to us. You understood our point of view about you and Steven, and we appreciated it. So we will let you go on this trip. We know it's hard to leave your home and all your friends and family. Your Mom will make arrangements for you to stay with Aunt Alice when you get there." Dad says like a executive, like he wants to get this settled, like he is selling a blouse in the store. There's no emotion whatsoever.

"I'll write Aunt Alice today," Mom says. "I'll airmail the letter and ask if you can stay there. I think a couple of weeks is plenty and maybe you'll want to stay with one of your friends for a few days while you're there. Once we get an answer from Alice, I'll make the airline reservations." Mom is also very cold, like she's helping me with homework.

"Thanks for letting me do this. I am so excited," I say graciously.

# 27
# FREEDOM!

Aunt Alice picks me up at the airport. While she's going on about all the relatives, I want to bounce up and down in the seat, I'm so excited to be here after a whole long year away. Her sentences fade into the background, like boring music on the radio, as my mind floods with thousands of special memories spurred by all the sights of my neighborhood: my old high school, Dad's store and the other shops, my friends' houses, the drug store, the public swimming pool. When we finally arrive at Aunt Alice's house, everything looks smaller and gloomier compared to sunny California. There are a bundle of emotions. Now, no matter where I live I know that I'm defined by what happens.

We don't drive by my old house or the country club yet because they're not on the way to Aunt Alice's. I think, just because time is the same mathematically from year to year, it really isn't the same in one's memory like Eienstein's Relativity Theory. If I didn't look at a calendar and know, I'd guess I'd been away from St. Louis for ten years. So many new things have happened, time feels slower because it takes more emotion to understand and put the new experiences in their proper place.

The next day I take the bus to Ruby's to get there before she leaves for work. I love her more than anyone in my life and I miss her love. I don't want to call Mitch or my old friends yet. I look at everything passing by.

As we approach the neighborhood, nothing looks nice. Everything is shabby and ragged, like it needs scrubbing and shaking out, like sand on a beach towel. I want to paint everything brand new in bright red, blue and green. I want to have all the window and shutters painted bright white. My insides scream, why do they have to live like this? Who is making them stay in these rundown rusty matchboxes? They didn't do anything wrong. Get out of here. Go be a princess or a king. Leave this jungle. You are not chained here.

I stand in front of Ruby's house with feelings of sadness, joy and guilt welling up. Joy for the love her, guilt for not taking care of her, and anger for her still living like this. I knock loudly, hoping she will be here.

When I see her behind the screen door, I scream, "Ruby!" That's all I can get out before the tears start coming.

"Hello, darlin'. Oh, my dear, now y'all stop that. I am so happy to see ya. I think you's taller—and I's fatter," Ruby says opening the squeaking door. "Come here while I grab my things. I's got to get on the bus."

I step into the dingy front room for a moment while she gets her purse and sweater and we both walk out. Ruby checks that the door is locked.

At the bus stop we talk about my breakup with Steven, and her life and family. The bus comes and I pay for both of us, even though Ruby has her money out. We sit in our seats and I notice her tired, splotchy red eyes. They still look at me intently as I talk but the creases are deeper everywhere—I hope from smiling. The grey hairs, forming a frame around her round face, weren't there when I left—or maybe I just didn't notice. I don't recall the big veins that look like blue rivers and valleys running through her worn old dry hands.

I ask about Ethel, Bernice, and Bill. Ruby says she doesn't know anything about Bernice and Bill. Ethel moved away after her husband died a few months ago and said she would call Ruby sometime, but she hasn't heard. That's all she can tell me.

I forget to ask if she ever read my letters. I just want to talk about the present.

I bring the letter I need to give her now so she doesn't talk me out of it.

*Dear Ruby,*

*I am going home after I see you but if you don't hear from me for a while, I joined the Freedom Riders. Ruby, I might not be able to stop myself and I didn't want to tell you about it because you would say I am too young or it is too dangerous or Mom and Dad will be so worried, so I am telling you now. I will write to you after I come home. It will be soon or maybe not so soon, but try to remember back when you were young and you just had to do something you believed in no matter what everyone else said. I love you with all my soul.*

*Rachael*

After the bus lets us off, we walk a few blocks to the house where she works. It's red brick and large, like mine was, but not English Tudor.

"Ruby, will you meet me at your church this Sunday, the one you took me to? I can't say goodbye here. Please?" I feel like I'm asking for a second helping of Ethel's caramel cake. "Also take this letter and read it later, okay??

"Sure, chil', I be goin' anyways. See you Sunday," she says, looking at the house, not me, like she's in a hurry to go.

We hug goodbye. I watch as she goes around to the back of the house. I hide behind a tree to gather my emotions. After a few minutes, Ruby comes out of the house with two young children—a girl about eight and a boy about six—and a jump rope. The boy and Ruby start turning the jump rope so the girl can jump. I think, she is me years earlier and Ruby loves them the same way she loves me. I should feel jealous but I don't. I wait a long time, hidden behind the tree, watching until they go inside.

Saturday, two days before I leave St. Louis, I finally see Mitch—not Tommy or any other friends. We meet at Steak 'N Shake where we always used to eat. Mitch is in the same booth, we order the same things, and Mitch looks the same—pudgy and disheveled, as ever. We are the same together—joking, laughing, feeling close. I feel totally myself and accepted with Mitch, just as I always did. When I tell him my idea of being a Freedom Rider, he is stunned. He remembers the store window he helped me with, but he says that was not risking my life.

I don't know now how I feel about going. Maybe it is stupid to die for what I believe in at seventeen.

"Mitch, do you have a girlfriend?"

"Yes, I do," Mitch he says shyly.

"I didn't expect to hear that. That makes me feel angry or jealous—I'm not sure—but I am happy for you, too." I give him my brightest smile. I have to be honest with Mitch; I've never lied to him. "I had a boyfriend, too, but we had to break up after one date. There were too many problems. Do you want to hear about it?"

"Not really, but you can tell me if you want to," he answers truthfully.

I love that he doesn't want to hear, like he may be jealous. "That's okay. Maybe I'll fill you in some other time."

As I sit and talk to Mitch I know why I came here. It wasn't to see Ruby and Mitch, but to decide what I must do next. I have no one to ask. When I go to Ruby's church I think someone there will surely know about the Freedom Riders. I can hardly concentrate on the rest of what Mitch and I talk about, I'm so preoccupied. Mitch drives me back to Aunt Alice's and we say goodbye.

Sunday morning I change and look dressy in my navy linen summer skirt, white cotton blouse, and white linen gloves with little buttons. I find the right bus to the church.

The church people are the same with me as they were before—friendly but curious when I walk in. They turn around to stare. I look for Ruby but I don't see her. I love the emotional service and how beautifully dressed everyone is.

After the service I wait at the end of the line to shake hands with the pastor and to ask him if he knows about the

Freedom Riders.

"How do you do? I'm Rachael Hirsch. I'm visiting from California and I want to thank you for the moving service. I was here once before about a year ago with Ruby—Ruby Smith. She was supposed to meet me here this morning, but I don't see her. I came to find out about the Freedom Riders. Do you mind me asking if you know about them?" I feel nervous, like I'm out of place here.

"Yes, I do know about them. What do you wish to know?" the pastor asks kindly.

"I want to know if they're coming to St. Louis to pick up people. I'm interested in becoming a Freedom Rider but I don't know if they will be stopping here."

"See that group over there?" the pastor points. "I'm pretty sure they'll know. Go talk to them."

"Thank you, Pastor," as I walk over to the group my nerves feel on fire.

"Wait," the pastor calls out, "I almost forgot. I have something for you from Ruby. She left a letter for me to give you. I would have found you if you hadn't found me. Being the only white girl, you were easy to spot." The pastor hands me a piece of paper as wrinkled as Ruby's hands. He walks away.

"Wait," I call out, stopping him. "Would you give these to Ruby next Sunday?" I take off my gloves and hand them to him.

The pastor feels the silky softness of them. "Yes, of course I will. I will be sure to give these to her next Sunday."

I walk away and over to the group the pastor pointed out. I introduce myself. "Hello. I'm Rachael Hirsch. The pastor told me that you might be able to help me. I'm trying to find out if the Freedom Riders stop in St. Louis. You see, I'm interested in being one," I say proudly as my nerves calm.

"Yes, dear. They do come to the bus station downtown, but I'm not sure of the schedule," a middle age lady answers sweetly. "My cousin is planning on getting on the next bus. I could telephone him and see when that is if you would like. My name is Ella Washington There's a phone in the church if you want to wait here for me to call." Ella's diction is so precise, she sounds more like a white person than a Negro.

"Oh, that would be so kind of you. I will wait right here." My heart starts pumping with excitement.

As Ella walks away and enters the church I stand near the group but far enough away so they don't think I'm trying to overhear them. They're all in their 40s or 50s and dressed just like Mom and Dad's friends did at the dinner parties they used to have at our house. The only difference is the color of their skin. And their hats and gloves are more colorful than those worn by the women at temple or at a fancy luncheon at the country club. The men's shoes and hats are not just grey, black or brown. Some are camel-colored or a light charcoal grey. It all seems to me to make a statement: they are colorful, expressive individuals, not just "colored folk."

"Rachael," Ella calls, coming back from the church, "I talked to my cousin Joseph and he's leaving tomorrow morning. The bus arrives at eleven o'clock in the morning but he isn't sure what time it leaves from the bus station downtown. Joseph is tall, about six feet, and skinny, and he said he will be wearing a red hat so that you can spot him and then sit with him." She holds her tan-gloved hand out toward mine and we shake. It feels like a warm hug.

"Thank you so very much. I look forward to meeting him and sitting with him."

The next morning, Aunt Alice drives me to the airport at seven o'clock in the morning to go back home. I'm dressed in the same clothes I wore to church to look nice for the plane.

After a sleepless night, scared to death to get on the bus, I decide not to go on the Freedom Ride. Aunt Alice drops me off at the curb. I get in line to check in. But when I get up to the front of the line I keep letting people go in front of me. I don't really want to get on the plane. Now I am the only one in line and I stare at the counter a few feet from the window. I don't hear anything—my ears have closed up. All I hear is a whooshing sound, like there's a vacuum in my ears.

"Hello, Miss, do you want help with checking in?"

I suddenly realize the clerk is shouting at me. I look at him, shake my head, and practically run out of the airport. I take a taxi to the bus station. I'm afraid I may be too late. I must find Joseph— Joseph with the red hat.

I don't know if I can do this. I reach inside the pocket of my skirt—the same one I wore yesterday when the pastor handed me Ruby's note. I unfold it carefully. It says: *You will ride for all of us, Rachael. Love always, Ruby.*

I need to cry hard but I don't have time.

# ABOUT THE AUTHOR

This is Mary Kinzelberg's first novel. She was a primary school teacher. She is now a writer and has always been a designer and artist. She lives in California with her husband, Jay, a meteorologist. She has a son, Matt and two stepchildren Wendy and Mike.